POINT DECEPTION

Also by Victoria McKernan
Osprey Reef

POINT DECEPTION

VICTORIA McKERNAN

Carroll & Graf Publishers, Inc.
New York

To Jon and Jacqueline for longtime support and new inspiration
Special thanks to Scott for many loving edits

First Carroll & Graf edition 1992

Carroll & Graf Publishers, Inc.
260 Fifth Avenue
New York, NY 10001

Library of Congress Cataloging-in-Publication Data is available.
Manufactured in the United States of America

One

The body was found at dawn, most of it anyway, entangled in a fishing net near the coast of Antilla. It was the body of a young white woman, with a dark Caribbean tan on her lovely shoulders. She was petite but shapely, that much could be seen, and she hadn't taken much care of her nails. At least on the one remaining hand. But was her hair blond or brunette? Naturally curly, stylishly cut, or badly permed? Was she a beauty queen or embarrassed by her nose? Were there dimples? Laugh lines? Had an orthodontist straightened her smile? No one could tell, for these features, and the color of her eyes, were lost along with her head.

Ranger tugged on the net and cursed the weight of it. He knew right away it was not simply a good catch. He could feel the deadness of it through the mesh. A large fish would be thrashing; even a big slow turtle would have some response. A log or other ensnarement would have a certain inanimate feel to it. This was something once alive, now dead—a big, vague, lump of deadness, a dolphin ensnared by mistake, maybe even a manatee.

Ranger tugged and swore under his breath. He was tired and hurting. Whatever it was, he didn't want to deal with it. A dead dolphin this close to shore couldn't just be left to drift away and couldn't very well be left to rot on the beach. Not this section anyway, so close to the island's brand-new resort, recently featured on "Lifestyles of the Rich and Famous."

"Oh, sheet, mon, come on—give a han'," he shouted to his father who was busy culling the fish they had already hauled in. The old man scuttled over and caught hold of the net with his sea-roughened hands.

His father pulled steadily, hand over hand, his forearms deceptively strong for all their scrawny appearance. How did the old man do it? he wondered. Ranger's back ached. He was too old to be up fishing this early. Or rather he was too old to be up working this early after dancing all night with four intensive-care nurses on vacation from Dallas. Damn white women have no business trying to lambada, he thought sourly.

Ranger was a strong man, stocky and broad chested, with sturdy limbs that could still get him up a coconut tree if challenged. As the island's new minister of tourism, however, he had no need to be climbing trees. He did, however, have a need for occasional extra cash. It was largely a ceremonial post, and Ranger had four nonceremonial children, the oldest of whom had just passed him in shoe size.

Together they pulled hard. The smaller fish flapped in a little silvery blizzard until they slipped through to safety. The bigger fish slid down and collected in a flopping pile in the bottom. The net coiled into the boat around their feet. A couple of crabs scrabbled away, a small sand shark flipped its tail in a last slice of bravado, clearing a swath through the trapped fish. Ranger grabbed it by the tail and threw it overboard. He braced his legs and pulled up on the net. One more tug, the last of the fish fell away, and the body, most of it anyway, rolled into the skiff.

Two

ALEX COULDN'T DECIDE if it was the sun that woke him or the dogs. Maybe it was the sun that woke the dogs and set them to wiggling and scratching in the sand, stretching their long-legged selves as they nestled like a pride of lions around him. Six bony dogs are a few too many to wake up with, he decided. At any rate, dogs and sun had both come too early. He leaned up on his elbows and squinted, ran his tongue around the inside of his lips, and expertly nudged away the sand that had collected at the edge of his mouth before allowing a yawn to escape. Dog-one immediately jumped up beside him and gave him a long lick on the face. Alex pushed her happy muzzle away, but this in turn roused Big-dog, Bug-dog, and Dog-four. They all leapt up at once, erupting in a series of vigorous sandy shakes.

It was a very effective way to get one's tired hung over body up and moving first thing in the morning, which was why Alex always slept on the beach when Miss Lilly held a fete and he had to fly out early. That was one reason anyway. The actual reason was that after Miss Lilly's fetes, almost everybody woke up on the beach; the more experienced above the tide line.

After almost a year in the Caribbean, Alex had still not fallen into the constant rum-drunk haze that seized so many expats, but his friends on Antilla—the Coboas band, Miss Lilly, and her dog-dogs—could always corrupt him.

Alex brushed the sand off his shorts, rolled his shoulders, and raked his fingers through his hair. Except for lack of hard drinking, he had "gone tropo" in other ways. His feet were hard from going barefoot, and his skin was tanned to a deep walnut. He had few clothes, mostly shorts and faded T-shirts, and one pair of khaki trousers to look presentable for the occasional tourist charters he flew. He wore his hair in a short ponytail. His walk had relaxed, and he had lost weight. It showed mostly in his face—a slight gauntness around the cheekbones, faint shadows around the eyes. He still looked strong, but another ten pounds would have fleshed out the muscles and given his six-foot frame an easier edge.

He looked around for his shirt and yanked it out from under Ugly-dog. Ugly-dog just lay there. He wasn't the frisky sort. If you called him things like "frisky," he would snarl. He wasn't all that uglier than the rest of the bunch—years of roaming on a small island had left most of the dogs looking pretty much the same—but he had a sour personality.

Alex sniffed the shirt: dog smell, piña colada, a hint of motor oil, sweat. The shirt could tell last night's story, but he wasn't sure he wanted to know it. Well, maybe the piña colada bit. This one, he seemed to recall, had been in the hand of a red-haired goddess with a Southern accent in a black-and-white-striped minidress that looked like a school tablet and made you desperately want to practice your penmanship. He again brushed the sand off his back. Ah, fleeting pleasures; the evening had obviously ended chastely.

"Sugah-sweet, come on fa coffee," Miss Lilly called from the bar. Most of the rest of the beach fallers were still solidly asleep. Alex was a restless sleeper in the best of circumstances, and had had the additional aid of the cuddling dog alarm to get him moving. He trudged up the beach, shaking the sand out of his hair and slipped onto one of the bar stools. Lilly handed him a steaming cup of coffee. "Gib me shirt," she commanded, her face as reproachful as she could make it. He handed it over, and she tossed it in the bar sink, turned on the water, and gave it a generous shot of Squeezy dish detergent. "Alex, you come heah neah ebery week, you maybe start to tink maybe you need an extra shirt, huh? You drink and dance, then you all be fightin', then makin' up and sweatin' on each other, then huggin' de ladies—so what you tink?" she chided him, laughing as she swished the shirt around and rinsed it.

Alex leaned over the bar and helped himself from the coffeepot. Miss Lilly went to hang the shirt on a bush in the sun where it would dry quickly. "I probably have an extra in the plane." He laughed. "But I know it would break your heart not to play mama to me."

"Boy, it ain't yo mama I thinkin' to be. I be alla time hopin' you finally get it troo yo head ol' Lilly may need hersef a young lover boy, hey?" She shook her ample bosom and tossed her head back in laughter.

Alex rolled his eyes at the thought. Miss Lilly was a mountain of a woman, a force of nature. Her bosom was planetary, her hips two shelves of high, solid padding that moved in a dizzyingly independent action. Alex wasn't sure he could get his arms all the way around her.

"Speaking of motherhood . . ." he broke in.

"Weren't motherhood I was speakin' of, sugah—"

"Isn't that Ranger coming in?" Alex nodded toward the bay.

Lilly shaded her eyes and watched the little boat chug up to the dock. "Must'a hab a good catch comin' in so early."

Three

The only good catch Ranger made that day turned out to be Alex. Somehow, within the next half hour, after a lot of pleading and bargaining, Alex found himself, against all his better judgment, sensible instincts, and gut feeling, agreeing to fly a dead body, most of it anyway, to Puerto Rico.

"It's like this, my friend," Ranger explained as he walked down the beach with his arm around Alex's shoulders. "Dis a bad, bad business. I don't know where dis body come from; I don't know how it get to be floating by my island or tangling itself in my fish net. God above knows"—and here Ranger put his other hand on his heart and looked speculatively toward the hot sky—"I've done my deeds to deserve punishment, but dis is just vexation. And dis not just my problem. Tink about it, Alex. She been half eat up from de sharks! What do people tink they hear a shark-bit dead body come floatin' by the beautiful island of Antilla? We just getting started in this tourist business, you know.

"Dem over dere now"—and Ranger waved a disparaging hand in the direction of Saint Martin—"Dey be having the tourist on a stick, grilled to order. Dey find a body, and no one care more den if once it got a good deal on a duty-free watch. But here, most the USA don't know dere even *is* an island here! What it going to be like if dat"—he gestured dramatically back toward the body, which his father and Miss Lilly were carefully guarding—"if dat show up on the front page of *The New York Post*! 'Shark Snacks on Tourist!' " Ranger had worked as a cab driver in New York for a couple of years; he knew his headlines. "And what you tink people is going to remember about Antilla? Is it the beautiful beaches? The lovely, secluded seaside hideaways? The friendly local people"—now he was quoting from his own travel brochure—"the miles of unspoiled coral reef? No, man, they gonna remember tree quarter of a dead lady wash up here! Just take her to Puerto Rico. I got friends dere can take care of details."

"How do you know she's American?" Alex asked, stalling, his head still too achy to reason his way out of this.

"Her legs is shaved—her leg and a half anyway, so she probably not German or French, and her shorts come from American store."

"And?" Alex prodded. He knew Ranger pretty well; he was an artful politician, reluctant to show all his hand.

"And, dere some notice paper been brought around couple days ago looking for American woman disappeared down here," Ranger added in a whisper.

"Ranger—"

"Come on, mon. It's no good to have disappeared ladies wash up on vacation paradises!"

"Aha. So you think this might be the missing girl?"

"If it not, no harm, right? She got to go somewhere, right? Where we gonna keep a body here—de hotel freezer?"

"No reward?"

Ranger's face brightened for a second. "I didn't notice that close . . ." Alex saw a ray of hope, but then Ranger shook his head. The Caribbean credo of "nuff problem" overtook any consideration of monetary reward.

"But if there is a reward, Alex, my friend, it will be all yours. Could be a big reward, yes, now that I think of it; it was a big important person looking for this woman, maybe a friend of the president."

Alex laughed at this. Flying a body to Puerto Rico was the last thing he had ever expected to be doing this morning, but three hundred dollars in pocket money plus fuel costs would make it worthwhile. Gilbey, the owner of Sky Indies, always wanted Alex back in Saint Croix early after the Antilla run in case there were weekend tourists wanting to charter the plane, but he could make up some excuse. Anyway, he could easily do the trip and be back by noon.

"All right, Ranger. But it ain't 'cause of your pretty face." They turned and walked back down the beach. A few more people had wakened and were gathered around the body, which Lilly was covering with tablecloths and an apron. A tourist boy of twelve or thirteen, bored with his hotel and out for a morning walk, had spied the commotion and was hanging around, trying to get a look at the gruesome corpse. Ranger shooed him away. Alex lifted up the cloth and took a look at the body. It wasn't pretty, but he had seen worse stiffs.

She was petite, about five two or three, curvy but with some decent muscles under that shapely flesh. While the skin was starting to suffer from exposure, Alex could still see that it was well toned, and guessed she was in her early twenties. She wore pink shorts and a bikini top, and her tan was uneven. Outside of some fading bruises on her thighs, there were no marks of violence, no wounds—except of course for the jagged edges around the missing limbs, the parts that had gone on to the inevitable next step in the wondrous process of life in the sea: food.

"Just think, Ranger," Alex pointed out, "another hour or so and you wouldn't have had any problem—the sharks might have finished her off." He was surprised at the cynicism in his tone. It was an awful thing to have happen to anyone, but Alex found himself strangely unmoved.

"What are we going to put her in?" he asked. "You don't expect me to strap her in the passenger seat, do you? That stump is likely to drip all the way if we sit her up."

"Alex, don't joke. I'm havin' a rough enough time as is. We'll pack her up nice and neat. Think, Faddah, what we got to box this lady in? Mama, you got some ice in the freezer? Let's do this deed before all the busybodies on the island wake themselves up."

The problem of a container was solved when Milton showed up. Lilly's bartender was a man known for his connections, solutions, and resources. A man like that is a valuable friend in the islands, and his methods are never questioned too closely. About the same time as the bars and restaurants along the beach were cleaned out of every available ice cube, Milton returned with a four-foot-long kidney-shaped goldfish-pond liner. It was made of heavy black vinyl, and the fact that damp sand and dirt still clung to its underside made Alex think that perhaps there were a few high and dry goldfish flopping around somewhere.

With the remaining leg tucked up and the body curved on its side to fit the shape of the pool, the dead woman looked as if she might be nestling into a cozy bed for the night. Long night, thought Alex as he turned away. He saw the tourist kid up on the roof of Lilly's with a telephoto lens, quietly clicking away. Alex nudged Ranger.

"Boy's got a future on *Geraldo,* I'd say."

Ranger swore under his breath, then pulled Milton aside for a quick conference. "Just bring me the film," he whispered. "I'll be sure he gets the camera back." Alex smiled. Maybe this was what he liked so much about the Caribbean. The sense that rules serve mostly to test your creativity. The ice was packed around the body, and a blue plastic tarp was roped securely around the pond. Then the whole package was loaded in the back of someone's truck, and in fifteen minutes, tucked securely in the back of Alex's plane.

"I'll be phonin' the gob'ment people in San Juan, Alex," Ranger assured him, still grateful but starting to wonder if he could have gotten the job done for two seventy-five, even two fifty. "I have friends there take care of such things. I'll have everything explained and such. All you'll have to do is slide the baby off! No problem!"

Four

Ethan Ruthwilde paced anxiously on the veranda, gazing down at the beach below. He had been up since dawn and was feeling tired. The Aurora Hotel was built on a bluff, overlooking the village of St. Simeon on one side and the beach on the other. With the recent tourist boom on Antilla, the village had started to blossom with cafés and guest houses, but it was still primarily a fishing village. Fishing boats docked near a long shed with a corrugated metal roof, fish traps were stacked on the dock awaiting repairs, and nets hung over pylons. Gulls screeched and dove for offal. He had been watching for hours, but had seen no sign of excitement. He paced along the veranda and looked down the other side of the bluff.

Here there was only a long white beach edging a sheltered bay where a couple of yachts were anchored. There were a few bars and restaurants on the beach, one of which had had a lively party most of the night. The music had disturbed him. Near the bar, a tall white man and a fat native woman were talking to two fishermen. Ruthwilde turned as he heard someone approach, and saw the young waiter who had served him breakfast.

"Do you ca-ah for more coffee out he-ah, sir?" He was about eighteen and spoke each word carefully with a slight British accent that hinted of nerves and missionary schools.

"No. No, thank you." The boy gave a slight nod and turned to leave. "Wait a minute. Excuse me." Ruthwilde called him back. "I was wondering if you had heard any news this morning."

"I haven't, suh. But there will be radio at ten o'clock, and sometimes there will be a papuh at the desk. From yestuhday though, suh."

"Oh, not that sort of news . . ." Ethan tried to sound convivial. "I meant local news. You know—what's been going on here."

The young man looked at him blankly. "Not much ever happen on this island." He shrugged.

"Well," Ruthwilde continued awkwardly, "if something did happen here, how would word get around?"

"Depend on what kind of someting," the waiter replied, relaxing out of his fancy hotel pronunciation. "Who won de football match is one ting, who did what at Miss Lilly's something else again."

"Aha. Well, yes. Thank you." The young man paused a minute, and Ruthwilde felt slightly embarrassed. "Well, I'm just interested in the island, that's all. I don't like to feel like I'm just a tourist."

"Yes, suh." The waiter smiled. "If I hear any news, suh, I'll let you know right away."

Ethan Ruthwilde didn't like the Caribbean. It was hot and sandy, and the water was full of *things.* Besides that, there was an infuriating sense that everyone was playing by some other rules. Or more exactly, that the rule book had been tattered and pages left to drift at will among the palm trees.

Ruthwilde was not the Caribbean type. He was fifty-three, paunchy, and pale. He had a big head. Not as in ego, but an actually large head. It wasn't grotesquely large, but it was enough that he had gone through school with cruel nicknames. His eyes were small and set close. All his features in fact were too close, crowded together in the center of his face, leaving a vast domed forehead, wide round chin, and cheeks padded enough to remove any suggestion of facial bones beneath. He wore glasses which made his eyes look distorted and which were a nuisance in the humid, salty air.

He took them off now, wiped the film of salt spray off on his handkerchief, replaced them, and gazed down over the beach again. It was quiet and empty now. Only nine o'clock. Too early for most sunbathers. He decided to stroll down to the wharf and see if there was any news in the air. Ruthwilde was a little nervous. It had all sounded simple in the planning, but of course, he had never planned anything like this before. His years in politics had given him a chance to handle many delicate situations, but never anything like this.

Ethan Ruthwilde was an unlikely, though effective lobbyist. Most of the men and women in the business were young and dynamic, slipping from careers in business or public relations into the halls of Congress; but he had come from science, moving up from the lab through the business side of industry and finally into politics as he eventually sought new challenges.

With a PhD in organic chemistry from MIT and a groundbreaking thesis on semipermeable polymer membranes for gas separation, he had been recruited by all the major chemical corporations. He had finally chosen a small Louisiana company when they offered him virtually free rein to run his own lab and pursue his own projects. No absentminded professor, Ruthwilde's scientific brilliance was counterweighted by a sharp business sense. He managed to retain percentages on all patents he developed for the company. After ten years in the lab, and dozens of patented industrial formulas, his shares had made him a fortune. About the same time, the chemical industry itself was suffering a slump and the mismanaged company was faltering. Ethan Ruthwilde collected a group of investors and bargained his shares into a controlling interest.

There were rumors of sweetheart deals and political manipulations, but whatever the reasons, the plant was turned around and began to flourish. In 1981 the company began to buy up smaller independent chemical plants in the Mississippi delta, and by 1984 Southstate Chemical Corporation was a federation of eight major chemical manufacturers. Once he was successful in business, Ruthwilde developed an interest in politics.

Now Ruthwilde was preparing for the outside world. He rubbed a generous slather of sunscreen on his face, buttoned his shirt all the way, buckled on his stiff new sandals, and picked up his straw hat. Thus armed, he set out on his quest for news. As he crossed the hotel lobby he heard a mixture of gay laughter and fierce mutterings. Three of the chambermaids were laughing as they knelt around the fountain, splashing like children.

Curious, he came closer and saw that the maids had saucepans and were trying to scoop up some goldfish. The fish swam in confused zigzags under the spilling waterfall. The maids were giggling over their efforts and trying not to get their heads splashed. The manager was ranting and raving and demanding to know who was responsible. Ruthwilde did not give it much thought, but bravely made his way out into the harsh elements of sun and sand, down the beach to find his news.

Five

ALEX PULLED BACK on the yoke and felt his plane respond. It was an older craft, but since he had taken over its operation, he had treated it well and tuned it up so the engine hummed. With so light a load he gained altitude easily, soaring up over the island into the clear sky. He banked left a little, gazed down on the sea below. He could see the pale green of the coral reefs, the light blue of the bay, and the little dots of sailboats anchored there. Farther out, the sea was a deeper blue, with whitecaps already forming. He glanced back over his shoulder to see if the wrapped-up body had shifted. It seemed secure enough, but splashes of water on the cabin floor told him that the ice was starting to melt. No worries. There were few clouds, and a slight tailwind; he could make Puerto Rico in an hour. Alex set the autopilot and tried to relax.

Usually once he was in the air, everything was perfect. For a little while, everything in the world fell into place. There was only the plane and the elements and himself, and he was good enough to know and trust all three.

But today he was having trouble finding that peace. He felt a knot in the back of his head and squeezed his eyes shut, opened them again, and concentrated on the blue horizon. What was wrong? It was a beautiful day for flying, and he was making an unexpected three hundred bucks. Why did he feel so stirred up? It's not the body, he told himself. What's one more body? He had certainly seen enough dead bodies in his life, though few recently. It wasn't like she was a friend or something. She was just some girl, probably down here on a package tour, went on a booze cruise, got drunk, and fell overboard. Of course it was tragic; he imagined her parents grieving, her friends crying, maybe a boyfriend. She was probably just an ordinary girl, maybe a cheerleader. She went to the mall with her friends and tried on lipstick.

She probably still had snapshots of high school boyfriends stuck in the back of one of those five-year diaries with the lock.

Alex realized he was clenching his teeth and grabbing the yoke hard with both hands. What was wrong? Why was he so angry? If he had to put it into words, he couldn't, but that's what it was: he was angry. He was mad at this unknown girl, mad at her for dying. Here she was, whoever she was, young and healthy, with nothing more to do than sip rum punch and lie in the sun. What *right* did she have to go and die? What a stupid thought, he chastised himself, but the thoughts wouldn't fade.

With all the danger in the world, with all the places where death was thick and ugly and too well known, how could this young American woman, this probably beautiful girl, just go and die . . . on *vacation*? It was just too absurd. He thought of young girls in all the dying corners of the world, peasant girls in Nicaragua and Chile, women who went to sleep every night with a prayer of thanks that no bullet or bomb had ended the day.

He remembered long ago a sudden glimpse of a girl in Laos, a young woman walking alone in a bright blue silk jacket and golden brocade dress, walking along a narrow road in the middle of nowhere, fifty miles from the nearest village, carrying nothing but a bird cage. He flew low and saw the sun glint off her jacket. She looked up at his plane, but she didn't run. She didn't even flinch or shade her eyes. There was a war going on, and he was the enemy. Why didn't she run? Why was she there? All alone, miles from nowhere, in a golden dress that seemed for a second to be on fire. She just stood there, calm and alone, watching him, hugging the bird cage to her chest.

He shook his head. He knew better than to rail against the vague and arbitrary reach of death. Alex looked out the window and could see the Virgin Islands sprinkled off to the right. Maybe another aspirin would help.

There are few secrets on an island. Despite Ranger's quick handling of the situation, news of the morning's bizarre catch had leaked out and made its way over the bluff to St. Simeon. Ethan Ruthwilde was examining some trinkets at a souvenir stand when he overheard two local men talking in a fruit stall nearby.

"Yeah, mon, I see it myself, a turrible ting. Wasn't noting lef but a few fingers an' toes."

"I hear de sharks eat all de arms and legs—leav'n noting but . . ." And the two men erupted in lascivious laughter.

Ruthwilde checked an urge to spin around and question the men. He held his breath and listened for more. The fishermen talked on about the details, about a man named Ranger who had pulled in the net, some good-natured slander about this Ranger, then finally, "So what he do wit it, eh?"

"I hear they put it in the beer cooler in Miss Lilly's." Another man had joined the conversation.

"No, mon, dey ship it out." Ethan's heart beat fast. "Send it on to Puerto Rico with that pilot from Sky Indies."

Ethan turned and looked around the village; he had to find a phone.

Six

Alex eased in for the landing, dropped gently on the tarmac, and taxied up to the service bay. Ten-fifteen, not bad. He should be out in forty-five minutes—an hour, max—depending on how many strings Ranger had been able to pull in arranging the whole thing. He looked around, spied a mechanic he recognized, and waved.

"Can you fill her, Raoul? I just got to make a quick drop and I'm out of here." Alex blocked the wheels, and Raoul dragged himself over and began to service the plane.

Alex plucked his sweaty shirt off his back and splashed water on his face at a stained basin. A glance in the cracked mirror showed him unshaven and red eyed. When dealing with officials, it always helped to look a little respectable, so he pulled off the broken shoelace that held his ponytail, scanned the shelf on the off chance there might be a comb lying around, and settled for smoothing his hair back into a slightly neater tie. His hair was thick and wavy, dark brown, almost black, with a few gray threads and one streak of silver shooting back from the left side of a cowlick. That annoyed him. He didn't mind the gray, it was about average for an almost forty-year-old guy with a fairly stressful past, but that one streak made him feel vulnerable.

He pulled up the hem of his shirt, wet it and rubbed it briskly over his teeth. OK, he thought to himself, ready for officials. But the officials, despite Ranger's sincere promise to arrange everything, were not ready for Alex. Two hours later, Alex had talked to the Puerto Rican police, the coroner's office, the chief counselor of Caribbean affairs, the assistant to the chief of agricultural inspection (how a body could be considered to be in the same category as souvenir pineapples Alex wasn't sure), three assorted United States customs' officials, and the governor's liaison for tourism. He had filled out seven different forms, handed his credentials over four or five times, and explained the details of his cargo more times than he could count, both in English and fluent Spanish. He was hot, tired, hungry, and hung over. There was still sand in his right ear. He was in a bad mood.

Now, feeling frustrated and on the brink of truly maniacal behavior, Alex was sitting in a holding room in the airport security office trying to explain why he should not be placed under arrest for murder.

"If I *murdered* her myself, why the hell would I be trying to drop her off here?" he argued logically.

"There are many things about the criminal mind I do not pretend to understand." The official smiled, enjoying his first chance at playing detective.

Alex was not a man prone to violence. He was not unfamiliar with the snarls of bureaucracy or the convoluted workings of the islands. He was, however, having a very bad day.

"So arrest me! Flog me in the public square!" he shouted as he stood and slammed his palms on the man's desk. "I don't care! But if you don't get this body off my plane in the next five minutes I swear I will drag you out there and drown you in that melted, rapidly warming pool of stagnant water and you can just bob for goddamn body parts!"

The officer, startled by the outburst, fell backward in his chair at the same instant two security guards, alerted by the noise, burst into the office. They saw their captain on the floor and an angry prisoner standing over his desk. They had received very little training dealing with unruly passengers with finesse.

The first one landed a flurry of blows with his truncheon, while the second one flung an arm around Alex's neck, crushing him in a very effective headlock. Alex checked the instinct to fight back, realizing it was his own mistake that had gotten him into this. They forced him back, up against the wall, with a hard fist to his stomach to subdue him. Alex gasped and lifted his hands in a gesture of concession.

"Fine—" he rasped. "Keep the corpse! I don't care! I'll just leave it here oozing on the tarmac!"

"Gentlemen, I'm glad I found you." A new voice cut through the tension. Alex looked toward the door to see a handsome Puerto Rican man in a well-tailored suit. He looked vaguely familiar. The two guards loosened their hold on Alex and stood still, not quite at attention but perhaps considering whether they should be. Alex glanced back toward the desk and noticed the portraits on the wall, and now recognized the man as the governor himself.

"Mr. Sanders? I'm terribly sorry for all this. I am Reynaldo Beiro." The governor nodded to the two guards and waved one hand. "Thank you, gentlemen. I am pleased with your prompt response," he said in Spanish. "I am happy to know our airport security is functioning so well. I'm sure we won't be needing you now. Mr. Suarez"—he turned to the official—"please don't worry. You have fulfilled your duties. It's just that there has been a small series of misunderstandings. I'm afraid it has caused our visitor undue annoyance." Speaking now in an easy and elegantly accented English he continued. "Now I wonder if I might impose on you to let us use your office for a few minutes?"

When they were alone, the governor motioned to a chair and Alex sat down.

"Well, I figure you're about the only person in this damn weeble farm left to deal with," he snarled.

"I am sorry. I was just notified about the situation a short time ago, and although I cannot repair the time and aggravation you have already suffered, I can help you on your way."

"Fine. Good." Alex tried for politeness, growling at himself for losing his temper. The guy was trying to help. He closed his eyes and rubbed the side of his chest where the truncheon blows were starting to throb.

"I have people repacking the . . . corpse right now. We have obtained a more, ah, suitable container and some fresh ice. As soon as that is ready, you have my personal permission to depart for Miami." The governor smiled. Alex sat up in the chair.

"What?"

"You are free to leave. We have even refueled your plane."

"You said Miami."

"That's right."

"I'm not going to Miami. I'm supposed to leave the girl here. I'm finished. I'm really sorry. I don't know what you've been told—"

The governor interrupted, "But you understand the situation?"

"No!" Alex replied, cringing. "Situation" was never a good word. "No, I don't understand any *situation.* All I know is my buddy in Antilla goes out fishing this morning, finds a body. It's been chewed on by sharks and he doesn't want the island to get bad publicity, so he asks me to take the stiff here where I'm suppose to turn it over to friends of his. Simple!"

"Your friend, he mentioned something about an American woman who was reported missing recently in the islands?"

Alex had to think a minute—reward, flyers—"Yeah, that's why he thought she is—was—American."

The governor looked properly reverential. "I had a call just about half an hour ago. It seems the missing young woman is the daughter of a United States senator. Someone on Antilla found out about the body. Evidently there were people looking for her in the area. Anyway, the senator was notified and called me personally. He is very anxious about his daughter, and although he is praying this body you are carrying is, of course, not hers, it unfortunately fits the general description. He wants it flown to Miami as soon as possible for an autopsy."

"So fly it there! Fly it to the moon—I don't care. There are a dozen pilots here who would be glad for the job."

"But you're already here; the body is already packed. Besides, they want to talk to you personally. I was told you were the first one to find the body."

"No! I was sleeping on the beach! I was drunk and sleeping with the dogs. Ranger found her. I was just there. I was just"—Alex banged on the arms of his chair—"a sucker."

There was a knock on the door. A hangar worker in an orange jumpsuit stuck his head in the door.

"Everything is ready, sir," he said in Spanish.

Seven

THE D.C. POLICE sergeant eased his car past the snaking line of waiting taxis to escort the limousine up to the front door of the terminal at National Airport. There were reporters from two local TV stations waiting. He saw Marcy DeLour, the blond reporter from channel five barking orders at her cameraman while she felt her hair for neatness. He laughed to himself. There was little chance of a stray hair on that head. He had seen her broadcasting from the inaugural parade when the winds were so strong half the floats were grounded and not a hair had moved. He pulled up to the curb and got out. The limo driver sprang out and went around to open the senator's door.

A senator didn't usually get a police escort to the airport, but when the news had come in there had been only forty-five minutes to catch the next plane to Miami. The sergeant watched amused as the two TV reporters vied for angles. Channel seven clearly wasn't all that excited over the event; they were probably just getting the footage in case anything did develop. They had sent Shana Phillips, a second-string consumer affairs reporter who had spent much of her career so far covering mayoral appearances at senior citizens centers and reporting on radon gas. Too bad, he thought, for in the few interesting pieces he had seen her do, she seemed sharp.

She was a petite black woman with close-cut hair who tended to wear clothing that was severe and conservative even by Washington standards. Now as the officer watched her in person, he could see why. She had a disarming prettiness, a doll-like appeal that made you want to pet her. There was nothing sweet and doll-like about her reporting; she was aggressive, and often blunt, but that heart-shaped face, those long eyelashes, hit all the puppy-and-chicks buttons.

Senator Wattles and his aide got out, and the two women thrust their microphones in his face.

"Senator Wattles, sir!" Miss DeLour tilted her stiff hair expertly in front of Shana's cameraman so he had to move for a clear shot. "Do you really think the body they found is that of your daughter, Angelica?"

The senator just raised a hand, obviously too distraught to answer questions. Darcy Sullevin, his administrative aide, stepped forward.

"Obviously, we are hoping and praying for the best. Of course it is a tragic situation whoever this young woman is. There's just no way to tell at this point. I'm sorry, but we really are in a hurry. I'm sure you understand."

Shana stepped up next to him. "Senator, do you have any reason to suspect that your daughter—" Sullevin practically knocked her microphone away as he kept moving.

"That's all. We have to catch a plane," he finished brusquely, glaring at Shana with an icy stare.

Eight

ALEX PICTURED THE city of Miami, the miasma of Miami, that vast, stewy, garish city full of brilliant excess. He had thought he was free from it, yet to be honest, he knew he had to return someday. But why today? There was a deep, hollow feeling in the back of his chest.

Of course, just because he was coming to Miami didn't mean he had to see Chicago. He could still turn around and fly back tonight. But he was almost there, and in a way, it was a relief. This way the burden of decision had been removed. Of course, he told himself, why the hell would Chicago want to see *me* at this point? He could picture her—black hair, pale blue eyes sparking all over like an electric storm. Alex remembered the first time he met her, she had cursed him up one side and down the other, then thrown him off her boat.

She would want an explanation. She deserved an explanation; but Alex still didn't know if he had one yet, at least not one that could fit into words, one that didn't involve his whole life and good and evil and pain in the universe, that is. He had to smile. He could just see her slap that down.

By the time he neared the Keys he was feeling waves of anticipation and doubt: relief, excitement, edginess, and something like seasickness. It was the feeling you have the day before you come down with the flu. His mind was crowded with memories: the feel of her body, her laugh, the mix of gentleness and hot temper that ruled her emotions.

They had been together for only a few months really. How in such a short time could he have lost himself so thoroughly? Could it have been just the drama of their meeting, the exotic, romantic tint of it all? He had plucked her from the sea one morning, bleeding from a shark bite, her boat cut adrift by smugglers. Almost immediately they'd been caught up in a dangerous adventure. Maybe that's all it really was—a brief adventure with a beautiful, exotic woman.

Alex was over the Keys now. From this vantage the islands looked like little green jewels, the roadside billboards and endless traffic snarls hidden by distance. The islands were like steppingstones, leading him on.

In a way, he wished that this were all there was to it, but he had had plenty of beautiful women and plenty of adventures. Chicago was different. In some ways he knew her so well, in others she would always be an enigma. Odd, Alex thought, he had loved her, fought with her, slept in her boat with his arms around her, and yet he could not say if she was tall or short. While swinging a scuba tank into a boat or starting up an outboard she seemed as sturdy as a Viking; but there were those rare unguarded moments when he thought of her as fragile.

Objectively, she was five foot eight inches tall. A mix of heritages had given her unusual features. Her father was a fair-haired Norwegian, her mother was from the island of Tobago, where Spanish explorers, Indians, African slaves, and Middle Eastern laborers had mingled their bloodlines over the years with stunning results. Chicago had fine, almost delicate features and skin the color of fresh bread crust. Her eyes were a startlingly light blue, but her long hair was black, thick, and straight. She had a swimmer's strong, lithe build: a little bony around the shoulders and knees, but otherwise well shaped.

Born on an island, raised on a ship, she craved the salt water like it was her lifeblood. She was a water nymph with a core of steel, and her steel had pierced his heart. He remembered the way she would sometimes smell him at night. After they'd made love and they lay together in the bow cabin and she thought he was asleep, she would sniff him on his back between his shoulder blades.

Alex saw the airport coming into view and radioed his arrival. He resisted an urge to circle around over the Pelican Bay marina for a chance at seeing her boat, the *Tassia Far.* He was given immediate clearance and directed to a priority runway. He landed and taxied over to the waiting entourage. There was an ambulance and TV van, people from the coroner's office and customs. There were several police cars. Alex didn't recognize any of the officers from his brief stint on the force here. That was a relief. Their regard toward him upon his departure was about fifty-fifty, about what you'd expect when you've stirred up trouble.

This little squad, armed with clipboards and radios and a stretcher, swarmed out to meet the plane. They unloaded the body, packed now in an official body bag, the fate of the goldfish pond unknown, and carried it away for the autopsy.

Alex was taken into an office for debriefing. He was hot and tired and still finding sand in his clothes from last night's sleep on the beach, but he resigned himself for more paperwork. He recounted the circumstances as he knew them from the time Ranger discovered the body.

"But tell us again how you got involved," one man asked him.

Alex sighed. "Look . . . this is the Caribbean. Things happen differently," he explained. "Ranger's my friend. He was afraid of the publicity. Shark stories are like wildfire. He just wanted to protect his island."

"How do you know this Ranger, Mr. Sanders?"

"I fly into Antilla at least once a week—usually every Thursday —delivering hardware, supplies, whatever." They all seemed a little suspicious at first, but Alex managed to convince them that Ranger's motives, if not his methods, were pure.

"So you were there when they brought the body in?" a customs official asked.

"What's the matter, you can't listen at the same time you're writing?" Alex sighed. The man stared at him stone faced. Guys like this brought out the worst in Alex. He was feeling a little punchy by now anyway.

"Yes, I was there. On the beach."

"And you saw the body?"

Alex resisted the urge to smart off again. "Yes."

"Mr. Sanders, sir . . ." A thirty-something man in a dark pinstripe suit who had been sitting quietly throughout the debriefing stepped forward. "Did you get a good look at the body?"

"A *good* look? Kind of an oxymoron there, don't you think?"

The man smiled dryly. "I understand this has turned out to be quite a long day for you, and we are sorry and most grateful for your help. It's just the, ah—circumstances, as I'm sure you can imagine, make identification difficult. I just wondered if you might have seen anything at the time—any signs, any clues."

"Do I look like Magnum PI?" Alex couldn't tell if it was this twerp in particular or just the day's overdose of the lot of them in general, but he really wished there were some sort of aerosol repellent.

"I think that's all we need, Mr. Sanders." The officer in charge wrapped it up. "We would like your address here in Miami in case anything comes up in the next few days. . . ."

"What 'anything' are you expecting to 'come up'?" Alex snapped in exasperation. "I'm just a pilot. I've made your delivery. I'm based in Saint Croix, with Sky Indies; the owner is a guy named Anton Gilbey. We have a phone. Now can I go? I was sort of hoping to get some breakfast before dark."

As the rest of the officials gathered their papers to leave, the pinstripe suit came up to Alex. "I'm Darcy Sullevin, Senator Wattles's administrative assistant." He extended his hand in a professional manner, the handshake perfected—not too hard, not too soft, just the right duration, slight squeeze at the end. "Senator Wattles asked me to tell you how personally grateful he is for your service." Sullevin spoke with a slight Southern accent, as if he had carefully erased all but the most gracious tones. "We will of course arrange to pay your company the transport fees and all extra expenses. I would think that with the unexpected flight here you might need some cash." Sullevin pulled out his wallet and extracted several fifty-dollar bills. "We will certainly arrange for a hotel for the night and take care of all that."

"No, thanks." Alex accepted the money. "I might have some friends around. Or I might fly back tonight."

"Whatever you like. At any rate, the senator wanted to thank you himself, but the stress of all this is very wearing, and he was eager to go to the morgue and try to identify—or we hope, not identify—the body."

"Sure."

"Good. We do appreciate your help." Sullevin continued smoothly, "Well, at any rate, let me give you this." The aide handed Alex a fat manilla envelope with a picture of the Capitol and the address of Senator Wattles's office. "It's just a little token of appreciation. We hope that if you ever come to Washington we'll have a chance to show you a little special hospitality. Just stop by our office and we'll arrange a special tour or something, show you how the government works." He flashed his brilliant up-and-comer smile, clapped Alex on the back, and was out the door.

Alex was too stunned to snicker. Incredulously, he lifted the flap and looked inside to find a standard constituent visit commemorative packet: a glossy photo of the senator with the President, a couple of letters to the home folks, listing all the wonderful things he was doing in Washington to benefit the citizens of Louisiana, a brochure on the history of the Capitol and another on "How your government works."

How my government works, Alex thought sarcastically. He knew only too well how the government could work. He was surprised at the wave of bitterness he still felt.

Nine

CHICAGO HAD HALF expected, half dreaded that he would show up again someday. She had played the scene over and over in her mind. Sometimes in these visions he would stroll up while she was working on the boat. She would look up, surprised, her heart pounding, remembering what he had meant to her, what they had shared. He would be so sorry. He would have in his hand a big bunch of flowers or something. She would have in her hand some solid tool—channel locks or a fifteen-inch crescent wrench. She would beat the shit out of him.

Sometimes in her imagination the scene was all fuzzy and pastel and romantic like a greeting card. She would run to him and fall into his arms. She would gaze into his dark eyes and run her hands down his lion-muscled back. She would lead him below to the bow cabin to make love. She would run her hands along his magnificent thighs and push him back against the piles of soft pillows. She would kiss him, then she would watch her eight-foot-long pet boa constrictor slither out from under the cushions and seize him by the throat.

The only good vision came in the dream. In the dream, she was underwater just before sunrise. She was hovering effortlessly before a beautiful coral reef with a beam of light playing over the colors. Then gradually, in the most gentle shiftings, the darkness faded, the shades of blue grew lighter all around her. The little reef fish that hid during the night started to appear. The sun rose and the first long-slanted rays pierced the sea. In the dream she always felt so completely at peace. There was no malice in the sea. The sunlight dappled on the coral, and she would spread her arms out and the little jeweled fish would swim through her fingers.

Then Alex would be there beside her. There was no sense of arrival in the dream. It was as if in this perfect place they had always dwelled together. In the dream, his absence was as natural and disturbing as the tide. In the dream they did not talk. They did not even touch except that in swimming side by side their arms brushed. They moved together in a surreal sort of nakedness, as if their bodies absorbed the sunlight and the water.

But the dreams came only at night, and there had been too many days now. There was still pain, a crescent-shaped pain that no matter which way she shifted would always work its way around to stab her someplace, but she had learned to live with loss. Almost any other way would have been better than this. One day he was just gone. A letter came; he was sorry but he had to go—couldn't say why, didn't really know. She had been frantic at first, afraid that something had happened to him. She knew little about his past, but enough to know there were people who could hurt him.

Then she heard news of him some months later, found out he

was flying in the islands for some two-bit charter company. It would have been easy to go to him then, but she didn't.

At least when her husband had been killed, almost four years ago, there had been an ending. It was a horrible ending, but once Chicago decided to keep living, there was at least a place to go on from. Death was like a solid board, once you summoned the strength you could finally push off and go on. This was like trying to stand on quicksand.

But time had passed. Now her boat was almost ready, and she had saved enough money to sail for at least a year, maybe two if the seas were kind. Now the memory of Alex had settled down to a dull ache in the part of her where such things were stored.

Ten

ETHAN RUTHWILDE PAID the cab driver, tipped him all the remaining Caribbean funny money in his billfold, and stepped through the airport doors. He had taken the ferry from Antilla over to Saint Martin, and now had a couple of hours to wait. The flight to Baton Rouge didn't leave for another two hours, but Ethan liked airports. He liked the miles of linoleum, the clean wide, blank hallways.

He bought three tickets and went to wait for Willie and Grant in the bar. He figured they would be using up every last minute on the beach, and was surprised when Willie showed up only a few minutes later. Ethan saw him pausing at the doorway, squinting into the darkness. He swayed a little. He seemed disoriented. Ethan waved, then when he didn't respond, left his booth to meet him.

"Willie," he started, then stopped, shocked by the sight of him. "My god, Willie, what happened to you?" Ethan took his arm and supported him back to the table. Willie Wallace looked nothing like the handsome young man who had graduated, with reasonable grades for a star football player, from LSU. If he had ever looked anything like this last spring he would never have gotten near a debutante, let alone be the choicest escort for the cotillion season. His blond hair was ragged; his handsome jaw was covered with a three-day growth of annoyingly red stubble; his blue-gray eyes were dark and his skin pallid even with the tan. Although he couldn't possibly have declined so severely even through the difficulties of the past few days, his strong young body appeared sick. He limped and he stank of bourbon.

"Willie, boy, sit down. What the hell's the matter with you showing up like this? Let me get you some coffee." Willie leaned heavily against the booth.

"I just want to get home," he said lamely.

"Where's your suitcase?" Ruthwilde pressed. Willie shrugged. "Where's Grant? Why isn't he with you?"

"He dropped me off. He went to buy some presents, I think. He kept putting it off, you know, the whole time we've been down here." Willie's speech was flat and edged with confusion. Ruthwilde grumbled to himself. He had always thought Grant a little too cocky. He glanced at his watch. They still had plenty of time.

"C'mon, son." He slid out and pulled the reluctant half-drunk Willie out of the booth. The boy's hands were trembling.

"We've got to get you cleaned up." They stopped at a gift shop to buy a shirt. Ethan flipped through the racks of garish or suggestive T-shirts until he found a relatively innocuous one with a little sailboat against the sun. He was about to buy a pair of Bermuda shorts too, but Willie stopped him.

"Can't wear 'em," he slurred, laughing unsteadily.

"Oh, it's just for the flight. So what if you look like a tourist for a few hours. . . ."

Willie just shook his head, edged his face close to Ethan. "Shark bit me," he whispered hoarsely.

Ethan just looked at him surprised. "What!"

Willie nodded. "On the leg."

Ethan was a detail man, an efficient and effective manager. He was not much on the emotional side. He hadn't thought of how difficult the past few days must have been for the boy. This revelation of injury aroused the closest thing he had to sympathy. "I'm sorry. Have you had it looked at?"

Willie shook his head. "Grant wrapped it up."

"We'll see about it first thing once we land. Come on now." They went into the men's room. Ethan snapped open his carry-on bag and found his cordless electric razor, soap, facecloth, deodorant. Soon, Willie looked simply like a half-sloshed, burned-out college student who had partied a little too hard in the islands.

Grant was waiting in the bar when they returned. Ethan gave him a disapproving glance. Grant had gotten a lot of those in his life and didn't much care. He was handsome in a strong-jawed, American way, with brown hair and good features. He was five eight, broadly built and muscular, with the sloping neck muscles of a wrestler. He carried himself with the slight swagger and dare of a guy a little sensitive about being too short. He had a couple of bags, a small souvenir steel drum, a straw hat, some shell necklaces, and two bottles of duty-free rum.

"I'm not sure you appreciate the gravity of this whole affair," Ruthwilde chastised him.

"Chill, professor. I'm here, everything's cool. It all worked out and you've got Sir Lancelot here looking pretty. Relax."

Eleven

As Alex walked down the dock to the end slip where the *Tassia Far* was moored he had a light-headed sensation, as if he were removed from his own body and watching himself walk. That removed part of him had the urge to fly on ahead and warn Chicago to flee. When he got close enough to see her boat he stopped. There was finally a new mast, he noted with elation and a bit of panic. And the deck looked freshly varnished. Chicago's father had built the boat almost thirty years ago, a sleek wooden-hulled ketch. She had spent the past two years refitting it, and converting it to a cutter rig to give more room on the aft deck for scuba gear. The sails were back on, and there were new sail covers. Dark purple. Where the hell had she found that color? The boat looked ready to sail. As Alex watched, Chicago came up from the companionway, sat down cross-legged on the deck and began bolting down some stanchions. From here, she looked small and gangly, her knees and elbows jutting out as she worked.

He walked slowly toward the boat. Chicago looked up. The sun was behind him, and it took a few seconds for her to realize who it was. She stood up. Alex tried to speak, but suddenly every word in the world seemed stupid. Chicago stood very still. He was carrying a bunch of flowers, a flat box tied with a red ribbon, and a paper bag. She was holding a large ratchet wrench. They stood silently for an eternity, then Alex looked away. He wiped a hand across his forehead and down the back of his neck, and it seemed to tremble slightly. He faced her again.

"I didn't know I was coming." His voice sounded scant. He wasn't sure she had even heard him. He tried to speak again, but Chicago interrupted.

"You shit." Her voice was shaky.

"Yeah." Alex smiled. Chicago seemed frozen. Alex set the brown paper bag down on the seat cushion. It rustled and shifted an inch of its own accord. Chicago looked at the bag. "That's for Lassie," Alex explained. "They were out of rats—I got her a guinea pig. I hope it's not too hairy or something," he added lamely. She was still gripping the ratchet wrench. Her knuckles were white. "These are for you." He handed her the flowers and the box. Chicago looked at them, and her eyes filled up with tears. This was the way she usually, though rarely, cried. No sobs and hiccups, no noise and weeping, just these silent, heavy tears.

"I know how much you love needle-nosed pliers," Alex offered feebly. Maybe this was all a big mistake. "Baby—I'm so sorry." He reached to touch her.

"Don't—don't you . . ." She threw the wrench down. She raised her hands, as if to strike, but instead pushed against the air. Her whole body was trembling, and Alex felt a crazy twist of pain.

"I'm leaving," she told him in an odd small voice. "My boat is all ready . . . and . . . I'm almost ready to go. . . ." There was a sense of pleading in her tone, laced with outrage. Her face was white, and he thought for a minute that she might faint. Alex touched her arm, but she jerked back. She yanked her arm away and jumped up to the dock.

"Wait—I'm sorry. Don't go." Alex felt so stupid. Why hadn't he at least given her warning? He should have sent a note or something. But he was also surprised. He had not expected to see her break down like this. She stopped for a second, and he hoped she would yell at him, curse him or something, anything, but she turned abruptly and ran down the dock.

Twelve

Senator Robert Wattles felt displaced by the Miami heat. It wasn't so different from a Washington summer, but it was October now and cooler up north. Flying down here back into the sultry air made him feel like he was in a time warp. He watched the sunset over the city from the air-conditioned comfort of his hotel suite.

"How long before they'll have anything positive, Darcy?"

"Depends," his aide replied. "We can go with your tentative ID of the body, the jewelry, her blood type, the appendicitis scar, and the scars on her knee, but if you want the irrefutable evidence, you're going to have to wait for the DNA stuff. That's a couple of weeks."

"Weeks! What weeks! What do we do—with her—in the meantime?" The senator got up and paced the room. "I can't just go on for weeks."

"Did Angelica ever break a bone?"

"Would it help if she did?" Wattles snapped.

Darcy raised his hands in a mild gesture of surrender. "Dr. Bolton just asked me is all."

"I gave him all her medical records." He sighed and rubbed his forehead. "No, she never broke anything."

"Look, we're all a little edgy over this whole thing." Sullevin tried to calm him. "Let's give it the weekend. Bolton has a lot to go on. If he's comfortable, we issue the results tomorrow. We may be able to have the funeral by Tuesday."

The senator nodded absently, went to the bar, and poured himself a generous shot of bourbon.

"Have you thought, sir," Darcy gently pressed, "where she should be buried?"

The senator looked wide-eyed, clearly surprised by the question. His hands shook, and his eyes filled with tears.

"You do have a family plot, sir."

"Well, but . . . yes, of course."

Thirteen

FOR THE SECOND time in as many days Alex woke with the first rays of the sun. He bolted awake and jumped up defensively. There was a six-foot-two, broad-shouldered black man with dreadlocks towering over him. The man laughed and nimbly dodged back.

"Hey! Alex, my mon! I don't believe my eyes. What you doing here?"

"Umbi! Christ Almighty." Alex flopped back on the cushion, heart pounding, and rubbed his eyes. He was in the cockpit of the *Tassia Far.* He was surprised to find it morning. What had happened to evening and night? What had happened to Chicago? Had he screwed up already? He must have fallen asleep while waiting for her to return, then just stayed asleep all night. Someone had thrown a light blanket over him. All this flickered through his mind as he was surveying Umbi.

Alex jumped up, and the two embraced. "Look at you. What is all this?" he joked, squeezing Umbi's arm. The last time Alex had seen Umbi, he was a tall skinny seventeen-year-old wiseass. Now Umbi had a good two inches over Alex, and at this rate would soon outweigh him.

"What are you doing still around?" Alex asked.

"Where else I'm gonna be? I'm a dive master now though," Umbi said proudly. "Chicago gettin' me ready for the instructor test in November." Umbi sat on the hatch and stuck his feet up on the helm. "So what *you* doing here?"

"It's a long story."

"Dat I believe." Umbi glanced down the companionway hatch.

There was no sign of Chicago yet, though they could hear sounds of her moving around. "So when you come back? And why you sleeping out here?"

Alex combed his fingers through his hair and searched his shirt pocket for a rubber band. "I guess I just fell asleep and stayed that way. It was sort of a long day. And I don't think Chicago was exactly what you would call happy to see me."

"Well, mon, you been gone almost a year, and you weren't like a sensitive sort of guy about leaving." Umbi shrugged. "She'll get over it. You two way too crazy for anybody else. Hey, and speaking of crazy"—he grinned—"they make me legal!"

"That's great. That's really great. So everything came through OK?"

"Yeah, I'm an alien though." Umbi laughed. "But so long as I'm a legal alien I don't care if they paint me green and give me pointy ears." The news made Alex happy.

Umbi was Haitian, one of the vast, unwanted sea of people who had made their way to Miami in tiny, overcrowded boats before the fall of Baby Doc. Chicago had found him one morning several years ago, sleeping behind a shed in the marina. She offered him a day's work, and when he proved a good worker, offered him another. Pretty soon he was pumping gas, filling scuba tanks, picking up odd jobs for boat owners, and diving with Chicago for her aquarium jobs. Alex had pulled a few strings in Washington to get the precious green card for Umbi. It was a small price to pay for someone who had pretty much saved his and Chicago's lives.

They sat silently a minute. The marina was already starting to bustle with weekend sailors.

"So"—Alex nodded toward the salon—"so, how's she been doing?"

Umbi lifted his hands. "She working a lot, same stuff—dive, fix boats, run the shop. She get paid two hundred bucks do some underwater modeling last week! Dis guy making a video for his resort. Two hundred bucks to hold her bubbles and look at sponges!" Umbi laughed and shook his head at the marvel of it. "We caught some nice eagle rays for the Boston aquarium last week—business been good. All her money go into this old boat."

"It's looking ready to sail," Alex admitted regretfully. "But how's she doing—otherwise?"

Umbi shrugged. "Do I look like Dear Abby?"

"You know her better than anyone," Alex pressed.

Umbi looked at him closely, cocked his head half a tilt. It was a particularly eloquent and maddening Caribbean gesture that said all at once yes, no, who knows, and why even ask. "You give her a hard pain, mon."

Chicago came up the companionway ladder. She looked perfectly composed, although tired. Her face was drawn.

"Hey, Umbi, you ready? We need to leave soon." Her eyes glanced off Alex and darted away as if they had been burned.

"Sure. Me'n Alex here just catching up old times."

She nodded. "Well good. But we have to go."

"I'm ready. Little problem come up though."

"Little how?" she asked warily.

"Brian call me dis morning—his dive master sick, stuff up yesterday and can't dive."

"Shit—oh, great!" Chicago slammed her palm against the helm. "Who? Who was it? I'll kill him. I'll bet it was Roger." Alex smiled in spite of himself as she punctuated her rage with punches to the boat. "Was it Roger? That gum ball! What a wimp! Was it Roger?" She stopped to glare at Umbi as if this Roger were a particularly nasty invention of his own.

Umbi laughed. "I don't know, mon. Brian just tell me see who you can find."

"Shit!" She swept a pile of manuals and charts off the ledge so they crashed down into the salon. "Who the hell am I gonna find on Saturday morning? Why the hell didn't he let me know last night? I could have called somebody. He knew we needed four of us. . . . I'll kill him. I'll choke him with his own snorkel—"

"Well, before you go planning your torture," Umbi interrupted, "Brian did try to get hold of you. You don't answer on the radio, and he say he call up and leave two messages at the office last night. But were you around to get them?"

Chicago leaned back against the hatch, crossed her arms and scowled at her feet. "All right. All right. But we'll never get anyone on a Saturday morning."

"Why, sure you will." Umbi flopped an arm around Chicago's drooping shoulders. "You see how luck is." He waved cheerfully in Alex's direction. Umbi felt her shoulders stiffen immediately in protest, but he squeezed tighter. "You want to dive?" He tossed the invitation in Alex's direction before Chicago had a chance to protest. "If we don't have him we have to sit some people out. You know they not gonna be happy. You know how hard to arrange the whole thing again . . ." Chicago was silent.

"Look at the day—water's like glass. We got to have a day like this—you can't cancel them out." He could see his argument was working on her. Today's class had taken months to arrange, and the conditions were perfect.

"So you say yes, mon?" Umbi glared at Alex over his shoulder, nodding an exaggerated encouragement.

"Yeah, sure. Yeah, I'd love to." Alex was uncharacteristically flustered. He felt hope and horror and a dreadful sort of thrill. It was a perfect chance. Diving made Chicago happy and peaceful. Lusty too, he remembered. Whoa—it would be miracle enough if she would simply talk to him.

Chicago pushed out from under Umbi's grip and turned to Alex. Her voice was cool, professional. "It's open water one and two. We've got eight students down in Pennekamp. It's a special class and we need one on two."

"Great." He knew he wasn't about to be absolved so easily, but it was a good start. "I, ah, didn't bring any of my stuff. I wasn't expecting to be here. . . ."

"You can use my extra mask and I'll get you gear from the shop."

They gulped some coffee and piled in Chicago's old truck. Umbi insisted that he wanted to stretch out in the back and nap for the drive, but even in the privacy of the cab, there was no great flood of intimacy. They finally did talk a little. Alex asked her about her boat. She told him about the new mast, about the autopilot she was installing, and a reverse osmosis water maker she had read about, plans for an extended sail.

After her mother died when she was five, Chicago had grown up on merchant ships with her father. She had never mastered the subtle feminine arsenals of behavior-like tantrums, pouting, guilt trips, and weepy hysterics, so useful in dealing with situations like scofflaw lovers who disappear without warning. It was this lack of game playing that Alex usually loved about her, but at the moment he wondered if it all might be a little easier if she just had a fit, cried, called him names, slapped him, stomped around, made him feel guilty, gone to a girlfriend's where she could talk about how rotten he had been, then either came back to him or told him to fuck off forever. This cool civility was driving him crazy. Alex had grown up watching his sisters go through operatic travails over boyfriends whose crimes were far less hurtful than his own.

He was wondering if he should just force the issue when Chicago turned off by the sign for Pennekamp, bounced along the gravel road, and pulled into a parking lot. He could see the calm blue water between two buildings and several dive boats moored along a dock. There was a large crowd of weekend divers. Some were already in wet suits, pulling gear out of trunks, loading the boats, while others stood around in groups trading dive stories. A young man with a dark tan looked up, smiled, and waved to Chicago. He looked about twenty-five and had sun-streaked curly dark hair just brushing his shoulders. Good teeth, a strong jaw, real shaving-cream commercial material, Alex thought. He wore baggy shorts, a small black coral stud earring, and a worn leather thong with some sort of amulet around his neck.

He strode over to the cab and kissed Chicago as she jumped out. "Hey, Brian, everybody here already?" It was just a friendly sort of kiss, a hello sort of kiss, Alex thought.

"Yeah, they're over by the boat. Calvin's been here since six A.M. Think he's excited? His dad said Calvin wanted to come down last night and sleep in the car, just in case there was a bridge collapse or something this morning." Brian laughed.

"Brian, this is Alex." The slightest pause. "An old friend." Brian glanced at Chicago with a touch of surprise. Alex knew the look; it was a so-this-is-the-guy? kind of look. "He can fill in for your worthless friend," Chicago continued. "What's he sick with—tequila or rum?"

"Actually, he's really got a cold. We were doing a lot of ascents yesterday with another class and his ears stuffed up." He turned to Alex with that friendly, easy smile and extended a hand. "Glad you can help out. You're a dive master?"

"No," Alex replied. Brian was shorter than Chicago. But well built. But he wasn't her type. *It was practically a brotherly kiss.* "I dove in the navy."

"He's good, Brian, and we're still more than fine on official ratios." Technically, only one instructor was needed to supervise eight students. They now had two instructors and a dive master plus Alex. Brian accepted her vouching for Alex and went to help Umbi off-load the gear from the back of the truck.

"Brian and I have been teaching this group together," she explained to Alex as they walked toward the dock. They walked around a parked van and Alex saw the assembled dive class. They were all lined up ready to board, all in wet suits and all in wheelchairs.

They ranged from a thin teenaged boy with orange hair who was chattering on like a stand-up comic, to a quiet woman in her early forties who was nervously adjusting the silicone strap of her new mask. A solicitous and nervous group of family and friends was looking over the scene, listening to explanations of the dive gear, seeking reassurances that their loved ones were going to be all right.

"This is your class?" Alex asked surprised.

Chicago nodded proudly. "A good one too. Hey, you guys!" She moved into the group, greeting, patting shoulders, meeting parents and husbands and wives. "How you doing? You ready? Yeah, you psyched?"

Once the tanks were carried over, each diver assembled his or her own gear on the dock, while Chicago and Brian watched. When every strap was tight and every connection secure, they carried the tanks onto the boat. After that Alex felt useless. The disabled divers needed little help in boarding. The boat had been altered slightly to accommodate the group. Two rows of benches had been removed from the center rear deck to allow for the wheelchairs.

It was a perfect day with no wind, and the bay was flat. The captain steered them away from the dock and through the channel markers to the open water. Brian and Chicago went over the plan for the day, then started firing questions at their class as they chugged closer to their initiation.

"What's this mean?" Brian placed his fist across his chest.

"Low on air," they chorused.

"What's this?" Chicago pointed to her ear, then waggled her palm.

"Trouble clearing my ears," a young woman responded.

"And what do you do if you have ear trouble?"

"Go up"—she made the sign for this with her thumb—"a little bit and wait for them to clear, then go back down a little."

"Right, good." They went over everything, the serious to the silly: a flooded mask, a dropped weight belt, farting in your wet suit. Brian worked the crowd like a warm-up comedian, and he was good at it. He had real charisma. It was just a casual kiss, Alex thought. He can't be more than twenty-five . . . Chicago is thirty-three . . . She's taller than him . . . but diving makes her incredibly horny.

"What do you do if you see a shark?" Brian asked.

The group looked skeptical and a little spooked. "You take out your dive knife, cut your buddy, and swim like hell!" Brian quickly answered. It was a worn-out diver's joke, but these were novices and they laughed.

"Hey, I guess we're really lucky there," the orange-haired boy quipped. "Shark can eat half of us and we won't miss it." There was a second or two pause while the comment hit home, then most of the group erupted in laughter.

"It'd be the top half of you we wouldn't miss, Calvin," somebody gibed. The older woman feigned shock at the remark, but had to work hard to restrain a smile. A pretty young woman, however, who looked like she should be a college cheerleader, was clearly jarred. Brian went over to her wheelchair. Alex watched as he casually eased down next to her and took her hand. They talked quietly for a few minutes, her head ducked and her face lost behind a thick mane of hair. Then Brian said something and she laughed, lifted her head, and was smiling, though her eyes were red. Brian jumped up, stood behind her, and began to fluff up her hair.

"Now the most important lesson, one we haven't really gone over," he started to say in a mincing tone, "is the importance of your underwater coiffure! Honey, we've just got to do something about these split ends!" The woman began to laugh. "Now, some women prefer the slicked-back look, but personally I go for the billowing tresses, the style made ever so popular by that luscious little mermaid. Now, we could go retro—you know, fifties Esther Williams, flowers on the bathing cap . . ." So mister handsome young macho stud was a sensitive guy too, Alex thought sourly.

The boat slowed and shifted to an idle. Umbi caught the mooring buoy, and suddenly it was time to dive. Chicago pulled off her T-shirt and shorts. Under it she was wearing a yellow tank suit. Even with her olive complexion, her legs were fairly pale. She never worked on a tan and could conceive of nothing so silly as lying around on the beach when there was all that water to get under. Most of her tan was across the back of her shoulders and arms, from working out in the sun or standing in the shallow water teaching a scuba class. She pulled on an old, faded wet suit, patched at the knees. Umbi wore only a spandex skin suit to protect from the scrapes and bumps.

Dive instructors, as a general rule, wear the oldest, rattiest equipment that can still qualify under safety standards. Alex was surprised to see Brian setting up his tank with some of the newest, brightest gear on the market. His bouyancy compensator, an inflatable vest for adjusting buoyancy that also held the tank in place, was chartreuse with black stripes. Both his primary and backup regulators had vivid plastic casings, and multicolored stripes wound around his hoses. His weight belt was one flexible ring filled with lead shot, instead of the standard clunky lead weights, and his mask was a new style that came with four different colored plastic frame clips to color-coordinate at will. He was wearing one of the new Darlex neutral-buoyancy dive suits, in a shocking shades of fuchsia and royal blue, and had not one, but two of the latest compact dive computers.

Alex felt happy over the excess. One thing he knew about Chicago, she hated gadgetry and excess. A guy with this many toys didn't stand a chance with her. Brian looked up as he was screwing the regulator on his tank and seeing Alex staring at the equipment, actually blushed in mild embarrassment.

"I do test marketing for a couple of the companies," he explained sheepishly. "They make me wear it!" Alex felt like a grouper had swallowed his heart.

Once everyone was ready, there was a palpable wave of apprehension among the group.

"Hey, what's with this?" Brian feigned surprise. "Did we take a wrong turn somewhere? You guys look like we're about to toss you into the snake pit of slimy vipers from hell!" He began to tease and reassure them; he revved them up like a game show host and clucked like a mother hen.

Alex slipped over by Chicago. He could smell the sunscreen on her nose and the old rubbery scent of her wet suit. He was shocked at the memories these simple odors stirred up.

"So what do you want me to do?" Alex asked.

"Umbi and I will get in the water; you and Brian can help them get in, then hand down their gear," Chicago suggested. "Brian and Umbi will take four, and you and I will take four." Her tone was all instructorial. "That's because I'm already used to you, and Brian has worked with Umbi." She made that pretty clear. "We'll go down the anchor line, then find a nice patch of sand. It's all about twenty-five to thirty feet around here." She was buckling on her gear as she talked. "While Brian and I go over their skills, you and Umbi just hover behind them to catch anyone who might start floating up. They're all good in the water, but only Lisa, the lady in the red BC, and Jim, over there in the green mask—can kick at all. If there's time I want to swim them around a little. They've had twice the usual pool work, but it's their first time in open water—they may not be so aware of buoyancy."

"Shall I help them get their tanks on or something?"

"Don't need to. Just watch." She smiled, her pale blue eyes

sparkling, the joy of adventure plain to see on her face. Chicago had been diving since she was ten, and part of the reason she liked teaching was the contact high she always got from seeing people discover it for the first time.

One by one the wheelchair divers rolled up to the gate. Brian had rigged up a small wooden seat there so they could transfer themselves from chair to seat, then do a backroll into the water. Chicago and Umbi waited in the water with each person's scuba gear. Once in, the diver paddled over and put the gear on in the water. Then Alex handed down a weight belt, and the divers strapped that on. The only assistance they needed was someone to help lift their legs as they rolled in.

In a little while, the whole group was ready. Masks on, regulators in, hearts pounding, two by two they slipped below the surface and began their descent down the anchor line.

Fourteen

SATURDAY AFTERNOON WILLIE Wallace finally felt good again. In fact, he felt blissfully happy. Whatever combination of sedatives and painkillers they had given him had managed to induce a sweet euphoria and finally blur the reality of the past few days. Their flight out of Saint Martin had suffered delays, then a thunderstorm over most of Texas and Louisiana had further stalled their arrival. By the time they'd landed in Baton Rouge, it was nearly 11 P.M. and Willie had drunk enough little bottles of bourbon on the plane to set up a miniature bowling alley in the middle of the first-class aisle. Ruthwilde and Grant had to almost carry him off. Since it was so late and no one was expecting them back, Willie and Grant slept at Ruthwildes', Willie on the couch where they dropped him upon entry.

It wasn't until Saturday morning, when he woke amid a variety of aches and pains, that Willie'd remembered about the shark bite. There was a hot throbbing pain in his leg. He tried to pull the pants leg up to have a look, but found it would not go. Finally he just dropped his pants. He hadn't checked the wound since Grant had doctored it, some twenty-four hours ago.

Grant was no Dr. Kildare. Grant had dozed through most of biology class, especially the bits about Antonie van Leeuwenhoek and his boring discovery of germs. He had cheated on his Boy Scout first aid exam.

Grant had, however, watched a lot of westerns, so knew what to do in the event of snakebite and gunshot wounds. It had taken him a remarkably few seconds to decide that the little shark who had fastened his jaws on Willie's left calf was probably not related to snakes at all and was certainly not poisonous and that the remedy would then be the same as for a bullet wound. He had poured a generous dose of Bacardi rum over the ragged wound and wrapped it up.

When they'd gotten back to the hotel, Grant bought some gauze from the pharmacy for a better bandage. He'd meant to buy some peroxide or something too, but didn't have enough guilders and that would've meant changing a fifty-dollar traveler's check, and since they were leaving that afternoon why bother. There was still a little rum left, so he'd simply doused the wound again and given it a generous wrap with the gauze.

Now Willie stared at his leg, red and swollen to the size of an inflatable bozo punching doll. The smell of rum was still vaguely recognizable through the stench of pus, and the red stain on the gauze had faded to a rusty brown. Willie was shocked, then he began to gag. The world began to spin. He took a step, the pants around his ankles tripped him, and he fell forward, crashing through the glass-topped coffee table, scattering copies of *Southern Living* and *American Gardener.*

A pretty nursing assistant came in with his lunch, and Willie gave her a drowsy, beatific smile. She was about nineteen, brunette, big green eyes. "Oh, Mr. Wallace," she purred. Willie was thrilled to hear the soft Southern drawl after two months of Caribbean accents. "Are you feeling better? Here, let me fix this pillow." Soft little hands rearranged his bandaged arm. The crash through the table had added a few cuts and bruises. The girl artfully arranged the blanket that was suspended over plastic hoops to keep the weight off his leg. Massive doses of antibiotics had started to reduce the inflammation.

"Is it ta-roo, you really got bitten by a shark?" she asked wide-eyed and admiring. "I just think you must have been so ba-rave!"

Willie hadn't the faintest idea what story Ruthwilde had told the doctors about the circumstances of his bite, so he wisely decided just to nod along to whatever she had heard. By the end of the day the gossip among the nurses had evolved to epic proportions which involved a shipwreck, some sort of valiant rescue, a daring fight with a pack of man-eating sharks, and ultimate rescue by dolphins.

Fifteen

THERE COMES A moment the first time underwater when you realize you are actually *there.* At first there are too many *things* to think about. Is my equipment right? Can I really clear my mask? Will something bite me? Which button do I push on the BC? Will my ears pop? Am I doing this right? Will I die? Do I look stupid?

Then suddenly, you are underwater and things feel right. You are floating effortlessly in the soft blue, and all around you are beautiful alive things, and you are *part* of it. You look up and see the sky far above, and realize you can *be* here. You are weightless, unbound.

Chicago and Brian eased the group slowly down the anchor line, then settled them into two semicircles on the sandy bottom. Alex watched as she guided each one through the slight adjustments that would get them perfectly neutral, hovering just above the bottom so that small regulations in breath could guide them up and down as desired.

The students gradually began to relax into this new world. Jerky and clumsy as all new divers at first, they soon began to move more gracefully, to play with their new freedom. Calvin was turning somersaults; one woman simply hovered over the bottom, her feet touching the sand, the first time she had stood erect in twelve years.

Chicago and Brian had prepared the group for every sort of circumstance except one. Crying. After years in wheelchairs, they could fly. Chicago thought at first one woman was having trouble breathing, for her bubbles came in hard little bursts, but when she swam up to her, she saw the tears. Emotion swept through the little group. Chicago worked hard to blink back her own tears. Umbi took off his mask and blew his nose. Then the tears became laughs, a major, and very contagious case of the giggles, causing everyone to get water in their masks, and so the first of the exercises, clearing a flooded mask, got underway.

After the training exercises were finished, Chicago and Brian led the group, half towing the weaker swimmers to the nearby reef. It was a perfect spot. A pair of stingrays, accustomed to the frequent traffic of divers in the area, swam around nonchalantly as if looking at tourists from another country. They found long-spined sea urchins in crevices, and coronet fish hanging upside down disguised among the corals. Then they saw the shark.

Six feet long, sleek and gray, it was a nurse shark. They might never even have seen it had not Brian led them right up to it. Nurse sharks had spliced off from their more aggressive cousins somewhere along the evolutionary way, developing proudly into the couch potato of the shark world, the basset hound of the species. They like to spend their days in quiet nooks, just waiting for dark to cruise around and munch a few crustaceans.

This one was a dependable actor. She usually hid in one of three holes. Lately, Brian thought, she didn't even seem to care to hide herself, and actually left her graceful tail exposed. Gently Brian reached out one finger and stroked the sandpaper skin on the tail, showing the new divers they had nothing to fear. Although far from vicious, nurse sharks are the most likely shark to injure a scuba diver. This is because divers, knowing the sharks are so placid and working for a show of bravado, often tease them, grabbing their tails and yanking them from their holes.

Alex watched as the group hovered by the reef, their eyes shining with fascination. Chicago hung just above them, looking like some guardian angel, perfectly at home here and forever out of reach.

Sixteen

ETHAN RUTHWILDE SAT in his study, watching the hummingbirds hover and sip from the bougainvillea that swept gracefully up the side of the garden fence. He loved their jeweled colors, their exquisite daintiness; and all his flowers were cultivated to attract them. There was something about the hummingbirds, the way they would be there, then suddenly gone, their flight all but invisible. He liked to do his thinking here.

He pulled off his glasses. The thick lenses made them heavy, and the earpieces pressed against the sides of his wide head. He rubbed his eyes, then rested his huge chin in his hands. Ruthwilde was not the fretful type. Although he had run a major corporation in a high-pressure business, he was not the Type A personality. He assumed an almost meditative state of relaxation for his thinking, and in this way he could view the pieces of whatever trouble he had to deal with and wait for the solutions to materialize like the hummingbirds.

He was worried about Willie. He hadn't expected the boy to be such a sissy about the whole thing. The shark bite was bad, but wouldn't necessarily cause any suspicion. But what else might go wrong now? He didn't like having to make plans so quickly, especially of this magnitude.

The phone rang.

"Yes," he answered tersely.

"Goot morning, Ethan."

"You goddamn bastard." Ruthwilde's voice trembled just a little, controlling his rage. "I didn't believe even you would do something this brutal—or this stupid. What the hell have you gone and done?"

Ethan waited, listening to the silence on the other end.

"Wot are you toking about?" Goerbel responded laconically, but with a note of surprise. The German's voice had a heavy cold quality. His accent was slight. He was proud of his *W's,* but still sounded his vowels round and low from deep in his throat.

"You said we had another week. I was working on things. There was no reason to kill her."

A pause. "We hovn't killed anyone. Wot are you talking about?"

"I'm not sure why you would choose to play dumb about it, *mein* friend. But just what the hell did you expect to accomplish? You think the senator is going to have any motivation now with Angelica dead?"

"Mr. Ruthwilde, Angelica iss not dead. She's hoppily bronzing her tits on a topless beach in Saint Barts."

"Yeah. When was the last time you talked to your goons down there?"

"Belief me, my men are not likely to miss information of this nature."

"When Goerbel?"

"I haf been traveling. I would say last week."

"Right. Eight days ago she was on Saint Barts. Then she got bored with the French and breezed over to Saint Maarten for some discos and shopping. Then three days ago she disappeared." There was silence on the other end. Ethan heard the sound of ripening worry.

"So she has met some other boyfriend and slipped away with him for a time. We will find her." A rude little chuckle. "She is not likely to be shut up with one boy for more than a week, don't you agree?"

"Oh give it up, Goerbel. They found a body."

"A body."

"The senator has already tentatively ID'd her. We're waiting for the autopsy to confirm."

"There was some problem with identification?"

"Yeah, some problem. You could put it that way. Where'd you get these goons of yours? The Dachau School of International Business?" Ruthwilde slammed down the receiver.

Seventeen

"DAD! HEY, DAD—I touched a shark!" Calvin's excited shouts could be heard over the chugging engine as the boat eased up against the dock.

"Oh, mon, by the end of this day he'll be telling how he stuck his head inside the mouth." Umbi laughed. Chicago smiled. The dive couldn't have been better, but she felt suddenly exhausted.

"But we should have figured," Brian pointed out as he popped a cork and poured Chicago a glass of champagne. "They've already gone through major traumas, a little water in the mask isn't going to scare them. And if it did, they can't bolt anyway." "Bolting," a panicked diver shooting for the surface, was every instructor's nightmare. Even a ninety-pound weakling has rare strength in a panic for the surface.

The ride back to shore was a merry one, and as soon as the gear was all packed away, the group reassembled at a local bar. The enthusiasm was ferocious.

"Yeah, it was like—eight or ten feet long!" Calvin was telling the shark story for about the fifth time.

"Yeah, like your nose is gonna be if you keep telling those stories." Brian laughed. There was champagne and pitchers of beer, much toasting, and a stream of excited stories.

"Did you see those great big parrot fish . . . oh, and then, those two orange fish? . . . What was that black one with the electric blue stripe? . . . I thought it would be harder! It was so *easy*. . . . Dad, you've got to try it. . . ."

Alex listened to the talk and marveled at the number of things he had missed. That gorgeous bright blue fish? A blue chromis, one of the most common tropical fishes, but come to think of it, they were pretty.

The bar TV was tuned to a baseball game, the regular patrons watched it attentively, only occasionally casting a glance over this strange rowdy group in wheelchairs. They were used to Saturday afternoon dive groups, but none quite like this. When the four o'clock newsbreak came on, the men left the bar and moved to the pool table or hit the toilets. Alex had a clear view of the TV as the story of Angelica Wattles appeared on the screen.

"The body, found Friday morning floating off the coast of the Caribbean island of Antilla, is suspected to be Angelica Wattles, daughter of Senator Wattles from Louisiana." This announcement was made over scenes of Angelica from a homemade video, shot at a party aboard a yacht. Angelica was a voluptuous blond beauty in a tiny orange bikini that showed off her perfect tan.

"Although the body had apparently been floating for some time and was not recovered in its entirety, the senator was able to recognize certain scars and jewelry." The bouncy Angelica waved at the camera, blew a kiss. Cut to another scene of her lying on a beach towel on the deck. She lifted her head up, peered over the top of her sunglasses, made a face at the camera. "The medical examiner said blood tests and other forensic evidence matched Angelica's. Cause of death has not been established, but it appears to be an accidental drowning."

Brian approached the bar, two empty pitchers in his hands, and looked up at the TV. "Some babe, huh? It's really too bad. I heard sharks munched most of her."

"Yeah?" Alex responded casually. "That so?" There was something about the video images that nagged at the back of his mind.

"A final identification may be issued soon," the newscaster finished, as a still photo of Angelica in debutante regalia was poised above his left shoulder.

It was five o'clock before they got the last of the happy divers packed off in the direction of home, and could start back to Miami. Umbi had decided to stay the night in Key Largo, Chicago would return in the morning for the final two dives with this group. She was clearly tired, and Alex offered to drive. She put her feet up on the dash and closed her eyes. He realized now, as they rode along in silence, that his sudden arrival had probably kept her up walking around all night.

This was all a big mistake, he thought. He should just leave in the morning and get back to his life. What life? Island hopping with crates of pineapples and plumbing supplies? Alex had put most of his year's salary into buying the plane from Gilbey, and figured to pay off the balance in another couple of months, but he still wasn't sure what he was going to do then.

Alex switched on the radio, spun the knob through top forty, some New Age harp crap, news, and a classical station that was playing something a little too violiny. He finally found some jazz. Chicago's eyes were closed, but he wasn't sure if she were asleep or just avoiding him.

What can I say? he thought. Where to start? I left you because . . . A dozen times he thought he might say something, but they rode in silence. Twenty minutes along the way, one of the tanks broke loose in the back of the truck. It rolled from side to side a few times, then shifted and rolled back against the tailgate with a crash. Chicago woke with a start as Alex pulled over.

"It's OK, just the tanks rolling around," he explained.

"Ah shit!" She climbed out and kicked the bumper in frustration. The tank had knocked an already-loose hinge halfway off. Roughly she unhooked the tailgate and smacked it back in place. Other tanks started rolling back, and she tried to catch them. The tailgate snapped open.

"Hold on, what are you trying to do?" Alex caught the rolling row of scuba tanks and steadied the tailgate. "Hang on—"

"Let go!" Chicago smacked his hand. "Don't *help* me! Don't you dare help me!" There was anger and defiance in her voice, but mostly there was hurt. "Just get the hell out of the way." She pushed him. Alex didn't even wobble, and this enraged her more.

"Don't you dare . . . *help* me!" Her voice was shaking. "You're just gone! You just up and disappear—and now you're mister big fucking helpful!" She cried as she tried to shove the tanks back in place. Her fury made her clumsy, and the tailgate fell open, all ten tanks tumbling forward. Alex grabbed her arms and pulled her back out of the way.

"Stop it!" she screamed. "Let me *go*!" He was so surprised he couldn't do anything but hold on to her. She was crying now. Real sobs and tears. The tanks rolled off and clunked in the weeds around them. He pulled her close, almost crushing her. Helplessly he held her, there by the side of the road up to their knees in goldenrod, as the thudding tanks sent up clouds of dust like bombs.

Chicago's sobs grew quieter. Alex loosened his grip and half carried her back to the truck where they both sat on the lopsided tailgate. Now he understood. Her composure had been to get her through the day. She had a job to do. Now that was done, there was room for the pain.

"I'm sorry. I didn't ever want to hurt you." Alex heard his voice flat. What stupid words he had. "I just had to go." Chicago wiped her face on the back of her hand and slid off the tailgate. The sun was setting with a dull smear of orange, and flocks of blackbirds whirred up around catching the evening insect bloom.

"Fine. Do it again," she said calmly as she grabbed one of the tanks and heaved it back into the truck. "Just go."

Eighteen

Frommer does not offer a guide to international accommodations for the rich and *wanted*, but somehow the wealthy fugitives of the world know where to go. Geneva, of course, for banking, and Liechtenstein if the marshals are particularly hot on the trail. Spain's Costa del Sol is a cozy place, especially if one has a yacht, for it has pleasant ports with quick access to North Africa. Buenos Aires is an old standby, but a little far for the Euro-centered criminal. Of course, if one really wanted to disappear there are remote places and ways to vanish, but one does not get to be a billionaire fugitive without a certain fondness for danger and the gamesmanship of pursuit, and so the Continent is littered with forged identities.

At the moment Peter Valascheck, bored by the indolent lifestyle and needing to meet with various business associates, had ventured out of his Austrian hideaway and taken a suite for the weekend in the Plaza Athenee in Paris. Hans Goerbel had flown down from Hamburg for dinner, and they were now enjoying espresso and snifters of Louis XIII cognac.

Things were looking grim. German reunification, a boon to legitimate business, had turned out to be something of a nuisance for Goerbel and Valascheck. The newly opened countries in eastern Europe were hungry for raw materials. German chemical manufacturing was up 2 percent in an otherwise depressed world market, and no one had much incentive to risk supplying them any more.

"Especially now with this"—Goerbel threw the newspaper on the coffee table.

BONN PROPOSES TIGHTER CONTROL OF LETHAL EXPORTS, the headlines declared. "The German government has approved a drastic tightening of controls on exports of chemicals today in the wake of several apparently illegal West German arms shipments to the third world," he read.

"It's nothing." Valascheck dismissed the report. "There will always be a market, and someone will always have to supply it."

"Meanwhile they're strangling me!" Goerbel said urgently. "Your friends in Singapore won't just stand around waiting for the climate to get better, you know. If I don't keep things rolling, all your networks will start to collapse. We'll have to start all over."

"No possibility of Rotterdam?"

"Rotterdam is tight as a virgin. The whole virtuous little country is up in arms since van Anraat was arrested."

"What about Pakistan?" Valascheck pressed. "Did you talk to the people I gave you there?"

"Pakistan's too dizzy these days. They have all the business they want with heroin and banking," Goerbel explained bitterly.

"So it is a test of your cleverness, my friend."

"Easy for you to say," Goerbel pointed out. "You've made your fortune."

"Ah, but living the life of an exile." There was a gentle irony in his tone as he waved the brandy snifter toward the elegant trappings in the lounge. "You don't know how it pains me to know I can never return to the United States again. Why, in all the time I was with Alsak I never did get over to see the Baltimore aquarium." Valascheck's tone was mocking. "But things will change." He tried to assure his partner. "It's just this Kuwait thing—no one wants to take the risk of supplying you right now. If we lose our networks, we can build new ones. Perhaps it is a good time to just lie low. Certainly you have other investments, interests, to keep you busy?"

Goerbel shook his head, and Valascheck saw there was something more urgent.

"You remember Abu Tahile?"

"He was Jibril's flunky?" Valascheck ran his finger down the side of his face. "A long scar here?"

Goerbel nodded. "But he's no flunky anymore. Did you know Saddam had Jibril executed?" Valascheck looked only slightly surprised. "It seems an occupational hazard of serving in the Iraqi cabinet."

"I never did hear the whole story, but they say his daughter went out to the family Mercedes one morning and found Daddy's head on the front seat. Anyway, Saddam brought Abu Tahile into the cabinet." Goerbel spoke quickly now in a low voice, although there was no one around to hear them. "Tahile came to see me shortly after the invasion, officially, to see about rearranging our supply systems around the sanctions. Unofficially, he's interested in obtaining more merchandise."

Valascheck looked puzzled. "They have enough stockpiled to gas the whole country three times over. What does he need with more?"

"Everything in Iraq is either in Baghdad or already moving south to the Kuwati boarder. Evidently, Tahile and a few others are hoping that if war does break out, Saddam's control will be weakened."

Valascheck's eyes widened with surprise and admiration. "A coup?"

Goerbel shrugged. "Who knows? Tahile is being realistic. He knows there are at least five or six other factions thinking along the same lines. He commands some loyalty, but his support is in the north. He's afraid of attack from Turkey, and certainly from the Kurds. If there is a civil war, he won't be able to handle Saddam's troops plus local opposition."

Valascheck smiled in appreciation of Tahile's foresight. He could use more such men in his network. "So he needs his own supply."

Goerbel nodded. "He can't move any stockpiles without arousing suspicion, and Saddam isn't good with suspicion these days."

"I see." Valascheck set his glass down and his posture changed ever so slightly as he quickly slipped from bon vivant to businessman. "So that is why the senator's shipments are suddenly so important?"

"Exactly. We've got him by the throat already. It's just a case of keeping him."

"And what is it that you need from me?"

"Muscle—and persuasion. First I need you to talk to Singapore—and Jordan—convince them you're still behind this. Then I need someone in the States to take care of a few loose ends. This thing with the senator's daughter is all screwed up, and I don't know what's going on with Ruthwilde."

Valascheck nodded. "Certainly. Anything I can do to be of help."

On the ride back to the airport, Goerbel was in a deep gloom. Things were falling apart too quickly. First those damn UN investigations, now the possibility of war in Kuwait. There was no way to predict how that would affect his business with Iraq in the long run, but Goerbel never believed for a minute that the market for his products would disappear completely. Syria was still buying—and Libya of course. And there was new territory: Burma—or Myanmar or whatever the hell they were calling it these days. There were all sorts of new despots cropping up every day. If he could keep the channels open, and get Abu Tahile off his back, he would be OK. All he had to do now was wait for the damn Louisiana shipment.

Nineteen

"TAX IMPOUNDMENT? WHAT the hell tax impoundment? You can't ground my plane." Alex was furious. "It's registered in the BVI, there *are* no U.S. taxes there, and besides, I already *own* half the plane!" He was trying to resist the black bubbling rage rising in his gut, the rage that began to simmer whenever he had to deal with officials of any rank, any country, in any capacity, ever.

"Mr. Sanders, the plane may have a registration from the BVI, and if you have any legal title to the property or a portion thereof" —Who the hell talks in *thereof's*? Alex cringed—"we will certainly consider your claim, but we have a previous registration in Florida in the name of Anthony Gibbs. There's a lien against it, for a bad loan for one thing, as well as several years of nonpayment of U.S. income tax."

Even as he protested, there was this small clear rhythmic thud going on in the back of his mind, an awful sinking feeling that, yes, it was quite likely true that Anton Gilbey could very well be Anthony Gibbs, and did indeed owe several thousand dollars in U.S. taxes and they had every right to impound his plane. At least half the expats in the Caribbean were hiding out from something or other.

"Well, who do I talk to? How do we start unraveling this"—he checked himself—"this little snarl?" he finished politely.

"I'm sorry, sir. It's seven o'clock on Saturday night. There's nothing we can do until Monday morning. The records do seem to be clear."

"Great. So what are the chances of me sleeping in my plane tonight?"

The woman smiled and shook her head. Alex sighed and stared out the window toward the grounded plane.

"Somehow I didn't think so."

Senator Wattles stared at the picture of Angelica propped against the mirror of his dresser. It was the one he had brought for the press, the debutante photo that made her look so lovely and innocent. Where had they dragged up those stupid bikini videos? How could they do that to him—to her? Oh sure, they were no more scandalous than half the commercials these days, but it was his daughter, his only child, his angel. They had no right.

Darcy stuck his head in the room. "I've got the press release about the funeral ready if you want to look it over." When the senator didn't respond, his aide continued. "It's just the basics—small funeral, immediate family only, privacy requested. Do you have a request for donations in lieu of flowers?"

Wattles rubbed his head and took another long drink of his bourbon. "God, I never thought there would be so many details."

"Cancer is always good, sir," Sullevin suggested, "or education. You could set up a scholarship fund in her name."

Wattles nodded. "That's fine. Yes." He walked over to the window and stared out at the lights of the city. "Oh God, Darcy, what am I supposed to do now? What do I say to everyone when I get back? How am I supposed to act?"

"I guess you just act like your only child is dead, sir."

Twenty

CHICAGO SAT ON deck staring out over the inky water with Lassie curled up on her lap. The night was clear with too many stars, the sort of night that made her want to be out on the open sea. She felt restless and exhausted and a little bit damaged. Too tired to walk, too awake to sleep, she absently stroked the snake's head and tried to think of anything but Alex.

She tried to remember the joy of the dive that day, how excited everyone had been—the look on Lisa's face when she found herself weightless and free after years in a wheelchair, the soft curve of the eagle rays as they waltzed around them—but the images were tainted by the picture she could not lose. Alex, oh goddamn you. She squeezed her eyes as if she could shut out his image that way, but it was more than a picture. It was as if he physically took up space even when he was nowhere around, as if his body pushed so hard against the air that it left the walls of space weakened around her.

For a long time Chicago had been able to displace the hurt, stoking up a sharp anger instead, but now that she had seen him again, that had crumbled. She felt adrift. To just leave like that, overnight; almost any other way would have been better.

She sat up abruptly and shook herself to stop the thoughts. Lassie, responding to her anxiety, began to move restlessly, and Chicago took the snake below to her favorite corner. "Maybe that's why I have you for a pet, sweetie," she spoke ironically to the snake. "You aren't going anywhere, and, don't take it personally, but you aren't all that damn lovable in the first place."

She switched on the cabin lights and looked around for something to do to keep busy. There weren't many little jobs left, and it was too late to mess with something big and greasy. Finally she decided to patch a small tear on the corner of the sofa.

The sofa was a huge, overstuffed antique with carved claw feet.

It was an absurd thing to have on a boat, but after much debate, she had decided, against all logic, to keep it. Her father had brought it back from a voyage many years ago, having won it in a card game in Brazil. It had been equally absurd in their home. She remembered most of the people from the village standing around laughing as her father and some of his crew tried to hoist it up to the porch. She could remember him lifting her up to sit on it the first time, and the strange hot texture of the brocade against the back of her bare legs. It had become too much a part of her life to see it go.

She had, however, bolted the feet down and made tough sail-cloth covers to protect it. Now she got out her sewing kit, cut a square from the extra material, and sitting cross-legged on the cabin floor, began to stitch it in place.

Sewing was about the only feminine skill Chicago was good at. Her mother, Tassia, had been a seamstress. Chicago remembered whenever her father would return from a voyage how excited they both were over the fabrics he would bring, glittery metallics, and the lightest prints, beautiful soft cottons that immediately were made into dresses, and velvets, impractical for wear on a tropical island, but lovely to touch.

Her mother used every bit of the fabric, first making clothes, then little stuffed toys from the remnants. Chicago kept every scrap in a basket and played with them, spreading them out in rows, lining them up according to color or pattern. Sometimes she rolled them up around marble sized fruit pits and made them into people, creating whole societies of children and fishermen, dancers, talking fish, sailors, beautiful ladies and handsome men, evil missionaries.

She was five when her mother died, and her father gave her the job of picking out clothes for the burial. Instead of a dress Chicago brought him the basket of scraps, and they tucked her into the wooden coffin in a cushion of confetti, with all the velvet bits soft against her face.

Chicago stared at the patch. Her sewing was uneven, and she had stretched the fabric on the bias so it was puckering in one corner. Annoyed, she ripped out the seam. It wasn't working; the crazy black wave was still there, hovering over her, threatening to crash in on her any minute. She got up again, popped a Patsy Cline tape in the stereo, got a beer, and sat on the cabin floor, leaning against the sofa with the idle needle in her hand.

Twenty-One

ALEX HAD NEVER felt so grounded. Stuck in the Miami airport, with no telling how long it would take to get the mess straightened out. Meanwhile, what to do with himself? He considered calling Wonton. Alex was certain his old partner would be glad to see him and put him up for a couple of days, but there would be things to talk about, inevitable explanations. He just wasn't ready for the whole scene.

Just let me take the plane, he thought. I'll fly to Saint Croix and get my hands on Gilbey and beat the tax money out of him. Alex was pretty sure his half ownership in the plane was good, but no telling what obstacles the government had in store for him before he was free to break away. There had to be a better way. There was always a way. All he needed was someone to pull a few strings out of this tangled ball. Someone like—Senator Wattles! Of course. Or at least his pompous little assistant. Alex went back to the hangar where he had noticed a bicycle locked up in the back room. He asked around and found out it belonged to a baggage handler. He found the man pitching suitcases onto a conveyer belt as if they were bombs and he liked explosions. It only took twenty bucks and Alex's watch for collateral to secure use of the bike.

A cab would have been logical, but cycling was a release for Alex, a tonic, a meditation. Once on the bicycle he was part of a machine, generating his own power, everything under his own control. He had developed an addiction as a boy back in North Dakota, where he would ride for miles and miles, swallowing up the endless flat highways and testing his limits. Later on he started racing.

He rode out of the airport, sprinting down the long service road until he found his pace, then out into the city. Alex was in a fairly good mood when he reached the hotel. He didn't even mind when the valet parking guy in the feathered helmet held him up at the front door, thinking him a courier. A phone call to the senator's suite got him through.

Darcy Sullevin met him at the door. Alex was even glad for this. He felt a little bad about bothering the senator with his own problem in the middle of the man's personal trauma, but hell, he figured, the guy *was* a politician.

"It's nice to see you again, Mr. Sanders," Darcy lied smoothly as he cast a fairly disgusted glance over the sweaty figure, now with a two-day growth of beard. "What can I do for you?"

"How about a drink of water to start, then maybe the senator can get my airplane unimpounded."

Darcy poured him a glass of ice water and listened passively as Alex sketched out the trouble with the officials and the seizure. "I can certainly look into the matter for you," he offered noncommittally. "Of course it's not so simple as a few phone calls. There are processes that have already been set in motion, as I'm sure you know, but I'll see what I can do. Why don't you give me a call Monday morning."

Alex was debating what further encouragement he could give the twerp when the bedroom door opened and Senator Wattles came in.

"I thought I heard a visitor."

"Senator Wattles, this is Alex Sanders—the pilot."

"Oh yes, yes." The senator came forward and shook Alex's hand. His eyes were bleary and tired, from grief and alcohol equally, Alex figured, and he felt a stab of compassion for the man. He was on the downside of that uniquely nineteen fifties brand of male handsomeness. The powerful jawline had gone jowly, the big hands were now pawlike. The lines on his forehead, which once lent an air of serious thought, had cracked and deepened over the years, and there was that all-over sort of puffiness that seizes bankers and businessmen around age fifty. His voice was still strong, the Southern accent still rich, but Alex could tell there was a certain tone missing.

"I'm sorry," the senator continued, "I was listening to the news. I didn't know you were here. I do want to thank you for going out of your way to bring my daughter home." Alex said nothing, but glanced at Darcy.

"I'm afraid we've just received news that a positive identification has been made."

"Oh. I'm sorry."

"We were just in the process of phoning the loved ones and

making arrangements." Darcy turned to the senator. "Alex has come to see if we could help smooth out a little trouble with his plane," he said, with timing calculated to make Alex feel like a heel for interrupting.

"Oh, well, yes, of course." Wattles seemed battered and tired. "Take care of it, Darcy, could you? Darcy here is a regular brick. Don't know how I'd get through all this without him."

Darcy gave him a thin smile.

"But if you will excuse me, I have to make some phone calls." The senator shuffled back to his bedroom, and Alex felt a little ashamed. So what if he was part of the power-grubbing, bloated, governmental bilge the rest of the time, right now he was just an old man with a heavy grief.

"Mrs. Wattles passed on some time ago," Darcy explained. "Angelica was his only child. She meant the world to him."

"Do you have any idea how she died?"

"The doctor is pretty sure it was an accidental drowning. Angelica was the type who—" he paused, and Alex caught a flicker of sarcasm in his tone, "was fond of good times. I'm afraid she could get carried away. We think she may have been out on a boat. We do know that she had met some boy down there; she had been seen with him for a couple of weeks. It's still too early to tell."

"A couple of weeks? How long had she been in the islands?"

"Oh, nearly two months. She had just graduated from college, and this was her little reward."

"She went alone?"

"No, with a girlfriend originally—they were just going to stay for a month, but then Angelica got into the life-style and decided to stay on."

"I see."

"Is there anything else I can do for you tonight, Mr. Sanders?"

"No. Thanks."

"Well then, call me Monday morning—say about eleven. By then I will have talked to my people in Washington."

Twenty-Two

Shana Phillips slumped back in the chair and gazed skeptically at her producer. The Saturday night news was over, and it was about the only time during the week they had to talk.

"I don't know, Harland. I'm not exactly high on Senator Wattles's hit parade these days, and his AA practically snarls whenever he sees me. Besides, I'm getting too old for crusades. I don't have an ounce of righteous indignation left."

"I'm not asking you to get righteous or indignant, or any combination thereof." Joe Harland laughed. "But the miscarriage thing you did got people interested. We've had a lot of calls. I just think we should follow it up. Channel four got a lot of mileage out of the incinerator pollution last summer."

Shana picked up the videotape of her three-part report on an area chemical plant. Although the plant was now operating within EPA limits, it had stored chemicals improperly for years and run-off had contaminated soil in surrounding neighborhoods.

"You really think this is a good time for another ecological scare story?" she pressed. "I mean—people are moving back to Love Canal; saccharin doesn't really hurt us; alar was a big joke. Why should they believe that a chemical plant is causing miscarriages in Prince Georges County?"

"We don't have to stay with the armless-baby angle," Harland offered. Shana scowled at the black humor. "But I do think Wattles's bill is interesting. If nothing else, it takes a lot of chutzpah to push for deregulation when ecology is so chic. You've already got the miscarriages"—Joe Harland paused dramatically—"*and* pesticide residue in duck eggs."

"Herons."

"Herons, whatever. They live on the *bay*." He exaggerated the revelation. "Chesapeake Bay is very big right now."

"Look, you know I'm interested. It's just that I don't know

where to go with it all. We've got daily murders, the mayor is on trial for using cocaine, war is brewing with Iraq, and you want me to feature some minor ethics thing?"

"I just want you to poke around a little, like in the good old days when you were an ambitious young reporter out for blood."

"I don't know, Joe." Shana seemed genuinely dejected. "I'm not sure there's a story there."

"What happened to rooting out evil and corruption?"

Shana laughed. "I guess I've just come to realize that I do more good for the world exposing bad roofing companies and insurance scams than I ever will uncovering the next government scandal."

"Let's start with Senator Wattles," Harland suggested. "You already talked with him on the last story. What was your sense of him?"

Shana rolled her eyes. "He's certainly close to the industry. His family owned a conglomerate of chemical plants in the Louisiana delta, but he divested when he was elected." Shana shrugged. "Supposedly—who knows?" She was dismayed to find herself thinking, who cares? "No one has actually ever accused him of any dirty stuff. He pushes pork to his home state, but who doesn't?"

"Well, let's just keep an eye on him. Talk to someone at EPA—try that guy we interviewed a while ago when we did the sick building story. That tall lawyer—looks like Frank Zappa, you know the guy, Jewish with some kind of Irish first name. I've got him in the file somewhere; he was sharp. Talk to him, get some background, you know, potential impact of the bill, stuff like that."

"Sure. OK. But do you think we can cool the investigation until the poor man gets over the shock of losing his daughter?" Shana asked sarcastically.

"They're sure it's her?" Harland looked surprised.

"It just came over the wire."

Shana gathered up her coat and briefcase and walked out through the newsroom, feeling strangely sad. What had happened to squash her zeal? Maybe she was just getting too comfortable. She had a nice apartment, reasonable creature comforts, a good audience share. She had a file of letters from grateful viewers who had avoided the phony credit card schemes and product rip-offs she had exposed.

Was it so bad to be happy and comfortable and respected and not save the world? Was it worse because she was a black woman? Sure, every young reporter wants a Watergate, but what sort of scandal could move the cynical hearts of America today? Hardly anyone could even follow the convolutions of Iran Contra, and besides, Ollie was too cute. The S and L scandals were never sexy; the Keating Five could just have well been a dance group. Even the old standbys—greedy officials stealing from widows and orphans as the Reagan officials in HUD had done—failed to inspire outrage.

When Shana Phillips was just starting out she had been told she was too pretty, too dainty looking to be an effective reporter. Her petite size, heart-shaped face, big brown eyes with thick lashes, and a tiny natural beauty mark over one lip, made her look innocent and doll-like. This charming appearance had been more of a barrier to Shana than either her sex or her race. Even now, as she careened on the edge of thirty, with a reputation as a good journalist, she still sometimes had trouble. But she had carved out an important niche in consumer affairs, and she was happy with it. She didn't need a crusade.

The air was cold and a stiff wind was still blowing as Shana stepped out onto Wisconsin Avenue. She was tired and dejected and frustrated, and she knew she was about to become more so. She stood on the curb outside the station in a well-lit area, so that every approaching taxi could see her clearly. One passed after only a brief glance in her direction. She could see two more stopped at a light and stepped into the street to wave at them. The one in the near lane switched over two lanes and sped away; the other driver didn't even make a pretense, just cruised on by.

It was a regular event. No amount of TV exposure, no amount of conservative clothing, not the leather briefcase or the professional demeanor, nothing was of much use to a black person trying to hail a taxi at night in Washington, D.C.

Twenty-Three

Alex decided to ride clear out of the city, zip down Route 1, and ride the causeways to the Keys. He could easily do fifty or sixty miles tonight, sleep on the beach, and just hang out down there until Monday. He could avoid the spandex nightmare of Saturday night Miami. He could leave behind the memories, the pieces of his life that had got all dragged out and jangled up here. He could have, that is, if the baggage handler had taken better care of his bicycle. Barely two miles along, the crank snapped in two, leaving him suddenly pedaling air. He pushed the bike under a streetlight and examined it. If he had a crank puller, this wouldn't be hard to fix, but there was little chance of finding the right tools this time of night.

Bad luck, Alex thought grimly. He wheeled the crippled bike down the shoulder of the road. He knew the general area. He was on the edges of a bustling Hispanic neighborhood. He had come here a couple of times with Umbi and Chicago to listen to reggae bands. Alex decided to go look for a cheap motel.

It was Saturday night in the barrio, and the streets were bustling. There was music careening out of every shop and bar. Posturing young men in their shiny polyester regalia flirted with beautiful girls in ruffled dresses and cheap party shoes. Huge rattling cars cruised the boulevard with dangling fringe in the windows and radios cranked to full. It could have been anywhere in the Hispanic world. The common elements were the same—that thick spilling swirl of music and macho and motherhood, family dinners and paper-bag booze. Sizzling oil, and spicy meat smells filled the air. Skittering children, currently armed with neon-bright clacker balls, ran wild, their laughter punctuated by the constant snap and clack of the toys.

As Alex walked along, he began to relax and enjoy the pageant. A day-long wedding reception was breaking up, the men weaving happily along, their jackets unbuttoned and wilted. A mother was trying to stuff her baby girl, dressed in voluminous ruffles and lace, into a car seat, but the baby was lost somewhere beneath the crinkly yards of yellow and white.

Two teenage girls, dark haired and lovely, caught Alex's eye. They smiled, then shyly dropped their gaze, giggling as they hurried past. The vivid colors of the women's dresses, their careful new-shoe stepping, no one on earth could carry off such excess with such style.

All week long they were maids and mothers, fry girls at McDonald's, steam pressers at the dry cleaners; now they were charmers. A small group of blissfully buzzed older men sat around a card table on shaky folding chairs and crates, watching the street activity. They shouted friendly abuse at Alex—*Es que tiene la berga tan grande que ni necesita un couche, para atraér a las hembras* (the man comes with his bicycle to impress the ladies—he must have a cock so big that he doesn't need a nice car). When he replied with his own good-natured retorts on their appearance, manhood, and plans for the evening, they hooted and declared him the aristocrat and offered to let him marry their granddaughters.

Although at six feet he was taller than most Central Americans, his hair and features were dark enough and his Spanish authentic enough not to mark him as an absolute gringo. In his last assignment, more than two years undercover, Alex had posed as the son of a wealthy Argentinian rancher. He knew the world, he knew the roles, he cruised easily along the streets.

Finally Alex found a little motel, a faded blue stucco building with a low cement-block wall decorated with unpruned plants growing in powdered-milk cans. Each can had been lavishly painted with flowers and animal faces. A skinny old man with three fearfully long yellow teeth grinned at him from the porch, where he was busy painting more cans while a fat raccoon watched passively from a child's rocking chair, also painted in wild patterns and colors. The porch light made the scene both eerie and inviting, so Alex wheeled his crippled bicycle in the gate and got a room for the night.

Twenty-Four

SUNDAY MORNING, CHICAGO was back on the road, returning to Key Largo for the group's final two certification dives. She hadn't slept well but felt almost calm. The focus of work, the prospect of another day underwater, all helped soothe her wounds. It wasn't until she was crossing the causeway and she spied a small plane flying south that she thought of Alex again. It was like a hot knife slashing out of nowhere. Chicago gasped with the sudden startling pain. "Oh, fuck you!" She pounded the wheel in renewed rage as she stared at the little plane. She knew it wasn't his plane. He was already back in the islands, out in the bright Caribbean sunlight, going on with his life, as she would go on with hers. Her shoulders began to shake, and the road grew blurry. Goddamn you, Alex! She had to pull over as the dam burst inside her. Goddamn you!

Alex sat on the front porch of his little blue motel drinking thick Cuban coffee and shooing the pet raccoon away from his breakfast. Luckily for the animal, Alex was really too involved in the front page of the Sunday *Miami Herald* to be very diligent about this, so the raccoon had managed to snatch an entire *chorizo* and half his toast, and now made his swipes more for the fun of it than from real hunger.

Angelica Wattles's perfect smile beamed out from the lower right corner of the page. It was the same picture he had seen in the senator's suite. He read the article, noting that Ranger would be glad that his island had indeed escaped identification. It only mentioned that the body had been found in the sea and flown to Miami for autopsy. Even the reference to the shark-eaten head and limbs was fairly decorous; Wattles must have some pull with the press down here to get that arranged. No matter, it would hit the scandal rags soon enough. "Headless sex kitten brutally dismembered by sharks in paradise!"

But that wasn't the only thing wrong. The whole thing was starting to feel weird. Something about how fast everything had happened. A little later it finally clicked. Alex had finished most of the paper and was gathering it up to put in the trash when the slick color circulars slipped out and spilled across the porch.

There was an ad for Camel cigarettes, with that lunky, scrotal, camel face smugly sucking on his cigarette as a quartet of bathing beauties posed in the background. The models all wore the same style bikini in four different colors, scanty arrangements of triangles and thread.

The body was not Angelica Wattles. Suddenly he knew it as certain as the day. It was the tan lines. Angelica was a sunbather. She was flirtatious and voluptuous and not embarrassed by an inch of flesh on her perfect little body. She had been in the Caribbean almost two months. What had she been doing—sitting in the shade reading *War and Peace*? No, she'd been out on the beach, day in and day out, in her bikini, getting a *tan.*

The body he had seen matched Angelica's description nearly perfectly in shape, size, and build, but it was not the body of a beach bum. The woman he'd seen had usually worn a one-piece suit, and hadn't bothered about a suntan. Her shoulders and arms had been dark, the front of her thighs brown but not the back. It was a tan like—yes, like Chicago's. She had the uneven tan of someone who maybe worked outdoors, but couldn't be bothered to sunbathe. Whoever she was, she was not Angelica Wattles.

Alex dropped the paper and remembered his intuition firing warnings from the very beginning of this mess when Ranger asked him to fly the body out. Now what?

Twenty-Five

DARCY SULLEVIN WAS fairly easy to divert. Alex called from the hotel lobby and pretended to be a reporter for a true crime show who was on his way down to the coroner's office to view the body.

Alex waited in the hotel lobby until he saw Darcy Sullevin hurry past, then slipped up to the senator's suite. After a minute or so of knocking, the senator answered the door. He looked more composed, but still under a strain, the harsh morning sun casting deep shadows on his face. He blinked once or twice, his mind clearly fighting the fog of last night's alcohol.

"Mr. Sanders, right? Our pilot," he said finally. "Uh, come in. What can I do? . . . Oh, there was something about your plane—"

"I haven't come about that," Alex broke in.

The senator looked skeptical, but stepped back and held the door. "Oh. Well, come in."

Alex stepped inside the room, glanced around quickly, a reflexive action more than anything, and got to the point.

"I won't keep you long. I'm sorry that what I have to tell you may be disturbing. I got Sullevin out of here because I don't know how well you trust him. And I don't really care." Alex paused. "I guess it's stupid to say I don't want to get involved in this, but believe me, I don't."

Wattles looked puzzled, but the canny political sense was already showing on his face. "I'm afraid I don't know what you're getting at."

"Whatever you've been told, whoever's been running this show," Alex continued, "someone's not telling you the truth." He wasn't all that interested in the senator's reaction. He didn't want any part of the puzzle. He was acting out of a sense, deep-seated from his Dakota farmland roots, that you do what needs to be done. Much as he disliked politicians, he felt compassion for the man. "I have serious doubts," Alex continued. "In fact, I'm fairly certain that the body I flew up here was not your daughter."

The senator's eyes widened and he seemed to choke a little. He waved his hand slightly "Please, I'm sorry. . . ." He went to the bar and poured a glass of water, collected himself. "Please sit down. I don't know. . . . What are you saying? The coroner made a very certain match with some medical records. . . ."

"Records can be fudged. I'm sure you know that. All I know is what I saw. I saw the videos on the news yesterday. Your daughter had been in the Caribbean for some time, right, Senator?"

"Yes. She wanted a little time off after college . . ."

"And she liked the beach?"

The senator nodded.

"In every one of those videos, Angelica is sunbathing. She looks like quite the devoted sun worshipper. Would you say that was accurate, sir?"

"Well, I—she liked the beach, yes. What are you getting at?"

"The body my friend found, the girl I brought up here had never worn a bikini, rarely lay out in the sun, was in fact relatively pale."

Wattles got up in a flustered way, went back to the bar, and poured himself a drink.

"Mr. Sanders—I appreciate your concern, but that's very little to go on. Why, she was a sensible girl; I'm sure she used sunscreen."

"Have you thought about the head, sir? Don't you think it's a little odd that the whole thing was supposedly eaten by a shark like that?"

"How the hell do I know how sharks eat, goddamnit!" He collected himself. "I'm sorry. You understand that's a rather horrible image for a father to think about. At any rate, I find it hard to believe this. What are you saying—that there's some sort of—conspiracy to make me think my daughter's dead? It's absurd. What did happen to her, then? Where is she? Kidnapped? Why haven't I heard any ransom demands?"

"If you had, sir, I'm sure you wouldn't be telling me about it," Alex said gently. "I'm sure you have people you can go to. I just wanted you to know that there is some doubt."

Darcy returned soon after Alex had gone. He found Senator Wattles well into his third drink and still shaking.

"That pilot was here," Wattles told him with an edge of hysteria in his voice, "to tell me he's certain it wasn't Angelica. That the body wasn't my daughter!"

Darcy kept calm, though his stomach twisted and a stab of pain rippled across his tensed shoulders. He sat down and drilled the senator on everything Alex had told him, then he thought about it for a few minutes in silence.

"So what do we do?" Wattles asked him almost frantically.

"I think we need to call Ruthwilde."

Twenty-Six

SINCE ALEX HAD to return the bicycle to the airport anyway, he decided just to ride out there Monday morning before he called Sullevin. He found a bicycle shop that opened at nine, borrowed a crank puller, fixed the pedal, and reached the airport by eleven.

He wasn't sure what the senator had been willing or able to do about getting his plane released, and walked into the office ready to face another bureaucratic morass. Because he wasn't expecting much, Alex was pleasantly surprised to find that everything had been smoothed out. The impoundment had been lifted, the permits were in order, and the plane had even been fueled up, courtesy of the senator. Finally life was back on track. Whatever the hell that was.

But now that the time had come to leave, he stalled. For most of the weekend he had eased into the timeless barrio rhythms, but he had been unable to push Chicago out of his mind. In a way, he was glad to have it ended. Now he *knew* it was over, and that was for the best.

Still, he was reluctant to go. He dragged out his checklist, fussed with his flight log, and checked the weather reports twice. There was a front moving in with low cumulus clouds and a wind from the east, but nothing major brewing. There might be turbulence, maybe a little chop here and there, but no real problem.

Finally there was nothing left to do but go. Alex started the engine and watched the propeller spinning in front of his eyes, a metallic blur that seemed to be severing forever his ties. The airport was busy with commuter flights and private planes. People were returning from weekend jaunts to the Bahamas, banking business in the Cayman Islands, corporate takeovers, and drug deals. He taxied out onto the runway, but then had to wait for clearance.

It was as if Miami were sucking on him for a final few minutes just to be annoying. He sat there and remembered how great it was to take off from a rural airstrip, with the smell of hot grass kicked back in his face and an excited crowd below waving and pointing. Alex had learned to fly in his uncles' crop duster when he was only fourteen. He still remembered every creak in that old plane and the glorious way he felt as he soared over the fields of North Dakota.

In addition to their crop-dusting business, Alex's uncles had a flying circus. They flew old biplanes and stunt planes, traveling to county fairs and air shows throughout the Midwest. When Alex proved competent in the crop duster, Uncle Phil began to teach him loops and stunts and tricks for the circus. There were three uncles who flew, and one daring aunt who stood on the wing and even hung upside down from a trapeze up until her fourth child.

Alex was finally given clearance for takeoff and the memories vanished as he focused on the controls. He taxied down the runway, felt his wheels leave the ground, and nosed the plane up. The city fell away, and he could see the line of haze as he passed into the clearer blue of open sky. In a couple of hours he would be back in the Caribbean. He had just glided out over the bay and started to gain altitude when he heard a low rough growl. It was a metallic groan of distress accompanied by a terrifying vibration.

Immediately he checked his gauges and pushed in on the control wheel to drop lower and to increase speed. He had just climbed through the leading edge of the clouds. Even on a hot day the temperature change there could be abrupt enough to cause ice formation in the carburetor. He checked the temperature gauge, but it was normal. The fuel level was fine, flow was fine, but the engine was skipping. Alex could feel the craft vibrating from the labors. He expected the engine to die any second.

He dropped to two thousand feet and turned into the wind, trimming the plane, feeling for a glide that would put less strain on the engine. He glanced once more at the gauges, glanced down at the buckles on his harness, and made sure his inertia reel was locked; it wouldn't do to go bouncing around the cabin like a pinball.

As he was reaching for the radio, the engine gave a final sputter and died. OK, Alex thought, this is not a problem. He glanced out the window. I'm close to land, the sea is choppy, but not impossible; 99 percent chance I come out alive. No, don't be smug, say 98. And let's see, 90 percent chance unscathed; bruises don't count.

The adrenaline surge was like wiping clean a window: everything became remarkably clear, his senses tuned up, the sequence of responses firing off rapidly. As he reached for the radio he kicked off his sneakers, glanced at his altimeter, then out the window to judge the wind direction from the whitecaps.

"Mayday, Mayday, Mayday. Aircraft in distress. My engine is dead. Repeat engine is dead. Cessna two hundred ten. Alpha Mike Foxtrot Delta; two nine four; altitude fifteen hundred feet, I just passed Virginia Key, heading one four zero—estimate water contact in five minutes." Alex waited for a response.

Umbi was in the marina shed cleaning engine parts. The marine band radio spurted and cackled in the background every now and then but didn't interfere with the Burning Flames tape until the Mayday alert sounded. He jumped to switch off the tape and turn up the volume on the radio, but he still missed the initial exchange. There was a spattering of squeals as he adjusted the squelch knob. He heard urgent voices, then the call for emergency radio silence. A controlled coast guard voice took over.

"Aircraft in distress. Expected water landing south of Virginia Key. All vessels in the immediate area please be advised. Rescue boats underway."

Chicago stuck her head in the doorway. "Hey, Umbi, can you radio over to . . ." Umbi waved a hand to silence her and pointed to the radio.

"Someone sinking?"

Umbi shook his head. "Airplane trouble." First Chicago felt a sigh of relief. An airplane crash was tragic, of course, but at least it wouldn't be any of the fishermen or charter captains she knew. She didn't know any pilots. Except—no. Of course not. He had flown back two days ago. He was probably delivering Spam and tourists to some island by now.

"Maybe somebody load up de plane way too many kilos," Umbi joked. Chicago nodded. It wasn't an uncommon event, but odd in the daytime.

"Look, I've got to run. I just got those parts for Captain Dee's bilge pump and I've got to take them over to Westbay. I'm taking the skiff. After the radio's clear will you give him a shout on sixteen and tell him to meet me at the slip?" Umbi nodded and began to wipe down the inside of the engine cover.

A second later she stuck her head back in the door. "Then call Swann on the *Lola Blue.* I'm sure he's speeding out to the scene to claim salvage rights. See if he wants us to dive for him."

Umbi's eyes brightened. Salvage paid well. "Thinking like that gonna get you far in this world, missy!"

Alex was in a good glide. He could see the waves below and if he glanced back over his shoulder, the shores of Miami not far away. He felt much more fond of those shores then he had an hour ago. He could see the little white trails of boats—three, no four of them—like spokes radiating in for assistance. What a swell morning for a crash, he thought with a frantic sort of glee.

When the plane felt stable, Alex reached behind the seat where the life raft was stored—was supposed to be stored. Flying so much over water, the life raft was always handy, bolted to the back of the seat. Unless—unless you had to squeeze a large rubber goldfish pond with a dead body in the space. He had been too tired and distracted to pay much attention to the loading procedure that morning, but now he clearly recalled Ranger and his father moving things around.

Alex looked back in the cargo area. There, neatly tied down in the tail of the plane, was his life raft. OK, he thought, this is not a problem. I won't be in the water that long. He reached under the seat and pulled out the life jacket, laid it on the seat beside him, and wrapped the Velcro tether strap around his ankle. He pulled the flare gun out and looped the strap around his wrist.

The sea was getting closer.

"Altitude two hundred feet. Final approach. Over."

"Roger. We have you in sight. You're looking good." The water suddenly didn't look so good. The whitecaps were bigger than he thought; whitecaps hell, these were waves. Alex pulled the nose up a little, wanting to set the little plane belly down and easy into the wind. It was a smooth move, a perfect touch. If the sea had been a little calmer, he might have coasted in like a pelican. But the wind was stiff now and the sea was harsh. A wave caught his wing, dragged it under, spun the plane. The other wing stabbed at the sky; the aircraft was jerked around and shoved nose first into the ocean. Alex felt his body slamming into the door as the plane was caught. A great wave of green water whooshed over the cockpit.

Nothing to do now but hold on. The rough sea was like a bullying child, grabbing at the toy plane, yanking it over, flipping it and slamming it down so hard the wings broke off. Alex was stunned. He hung upside down, then upside down and backward; then he was swinging to one side as the cabin went crazy in the surging sea. He tried to unclip his harness, but the buckles kept moving out from under his hands. Water was pouring in from cracks and rusted rivet holes, splashing over his face and starting to pool in the bottom, or top, or whatever it was at the moment, of the cockpit.

Well, this might be a problem, Alex acknowledged, and he tried to make his hands work and quell the urge to vomit. Always had been prone to seasickness. Finally the buckle yielded. Alex fell out of the seat and crashed against the instrument panel. The force of the collision set the wingless plane to more crazy rocking. He felt for the door handle, took a deep breath, pushed the window open, waited just long enough for the force of the inrushing water to subside, then pushed his way out into the sea. He was only about ten feet down and could see the sky through the water, a bent blue heaven shimmering just above.

He had almost reached it, was sure in fact that one hand broke the surface, when there was a tug on his ankle. Alex was being dragged back down. The tether line of his life jacket had become entangled during the rolling of the plane and was pulling him under. This is not a problem, Alex thought, even as his lungs burned from the pressure and the blackness was starting to swarm in around the edges of consciousness.

He reached down and unpeeled the ankle strap. He felt himself drift up, up into the sky.

"This is *Lola Blue.* We're in sight. The plane is breaking up and sinking. No bodies yet. Over."

"All vessels be alert. Watch your props. Just idle out there, wait for the helicopter to direct."

Alex hit the surface semiconscious and choking, his whole body stunned into one general log of pain. He lifted his head but couldn't see anything. He could hear noises, but he couldn't see more than white-capped waves and foam green troughs of water. He moved his arms and legs, but he couldn't manage to make them swim somehow. One arm would sort of flop here; one leg kicked weakly, then the other. He couldn't get anything to work together. Why couldn't he see anything? His eyes stung from the salt. He wiped at them and noticed blood all over his hand. Waves hit him in the face, and he choked on the water.

Swann stood on the bow and searched the sea in a rhythmic sweep while his son Peter took the helm. He was not so much of a scavenger that he didn't want to rescue the survivors before he got to work on the wreckage. Besides, a live owner is easier to hit up for salvage payment than an estate. He looked for flares, for the orange of a life jacket, for pieces of clothing, but he knew that in rough seas you can be right on top of an object and not see it.

From somewhere Alex could hear the sound of sirens, something else, a helicopter. Signal them. He felt for the flare gun. The other hand. No, not there either. OK, all he had to do was not drown for a little while. Now how do you do that? Alex relaxed, he let his body ease along with the surge, put his face down in the water, almost automatically, he started the survival float. Arms up, one slow easy push, one easy scissors kick, lift your face, breathe, relax, face in the water again.

"Approaching vessel, we have a body," the chopper pilot called urgently to the *Lola Blue.* "Twenty feet forward to starboard. Over."

Swann felt the boat shift into gear and looked back to the cockpit.

"We've got him!" Peter shouted as he eased the throttle up.

It was nearly four when Chicago got back from her job. It had been longer and messier than she had hoped, and there was still grease under her nails. She would be glad when all this scrounging-out-a-living business was over for a while. As she eased the skiff up to the dock Umbi came running out to meet her. One look at his face and her heart jolted.

"Wonton call from the hospital," he said as he caught the bowline. "The plane wreck was Alex."

Twenty-Seven

WONTON HEARD CHICAGO's truck screech to a stop in front of the house and went to open the screen door. She walked across the lawn looking slow and skittish, as if there were weights on her shoulders, mud up to her knees, and balls of doom everywhere that she wasn't sure how to dodge. Although she was composed, he could see she had been crying. He could only guess at the storm of her feelings.

"Hey, babe. How ya doin'?" The moment she felt his bulky hug Chicago broke down. "It's all right. He's fine, baby. He's going to be all right." Wonton was one of the few people big enough and close enough to Chicago to get away with calling her things like "baby." He was six foot four and blocky as a refrigerator. Wonton was a detective with the Dade County vice squad and had been Alex's partner for six months before discovering that Alex was on an undercover assignment for the FBI.

He just stood there on the front stoop with her until her sobs quieted.

"Goddamn him, I know he's OK. I was half hoping for a couple days of coma," she sniffed. "Let me get used to the fact he's still here."

Wonton laughed and gave her a handkerchief. Her sentiment didn't shock him. He had known Chicago and Alex from the beginning of their relationship and agreed with Umbi that he had never seen two people more right for each other, or two to make each other crazier. When Alex had disappeared suddenly last year, it was Wonton Chicago went to, thinking at first that he was in trouble somewhere.

"Yeah, I was pretty surprised to hear from him myself."

"They said you were taking him home. He's here now?"

"He's sleeping—they gave him some painkillers."

"What did he hurt? They weren't very specific at the hospital."

"Just some cracked ribs and stupendous bruises, a few stitches, but what's another scar or two? He swallowed a lot of water too. They wanted to keep him there, but you know Alex."

"Do I?" She shrugged.

"Come on inside. You want a beer?"

Wonton's house was a comfortable little bungalow betraying a cozy family with more interests in life than housekeeping. Chicago went to the bathroom and splashed cold water on her face. She noticed something soaking in a pail of water under the sink, a swirl of color in reddish water. With a stab of pain, she recognized a scarf she had woven for Alex. It was raw silk, her first attempt with the fine threads and a little clumsy, but the pattern in blues and purples was nice. She picked up a corner and drew it from the water; it was still stained with blood. Chicago felt her knees weaken. She slipped down to the bathroom floor and banged her head against her knees in frustrated tears.

Wonton brought two beers out to the back patio where Chicago was sunk listlessly in a partially unraveled wicker chair. There were toy soldiers stuck in a line down one arm, their feet wrenched down into the rattan. Ellen and Dusty had gone out to the store to get some clothes for Alex.

"Dusty says Alex needs Superman underwear." Wonton laughed. He looked out over the yard and felt a small chill. It looked oddly disturbing, dotted as it was with the bright plastic toys—Tonka trucks and a big wheel—all left exactly where they had been dropped, and the child nowhere to be seen. He had planted hedges all around the yard, as if that were enough to cushion his son from danger.

"You know . . ." he started hesitantly, unsure about how much to bring up right now, "after we spent those first weeks trying to find Alex, I learned a little more."

Chicago shifted; her body tensed. For a few months after Alex disappeared, she went through every extreme and irrational fear every spy movie had ever dreamed up. Someone from his past had tracked him down, or some evil government agency wanted him dead because he knew too much. Wonton had quietly tapped a few connections from his own military past, but they had found out little. Then when Alex had turned up safe and sound in the Caribbean she had been so crushed and angry she didn't want to know more.

"It might help make more sense of things. It might make it a little easier for you." Wonton wondered if it could. "This wasn't the first time Alex disappeared."

Chicago put her beer down and leaned forward. "Tell me."

"What had he told you about his past?"

Chicago shrugged. "Most of what I told you back then. The navy, then he was with the government; Southeast Asia, then Central and South America."

"Did he ever tell you which agency—how he got into it?"

"He didn't like to talk about it. I guess I kind of knew it was CIA. He enlisted in the navy when he was seventeen and went to Vietnam, but the war was almost over. He mostly flew cargo and transport. Then he got recruited into the"—she waved a hand as if wanting to dismiss the idea—"spy stuff."

Wonton nodded. "It looks like Alex was what they call 'sheep-dipped.' Soon after he was sent to Vietnam, someone realized his potential. He was young, naive, adventurous, and patriotic—a bad combination. He was apparently a hell of a pilot, especially with small planes and tricky flying. He was discharged from the military. That's how the CIA got people. They had to be civilians, so they made up some reason to have them discharged. The soldier would go through a formal resignation and all his files would go top secret, and soon he would be hired by a 'civilian' cover company. Officially, in Alex's case he was released for a family hardship case.

"Then there's many blank years, and it seems he left the company in the early eighties. He disappeared for a while, but then seems to have been recruited as something of a free agent. That's the South America years. What do you know about that?"

"I know he was infiltrating rebel groups. I knew something bad happened there, something horrible. And then he quit. He told me he just sort of floated around a while, then a friend in the FBI wanted to help him out with something, and brought him in to do the corruption investigation down here. It was supposed to be a little job."

Wonton gave an ironic half laugh over this. The "little job" in Miami had wound up toppling a major drug lord, exposed over seventeen cops on the take, and led to the suicide of the precinct captain.

"So what else did you learn?" Chicago pressed.

"Not a lot more, but I think it'll help."

"Go on." Her voice was composed. She could deal with this; anything she could grab on to, no matter how bad, was better to her than not knowing.

"Do you remember about three years ago, there were a couple of DEA agents kidnapped in Colombia—it was big news for a while?"

Chicago shook her head. "No, I wasn't here then."

"They were missing for two months. Alex had, as you know, been in deep cover for over two years. I don't know who he actually reported to, but DEA asked him to use his cover to go in and arrange the release of the agents. Something went wrong—Alex was exposed." Wonton couldn't read the effect this was having on Chicago. He had wanted the story to be simpler; he had just wanted to give her a way to see Alex's desertion in a different light. He decided she didn't need to know all the grisly details.

"I mostly dug up some old newspaper clippings, then checked

with some friends in DEA, so I still don't know all the details," Wonton explained a little too hastily. "But basically, they held him captive there. One of the DEA guys was killed, but Alex finally escaped and got the other one out. That part was in the papers. It didn't list him by name, but I could figure out that it was him." Wonton paused. "Then after that, he was in a . . . a place—a hospital—in Texas for a while."

"OK." Her voice was small.

"After that I'm not sure. He just disappeared."

"Until?"

"A couple months later some guy was doing a documentary on the plight of Jamaican migrant laborers in Louisiana. One of those pesky, liberal, human-rights kind of guys." Wonton's sarcasm was thick.

"The documentary guy wound up inciting a riot in the cane fields. It showed on public TV, and one of Alex's old CIA handlers recognized him getting clubbed and stuffed into the back of a paddy wagon. Turned out he had been living in a shack, cutting cane for months. They sent someone down there, got him out of jail, and brought him to Washington."

The story was interrupted by the sound of a door slamming, followed by retching noises. Wonton and Chicago jumped up and ran in the house. They found Alex leaning against the wall, holding his bandaged ribs, throwing up into the bathtub. Wonton kicked the toilet seat cover down and steered Alex to sit there.

"I'm sorry, man. I couldn't bend enough to aim for the bowl." Alex smiled weakly as he wiped his nose and coughed.

"It's all right. At least it's not too chunky." Wonton handed Alex a glass of water.

"You know how seasick I get." Alex's voice was slow, his eyes still heavy. He looked up just then and saw Chicago standing next to Wonton.

"No worry. I'm used to this with a kid." Wonton was wetting a washcloth. "We'll clean you up and get you back to bed."

Chicago laid her hand on his arm. "It's OK, Wonton. I'll take care of him." She took the washcloth, and Wonton left them alone.

Twenty-Eight

Shana Phillips was grateful when Finneaus Lincoln finally sat down at his desk. The EPA lawyer was six foot five, and she was getting a crick in her neck looking up at him.

"So you're interested in Senator Wattles's new bill, eh?" he asked as he turned on the computer.

"And a general look at his record on any legislation that has to do with the chemical industry, if you have it," Shana added.

"We track legislation that might have any impact on environmental policies," Finneaus explained as he called up the index. "But it's arranged by subject or year, not by who introduced it or voted for it. I can't tell you exactly what kind of stuff Senator Wattles has personally supported." He gave her a cynical smile. "But you can generally assume Bambi and Thumper wouldn't be leading his parade."

"How about some of the private groups—Earthwatch, Greenpeace—someone like that," Shana suggested. "Do they track individual legislators?"

"Probably." Finneaus punched some more keys and called up an index of environmental groups. "I can print out a list for you, and give you people to call. What are you after Wattles for, anyway? Do we get to screw him?" He scowled with conspiratorial glee.

"I take it the senator is not high on your list of most admired men in Washington."

"Wattles is a whore. Him and that puffy little Ruthwilde."

"Ethan Ruthwilde the lobbyist?" Shana's interest picked up. "What is their relationship?"

"Major cash cow," he explained simply. "Plus he's probably the real engineer behind most of the legislation. The trouble with Ruthwilde is he's so"—Finneaus leaned back, searching for the right word—"insidious. He's never pushing the big stuff. You won't find Ethan Ruthwilde within a hundred miles of a spotted owl. His forte is technical, and the issues definitely dry. Negotiating allowable solvent evaporation rates doesn't usually stir the greenies. And I'm not just one of those vile tree huggers myself," Finneaus added in his own defense.

"Yes." Shana smiled as she looked at the jumbled failure of the lawyer's office recycling bins. WHITE PAPER ONLY held the remains of what looked like moo goo gai pan, and ALUMINUM was littered with junk mail. Finneaus followed her gaze and looked momentarily chastised.

"Yeah, well, I'm pretty good with newspaper and green glass." He smiled. "Anyway, back to Wattles and his evil bill. You know the basics, right?"

"He wants the Commerce Department to reduce the number of controlled chemicals for export."

"Right." Finneaus nodded. "In 1989 it went from seventeen to twenty-three. All the chemicals on the list are dangerous substances."

"But you know that most of the industry is in support of his bill? And from what I've read, besides the deregulation of the six chemicals, the changes don't seem all that significant."

"Tell that to the Kurds or whoever the next bunch of poor stupid peasants to get gassed turns out to be."

Shana was surprised at his vitriol. "How did gassing Kurds get into this?"

He swiveled around. "It's a Jewish thing. You wouldn't understand." Shana wasn't sure what to make of that remark.

"Sorry, that was probably rude," he said sincerely. "But you have to consider that all these controlled chemicals can be used to make chemical weapons."

"As well as pesticides and industrial solvents," Shana added evenly.

"Nothing worse than a fair reporter." Finneaus gave her a dry smile. "But you're right. The real problem isn't with the export regs. There's way too much international manufacture and trade already going on for this to make much of a difference," he explained as he flipped through a few pages in the bill. "The most the deregulation will do is maybe boost a little Louisiana industry. But as you usually say on TV when you're doing those consumer affair bits, read the fine print."

Shana read the lines he pointed to. "So? It says the government supports compliance with the recommendations of the Australia group." She looked puzzled.

"There was an international conference held in Australia, oh a couple of years ago, maybe 1988," Finneaus explained. "Negotiators met to figure out ways to try to control the spread of chemical weapons. They called for an international treaty—sort of like the Nuclear Nonproliferation Treaty. It would allow inspection teams to drop in on plants that were known to be capable of producing what's called Schedule Four—supertoxic lethal chemicals."

Shana read the dense paragraph and looked puzzled. "So this says we support that."

Finneaus shook his head. "It says, in its usual governmental doublespeak, that it's a nice idea, but there's no way in hell we're going to let anyone inspect our plants. This bill is just a nice, innocuous way to kill the issue."

"And you're saying that's why Wattles is so keen on this bill?" Shana pressed. "By which you are implying that he has some stake in allowing U.S. chemical manufacturers to produce . . ." she stalled, trying to absorb it. "To produce what? Nerve gas?"

"Not the gas, no. Just the precursor chemicals." He rocked back in his chair and pressed his fingers together. "But, since we're being honest and fair—no. I can't say that. I don't like the guy, I think his policies stink, but in all fairness, most of the industry does oppose plant inspections. It's a competitive business; there are trade secrets. And you're right: most chemicals that go into nerve gas also have legitimate commercial uses."

Shana looked dejected. Finneaus caught her eye, and suddenly they both laughed.

"Listen to us," she admitted sheepishly. "We're like disappointed kids."

"Yeah—like all the fireworks we stole turned out to be duds."

Shana sat back and stared dejectedly at the dense stack of information on her lap. The story wasn't going much of anywhere. Finneaus was definitely right about this not being a sexy topic. She clicked off her minirecorder and tucked it into her briefcase.

"Whatever happened to good old bad guys?"

Twenty-Nine

"Look, Grant, it was naive of us to assume we could just get away with a dead body floating around. There was sure to be an investigation."

Grant sat impassively in Ethan Ruthwilde's office. He could see the hummingbirds buzzing around the patio. He was enjoying the convolutions of Ruthwilde's fleshy globe of a head as he alternately rubbed his forehead and massaged his chin—his way of concentrating.

Ruthwilde's strong suit was not in personal relations. He was best as an orchestrator. He was still a chemist who enjoyed the orderly, predictable arrangement of matter. Grant knew that Ruthwilde's true agony here was because he had failed to really *think the thing through.*

"This is how I see it," Ruthwilde continued. "I'll arrange the announcement and get a lawyer. All we need you to do is show up and confess. You were hanging out with Angelica on Saint Martin, the two of you went on a night sail. You were drinking; she fell overboard. It was an accident. A little hard on her image, but forgivable."

"And how about my image?" Grant asked coolly.

"Your image is already perfect for the job." Ruthwilde smiled sarcastically. "Two DUIs and that unfortunate episode with the cheerleader? You're a reckless rich boy; basically good and wholesome"—Grant snorted at this—"but a little on the wild side. You call up the police now because your conscience is bothering you; you feel sorry for her father. You're terribly sorry; you tried to rescue her. We can provide the records that you did take a boat out that night."

"I'm sure you can."

"We're not asking you to take a fall, Grant. There won't be any charges."

"How do you know that? Why the hell should I trust you?"

"Have I ever been less than straight with you?"

"You haven't exactly been very informative."

"For your own good. Look, there might be some sort of investigation, but we can finesse that too. The worst that can happen is 'Hard Copy' camps on your doorstep and people look at you funny for a while."

"And I just go on with my life?"

Ruthwilde stifled a sneer. What life? The boy had barely slid through college. He had no interest in the minor positions his father's company had offered him. This had been his first real job, and some job—hanging around the Caribbean all summer spying on a girl for her daddy. It wasn't spying exactly; he and Willie had been hired by Wattles to "look out for her." Willie Wallace had been more of a Boy Scout about the whole thing. He'd done it out of an honest sense of obligation. The senator was an old family friend, and it was his duty as a Southern gentleman to protect a lady. Grant had been moved more by the prospect of an easy job and a free vacation.

They had followed her from island to island, keeping in the background, watching who she got involved with, intimidating a young guy here and there who seemed the wrong type for involvement with the precious deb queen.

"I just don't think I'm that eager to get involved," Grant shrugged. "It's already turned out to be way more than I bargained for."

"And I don't have to remind you whose fault that was," Ruthwilde replied coolly.

The boy glared at him. "It was an accident."

"Rape is not an accident."

"Oh come off it, Ruthwilde!" Grant got up and walked over to the window. Stupid little birds looked like gnats. "We were messing around; I wasn't about to *rape* her."

"Well, maybe you should have explained that to her before she ran away and fell down the stairs."

"I feel bad about it, OK? I feel like shit about it, but it happened. She was dead. You want to go to the police about it right now? Huh? You really want to?" he said with snide challenge. Grant knew that whatever the hell was going on here, he held some powerful cards.

There was something about Grant that Ruthwilde both identified with and found troubling. A certain moral passivity. "I think it is in both our best interests to see this thing resolved without more investigation," Ruthwilde replied calmly, ignoring the boy's threat.

"So say I'm convinced," Grant countered. "Say all this won't get me in any kind of long-term trouble. Say I decide to go along with this, play your—what is it—accessory? Let's talk bottom line."

Ruthwilde was a shrewd man who knew what things were worth and what people would pay. It was how he made his living. The negotiations didn't take long. He was almost contemptuous of the boy for accepting too low an offer; he had been ready to go to fifty thousand. They had settled at thirty, plus legal expenses and a guarantee of some "career placement" once it all blew over. They spent the next few hours going over the details of Angelica's unfortunate accident.

Thirty

PHONING THE CARIBBEAN was never easy. The connections were sometimes wobbly, the operators capricious, and inevitably, whomever you were calling was out on the beach somewhere and had to be found. So it was not until late Wednesday afternoon that Alex was finally connected to the old black dial telephone that sat on the bar at Miss Lilly's between the cash register and a jar for donations for Luther Peache's new artificial eye. (He had lost the old one in a card game.)

"Ranger? Ranger is that you?"

"Alex—glad to hear you, mon! I be wanting to tell you how sorry I am about your troubles."

"Well, save it. They aren't over yet."

"What you mean? Where are you?"

"I'm still in Miami."

"What for?"

"Well, mostly because my plane sank."

"Dis not sounding so good, Alex. You in trouble dere?"

"Yeah, you could put it that way."

A rustling static, then ghost voices on the line split their conversation for a second.

"Look, Ranger, I'd love to chat and tell you the whole story, but I don't want to lose the line. Listen up. You know that film you swiped from the kid? That little tourist twerp with the telephoto on the roof? I need it."

"I din get it developed, Alex. . . ."

"That's fine. I'll do it here. Just get it to me tomorrow. Get it to St. Martin and Federal Express it.

"I try, Alex, but—"

"Go, Ranger." Alex glanced at his watch. "The evening ferry leaves in fifteen minutes. If you're not on it, build a raft, swim, sprout wings and fly. I don't care—just get it to the Fed Ex in St. Martin and send it to me!"

"OK. Yes, OK. I'm going, mon, and really, Alex, I never tink of all this dat day. When dat man show up, he get things all on delay."

"What man?" Alex sat forward all alert.

"Da big-head mon. Da mon from da senator office."

"Ranger." Alex raised his voice; the static was a constant rustle in the background. "Ranger, this is important. Tell me about this man."

"American man wid a big round head and thick eyeglasses. His name I don't remember, Rough-something. He show up an hour or so after you leave. He say he hear about the body and he from the senator's office supposed to be down here looking for a girl, daughter of the senator. That's what de flyers I was telling you about was for. Dis missing girl. He come to look for her. He hear about the body and want to look to see was it her. But you already gone."

"Had you already called your friends in PR?" Alex asked.

"Well, I—" There was a twinge of evasiveness in his voice.

"Ranger, I don't care if you slacked around. I just need to know."

"Yah, well, truth is, I need to eat me breakfast, and Momma, she can't get no luck in the calling for a while, so—"

"OK." Alex broke in impatiently. "So this Rough-something guy shows up before you had a chance to call. And says what?"

"I don't tell him anything at first, but then he say how her father desperate, and so I tell him all what happened."

"And then what did he do?"

"He say he take care of tings. Dat it was a U.S. government

investigation now, and I didn't have to worry about calling Puerto Rico."

Alex hung up the phone. Wonton looked at him and shrugged. "It's still not much to go on. The senator was worried about his daughter and sent people down there to look for her. One of them happened to be nearby when she washed up. He knew she was last seen around Saint Martin or Saint Barts. It's not so farfetched."

Alex shook his head impatiently. It had been three days since his wreck, and he was starting to feel whole and energetic again. Attempts at his life tended to stir the old blood. Moving out of Wonton's guest room onto the *Tassia Far* didn't hurt his spirits much either. True, they were sleeping at opposite ends of the boat, but at least they were talking.

"OK, here's two possibilities." Wonton drew a line down the middle of a page. "Story A—it's all legit."

"OK." Alex sighed. "The body really was Angelica, even though I know it wasn't—"

"Without the editorializing."

"She really did drown accidentally, wash up on Antilla where one of the senator's aides happened to be waiting, on the lookout for her. Which means there should have been people looking on the other islands too."

Wonton nodded and wrote this down.

"And I was just mistaken in thinking the tan lines had anything to do with it. And my plane's engine just quit cold for no reason. And everything's swell," Alex finished.

"OK now. Story B—everything's fishy." Wonton smiled because he knew how much more interesting this one would be.

"Story B. The body is *not* Angelica, but someone wants the senator to think it is. Probably someone he trusts, because he was the only person I told about my suspicions."

"The aide?" Wonton looked at the notes. "Darcy Sullevin?"

"Maybe. So then this Rough-person is either in on the conspiracy, or another dupe, planted somehow to get the process moving along to the desired end. The coroner is crooked; he fakes the autopsy report. When I start to question things, they sabotage my plane and try to kill me."

"How easy would that be?"

"Too easy. The way the engine failed it would probably have been contaminated fuel. From the time it took to choke, I would guess it was probably water."

"But you checked for that before you took off, didn't you?"

"I checked, but the plane had just been fueled up. If someone poured water in the tanks, it would have taken a half hour or so to settle before it would show up."

"OK. So who are the bad guys—Darcy Sullevin and Mr. Rough-whatever?"

"Or someone we don't know about. A senator could have lots of enemies."

"Let's think simple right now, OK, pal?" Wonton suggested.

"OK. Let's say Darcy Sullevin is double-crossing the senator. I don't see him sneaking down to the hangar himself with a jug."

Accomplices, Wonton wrote down. "And motive?"

Alex shrugged. "What's Wattles got that people want?"

"Besides a daughter so hot she could poach an egg in her navel?"

"I wouldn't see the buxom fluff as your type, Wonton."

"Maybe not today, but you got to admit, she's every young man's dream bimbo."

"But getting back to motive," Alex laughed. "I called a lawyer friend in D.C. He's getting me the whole poop on Wattles. His committees, involvements, campaign contributors—everything. We'll just have to wait and look it over." Alex flipped the notebook around and stared at the two sides. "Meanwhile—"

"Meanwhile," Wonton broke in, "this isn't even an official case. Meanwhile, I've got plenty of official cases, so meanwhile, we assume that everything is on the up-and-up, and you just had a real bad day."

Wonton's desk phone rang. He picked it up, listened; his face changed. He was getting up and buckling on his shoulder holster even as the caller was finishing.

"We're on our way." He hung up the phone. "That was homicide. There's been a shooting at the marina."

"Who?"

"I don't know, buddy."

Thirty-One

THEY SCREECHED TO a stop, siren screaming. Alex was out of the car before it fully stopped and sprinting down the dock before Wonton had it in park. Over the heads of the police and onlookers, he spied Umbi's shaggy hair, and pushed his way toward him. When he got there, he saw that Umbi had his arm around Chicago. Alex felt cold with relief. Chicago turned and staggered a step into his arms. Her shirt was spattered with blood. She was shaking all over. He could feel her hands clutching spasmodically against his back, her feet making small stamping motions. She was nearly hysterical.

"What happened?" he shouted at Umbi over the noise. Wonton stepped up beside him, clapped one hand on Alex's shoulder.

"She OK?" Alex nodded. Wonton left them, flashed his police badge, and was let through the yellow tape that now roped off the end of the dock where the *Tassia Far* was moored. Police officers were already surveying the scene, marking evidence, stepping carefully around the body. It was covered with a sheet and lay half in the cockpit, half across the seat, one arm caught between the spokes of the wheel. There was blood everywhere.

Umbi was wide-eyed with the shock. "Brian been killed. Somebody shot him back of the head while he sitting right there."

"Did you see it?"

Umbi shook his head. "I was in the shop. I hear the shots and come running out. I seen two men in a boat speeding away."

Wonton and a homicide detective came up.

"They need to talk to you, baby. Can you tell us what happened?" Wonton spoke in a soft, comforting tone, the tone he used when his child had suffered some trauma. "Can we go somewhere?" he asked Alex.

Alex nodded toward the dive shop. He steered Chicago through the crowd. Once inside Chicago began to calm down. The rubbery dive-shop smells, the soft rumble of the compressor in the next room made a sort of cushion against the horror outside.

"OK. Just tell us what happened. Take your time," Wonton urged her.

Chicago looked down at the floor and spoke in a flat voice. "Brian came over with some PICs for me to sign. Scuba paperwork," she explained, "for this class we taught. We were talking. Then I had to go below—"

"How long was he there?" the other detective broke in.

"Uh, about a half hour. He was working on fund-raising stuff for the permanent mooring project in the Keys." Chicago halted, and fought back tears. How strange it was that he had been making plans like that just an hour ago. The detective stopped taking notes as she collected herself.

"But then he had to leave, and I went below to get a pen to sign the forms and to find some addresses. That's what took a few minutes. I had to find these addresses of people. For his project. Then I was coming up the companionway. I was at the bottom step, looking up. I heard a noise. I thought it was an explosion, and I turned toward the engine room. But then there was . . . blood."

The compressor chugged to a stop. There was a thin, painful silence.

"Did you see anyone?"

Chicago shook her head. "When I got on deck I went to help Brian. Then I looked up and saw a boat, but it was speeding away —there was a high wake, I couldn't see anyone. He was already dead."

"You say you saw the boat leaving?" The detective turned to Umbi.

"I saw, but not good. There were two men. One I know was a white guy, brown hair. The other I don't know, dark skinned, maybe Hispanic, maybe just tanned."

"I'm sorry to have to keep at this right now, but there's just a few more things I need to know. Do you know of any trouble Brian may have been in? Any enemies?"

Chicago shook her head, and something like a smile fought its way through her tears at the thought of Brian having any enemies.

"Anyone at all—even trivial. Someone he failed for their dive certification, a jealous girlfriend?"

"No."

"Was he, to your knowledge, using any sort of illegal drugs?"

"Nothing. He never did anything. He hardly even drank."

"Were you very close to the deceased?"

Chicago seemed taken aback by the term, but nodded. "He was a good friend. We taught dive classes together. I've known him awhile. Yeah, we were close."

"Were you—ah, romantically involved?"

"Oh shit." A sob caught in her throat and her eyes glistened with fresh tears. She wiped her eyes and looked up at Alex. He saw with a sad shock that she was oblivious of the pangs of jealousy he had felt. "I have to call someone. No—" she said distracted, turning back to the questioning officer. "We weren't, he wasn't . . . Brian lived with this guy— How do I tell him this?" She started coughing. "Brian was gay. They've been together for years. I don't know how to tell this to—him."

She looked up, glanced around the room as if she were in a hostile place. Her face was pale and drawn. "I—I'm sorry, I'm going to be sick."

Chicago sat hunched in the back of the car while Wonton and Alex walked back down the dock to her slip. Brian's body had been carried away. There hadn't been much evidence to collect. The shot had come from behind, a high caliber rifle shot that had blown most of his face off.

"I had Pearson radio in for a cleanup crew," Wonton told him in a strange, casual tone. "Did you know there are professionals down here for that? Found a good team a couple of years ago. Young guy, no sense of smell, cleft palate. Maybe that's why. Anyway, this young guy and his father. They're great. They can get blood off anything. Blue satin chairs at this one penthouse—a real mess. Wife came home and found hubby in bed with one of those girls takes care of plants in office buildings."

Alex recognized the evasive rambling. It was a defensive parry against the murdering reality. They fell silent, looking over the boat, staring at the spot where just an hour ago, Brian had been sitting.

Finally Alex pressed. "What are you thinking, Wonton?"

Wonton rolled his shoulders, exhaled a deep breath, and turned away from the gory mess. "I'm thinking, that, with Brian's build, with his hair in a ponytail like it was, from behind, sitting here on Chicago's boat, one could easily mistake him for you."

"Yeah. That crossed my mind too."

Umbi came up beside them. "Chicago don't really want to stay on the boat right now. I got her some clothes. I told her I'll stay here and look after things."

"You guys want to come stay at the house?" Wonton offered. "You're always welcome."

"No thanks, Wonton." Alex looked around. "I think I need to be someplace low profile."

Alex took Chicago to the blue motel. They got a room in the back, where the afternoon sun beat in with a heavy ocher glow. The air felt burnt. A ceiling fan whirred and spilled a warm breeze down on them as they lay side by side on the bed. There were more of the painted milk can planters in a line outside the window, with untamed geraniums that had grown long stemmed and twisted.

Thirty-Two

WEDNESDAY WAS A big news day in Washington. There was shocking new testimony in the mayor's cocaine trial, and two local reserve units had been called up for Saudi Arabia. Shana always hated distraught-loved-ones segments, and these were even worse. She still felt raw from watching her own brother leave. His unit had been one of the first ones called up. It had seemed so absurd. Never in her life had Shana expected to see her little bother go off to war. It wasn't until after the 11:00 broadcast that she finally had a chance to sit down with her producer.

"OK, what do you have?" Harland asked. He saw a light in her eyes that he half missed and half dreaded.

"Lots—but it's all a mess." Shana dropped a stack of notes on his desk. "Finneaus has been digging up lots of stuff at the EPA, but all we really have is some suspicious associations and possible conflict of interest. Senator Wattles's family used to own a controlling interest in Southstate Chemical. It's the biggest conglomerate in the region, one of the biggest in the country. He supposedly sold his stock and put all his money in a blind trust after his first election eighteen years ago."

"You know what words like 'supposedly' do to me, Shana?" Harland shuddered.

"Wait, hear me out. Wattles has been on the Commerce Committee for two terms and sponsored all kinds of prochemical legislation."

"It's an important state industry," Harland pointed out. "Of course he's going to legislate to support it."

"True enough."

"What else?"

"It seems Wattles is tight with Ethan Ruthwilde, also formerly a major shareholder in Southstate, now a lobbyist for the chemical industry."

"Oh well, *that's* a shocker . . . a senator and a lobbyist—oh my!"

"Don't." Shana cut him off. "I know, I know, but hear the rest. Wattles's bill would deregulate several chemicals that can be precursors for chemical weapons. Ruthwilde's name came up in the recent UN investigations of German connections to chemical warfare production."

"Lots of names came up."

"True."

"And nothing stuck."

"Except Alsak." Shana seized the opening.

"Ahh . . ." Harland searched his memory for that news. "The Baltimore plant, selling chemicals to Iraq for nerve gas or something?"

"Right. A guy named Peter Valascheck who worked for Alsak was indicted for shipping precursor chemicals overseas. Thiodiglycol; it's a precursor chemical for mustard gas. He would send the stuff through Singapore, Holland, and Jordan." She pulled out a clipping covering the story. "Ruthwilde lobbied for Alsak."

"OK. Ruthwilde lobbied for them. He lobbies for *everyone* in the industry. That's his job. He's a lobbyist." Harland glanced at the notes. "Was this Ruthwilde indicted? Implicated? Did he actually *do* anything? Arrange anything? Promote the shipments? Staple the boxes? Anything at all?"

Shana hesitated. "I haven't finished investigating it." She felt chastised by Harland's silence, and realized he was right. She had no tangible evidence of anyone doing anything wrong.

"I know this is all very vague," she admitted, "but I think there's more to this than just lobbying for constituents."

"Possibly. So what do you propose to do next?"

"Go to New York." She hurried on to stop his protest. "Fineaus Lincoln gave me some names of people at the UN who investigated the use of gas during the Iran-Iraq war. If nothing else, I'll just get some good background. Everyone's interested in poison gas these days. We've got three hundred thousand troops in Saudi Arabia who might get hit with it."

Joe Harland winced. "Was this all really my idea?"

Shana smiled sweetly. "I was very happy exposing unsanitary conditions in sidewalk hot dog carts."

"OK," Harland laughed. "Go to New York, but no muckraking. No allegations, no innuendos. Talk to people about the bill, get some background on the poison gas business. Leave the rest to '60 Minutes.' "

Senator Wattles flew back to Washington the day after Angelica's funeral. He was accompanied by Darcy Sullevin and the newest member of his staff, William Wallace. Willie was excited about working for the senator. He had been promised the job if everything turned out well over the summer, and now it looked like everything had. He still wasn't sure exactly how it had worked out, but everyone seemed relieved.

Willie had long grown used to the sensation that he wasn't always, well, as *aware* of events as others. He did OK enough in school, but when it came to the complexities of life, he felt as if he were always tripping over the edges of the carpet. Maybe it was some kind of learning disorder. It didn't bother him. In this case it was enough to know that he had done well. It was romantic in a way. It sort of made him a hero, didn't it? He leaned back in the seat and watched the clouds dreamily. Most of the grisly details had faded by now, and his leg was healing nicely. He would be living in Washington and working for a senator. He had a bright and happy future.

Darcy Sullevin watched Willie drift off to sleep. Sullevin was not happy, and he was not relieved. There were too many details still dangling. All he needed was an airhead in the office answering constituent mail. He agreed that it would be better to keep the boy close by for a while, but this meant Sullevin wouldn't get to hire anyone else from the thick file of bright beautiful young female applicants he had so carefully compiled.

Thirty-Three

Chicago was standing at the base of the companionway ladder, looking up from the salon. The sky was blue and clear, with fat white clouds. Two pelicans soared across the view. Then the explosion: a fountain of blood, each drop vivid and red against the blue sky, the body flying, arms limp, not even a push against death. How heavy a body was in death. Blood was pouring out of him. It spilled across the deck in a thick pool and rolled down the hatch. It poured down on her, swirling around her ankles, rising fast. She tried to climb out of it, but her hands were slippery with blood. She fell back, grabbed the ladder again, and struggled up. She reached her hands into the bloody mess seeking to stop the bleeding. The boat rocked, the head turned, and she could see the face. Alex's face. Chicago screamed.

Alex woke, hurling his body instinctively over hers. She flailed at him and wrenched herself away. A few seconds of panic, then they were both fully awake, hearts pounding, gasping for breath.

"It was you, wasn't it?" she asked finally, her voice flat. "It was you they were trying to kill." She rolled over and reached for the light, but Alex grabbed her arm and pulled her back. It was a harsh movement, almost violent. Chicago fell against his chest, feeling the heat of his body an instant before the flesh of it, feeling a heave in his chest that might have been sound.

"Why!" she screamed. "Why?" She sobbed and pushed away, her fists against his chest. Alex caught the weight of her hair in one hand and pulled her back, rolling them both over so he was cradling and crushing her all at once. She grabbed him as if he might dissolve. Chicago felt panic like a leopard hovering in the dark room, urgency, pain. The world was breaking up and this was all that was left—this room, this moment, their bodies crushed between passion and fear.

They made love without speaking in a confusion of love and desperation, passion and punishment. In blue shadows and the strafing light of passing cars, their bodies remembered the pleasure, but had to exorcise the pain. Deep bruises were seeping out now, aching through their bones, a year's worth of hope and anger and why. It was almost brutal. At the end, they lay side by side, exhausted, skin numb, only arms touching while the first blue of dawn tugged at the sky.

The scraggly geraniums in the window box were silhouettes against the faint light. Alex stared at them. They looked twisted and sinister, as if they could strangle. He draped his arm across his eyes and turned away. Chicago lay silently for a long time. Finally she spoke.

"Now tell me why."

Alex pulled away and sat up. The bed was old and the springs popped; the sheet had come off and was swirled like a tangled scar across the mattress. Chicago waited. She would wait all day now. She would wait the rest of their lives in this little room until he told her or she killed him.

"Do you remember the day before I left?" he finally said. "We went snorkeling—do you remember?" She was watching his face for clues, seeing only a distant pain.

"The sun was bright; so terribly, strangely bright." His voice became a quiet monotone. "And there were all these ripples underwater. I was watching you. You would just dive down and hang there. Your hair came undone and was swirling up. The way the light was on your skin, you looked—the way you looked—" Alex stared out without blinking at the lightening sky. "It made me feel —some way—desperate."

How to explain? How to describe the mass of the universe, the sheer weight of malice, the danger that hung over everything beautiful and precious? How to describe the brittle helplessness he had learned, the pain of being strong—but finally not strong enough—of knowing how ready harm was, and how helpless he was against it?

"I looked at my hands, underwater. They looked so—feeble. So absurd." He stood by the window, watching the blue rim of day swell a little further. "I can't fix"—he groped for what he was trying to say—"things."

Chicago went to him. She couldn't see his face. She rested her chin on the back of his shoulder, one arm around his chest.

"Did you ever think you could?" she whispered.

"No," Alex replied sadly. He caught her hand and pulled her tighter around him. "But before—it didn't matter."

Thirty-Four

IT WAS A ragged morning. Alex, Chicago, and Wonton sat on his back porch looking over scattered stacks of paper and clippings they had collected on Senator Wattles. They were trying to sketch out a scenario, a plan, a list of possible suspects, anything. The TV was on, tuned to the morning news with the sound low. A newspaper photo of Senator Wattles and Ethan Ruthwilde was tacked to the wall, Ruthwilde finally connected to the vague "Rough-somebody" Ranger had mentioned.

"Senator Wattles is, according to who you talk to, 'an effective legislator committed to strengthening our country by restructuring the American industrial base' "—Wonton read from a news clipping—"the American Society of Chemical Manufacturers; or"—he picked up a second clipping—" 'a grubbing special-interest chore boy, who has bullied the most egregious bills through Congress with no regard to public interest or welfare'—Greenpeace." He tossed the samples back into the pile. "There's more, but it's all about the same."

"So someone could hate the guy enough to threaten his daughter," Chicago mused. "Maybe lots of people."

"Yeah, but not many people with the ability to mount this kind of effort," Alex pointed out. "Whoever it is, they can move fast. They've sabotaged a plane and arranged a hit in broad daylight. These have been pretty sophisticated moves."

"Not to mention fudging an autopsy report. And arranging for a matching dead body in the first place," Wonton added.

"If it really isn't Angelica," Chicago reminded. She was glad for the intensity of the investigation. It was a way to deal with the shifting pits of emotion. "How soon will we have the pictures?"

"This afternoon, if Ranger got moving on it. Then we develop them, and what—another day for enhancement?"

Wonton nodded. "Maybe sooner."

Chicago pointed to the TV suddenly. "Turn it up." Alex and Wonton turned and saw a picture of Angelica on the screen, then a live picture of a young man sitting at a desk reading from a paper. He looked worried and sad. He was handsome, well groomed, the young-corporate-executive look. A man with a law-yerlike posture stood beside him. Wonton punched the sound button.

"I regret any pain my delay has caused the senator's family. I'm sure you can understand that I was personally traumatized by the accident. I am embarrassed by and regretful of my behavior. It was totally irresponsible of us to go out in a boat when we were both intoxicated. I tried my best to rescue Angelica." And here he seemed to lose his composure for a minute; his voice broke. "These were the most horrible hours of my life."

Alex, Wonton, and Chicago watched in stunned silence as the young man finished his statement. The newscaster came back on.

"That was Grant Darlington from Baton Rouge, Louisiana, who has just come forward with a statement about his involvement in the death of Angelica Wattles, whose body was found in the Caribbean last Friday. According to Mr. Darlington, the two had gone out on a small sailboat at night after some heavy drinking. Angelica fell out of the boat and drowned. The senator was informed of the matter late last night, but has issued no statement. Mr. Darlington had known Angelica since high school. When we come back—"

Wonton switched off the set. "Well, which list does he go on?"

Thirty-Five

WHEN SOPHIE VON BRAUER entered the foyer of the Spitalerstrasse office the lobby guards instinctively shrank back against the marble walls. Sophie had that effect on people. She strode into the private elevator and punched the button for the twentieth floor. Sophie did not need to be announced.

Hans Goerbel looked up as the woman entered and felt that indescribable thud that only Sophie could inspire in a man. She was stunning in a brutal sort of way. She had a thick carpet of blond hair that brushed her hips as she walked. Her nose, once broken, was a little too long and crooked to one side, but poised as it was over full, snarling lips, it gave her face an arresting, erotic quality.

She was six one and one hundred eighty pounds of daunting flesh. Her muscles were amply upholstered, but the flesh was firm; so firm it hummed. Sophie did not diet. The only use Sophie ever had for a celery stick was to ram one once in the eye of a drunken sailor in a bar on the Reeperbahn. And that wasn't because he'd made improper advances, but because she hadn't considered his offer exciting enough.

Sophie was wearing a stretchy red miniskirt and sheer black stockings; a black leather jacket was unzipped to her cleavage, so that when she bent a certain way, one could glimpse the lace edge of an impressively engineered bra. She strode across the thick carpet and perched on the edge of Goerbel's desk, sliding one leg up and propping a size eleven high-heeled red shoe on the arm of his chair.

"Missed you, darling," she crooned sarcastically. Her voice was carnivorous.

Goerbel patted her ankle, ran his palm up the back of her calf, and smiled. "I have a job for you."

"Ja?" She smiled, then her eyes narrowed with suspicion. "No more sex with kinky little Japs," she growled. "Why don't I ever get to seduce secrets out of sexy young businessmen?"

Goerbel laughed. "I wouldn't think you could be so choosy these days, my *shatze.* Most of your Stasi friends would be happy to have any work at all."

"Peter paid me nicely for the last job," she reminded him haughtily.

"I heard it was messy."

She bristled slightly, then shrugged. "I ruined a pair of suede pumps, but the dry cleaning was successful."

"Maybe you're losing your touch."

Sophie smiled suddenly. "Sweetheart, you wouldn't be trying to bargain me down, would you?"

Goerbel felt a little shiver. Sophie enjoyed her work just a little too much. She came from a long line of East German agents. Her grandfather had trained with the Gestapo, and both her parents had been top agents with the secret police, but Sophie was a breed apart. She had grown up in the steely bosom of the German Free Youth, East Germany's training school for Communists. She was cunning and smooth, an exceptional operator who spoke Russian and English flawlessly, and now, with new horizons to consider, was rapidly learning Japanese.

Since reunification had brought her career to a halt, Sophie had been recruited by Peter Valascheck as a "personal assistant." She wasn't thrilled with the world of international corporate subterfuge, mostly because her victims didn't usually prove to be much of a challenge, but it was a job.

"So who's the lucky guy?" She pulled a cigarette from a jade case, and Goerbel lit it for her.

"It's a girl."

"Pretty?" Sophie's eyebrows rose in interest.

"A baby doll," Goerbel assured her. "But I don't want you to kill her, just find her." He handed her a file of photos. "Angelica Wattles. Her father claims she's dead. I don't believe him."

Sophie gazed at the pictures. "Who's the daddy?"

"Senator Wattles. A business associate. He's become rather uncooperative lately. You remember Ethan Ruthwilde?" She looked blank. "Guy with the fat head?" he prompted.

"Bread dough face?"

Goerbel nodded. "Ewwww—" Sophie made a face. "If I have to do him it's from a distance, baby. Give me a night scope too. Guy gave me the creeps."

"I don't want you to kill him either, just talk to him."

"I thought he worked for you."

"Not exactly. He's an intermediary. But now I'm not sure whose side he's on."

Sophie shifted her statuesque hips around on the desk and swung her other foot up on Goerbel's chair so she had him pinned casually between her legs. The red skirt didn't have much farther to ride up, but the few inches had a stirring effect and she damn well knew it.

"You want me to go all the way to America and not kill anybody?" Her voice had an almost childish disappointment.

"Not right away, but if you're good I'll see if I can scrape up someone," Goerbel offered.

"So what's in it for me, dumpling?"

He caught a scent of her, ran his hands up the inside of her thighs, and twisted one finger into the taut nylon. "Your usual fee," he said coolly, as he pulled the stocking away from her leg, jabbed his middle finger through the fabric, and roughly tore a hole in the crotch of her panty hose. "Plus a bonus in advance."

Thirty-Six

ETHAN RUTHWILDE CAREFULLY measured some of the dark liquid into the eyedropper and squirted it into the glass beaker. He swirled it gently and watched the solution turn bright red. He felt the container to see if it had cooled enough. The tubes were ready, scrubbed clean and drying in the rack. Carefully, with the practiced hand of a chemist, Ruthwilde poured the mixture into the tubes and screwed the special caps back on. Then he gently placed the containers in the box, being careful not to tip them over. A spill would be messy.

He put on his sweater and took the box out to the patio. It was a beautiful October morning in Baton Rouge, and he felt a wave of weariness at the thought of another trip to Washington. The phone rang. Carefully, he set the box down on a chair and went back inside to answer it.

"Yes."

"You are leaving today?" It was more a statement than a question.

Ruthwilde had little patience for Goerbel's grand, dictatorial style. "Yes."

"Very good. I just wanted to be sure you understand our situation. I want you to have a good picture in your mind when you sit down with Wattles."

Ruthwilde sighed audibly.

"Before you get exasperated"—Goerbel laughed in that irritatingly good-humored way—"I just thought you would want to know the whole scene at the moment. Singapore is giving me another week, they can't afford indecision; and I have a rather urgent request from a rather aggressive buyer."

"I know my job, Mr. Goerbel," Ruthwilde broke in. "And I know your situation. I'll do what I can." He hung up and glanced at the clock. He had just enough time. Ruthwilde hurried back to the patio. The garden was a soothing place. He wished he had time to sit here now and watch the tiny birds flicker in the sunlight. He went back to the box and picked up one of the tubes, holding it up to the light to admire the ruby-colored liquid. One of them had tipped over and some of the fluid was leaking out around the stopper. Ruthwilde ran his finger over the droplets, then licked the finger. Carefully and precisely, whistling a little off-key as he worked, Ruthwilde hung the hummingbird feeders, filled with fresh red sugar water, back in the trees.

Thirty-Seven

"OK, SHE CAN'T be a tourist." Wonton scratched it out with solid strokes. "Someone would have reported her missing by now. Same with hotel employee, bartender, anything like that, right?"

"Not necessarily," Alex broke in. "People come and go all the time in the islands. Some bartender not showing up for work for a week wouldn't be cause for a report unless the till was empty when she left." He tapped the row of photos spread out before them on the desk. "Look at the tan. That's what first struck me."

The photos Ranger sent had lost their initial grisly shock by now. Most were of no help. The kid hadn't had the steadiest hand, and there were usually palm fronds or people in the way; but there were a few shots that showed the dead woman's body in good detail.

"She was tanned darkest on the back of her shoulders," Alex repeated. "And usually wore a one-piece swimsuit. I'm sure she worked outside in the sun."

"She could have been crewing on a yacht," Chicago offered. "Did you notice her hands? Any calluses, rope burns?"

Alex thought hard and tried to picture the girl's hands—hand. He remembered a watch, nothing special, just a basic Cassio—but there was something about that—what had he noticed?

"OK, she worked outdoors," Wonton agreed. "But don't make her crewing a yacht. How the hell would we ever track that down?" he pleaded dejectedly.

Chicago picked up the two good photos and looked them over once again. She held one under the lamp, tilted it back and forth a couple of times. She squinted.

"What do you see?" Alex leaned over her shoulder to look at the photo.

"I think she was a diver. It's faint, but I think that's the outline from a skin suit. The old zipperless kind. Like the one Umbi was wearing that day we went out."

Alex and Wonton examined the photo. "She's right." Alex traced the line on the woman's chest where the lycra suit had left a tan line. "The older style skin suits have a neckline like this—off center," he explained to Wonton. "And—that's it—her watch! She had an O-ring on her watchband." He grabbed Chicago's arm and unceremoniously held it out to Wonton. "See. Divers often carry extras on their watchbands."

"Great. So she's a diver. How many thousands of people dive in the Caribbean?"

"But how many aren't tourists?" Alex was excited by the idea. "The tan on the back of her shoulders, pale legs." He nodded to Chicago. "She had a tan like yours—from standing around in the water teaching classes. Let's make her a dive instructor. How easy would that be to track down?"

Chicago shook her head. "Not impossible, I guess. But without a name or a face . . ." She shrugged. "There are two main certifying organizations, PADI and NAUI, plus a few smaller ones. They would have records, but you need a name."

"Well, look at her, she's so little. Someone might remember her just from her appearance."

Chicago shook her head doubtfully. "I guess you could talk to all the course directors to see if anyone remembers a woman of this physical description, but that seems a lot to ask. She's what, twenty-five at the most? She could have gone through instructor training as long as seven years ago. That's a lot of faces for anyone to remember."

"Yeah, faces," Alex mused. "You know what else I'm thinking. They cut off her head so she couldn't be recognized, but what about the arm and the leg?" He dropped the photos in front of Wonton. "Look, doesn't it seem strange that sharks would just bite off these limbs so neatly and leave the rest? Besides the missing parts there were no bites anywhere on the body."

"How the hell do I know how sharks eat." Wonton broke in. "I never had one over for dinner. Anyway, she wasn't in the water that long. And she was tangled in a fishing net—maybe that's all the sharks could get to."

"No." Chicago shook her head. "He's got a point. The shark stuff doesn't fit." She looked intently at one of the photos. "I mean, sharks certainly did get to this body, but something's wrong. Look at it. Sharks are pretty violent eaters. The limbs are off below the joints. Wouldn't you think there would be more damage to the knee and elbow?"

Wonton groaned. "Could you be a little more graphic?"

Alex jumped up. "She's right, Wonton. A shark does like this" —he grabbed Wonton's arm and jerked it as hard as he could back and forth in a whipping motion.

"If a shark really did bite her arm and leg off," Chicago continued, "especially if she were already held in place in a net, I would expect to see the joint messed up somehow."

Alex whistled in surprise. "You're right. When did you take up forensic pathology?"

Chicago shrugged. "I saw a cow carcass get eaten once. The shark would grab a leg and just yank the hell out of it. I could see the bones pop out of the sockets. The hide was all torn. It was more ripped apart than just bitten off. Look at her skin, it's not ripped at all."

"What if someone cut her arm and leg off first," Alex suggested, "then made it look like a shark meal?"

"Why go to all that trouble?" Wonton pointed out.

Alex shrugged. "Scars, marks, identifying features"—he tapped Wonton's forearm where there was an old, slightly blurry cobra curled around a rose—"tattoos."

Thirty-Eight

SOPHIE WAS BORED. She had waited outside the American Chemical Society on Sixteenth Street for two hours. Absently she picked the last of the flowers that grew in the little boxes by the driveway, plucked the leaves off, peeled the stem, and stuck it in the bosom of her sweater.

The wait for Ruthwilde would have been desperately dull if not for the heavy traffic of bicycle messengers zipping by. Washington was enjoying an extended Indian summer, and most of the riders were still in spandex shorts. The display of fine musculature kept her life bearable. It also gave her an idea. When one of the messengers finally wheeled up to the front door of the building, Sophie was ready. It was a lucky catch. He was tall and exquisitely built, and Sophie would rather have their destinies entwined some other way, but she had a job to do.

She silently followed him into the stairwell, knocked him out with a quick blow to the back of the neck, and stripped off his green and purple cycling tights.

Oh my, she sighed to herself as she slung his knapsack over one shoulder and picked up his helmet. What a shame to just leave him here. She pulled the flower out of her bosom and tucked it into the elastic of his jock strap, then she sprinted up the stairs.

In the guise of a messenger she cruised the floors easily. She glanced in offices and opened doors at will. There was no sign of Ruthwilde. Finally she noticed a tray of coffee cups outside a conference room. Sophie strode up to a receptionist.

"I have a delivery for Ethan Ruthwilde. I think he is in this meeting, can you check please?" There was no hint of German accent in her voice; years of training had taken care of that. She also knew how to walk like an American. The receptionist stammered a little, glanced at the conference room door, then back at the towering woman in the flashy tights.

"Ruthwilde?"

She consulted a list on her immaculate desk. "Why, yes, he's on the agenda. You can leave that here for him."

"Sorry, I need a personal signature. Do you know when they're getting out?"

"They adjourned ten minutes ago, he should be out any minute."

"Thanks, sweetie." Sophie cocked one eyebrow and blew the woman a kiss. It was meant to disturb her and it did. She turned on her heel and strode toward the conference room before the receptionist could object. Sophie pulled open the tall oak door as if it were a garden gate. Two men who had been about to push from the inside stumbled forward slightly. One of them was Ethan Ruthwilde.

"Mr. Ruthwilde, package for you, sir." Sophie adroitly stepped between the men so that her bulk was preventing Ruthwilde's progress while almost bumping the other man into the corridor.

"I just need a signature. Here, let's use this table." She gripped his arm and steered him quickly back in the room, kicking the door shut behind her. Once inside she flipped up the latch to bolt the door. Ruthwilde was calm. He knew she had to be connected to Goerbel. Sophie flipped the package on the table and put one foot up on a chair.

"What do you want?" Ruthwilde spoke calmly.

"Ooooh—I didn't figure you for the direct type. You're impressing me." She sauntered over to the man, pressing close, towering over him so that he had to look up or remain eye to chin.

He sighed. "Hans Goerbel clearly doesn't know me very well if he expects you to exert either physical intimidation or bizarre sexual allure toward me."

Sophie laughed, conceded the point, and backed away unrebuffed. "I love it when you talk dirty."

"Tell him I'm still working on the shipment. Meanwhile, I can probably divert something else his way if it will help . . ."

She shook her head impatiently. "Shipments bore me. Tell me where Angelica Wattles is."

Ethan felt his hands go cold, his heart start to palpitate.

"And don't say dead," she added with a growl as he opened his mouth.

"I don't know what you're talking about," he tried lamely.

Sophie reached her broad hands to his face and pinched two

great slabs of his flabby cheeks between thumbs and forefingers. She twisted hard. His eyes began to water.

"I can take you back to my hotel and use you up, you sweet little puff pastry." She jabbed her knee viciously up into his crotch. Ruthwilde gasped and collapsed to the floor.

"I'll give you three minutes to recover your voice." She patted his suit pockets and pulled out his cigarettes. Sophie smoked one, standing over him, letting the ashes fall on his great, quivering head.

Finally Ruthwilde pulled himself up. He straightened his clothes. "I don't know where she is."

"You're no fun, Mr. Potato Head. That's what you look like, you know. How about I get some little plastic eyes and little plastic nose and little plastic lips and jab them all into your face?"

"I'm telling you all I know."

Sophie grabbed the man's fleshy chin in her iron grip, thumb on top, three fingers digging in from below. She dragged him up, pressing up through the loose skin until he could feel her forcing his tongue against the roof of his mouth.

"But you know she's alive."

"Yes," he gasped.

"Go on, precious."

The pressure was cutting off some blood to his head. He saw stars. "I don't know where she is. I think Wattles sent her away somewhere. I think to Europe."

Sophie let go and his head fell forward. She pushed him into the chair. He felt sick, but slightly triumphant.

"If you are lying, I'll know very soon." She didn't waste her breath with threats. She was gone in a blur, her blond cape of hair swirling behind her.

Ruthwilde shakily poured a glass of water. It hurt to swallow. The wounds to his pride he swallowed with his usual odd tranquillity. Well, he thought with some pride, I may be ugly, but I'm not a fool.

Thirty-Nine

"Did you ever think there were so many tattooed ladies running around the Caribbean?" Wonton slammed the phone down in frustration. "This one's on Saba. A hibiscus on her shoulder. But she's still alive." Alex scratched the dive shop off the long list. Chicago had just connected on another line. Wonton had managed to get them into the police station where they could use multiple phones.

"Hi, Island Divers? Yeah, I need to find out the name of one of your scuba instructors. I'm really embarrassed that I forgot her name, but she was really nice and I wanted to recommend her to a friend." Chicago rolled her eyes, bored now with the story. "Actually, I'm not even sure she worked for your shop. We hired her privately through our hotel, but she mentioned the name of a local operation, and I thought it might be yours. . . . Well, she was short, about five two, and she was well built, not skinny . . ." Alex and Wonton were using "curvaceous," or "voluptuous," but Chicago felt stupid saying that. "And she had sort of blondish brown hair. . . ." A good guess. If that description alone didn't strike a bell with whichever dive shop they were talking to, they would toss out the next suggestion. "Oh, and she had a tattoo. . . ."

The photo enhancements had arrived from the lab. Wonton had shown them to a medical examiner who agreed with the joint-damage theory of shark bite. In the enhancements, however, he pointed out bruising and bulging muscle tears in the arm stump that could be the result of a real shark bite.

"The leg though, I can't really tell from the photo," the examiner mused. "I'd have to see it in person. But it looks pretty clean. There doesn't seem to be enough of the sort of tissue injury I would expect." So, if she had a tattoo, it was probably on her leg. The search was further complicated by the fact that they had no way of knowing what the design of this supposed tattoo was. Fortunately, however, they had found if they mentioned it a certain way, and there was in fact such a person, the respondent would volunteer the information.

So far they had found several flowers in assorted locations, and a snake on an upper thigh. An instructor in Saint Lucia had matched the general description and had gone off suddenly two weeks ago with a new boyfriend, but she didn't have a tattoo. Another possibility was a woman who had worked recently in Saint Croix. She had crudely tattooed letters spelling out "Steve" across her fingers, a faded remnant of younger rebellious days. She was reportedly almost five seven, however, and was supposed to have gone back to the States for college.

"But we still don't even know if it *was* a tattoo," Chicago pointed out after another dead-end call.

"Look"—Alex tried to boost their morale. It was a big hunch, but a good one, he thought. "It seems they had someone down there waiting for the body. Someone was expecting it to be found. Obviously, they hoped a whole lot of people wouldn't see it, but they took pretty elaborate precautions to remove some sort of evidence in case someone did."

"But that still doesn't mean it's a tattoo," Wonton pointed out. "It could have been a birthmark, a deformity—anything."

"True, but . . . a casual observer wouldn't notice a scar or a birthmark, and if the autopsy was rigged anyway, they wouldn't need to remove it for that. A tattoo, especially on a young woman, is memorable. Let's just go with it a while more."

Chicago hung up her phone and scratched another name off the master list. Across the room Alex had reached another dive shop and was starting a similar query. They had been at it for hours. They had covered twenty-two dive operations on twelve islands.

Out of the corner of her eye she saw Wonton suddenly swing his feet off the desk and sit upright. "Yeah, pretty girl around twenty-three. Yeah, that's right . . . a butterfly on the ankle—right! . . . Uh-huh . . . uh-huh . . . Do you remember the name of the boat? . . . No, that's OK . . . hey, thanks a lot . . . yeah, OK, thanks." Wonton hung up and practically whooped.

"Yah! A dive instructor in Antigua remembers a girl who came to see him at the end of August. She had been teaching at a summer camp." He glanced over his scribbles. "Antigua Adventure—it's a scuba camp for teenagers. He thinks the office might be in New York. Anyway, this girl decided she wanted to stay in the Caribbean a while after camp finished. He doesn't remember a name, but maybe Katie or Karen or something. He heard later that she got a job cooking on a charter yacht, but doesn't know which one."

Alex was already calling information for the New York office of Antigua Adventure.

Sophie took the stairs, listening first to make sure they were empty. She didn't think the mugged messenger would have called the police. Who was going to admit that someone had knocked you out and stolen your pants? She ducked under the basement landing and changed back into her own clothes, stuffed the tights into the knapsack and walked out into the street.

There were three bike messengers outside, no cops. Her victim wore a borrowed pair of khaki shorts and sat rubbing the back of his head. He was stabbing the air every now and then in anger as he told the story to his friends. Sophie's heart flamed with lust. She'd love to admit her guilt and offer to do a little penance, but she had to go. She quietly dropped the knapsack at the bike messenger's feet.

"I found this in a trash can in the basement," she told him. "The lady at the front desk said you lost it." Although Sophie had no trouble being a hired killer, she hated to cause people inconvenience.

Before the surprised messenger had a chance to question her, Sophie was gone. She walked a few blocks, then found a pay phone and quickly punched in the overseas call.

Hans Goerbel answered on the second ring; he was pleased to hear that things had gone well, although disappointed that Sophie had not yet actually located Angelica Wattles.

"I'm not sure I believe the trip to Europe," Goerbel mused. "Ruthwilde is not exactly the cultured type."

"I can twist him some more if you like," Sophie offered reluctantly; torturing fat old men wasn't much fun.

"Let me see what I can find out through other channels. I have something more pressing for you." He could almost feel Sophie smiling at the other end of the line. Despite his own relative lack of morals, the zeal Sophie displayed, the absolute relish she had for violence, gave him a chill.

"I've discovered that some silly reporter has been poking her nose into Senator Wattles's business. We haven't been worried about it before, but evidently she went to New York recently and talked with one of those goddamn UN investigators."

"I could blow her up," Sophie offered casually.

"No, no, it's not her I'm worried about, although a little intimidation might be in order. It's the UN fellow; he was one of the team that brought Imhausan down. We've been keeping an eye on him, but he hasn't done anything too threatening until now."

Sophie leaned against the phone and felt a warmth spreading through her body. This was like a sexual thrill to her, the anticipation, the planning, the stalking, finally the climax.

"Tell me what I need to know, darling," she crooned.

Forty

CLARA GREENWAY'S CARIBBEAN adventure was sketched in pencil on the map. On the desk were two photos the director of the camp had faxed down. Next to them were the newspaper photos of Angelica Wattles. It was hard to see much detail in the fax, but one thing was obvious; this petite, curvaceous scuba instructor bore a remarkable physical likeness to Angelica Wattles. Her easy, crooked smile made her look like she would rather play Frisbee than go to a debutante ball, but aside from that, the two could be twins. And she had a tattoo.

"OK." Wonton plopped his finger on the island of Antigua. "Camp finished August seventeenth. Clara finds work as a cook on a charter yacht. They leave August twenty-second from English Harbor and sail for three weeks south to Saint Vincent and the Grenadines, back to Antigua, then Saint Barts and Saint Martin. According to the skipper, they had all sorts of trouble with the boat, breakdowns and stuff, and Clara finally jumped ship on Saint Martin. That was the second week in October."

"And she's been missing since?"

"We don't know yet. She hasn't been declared a missing person," Wonton pointed out. "The camp director said he would call Clara's parents and ask after her, then let us know."

"Do you think we can get an exhumation order on that?" Alex asked.

"We can't get shit with that," Wonton admitted bluntly. "I doubt we can even open an inquiry."

"What if Clara Greenway's parents could identify her from the photos?" Alex suggested.

Wonton looked doubtful. "I don't know. There isn't really much to go on; one little scar on her shoulder. The clothing can't help much, shorts and a bikini top—come on. The autopsy says it's Angelica; Wattles says it's Angelica. Why would he lie?"

"Why would he try to kill Alex?" Chicago broke in angrily.

"We don't know who tried to kill Alex," Wonton pointed out. "Meanwhile, we've suppressed Brian's identity about as long as we can. Whoever has tried to kill you so far is going to find out real soon that he missed again."

Alex shrugged. Chicago was leaning back in a chair, her feet on the window sill. Brian's funeral was still too vivid in her mind.

"So we just have to find out what's going on with the senator," Alex suggested. "Who would want to make him believe his daughter is dead."

"Now *that's* a good idea," Wonton said sarcastically. "Poke around some more and see how many more ways they can think of to kill you!"

Forty-One

WHEN SHANA PHILLIPS left the studio after the eleven o'clock news she had two big surprises. The first came as soon as she stepped to the curb. A passing taxi stopped for her. There was already one passenger in the back, and she was a little surprised that the driver didn't ask her destination before he let her in, but she was so happy to be picked up that she didn't question it.

"Whea yo go?" the driver asked in a musical baritone with a heavy Somilian accent.

"Mt. Pleasant—Eighteenth and Newton, please," Shana requested. She nodded to the other passenger, a woman in a stylish raincoat with an expensive-looking woolen shawl tossed over her head. Shana didn't notice her height; almost everyone looked tall to her.

"You're the lady on the news, aren't you?" the woman asked politely.

Shana smiled and offered her hand. "Yes, Shana Phillips."

"Yes—Shana Phillips," the woman echoed. She held Shana's hand a beat too long. "I'm familiar with your work." Another long beat. Shana didn't know what to say. It was just a statement, not exactly a compliment. "I imagine investigative reporting must be a very exciting job," the woman continued. The taxi driver passed Hechinger's and turned left.

"It's mostly routine—a lot of research, footwork, stuff like that."

"But sometimes you discover something exciting, don't you?"

"Sometimes." Shana smiled and settled back into the seat, looking out the window to discourage conversation. Something about the woman was giving her the creeps. They turned right onto Reno Road. At least the driver knew the quickest way home.

"Sometimes," the woman repeated. "And tell me, Miss Phillips, do you ever start to feel nervous when you are investigating something? Something maybe that other people would not be happy to have you investigating?"

Shana turned, her senses growing alert. She glanced at the driver. He saw her in the rearview mirror and smiled. He probably didn't speak enough English to understand what was being said. Calm down, Shana told herself, what has this woman said that was really so threatening?

"I personally know of several people who would not be happy to have their affairs made public on one of your little exposés," the woman continued.

"Honest people have nothing to fear," Shana replied steadily. As a broadcaster she had plenty of control over her voice.

"So true. And you have nothing to fear from honest people, do you?"

Shana watched for clues. Maybe she was just overreacting.

"But it follows logically," the woman went on smoothly, "that you wouldn't be wasting your pretty young life reporting on honest people would you? They're not quite as exciting as say, the sinister international chemical industry." Her voice took on an edge.

Where are we? Shana thought. She found the door handle and casually switched her briefcase to her other hand. A few blocks to Connecticut Avenue. What was there? Apartment buildings, some stores; she couldn't run in heels; she would have to kick off her shoes.

"Are you threatening me?" she asked steadily.

"You are a bright young woman. It is a shame that only the lowest class of your people tend to procreate. I'm suggesting that your race could benefit by your living long enough to pass on your pretty little genes."

The cab stopped at the light on Connecticut Avenue. From here they would go down a long hill into the emptiness of Rock Creek Parkway. Shana grabbed the door handle. The woman grabbed her arm. Her grip was like iron, long red fingernails pressed into Shana's skin.

"Don't bother." She smiled. "I'm getting out here." She pulled out a twenty-dollar bill and handed it to the driver. "Take my friend home, please, and keep the change." She got out and held the door open. "Oh and, driver"—the Somalian looked back, his face bright with the generous tip—"wait until she's inside her door. These streets are dangerous for a pretty woman."

Forty-Two

ALEX PHONED WONTON the next morning from the marina. The *Tassia Far* had been cleaned of all traces of blood, and he and Chicago had moved back on board.

"No cards. No letters. No calls in over three weeks," Wonton informed him almost happily. "According to the camp director, Mom and Dad Greenway are starting to worry. I just talked to the skipper of the boat she worked on. He confirmed that Clara got off on Saint Martin. They ran aground in the harbor there and were stuck for two days. She got tired of waiting and split."

"So she's there—right place, right time, and unattached, drops out of sight at the same time Angelica supposedly disappears."

"Looks that way."

"Did you talk to her parents?"

"Sure, Alex. I called them up this morning and asked if they had considered the chance that their daughter might be dead and mutilated and buried under a false identity."

"Sorry, pal. Listen—you got an address?"

"Potomac, Maryland. Her father is president of some bank in Chevy Chase."

Alex wrote down the exact information. He tapped the receiver absently, looking out over the low tidal mud.

"You still there?"

"Yeah, I'm here. I was thinking."

"I was afraid of that."

"I was thinking, since Miami hasn't been exactly hospitable lately to me these days, it just might be a good time for a visit to Washington."

"Alex, they can kill you just as easily up there as here. Hell, with all the regular murders there they might not even have to try. I think we've got enough to start an investigation here—"

"What here? C'mon, Wonton—the body was found in the Caribbean, and the senator is in Washington. Even if you could open something here over Brian's murder it would just raise more heat for me."

"So call in the FBI," Wonton suggested, even though he knew this was futile.

"Look, the easiest thing as I see it is to find out if the dead woman is actually Clara Greenway. If I can get a positive ID from the parents, they can get an order to dig up the body. If it's not Angelica, we have evidence, and we just toss the whole mess to the feds."

"I don't know, Alex . . ."

"Look, I've got to make arrangements. I'll call and let you know when I'm leaving."

"Leaving for where?"

Alex hung up and turned to see Chicago standing in the doorway. She had a bunch of regulators over one shoulder. He could tell by her expression that she had heard the end of his conversation. They stood silently for a few beats, then she exploded.

"What the hell do you think you're doing?" She threw the regulators down on the bench. Alex hadn't expected her to embrace his plans either, but had at least hoped for a better time to discuss them.

"I just need to talk to some people." He tried to make it sound routine.

"Talk? You're just going to fly off to Washington and talk to them?" Her hair snapped across her shoulders as she began slamming drawers in her workbench. "Like suddenly you're a priest or something, and they'll want to confess all their sins?"

"It's not like that—"

"It *is* like that!" She stabbed a Phillips-head screwdriver down so hard the point stuck in the plywood. "But fine. It's your damn life." She spun around and headed for the door.

"Cut it out. You're getting all worked up." Alex grabbed her arm.

"I'm not worked up! I don't get worked up! I am mad. You're a shit and I hate you!"

"Hold still and talk to me, damnit!" Alex shouted.

"Talk to you? I've had it with talking to you!"

"Illy—"

She cringed at the use of the nickname. It was a private pet name, short for Miss Illinois, a mock title he had awarded her at a dismember-your-Barbie-doll party in a local bar during last year's Miss America pageant.

"I have to find out what's going on." Alex loosened his grip.

"Why?" she challenged. "Why the hell don't you just back off?"

"Back off where? Someone is trying to kill me—"

"Oh, you noticed!" She jerked her arm away. "So doesn't it seem a little stupid to just march yourself up to their front door?"

"I've just got to get a little information."

"What about the police? What about the goddamn FBI?"

"The police have nothing to go on. And even if they did, Wattles isn't going to let it go anywhere."

"Oh, but he's just gonna spill his guts to you, right?"

"Oh, cut it out!"

"No, you cut it out!" she shouted. "You want to screw up your own life go ahead, but don't get all—don't get all—*snarled up*"—she stumbled over the word—"with me first." She turned away, trying to dismiss him with her back, but Alex saw her shoulders were shaking. She hated anyone to see her cry.

"It's not a big deal—"

"Not a big deal?" Chicago turned back and stared at him. "Which wasn't a big deal?" Her voice was tight. "Them wrecking your plane or blowing Brian's head off?" Alex saw the fear in her eyes and felt a wave of guilt.

"What do you think?" she whispered through her tears. "I need to see another murder? Make it three just for good measure?"

There was a horrible quiet in the shop. He hadn't thought how she must feel. He had walked out on her once already, and now was threatening to do it again. She had just buried a good friend, and she had lost a husband to a violent death.

"Why don't we just go away?" she pleaded. "The *Tassia Far* is almost ready." She was surprised and embarrassed at her own suggestion and talked faster to keep from changing her mind. "We can sail for months, years. Whatever is going on with this whole mess will be over; they won't get you."

"I'm sorry." Alex put his arms around her and was almost surprised that she let him. She butted her forehead into the hollow of his neck, like some animal seeking the scent of another. Why not leave? Alex thought to himself as he stroked her hair. It was a reasonable option. What did he owe anyone, anyway? It wasn't his job to solve a murder. Why not just sail away? Why the hell not?

Forty-Three

WHEN ALLEN DRAY was stabbed to death by a deranged panhandler in the Fifty-ninth Street subway station during rush hour on a drizzly October afternoon, the New York public's sense of outrage had already been worn thin by a summer full of violence. Dray did not seize attention the way a teenaged boy from Kansas who had been killed defending his mother had. He was just a man in a suit who happened to be in the wrong place at the wrong time.

The incident would probably not even have made the papers except that Dray held a moderately noteworthy position with the United Nations. Even so, the press had been getting a lot of flack for writing too many stories about brutally murdered white business people and ignoring brutally murdered poor blacks, so the *Times* gave it a few inches and that was the end of it.

The doctor in the ER who pronounced him dead on arrival was a smart, capable surgeon who had already seen far more than her share of stabbings and gunshot wounds. It was clear to her that Dray had died almost immediately from massive bleeding caused by a stab wound to the heart.

An expert looking for such details might have noticed a few odd things: that there were no peripheral scratch or bruise marks—the sort of thing one might expect from the clumsy attack of a madman. The fact that this blade was thrust up under the man's ribs on the left side, piercing the heart in one clean stroke seemed like just a lucky hit. The doctor knew her trauma, but she had never had cause to study the uniquely refined techniques of a trained assassin.

The police had no reason to suspect anything. Dray had no criminal attachments. He was an unremarkable mid-level civil servant with a rent-controlled apartment and a steady girlfriend. There were witnesses who had seen the panhandler harassing other people before he stabbed and robbed Allen Dray.

The panhandler was a big man and seemed drunk. He'd worn a dirty coat and a knit cap, and he smelled bad. A few people had seen him run out of the station, but by the time the police had arrived to scour the surrounding streets, they found nothing but Dray's empty wallet in a trash bin. Only a few people lingered to watch as the ambulance arrived and Dray's body was carried out: an elderly woman walking her terrier, a few joggers, a couple of tourists, and a tall woman on her way home from work.

Except for her height she looked like any average business woman on her way home from the office. She wore a blue suit with white socks and Reeboks on her stockinged feet. Her blond hair was done up in a neat bun. But she was no ordinary secretary. As she watched the body being loaded in the ambulance, she felt slightly dizzy, almost drunk with the thrill of it. Her hands tingled, colors and sounds seemed overly sharp, and there was a heavy sexual ache in her groin. She stood and watched as the doors closed and the vehicle rolled away, then she went on her way, a chic leather purse over one shoulder and an eight-inch spring loaded knife in the pocket of her coat.

Forty-Four

Ethan Ruthwilde stopped between a banana tree and a display of orchids to wipe the steam off his glasses. It was humid in the greenhouse, and his suit jacket already felt clammy. It was 10 A.M., and the botanical garden was largely empty. There were a few tourists and a few students who came to read or study in the tranquil garden setting, but no one who was likely to recognize either of them.

Ruthwilde hurried past the pond, through the fern house, the palm house, and into the cactus room. There was Darcy Sullevin, already waiting, pretending great interest in a variegated century plant.

"I'm sorry, I don't have too much time," he said by way of greeting. Ruthwilde gave him a bored, blank glance. Sullevin never had much time. The less time you claimed you had in D.C. the more important you seemed.

"Goerbel has sent someone to look for Angelica." Ruthwilde could make his business equally blunt. There was a whirl of gears behind Sullevin's professionally composed face as Ruthwilde told him briefly of Sophie's visit and the threats she bore.

"What do you know about this woman?"

"She's German but passes for American. She's big."

Sullevin loosened his tie and ran a hand through his hair, brushing the wilting strands off his forehead. "But she doesn't know anything yet?"

"I offered a few red herrings. But it won't be that hard for her to track them down and come up empty." They strolled in silence a few minutes, stopping under the huge, branching arms of a *euphorbia neglecta.* The dark spiny limbs were so extensive that they were wired to the ceiling for support. The plant looked way too bizarre to occur naturally.

"It won't be that hard to have Goerbel call her off, either,"

Ruthwilde suggested smoothly. Sullevin ignored the hint. "I'll have a customs alert issued. If she tries to leave the country we can detain her."

A gardener entered the hall with a hose and started to hook it up to the tap at the far end of the room. Ruthwilde nodded toward the exit, and the two men walked into the empty palm room.

"I'm not sure the senator understands exactly how complicated this has become," Ruthwilde explained in his soft tone.

"I'm not sure *you* understand, Ruthwilde!" Sullevin broke in, almost hissing. "There's no way any more shipments are going out —nothing—no more—no ties, no connections." He slammed his hands angrily against the stone balustrade. There was a small waterfall spilling over rocks into a pond, making a soft burbling sound. The setting was lush, with a thick green silence that made him need to whisper. "Think, man! Think for yourself. We're probably going to *war* with Iraq. A month or two maybe—that's all. It's going to happen. It's got to. What happens if just one shell of mustard gas hits our troops?"

"The danger of gas attack, as I'm sure you know, is vastly overdramatized," Ruthwilde replied coolly.

"Oh, tell that to the *Washington Post*!" Sullevin was feeling sick. "That's exactly the point! Poison gas is great drama. The press is already lapping it up and churning it out. Do you realize what would happen now if the senator is connected . . . in any way?" Sullevin's eyes were wild at the thought. "Why—why, we wouldn't just be out of office . . . we'd be drawn and quartered. There would be a riot on the Hill, and we'd be thrown to the mob."

"That's exactly why I am suggesting you comply. Goerbel needs your product right now. Needs it so desperately, he might as well sink himself if he doesn't get it. And if that happens, I can guarantee he will drag you down with him."

Sullevin shook his head. "No—uh-uh. I don't buy it. We're not the only producers in the world. He can get it anywhere."

Ruthwilde sighed. "We've gone over all that. German producers are being heavily controlled right now. And, as you've pointed out, this Kuwait thing has disrupted all kinds of commerce."

"No deal," Sullevin said, slinging his jacket back on. "You go public with anything so far . . . we can handle it. We can still put up for ignorance—the stuff was sold for pesticide production, et cetera, et cetera. There was no way for us to know where it would wind up."

"Calm down, Darcy. We all have our stake in the matter. Let

me remind you that the cover-up has often proven more damaging than the crime. What about the body? What about that pilot?"

"No. You can't tie us to anything else."

Ruthwilde scoffed. "Just because I have handled all the dirty work doesn't mean it won't contaminate the senator."

"We never asked you to kill that pilot."

"Why did you call me then?"

"Goddamnit, man, you could have paid him off and sent him back to the islands. I know these types; they're all pirates."

Sullevin was silent. Half his mind was already off thinking up plausible deniability, press releases. Could they get Brendan Sullivan to represent them? How could he salvage his own career in the midst of it all? There was no reason it had to explode now.

"Goerbel is being very reasonable." The calm voice coming out of the huge fat face bothered Sullevin.

"Go on."

"One more immediate shipment of thiodiglycol—two hundred tons."

Sullevin was silent. This was a possibility, but he could tell by the inflection that it was not all Ruthwilde was seeking.

"And a small amount of Dichlor."

"What? What the hell! Are you crazy? Damnit, Ruthwilde, there's almost no commercial purpose for that. We couldn't ship that anytime, let alone now."

"Goerbel needs the thiodiglycol immediately. I know Southstate has it in the warehouse. I can make the arrangements."

"Wattles will never agree," Sullevin insisted. But maybe he didn't have to, Sullevin thought. He knew enough people by now. He could let Ruthwilde arrange everything and keep Wattles out of it. He could insure that his own name stayed clean. "What do you need to arrange that?" Sullevin asked skeptically.

Ruthwilde smiled. "I'll let you know."

One of the few people who still remained interested in Allen Dray after his death was Shana Phillips. She stared at the *Times* clipping. Slowly she opened the file folder and added the obituary to the rest of the material.

Her reporter's heart was on fire; her personal heart was terrified. This was exciting; this could be Pulitzer Prize stuff; this could be her Watergate; this could get her killed! This could actually be just a freak accident, she reminded herself, but a cold shiver spun down her back as she remembered the woman in the taxi. What was going on? Her brain swarmed with questions, fears, ideas. What if it really wasn't an accident. What did it all mean? What could Allen Dray have known that was so important? Nothing he had told her, none of the reports seemed that earthshaking.

Allen Dray wasn't a crusader. His "bleeding heart" had been well staunched long ago by experience. He had liked his job with the United Nations. He didn't expect to save the world, but when Shana had expressed interest in his investigations, Dray had been only too happy to oblige. He had been disappointed in the UN's resolution; he didn't think it went far enough. There were so many loose ends. He had provided Shana with copies of his reports and helped steer her toward other sources.

Now Shana poured over the reports and statistics in the file. If Dray really had been murdered, what had he known that was so important?

Forty-Five

CHICAGO LOOKED ONCE more around the salon of the *Tassia Far* to see what she might have forgotten. Lassie was draped placidly around her neck. Chicago had had the snake for almost twenty years and was as silly as the mushiest cat owner over her pet.

"OK, you remember about the rats? Two this weekend, then just in case we're not back, she needs a couple more in two weeks. But she'll let you know when she's hungry."

"Wait a minute," Umbi interrupted. "How exactly this snake gonna *let me know* she's hungry?"

Chicago laughed. "She'll start poking around the starboard cabin—that's where she gets fed. And don't forget to leave her hot rock plugged in. The nights are getting cool enough that she may need it."

"Yeah, yeah—anything else you want to tell me about for the fiftieth time 'fore you go?"

"Well . . . don't forget—"

"I won't have any need to forget anything if you don't leave!" Umbi nodded toward the dock. "Go now. I take good care of this old boat." Chicago hugged him good-bye, grabbed her bag.

Finneaus Lincoln was easy to spot in a crowd. Partly because he was so tall, and partly because he was utterly unembarrassed to shout and wave in public. Alex saw him the moment they entered the terminal at Dulles Airport.

"Yo, Alex!" He threw a long arm across Alex's shoulder and took one of the bags. "And you're the shark lady," he greeted Chicago. "I'm glad we meet at last. I hope Alex told you what an important part I played in your last dramatic caper."

Chicago cast a doubtful glance at Alex. "Uh, yeah."

"You remember," Alex prompted. "Finneaus is my garbage expert. He got me the list of ships cited for offshore dumping."

"Oh, yes. The rock-and-roll lawyer for the EPA." She looked him over anew. "Alex has told me a lot about you."

"Don't believe it. C'mon, Jacquie's waiting in the car."

There was something brash about Finneaus, something flung out and almost rude, but it was backed by such a genuine sense of good nature and affection that it was winning. He and Alex had become friends when Alex was living in D.C. a couple of years earlier. They met on the Mount Vernon bike trail one day, when in an unofficial and spontaneous race, Alex caught a loose board on a bridge and crashed. They had shared a taxi to the hospital for stitches and became friends. Jacquie was leaning on the trunk of the car, a beat-up 1972 Impala. She jumped up to embrace Alex.

"God, it's been ages. You look great." Jacquie was tall and willowy, with tiger-colored hair and a fair complexion. She would have been frail looking except for a steady energy and curious alertness that made her seem strong. They contrasted physically, but there was something about them that seemed right together. She was much quieter than Finneaus, but hardly suppressed by him. Alex introduced Chicago, and they all piled in the gigantic old car.

Finneaus and Jacquie were renovating an old house in Mt. Pleasant, one of Washington's few remaining eclectic neighborhoods. The blocks here were lined with large row houses, where one could find a combination of middle-class black families, upscale yuppies, group houses of vegetarians with causes, radical nuns, and basements full of Central American refugees.

"This is weird. You know, to be talking about heat pumps and wallpaper and shit," Finneaus confided after he had given them the tour of the place. He and Alex were sitting on the front steps. "I mean, the last time I saw you we were into geopolitical affairs and the essence of democracy. Or something like that." It was early evening and the Indian summer day was still warm.

"Yeah, well if this is what buying a house has done to you, I can't wait to hear you once the kids come along."

"Hey, at least let us get married first."

"Yeah, aren't you doing all this a little backward?"

Finneaus shrugged, pulled out a couple more beers, and handed one to Alex. "Well, the house came along. I knew there was no way I could ever hope to buy anything this side of posumville on a government salary if I didn't jump on it. And Jacquie and I are solid. Marriage is just details. I tell you though"—Finneaus sighed as he fumbled with the bottle opener—"more than once I've thought about you hanging out down there in the islands doing the grass skirt scene."

"That's Polynesia." Alex laughed.

"Yeah, well, it ain't D.C."

"I thought you liked it here."

"Oh, I'm happy here. EPA gets stifling, the bureaucratic end of it, but I still get to feel like one of the good guys." He gathered up the empty bottles, leaned over the railing, and dropped them one by one into the glass recycling bin by the basement door. "You just raise my wild streak."

They saw Jacquie and Chicago round the corner on their way back from the market. The sidewalks were carpeted with autumn leaves, and a small wind sent a flurry of color swirling around the women. The end of day light gave the scene a golden touch. It was an accidental pocket of beauty, the sort of moment that steals away sound and makes you feel hopeful and frightened all at once. Hallmark might write a card about it; kids get wild and jump on the furniture; men change the subject.

"So what's up with this Wattles thing?" Finneaus asked. "Was the information I sent you any help?"

"It was a start. It narrowed our focus; now all we need to know is who in all that mess wants to blackmail Senator Wattles."

"Can't tell you that, buddy, but I might have a lead for you. A couple of weeks before you called, a reporter came around looking for information on Wattles too. Shana Phillips, with channel seven. She was investigating miscarriages in women who live near a chemical plant in Maryland. Wattles has a bill before Congress to further deregulate and ease export restrictions. I helped her find some people to talk to, steered her toward references, stuff like that. I don't know what ever came of it. Haven't heard anything on the news."

"What was her angle?"

"Ethics mostly, I think," Finneaus said. "Wattles supposedly sold off his stock in Southstate Chemical years ago when he was elected, to avoid conflict of interest. The money is invested in a blind trust." Finneaus took a swallow of his beer and gave a skeptical nod. "Of course, the money is still in Louisiana industry, and I somehow doubt it's financing crawfish farming."

Jacquie and Chicago kicked open the little gate and carried the bags up the steps.

"What did you get for dinner?" Finneaus greeted them.

"Work for you, lazy butt," Jacquie said as she dropped a bag of string beans on his lap. She and Chicago went on with their conversation as they disappeared into the house. Finneaus and Alex stayed out on the steps, drinking beer, catching up, and snapping beans.

As they lay together that night in the newly finished guest room, which still smelled faintly of sawdust and paint, Chicago felt calm. The danger seemed far away now. Here at least was a temporary peace, the simple peace of clean sheets and just-washed dogs, of sweet oranges and favorite sweaters.

They made love slowly, gently, as if only now, were they discovering each other. Her hands remembered places; the span of his back, the curve of his heel. He ran his finger over her eyelashes, barely touching. They kissed forever; they did not speak. Alex fell asleep in her arms, and she did not want to move them even when one went numb.

Chicago could not sleep. The sounds of the big old house settling itself for the night were strange. Houses seemed so enormous to her, and to fill one up such a task. She was used to small island houses and ship's cabins. She felt a little out of place here, even, she realized now, a little intimidated. Jacquie seemed to be flawlessly sailing along on those mysterious seas of womanhood that Chicago couldn't even navigate. From the way she pulled out clean towels to the way she wore bracelets, she just seemed to *know* more about mysterious things. Chicago had never spent much time in the company of women, and felt a mix of awe and awkwardness being around her.

And Jacquie and Finneaus seemed so easy together, even in the silly ways they squabbled over details of dinner. He cut the carrots too thick, she took liberties with his mother's chicken recipe; he had put the colander on a shelf she couldn't reach, and who had forgotten to buy cat litter? It was all so sweet, so attractive, in a horrible odd way.

She turned and watched Alex as he slept. He lay on his back, his strong body sunk slightly into the mattress. He looked like a statue only half loosened from the stone. What would become of them? The immediate danger suddenly seemed tiny compared with the rest of it, the stuff of life and love; that was as big as a house. How would they ever figure it out?

Chicago's marriage to Stephan, like the rest of her life, was far from traditional. He'd been a marine scientist and they were usually either living together on a crowded research boat or apart for weeks at a time. She tried to remember if they had ever gone to a grocery store together.

She had loved Stephan, and now she loved Alex. Stephan had been her first real love, and she was certain, whatever happened, Alex would be her last. Chicago suddenly understood what he had been trying to explain that night in the blue motel: the feeling of having something so precious that it terrifies you.

She was still awake when Alex began to dream. His body grew tight and his hands twitched. Why did it come tonight? Chicago thought sadly. Everything had been so easy, so calm. She put her hand on his chest. His fingers curled in and he shook his head back and forth as if in pain. He was sweating and breathing hard, though he made no sound except a sort of harsh catch in his throat. She was frightened; she had never seen it start. Usually she woke to find him thrashing, then suddenly he would burst awake in terror. He never cried out.

"Alex, Alex," she whispered, thinking to soothe him without waking him. "Alex, it's just a dream." She stroked his chest as if she could smooth away the terror, but he woke suddenly in a panic, throwing her away so she nearly fell off the bed.

"Alex! Alex, stop, you're dreaming!" Chicago knelt on the bed, frightened by the power that held him. He sat tensed, and looked around the room. "We're safe, we're at Finn's house. In Washington, remember?"

Alex looked at her and she saw the terror slowly fade. "I'm sorry, I'm—" His voice was choked, then he shook his head and let out a breath. Chicago hugged him, burying her face in his shoulder. Alex took a deep breath. She was all right. It hadn't really happened. Nothing had happened, the girl was safe. But no —it wasn't her. It was Chicago. His thoughts were still tangled, still half in the cold dream world. He reached out and took a handful of her hair like a rope. The other girl was dead, but Chicago was safe. Her body was warm; he could feel her breath on his neck. Alex pulled her down on top of him and dragged the quilt up over them both. The peace was gone.

Forty-Six

"MR. SANDARS, THANK you for coming over." Philip Greenway rose and crossed the room to greet Alex. He looked calm and alert, but there was a hint of wariness in his posture, as if he were expecting to dodge blows. The office was large and elegantly furnished with traditional bank decorum. There were pictures on the desk, more on the walls, a groundbreaking ceremony with the mayor, handshaking with various public figures, a big dog with three little children draped on top of it, a sailboat, a younger Philip Greenway in a marine uniform with his bride.

"I appreciate you meeting me here. As I explained, I'd rather not upset my wife if it's not necessary." Alex felt closed in by the office and weighted by the task. Greenway was in his late forties, with thinning salt-and-pepper hair, mostly trim with a little paunch. Alex was not usually fond of bankers. It was an admitted prejudice, and not entirely justified, but he usually included them along with lawyers and politicians in the category of stupid men who screwed up the world and walked away richer for it. But there was something straightforward and likable about Greenway.

Alex had heard him speak warmly to his receptionist. Among the pictures was one of him at a benefit dinner for an AIDS organization, not one of the safe kiddie ones. His bank had a reputation for financing inner-city rehab projects, and he had caused some stir in the Washington power circles by quitting his membership in a country club because it refused to admit women.

Maybe the body would turn out not to be Clara at all. Up until now Alex hadn't even thought to wish this. Identification would help clear things up as far as his own life was concerned. But until now he hadn't really thought of the body as having parents.

"You have some information about my daughter?"

"I have some information about a young woman. I'm not sure if it's your daughter."

"These are photos of Clara." Greenway turned a frame on the desk so Alex could see. He wished he hadn't.

"I'm sorry, Mr. Greenway, the young woman in question wasn't —easily identifiable."

Greenway gave a little cough, unbuttoned his suit coat with a slight tremble in his hands, and sat down.

"Please," he said quietly, indicating a chair. "This woman is dead, then."

Alex nodded. Succinctly he sketched out the essentials of the story. "I have photos of the body here, Mr. Greenway, and some computer-enhanced enlargements. I'm sorry, but they're pretty hard to look at."

"Yes. I understand." He held out his hand for the envelope. He looked at the top photo which showed the body lying on the sand. Miss Lilly had been stepping up to cover the girl with an apron when the frame was snapped, and there was a ripple of bright cloth along one side as if a curtain had just been drawn back. The enhanced photos were next. He looked them over, pausing once for several seconds to examine something closely. Then Alex saw the color drain from Greenway's face. He closed his eyes and turned his chair around toward the window. "Yes." The word came out cracked. "This swimsuit—this bikini—it was the first one she ever wore." He turned the leather chair halfway back around. He smiled, but his lower lip was shaking. "Clara was always a lifeguard. And a diver. Springboard diving," he explained, inscribing a little whirl with one finger in the air. "She wasn't into these little bikini things. Twenty-two years old and still sort of a tomboy. Her mother bought her this one when she went to Antigua. I think she was a little embarrassed to wear it at first."

"Besides the bikini top, is there any other way you would know that this might actually be Clara?"

Greenway nodded. He turned back to one of the enhanced photos. His voice was very quiet now.

"She hit the diving board once in a meet. Doing an inward—you know?" He demonstrated the dive with his hand. "She cut her shoulder on the edge of the board, had seven or eight stitches. God, I was glad it wasn't her head. Oh, God—she could have hit her head. . . ." Suddenly he couldn't contain himself; his face was twisted in grief. He got up and went into the bathroom.

Alex waited in the office until he returned. He got up and wandered around, scanned the bookshelves, the photos. When Greenway returned he looked half dead.

"I'm sorry to have to bring you the news."

"No. I appreciate that you went to . . . the trouble. It's just—we were only just now starting to think there might be something wrong. We thought she had just gotten another boat job and the mail was slow. It often took three weeks for her letters from Antigua." He wiped his glasses and put them back in his pocket. "So, we didn't—" He made a vague gesture of frustration, then rested his head in his hands. "I don't know what to do. I don't drink." He said this almost apologetically, looking vaguely lost now in the quiet office. "Do you have any children, Mr. Sanders?"

"No."

"I want to know what happened. Where's her body now?"

"Mr. Greenway, what I'm going to tell you might not make much sense. And I'm going to have to ask you to keep it confidential. At least for a few days until I figure out the best way to go from here."

"Confidential? From whom?"

"This young woman, the body that you have just identified as your daughter, was buried last week in Louisiana, identified as Angelica Wattles."

"Senator Wattles's daughter? But she drowned—"

"No," Alex broke in. "I think she's alive. But for some reason, someone, maybe the senator himself, wants the world to think she's dead. Angelica and Clara have very similar physical appearances. We don't think sharks ate . . ." He cringed at his words and tried to put it differently. "We think someone—removed—the only obvious physical identification, Clara's tattoo, and that the autopsy report was faked."

"But why would . . ." A look of fierce anger infused his body with a new strength. "Are you saying my daughter was *murdered*?"

"I don't know that. We haven't been able to get very far because we couldn't prove the body wasn't Angelica."

"Who's we? Why are you involved?" he asked suddenly.

Alex liked that. The man was sensible and alert. "When it dawned on me that there was something going on, that the body I originally saw didn't really match up to what I learned about Angelica, I first thought someone was trying to dupe the senator," Alex explained. "I was just sort of being a nice guy. I was on my way back to the Caribbean. I figured I would let him know what I thought, then he could go with it wherever he wanted. After I told him, someone tried to kill me."

"You? They tried to kill you?"

"Twice. They did kill another man. Someone they mistook for me. He was visiting my—a lady friend of mine. It was a very professional hit."

Greenway sat down heavily. "This is too—unreal. I'll call my lawyer. I can have the body exhumed. Then, we just have another autopsy. And that will clear everything up."

"Mr. Greenway, sir. I'm not sure that would be a good idea. I don't want to sound—well, like a movie or something, but I think there are some dangerous people involved. Whoever is behind this is well connected and very powerful. They've been able to pull off some very complicated stuff. I'm afraid that if you just burst in with allegations, it might not be good."

"I don't care! What the hell can Wattles do to me? I'll have my lawyer talk to him. I'll go to the press if I have to."

"It's not Wattles I'm worried about. I don't really think he set this up. I think someone else might be putting a squeeze on him. Blackmail or something."

"I don't care! This is my daughter we're talking about!"

"It's his daughter too, sir, and it might be that her life is in danger."

"So we'll go to the FBI." He grabbed up the telephone. Alex recognized the man's need to act, to *do* something. Alex put his hand on the phone.

"The day after I talked to Wattles, my plane was sabotaged. Then when that didn't work, two men rode up in broad daylight and shot this guy's head off."

"Are you trying to scare me?"

"Yeah. Yeah, I guess I am," Alex responded sadly. He turned the family photo around on the desk. "Your youngest—he's in Scouts or something? Maybe plays Little League? One day he disappears on the way home from a game. Your wife has her own car, right? Does she have any regular meetings or appointments she drives to every week?"

Greenway looked like he might be strangling. "So what do you suggest I do?" he asked bitterly.

"Wait a few days. I'm trying to scrape up leads on Wattles. I'm meeting with someone this afternoon who might have information. If we can get a handle on who's threatening him, maybe then Wattles will talk."

"Who are you?" Greenway interrupted. "Excuse me, Mr. Sandars, but you came in here saying you were a pilot or something. Now you want to conduct an investigation."

Alex smiled. "Ah, yes." He glanced once more around the room. "I've had some experience in this sort of thing." Greenway remained silent, an unusual power move for a D.C. guy, Alex thought. It was subtle; let your opponent feel the void and fill it up. It only really worked on the nervous.

"You were in the marines. You know Colonel Cary Brewer?" That made some impression.

Greenway looked at Alex with a mixture of relief and suspicion. "He was with the government last I heard. CIA or something?"

Alex nodded. "The extension is three nine one. He'll vouch for me."

Forty-Seven

FINNEAUS ARRANGED FOR Alex and Chicago to meet with Shana Phillips that same afternoon. They met in a coffee shop near the news station after she finished taping a fluff piece on local school children writing letters to the soldiers in Saudi Arabia. Shana listened to the story of the body switch and the murder attempts, holding back her own cards until she was convinced that this *was* the other half to her own puzzle, and that it was going to be a shocker. Then she brought Alex and Chicago to her apartment to show them what she had.

Now Alex sat on the rug with the files and clippings and stacks of photocopied articles. They were arranged all over the floor under torn slips of paper labeled "Southstate Chemical," "UN," "Leg/ship reg," "Germans." Alex felt like they had fallen into a gold mine, but without a light or much of a pick. Chicago sat on the couch with the biggest file on her lap, looking through every bit of information Shana had gathered on Senator Wattles from his high school record to his current list of speeches and honoraria. It was four inches thick and mostly boring.

"Is there someplace else you can go for a while?" Alex looked up from the papers.

Shana stared at him. "I'm sorry. What?"

"It might be good if you had somewhere else to stay."

"You mean like hide or something?"

"Well, you could put it that way."

"You really believe that Allen Dray was murdered because he sent me this information?"

"I don't think he was killed for his wallet by a dirtball with a lucky stick. No," Alex replied. It was after midnight and his eyes were beginning to ache.

"But the stuff he sent me wasn't any big deal. Just some people and companies he thought were suspicious."

"But the bad guys don't know that."

Shana thought about the threat in the taxi. She hadn't mentioned it, and now decided she wouldn't. She didn't need anybody pressuring her to quit now.

"If you haven't really left a trail or stirred up too much suspicion, you might be OK," Alex offered reluctantly. "They were probably already keeping an eye on Dray. He put his head on the block when he decided to go to the press. But if they know who you are, they're going to be wondering what you're up to."

"Alex, *I* don't have any idea what I'm up to at this point. And we still don't know who 'they' are!"

"Too right." Alex leaned back and stretched his legs out. He was impressed. He was also worried. He could see in Shana's face the rabid excitement of a reporter on a juicy case. It was starting to affect them all: the zeal and passion of a good hunt. Finneaus was digging through EPA files and Chicago was chomping at the bit. Alex had to admit, even he had the bug. He was feeling more alive and centered than he had in a long time.

"How many people know you've been researching this stuff?"

"Just Harland, our director, and a couple of research aides."

"What about all your sources? You've gone to Defense, NSA, American Chemical Society, Brookings, ICC . . ." He scanned the notebook of sources. She was a meticulous researcher, noting names, positions, phone numbers, times of calls or visits, even a reference number to coordinate with her computer notes.

"You have over twenty contacts just in this book. That's a lot of people."

"Yeah, but most of it's just basic stuff. I didn't tell everyone what I was looking for. It started out with the miscarriage thing and Wattles's connections to the chemical industry and his work on this bill. It wasn't until I got to Ruthwilde that I began to turn up real dirt. I sure as hell didn't want anyone else putting my story together once it started to look good."

"You talked to Borkowsky himself at the Defense Department?"

"For about thirty seconds. And I had to pull a lot of strings to get to him. But I just asked him about their position on further plant investigations. According to Allen Dray, the UN found six or seven other German plants that are probably making nerve gases, only disguising it too well. They've also been supplying technology, equipment, and precursor chemicals directly to client countries. Iran, Iraq, Egypt, Syria, probably others." She pulled a list of countries out of one of the files and handed it to Alex. He looked it over and passed it back to Chicago.

"They ship it legitimately to someplace like Singapore, then turn it around and ship it out again. A company in Maryland, Alsak Chemicals, was busted last year—they were transshipping through Jordan."

"What happened to them?" Chicago asked.

Shana shrugged. "A few minor managers were indicted, appeals still going on, but the main guy, Peter Valascheck, got away. Only one German company, Imhausen, has ever been convicted, but there was evidence on several others. I thought Defense might be picking up the ball. So I asked Borkowsky what they were doing about investigating it."

"And he said . . ." Alex picked up her notes. " 'Manufacture and distribution of chemical warfare agents continues to be of concern to the United States.' "

"Yeah," she added sarcastically.

"Wow!" Chicago exclaimed as she looked over the data. "All these countries have chemical weapons? Iraq, Iran, Egypt, Israel, Syria, Burma, Ethiopia . . ."

"We can't prove it, but it looks that way. Also France, Russia, North and South Korea, China, Libya, Vietnam, Thailand . . .

and of course, Uncle Sam," Shana recited the rest of the list from memory.

"I thought we were getting rid of it all. I thought there was a treaty for disposal. Didn't they do another Geneva thing about this?" Chicago asked in frustration. "I mean—it doesn't make sense. No one's supposed to use it anyway; everybody has way too much of it already. They're trying to get rid of it, and they're making more. This doesn't make a bit of sense."

Shana smiled sadly. She had lived in D.C. a long time and wasn't used to people who still worried about government not making sense.

"It's nuts." Chicago shook her head. "And now they're all pissing in the sand over there."

"Oh, don't even get me started on that," Shana said as she jumped out of her chair and headed toward the kitchen. "But on the other hand, what did any of us really care about the whole issue before this?" She stopped and leaned in the doorway. "Did you know that since 1984 we had proof that Saddam Hussein was gassing people? The Senate tried to pass sanctions against Iraq *three years* ago because of it, but only *now* is it a big horror, because our own people might get a taste of it."

Shana returned with a bottle of wine and three glasses.

"We can't really claim much righteous indignation." Shana poured the wine and handed them each a glass. "Anyway, I don't know about you guys, but I've had it for tonight. I'm lost with this stuff. There's something going on—and here it is." She shoved one of the piles with her toe. "But darned if I know what it is."

Alex smiled at the demure expletive.

"You're just too close to it right now," he consoled. "You need to put it down entirely for a week or so. Get away . . ."

"Ah, so we're back to that." Shana smiled grimly. She turned back to the notes on her computer screen, and scrolled quickly through the list of her sources.

"I don't know why anyone would think I was a threat. Especially since I still don't know what's going on."

"But they don't know you don't know," Chicago pointed out.

"True . . ." Her voice trailed off.

"Have you filed anything under FOIA?" Alex pressed.

Without looking up Chicago kicked him. Her shipboard education had been weak on American government. She was unfamiliar with many of the organizations they were referring to and starting to go crazy with the number of acronyms and initials they were throwing around.

"Sorry, dearest." Alex laughed. He caught her foot and rested it on the back of his neck. "FOIA is the Freedom of Information Act. It's how you get to look at stuff nobody wants you to. So did you?" he quizzed.

"Just one," Shana replied. "On some research the government was doing in the sixties on our own nerve gas development. I wanted to find out if any of the chemists came up anywhere interesting now."

"Did they?"

"A couple."

"Like?" Alex prompted.

"Like Ethan Ruthwilde."

Alex dropped the stack of papers and looked up at Shana. "Ever consider a career as a spook?"

Shana laughed and leaned back against the brick wall, propping one foot on a half-open drawer. Dressed in sweatshirt and old jeans, her smooth brown face relaxed for a moment, she could have been a college kid cramming for an exam.

"I like a byline too much for that," she admitted. "My mama used to call me haughty. Who you think you are, missy?" Shana mimicked a righteous Southern scolding. "Who you think you are, the queen of Sheba?" They laughed.

"So you think Ruthwilde is deep into this?" Shana pressed.

"He has been turning up," Alex mused. "If you had to guess, what would be your scenario?"

Shana stared over the piles of paper. "Someone is pressuring Wattles to get this bill through, and the most likely candidate is someone with something to gain. But that could be anyone from a paint factory in West Virginia to Saddam Hussein himself."

Alex stretched and rubbed his eyes, pushed himself up off the rug, and flopped on the couch next to Chicago. "How you doing? You find anything in there?"

Chicago gave him that half-smug half-triumphant look he had come to know, love, and worry about.

"Well, I think I know where he's hiding Angelica."

Forty-Eight

Even the riotous crowd in New Orleans on Halloween night was a little impressed with Sophie. In a city used to glorious debauchery, where wretched excess is the right, if not duty of every citizen, on a crowded street filled with ghouls and goblins, this was no small feat. She wore no costume except for a certain palpable evil that caused people to shrink away as she passed and feel a pang of some foul dread in her wake. Sophie was stalking Grant Darlington.

Grant had driven down from Baton Rouge with some friends for the festivities. By now his notoriety had faded enough that people no longer stopped and stared on the street when he passed, but there was still talk. Scandal in the South is an art form. There were the little sidelong looks, the quick hush that happened when he passed.

Not that he minded. Grant really didn't care one way or the other what people thought of him, but it was starting to cramp his social life. The girls were still willing, but their daddies sure weren't; and in the deep South daddies still count.

With Ruthwilde's generous payoff, Grant had no need to find a job, but with all his other friends either working or in grad school, he now found himself adrift and bored. And at the moment, very drunk. He was leaning against a brick wall on a narrow piece of sidewalk waiting for his head to stop spinning. He had long ago lost his friends in the crowd, but figured they'd all wind up back together when they swept the streets at dawn. Meanwhile, he would just chill out and watch the pageant.

A flock of staggering college students dressed as Arabs in their bedsheets jostled him as they passed. Batman was dancing with Tinker Bell, while a rubber-faced George Bush paraded with a rubber-faced Maggie Thatcher.

Grant closed his eyes and slid down the wall so he was crouching on a stoop. The world eased out of its careening tilt into a milder swaying motion. When he opened his eyes again, he was staring at Goliath's kneecaps. He blinked and tried to focus. These were big legs, and they went up a long way.

He tilted his head back and tried to follow them up to the body that he felt sure had to be attached up there somewhere, but the wall got in the way of his head. No matter, the body reached its hands down, tucked them under his arms like he was a child, and lifted him to his feet.

"Well, well, what do we have here?" Sophie smiled. The voice was still coming from somewhere above his head, and Grant's brain lurched through the drunken haze to figure out why. He was eye to eye with an immense arrangement of flesh.

"Looks like Peter Pan."

"No!" he snapped. All night he had been getting that Peter Pan crap. "Goddamnit—I'm Robin Hood!" And with a supreme effort Grant raised his heavy head and fixed his eyes on the stuff of Sophie. He nearly passed out. Before he could, Sophie's lips fell over his like a plunger, and she flattened him against the wall.

Forty-Nine

"I WOULD LIKE you to find out what happened to my daughter," Philip Greenway said quietly. Since they had last spoken, the man's appearance had changed. There was something looser in his posture, a tightening around the edges of his mouth, a flatness in his once keen eyes. He looked broken.

"I checked with Cary Brewer," Greenway continued. "He was surprised that you were in the city. He asks that you call, and said to tell you he understands if you don't. He did back you up." He noticed Alex tense a little at this. "Of course, he gave me no details." Greenway got up, then leaned against the back of his chair as if he didn't quite know where to put himself in his grief. "I am familiar with—things. I'm not interested in the details of your government career," Greenway assured him. "Colonel Brewer did say that you were to be trusted, and that if he had anything that needed to be done anywhere you would be his first choice to do it."

Alex shrugged. "Well, he's a generous man with praise."

"Be that as it may. I trust his judgment. And I need someone. I want you to find out what happened. The photos—" His voice caught a little, then the firm authority of the bank president took over again. "I haven't told my wife yet. It's still too unreal this way. I have to know what happened. Who killed her? I want you to find out. I can only respect your wishes to keep quiet about it if I know something is actually being done."

"Mr. Greenway, we actually have found out a lot of information since yesterday. Someone else was already investigating some suspicious things about Wattles."

"I know how this city is." Greenway sighed. *"Suspicious things* take months to unravel—years if you've got enough clout to repress them. This Persian Gulf thing is already starting to dominate the news. Unless you have Senator Wattles sleeping with Saddam Hussein I doubt your suspicious things will get much attention. I want my daughter. Dead or alive, I want her to"—Greenway's eyes looked electric—"I want her to *exist.* Right now, she's just . . . nowhere. I'll pay you ten thousand dollars plus expenses." He opened a drawer and pulled out a ledger. "I'll write a check for five thousand right now. Or I can get cash if you prefer."

"Wait a minute." Alex leaned back in his chair. "I understand your desire, but I'm not sure what else I can do, even with the money."

"You could find Angelica. When the world sees she's alive, whatever Senator Wattles is up to has to come out. What better catalyst could you want?"

Alex hesitated. "I can find Angelica. . . ."

"But?" Greenway caught on his reluctance.

"I'm not sure it would be the best thing."

"What do you mean?"

"If all this started out with someone threatening to kidnap or harm Angelica, she's probably safer where she is."

Philip Greenway was wrestling with the question. The need to have some resolution on his own dead daughter vied with the duty to protect a living girl.

"You say you might know where she is?"

Alex nodded.

"Think a minute, Mr. Sanders. Has it occurred to you that if you know, the enemy probably does too?"

Fifty

Belize is a good-natured jungly little country nestled on the Caribbean Sea in Central America. Rare among its neighbors, Belize has managed to escape the more pernicious effects of its colonial past and emerge with a stable government, a reasonable economy, vast acres of still untrammeled land, and a gentle, friendly population. The Belizians are a handsome race of African and Mayan ancestry, with some English and Spanish blood mixed in along the way.

Off the east coast, a string of cays border the longest coral reef in the Western Hemisphere. Tarpon, bonefish, and marlin challenge the serious fisherman. In the early 1980s Americans, mostly from Texas and Louisiana, began to discover these cays. Belize offered all the charm but few of the drawbacks of Mexico, and everyone spoke English. Ambergris Cay, the largest and most developed of the islands, was a short flight from the United States and land was cheap. Vacation homes and fishing lodges sprang up, and Ambergris Cay gradually became a haven for tourists. Sport fishermen, scuba divers, and general paradise seekers loved it. Angelica Wattles hated it.

She might have liked it better if she were not being held there against her will. But she was stuck in isolated luxury with only a grouchy housekeeper, a few boatmen and grounds keepers, and Buster Cray, the morose, ugly guard her father had trusted with her protection. Protection, hell—what was there to protect her from except mosquitoes and boredom? No one could land on Turtle Island except by the one channel or helicopter.

The land was not exactly an island, but a fragment of land at the northern end of Ambergris Cay separated from the mainland by dense mangrove swamp. Senator Wattles had bought the place in 1975, when Belize was still a treasured secret among serious fishermen, and built a grand lodge where he often hosted groups of political cronies.

While it was a very popular place among her father's friends, Turtle Island held little appeal for Angelica. The clear waters of the shallow lagoon were not nearly so much fun as a good swimming pool, and there was no parade of boys to hold her interest. She had been here three weeks and there was still no glimpse of reprieve.

"Tobo, what the hell is this?" The man cringed instinctively at the sound of her voice. Angelica hurled the stack of videotapes on the floor. *"Fletch Lives, Friday the Thirteenth Part Five,* and *Conan the Barbarian*!"

"Miss Angelica, there are no more tapes left in town you haven't seen," he pleaded. "I even ask my friends at the hotels." Marion, the housekeeper, just sat impassively reading a romance novel. She did not trouble herself with the young lady's tantrums. She ran the kitchen with an imperious autonomy. "Tell Daddy to send some tay-ypes. Did you give him the list? I cannot believe this! Wheah are they?" she demanded. When annoyed, which was most of the time these days, Angelica's cultured Southern drawl took on a shrewlike pitch.

"I got all your nice magazines, Miss Angelica. Why don't you look at them instead?"

"I can't believe my own fathah would be so callous. It's bad enough I'm a prisinah heah on this godforsaken desert island. But y'all just are not very nice!"

Angelica stomped up the stairs to her bedroom and slammed the door like a child. The first thing she saw was her own reflection in the wall mirror. This further depressed her. She had been so bored here that she had put on at least five pounds. When you're only five foot one that's a lot of extra flesh. She flopped back on the bed and stared at the ceiling. She couldn't even work up a good cry. Boredom and stupid videos were fairly minor traumas of her confinement here. Finally she flipped over and lay on her stomach and began to look through the new magazines.

Fifty-One

Grant Darlington woke up while speeding down the highway in the front seat of a convertible with coarse hanks of blond hair snapping at his face. His Robin Hood hat was long gone, but he was still wearing the green tights and terry cloth bathrobe that served as his costume, and his bow and quiver still dangled from one shoulder. All the arrows, however, were gone. He groped at the hair in his mouth and dragged it away, sat up in the seat, and squinted at the harsh morning light. Then he saw Sophie.

She turned and probably grinned at him. Her rocket-red lips curved up on one side anyway, but there was so much going on in the rest of her face—a contemptuous sort of appraisal in her eyes and a lusty slackness in her jaw—that Grant didn't know what to think. But he wasn't going to be intimidated by the woman no matter how big she was. He pulled himself upright and looked at her directly. He felt sick.

"So who the hell are you?" His voice was hoarse, and the effort made his head throb.

"Ooh, baby, you don't remember? I thought I made a better impression than that," Sophie crooned.

"Oh, sure." Grant laid his head back on the seat and sneered. "Well, it was good for me; was it good for you?"

Sophie gave him an imperious, pitying gaze. "If we had slept together, sweet pea, you would remember it." She reached over and laid a palm on his thigh. Slowly she let her fingers creep up under the hem of his costume. "You have a hole in your stocking."

He pushed her hand away. He tried to remember the events of last night, but it was all just a fog of revelry, noise, costumes, and beer.

"Where are we going?" he asked.

"There you go right away getting ordinary. Don't you like that sense of"—Sophie widened her eyes and ran her tongue around her lips—"magic?"

"Not when I have a shit-kicking headache." He groaned, sinking back and letting the wind soothe his face.

"There's some aspirin in your suitcase," Sophie replied nonchalantly. Grant twisted around in surprise to find his suitcase on the backseat. He turned back to confront her when he saw a highway sign for the airport.

"What the hell's going on? How did you get my bag?" He reached suddenly for the wheel and turned it so they skidded off onto the shoulder. "Where are we going!" he yelled. Sophie flung him off with one hand and steered the car to a stop.

"Where we are going," she bit each word off like she was snapping chalk, "is to find Angelica Wattles."

Grant was startled. He waited a beat too long. "She's dead. Angelica drowned. What's the matter, don't they have news where you come from?"

"Do they have brains where you come from?" she replied icily. "I'm sorry, cookie, I know your little head is aching. But try not to be so stupid. I found you for a reason. I already know where the girl is hiding. And I know that you will have no qualms about playing another little part in this silly game for the right price."

Grant remained impassive, but there was interest in his eyes. "If you know where she is what the hell do you need me for?"

"To get me onto Turtle Island. Angelica knows you. She won't be frightened if you show up. You just don't know"—Sophie looked at him with a beleaguered expression—"how much trouble it is to have to kidnap someone and then have to haul them around, and find someplace to put them, and tie them up. I'm not very good with knots, and then, oh, you know, probably you have to shoot some people, and then you have these bodies to get rid of. I strained my back once that way." She smiled. "You're going to help me."

"Well, I hate to mess up your fantasy here, but what about you? I mean she's not going to think you're her fairy godmother or something."

"She will think her loving daddy was worried about her and sent some extra guards to protect her. She will think whatever I want her to think."

"Forget it. Uh-uh. There's no way." Grant folded his arms and closed his eyes. "I'm not getting into this shit."

Sophie reached casually across the seat and wrapped one hand around his neck. With an iron grip she began to squeeze and pull upward, so Grant felt his breath go and his body rise out of the seat.

"Would you like to hear about your alternatives?" Sophie asked sweetly.

Fifty-Two

Chicago heard Alex coming down the hall and quickly pulled some papers over the book she was reading. She looked up and smiled as he walked in, still rubbing sleep from his eyes.

"Hey," he greeted her. "When I asked you to look at those manifests I didn't mean at the crack of dawn." He bent and kissed her.

"I just woke early and couldn't get back to sleep." She leaned back and stretched. "It's weird sleeping in a room that's bigger than my whole boat. There's too much space."

"I'm sure Jacquie could give you a mat in the closet if you want. Is there any coffee?"

Chicago waved toward the pot. "I, ah . . . I made you some breakfast," she offered hesitantly. Alex stared at her. "Scrambled eggs," she added quickly.

He yelped as the coffee spilled over onto his hand. "What did you say?"

"I said I made you scrambled eggs. For breakfast." He was looking at her as if she had just offered to fly to the moon. Chicago began to feel embarrassed. "Well, so you want 'em or not? You don't *have* to. It's not like national egg day or something."

"No—yes, I mean yes, sure I'd love some scrambled eggs." He stumbled to the table. What the hell was going on? Chicago did not cook. She couldn't make toast if the directions were stamped on the bread. Early in her shipboard life, she had realized that it would be too easy for her to get stuck with the job, and so had carefully avoided all contact with the galley.

"They got cold. I'll just heat them up."

"Sure, fine." He gulped his coffee and picked up some of the papers, uncovering the book underneath. It was Jacquie's well-worn copy of the *Joy of Cooking.*

"Oh, goddamnit . . ." he heard Chicago muttering from the stove, then some vigorous scraping, then a strange plopping sound. She set the plate down in front of him, then slid into the chair. "I guess they don't reheat so well." In the center of the plate, unadorned and unaccompanied, lay a stalwart mound of hard pale eggs dotted with shards of burned crust. Alex took a big bite.

"Ummmm!" He nodded and raised his eyebrows, hoping for a good show of enjoyment without having to outright lie. She wasn't convinced.

"Shit," she declared simply as she snatched the plate away and emptied the eggs in the sink.

"Wait—they're not that bad. Really," Alex offered as he tried to select the appropriate response. He was sure there was some kind of female thing going on here, one of those pop quizzes that come along just when you think you've been keeping up with the reading. The trouble was, Chicago had never thrown anything like that at him before.

"I mean, they were probably better when you first made them. I should have gotten up earlier." He heard the garbage disposal groaning with the load. "And I don't like eggs all that much anyway," he shouted over the noise.

She came back to the table perfectly calm. "I don't care." She smiled. "It's just eggs."

"Right." Alex reached for her hand, but she was already reaching for the papers.

"So let's go on to something I *can* do."

"Illy, I'm sure you can cook eggs . . ."

"It doesn't matter. Now look at these papers."

Alex was glad to let the matter drop and seized upon the diversion. Finneaus had managed to get them copies of shipping manifests and records for the major Louisiana cargo ports for the past year. Since Chicago was the most familiar with the industry, she had been the one to look them over.

"Did you find anything?"

"I don't know." Chicago handed him a few manifests with highlights. "There is way too much traffic and cargo to be able to check for faked manifests. I mostly looked at the small freight companies; if you want to smuggle something you usually try to turn it over through an intermediary; but nothing clicks."

Alex grunted and sipped his coffee. "So no million-barrel midnight shipment to Iraq?"

Chicago shook her head. "The only thing even faintly suspicious is this." She pointed to a circled item on a manifest. "Southstate Chemical sold a lot of pesticides to companies in Malaysia, shipping them to Singapore. Shana did say to keep an eye out for stuff going to Singapore, and besides that, remember what Finneaus was saying about pesticide dumping in third-world countries?"

Alex shook his head. "You know," she prompted, "how even after the U.S. banned a lot of chemicals for use here, the companies can still sell them abroad?"

"Oh yeah, something about villagers in Africa sprinkling DDT around their huts?"

"Yeah. Well, this doesn't fit, that's all. Why sell half a million dollars' worth of brand-new pesticides to a poor country like Malaysia, when they can probably get other stuff cheaper?"

Alex called Shana at the station later that morning. "I want to talk to Wattles. Got any ideas?" He was tired of papers and diagrams and second-guessing. "I think it's time to force his hand."

"I guess you guys didn't come up with anything new."

"Just that there are too many holes. But the holes made me think. I don't believe the senator would have another girl killed to protect his daughter. He's stupid and he's greedy, but I don't think he's a killer."

Shana tried to think. The senator's office was no good; Alex would be thrown out, as she herself had been on two occasions, at the first hint of trouble. "There's a couple of bars and restaurants on the Hill he frequents." She had the phone cradled on her shoulder as she sifted through her "to do" pile that had been neglected lately. There was a journal renewal notice, letters on a story she had done, results of a follow-up survey on radon gas detectors, an invitation to a dinner, a notice for a baby shower. "Wait!" Shana almost jumped out of her seat; she flipped back and pulled out the invitation. "Go to the ball!"

She heard a lump of silence. "Alex? Did you hear me?"

"Yeah, I heard you, but—ah, I didn't bring my glass slippers."

Shana laughed. "No, listen—there's a big dinner at the Corcoran Gallery tomorrow night for the International Federation of Engineering and Manufacturing Industries. I'm sure Wattles and

Sullevin will both be there. I could get you guys in. You could do one of those Agatha Christie deals—you know, with the cunning conversation revealing the murderer."

"Hmm—sounds good, but I don't think I could pass for Agatha."

"No, Alex—but seriously, think about it. It's a social affair; Wattles will be drinking; at least you can talk to him."

"It might work, Shana, except for the fact that Wattles and Sullevin have both met me. Even with my haircut and mustache, they're bound to recognize me."

"Oh, right." Shana started to think. "But they don't know Chicago, do they?"

"Forget it," Alex cut her off. "She's staying out of it. I didn't even want her to come here."

"All she'd have to do is talk to him. And you can be there anyway. You could be a waiter! No one looks at the waiters. I'll find out who's catering. With this big an affair they'll have fifty or sixty waiters. You can just show up and blend in."

Alex was starting to like the idea.

"You could have Finneaus take Chicago," Shana went on. "And I'll have Harland, my producer, introduce them to the senator as old friends . . ." Shana was suddenly scripting the event with all the zeal of a soap opera writer. "And then she can just sort of work the conversation around to . . . to something."

Alex felt a new thrill starting to displace his fatigue. It sounded good. The senator was likely to have his guard down at a party surrounded by friends and associates.

"Alex? Are you still there?"

"Yeah—listen, I only see one problem."

"What's that?"

"Getting Chicago into a dress."

Fifty-Three

"I LOOK LIKE a goddamn nudibranch!" Chicago scowled into the mirror as she stood awkwardly in the swirl of flowery ruffles.

"A what?"

"Gag—get it off me!" She stamped impatiently as Jacquie laughed and jumped toward the zipper. "It's a mollusk," Chicago continued as she wiggled out of the flounced taffeta. "But soft like a worm. They're all ruffly and bright colored like this. Actually, they're kind of cool," she explained as she tried to figure out how to get the gaudy dress back on the hanger.

"That's very interesting," Jacquie replied skeptically as she gently took the hanger out of Chicago's hands before she mangled the dress entirely.

"How's that one, girls?" The saleslady interrupted with a strained brightness. She appeared at the dressing room door, a woman with a drum-tight face-lift and lipstick the color of cough syrup. Philip Greenway had sent them to this boutique at his wife's suggestion. Mrs. Greenway spent quite a lot of money here and the clerk had orders to please. "Have we found that perfect little gown yet?"

Chicago glared at the woman and thrust the rejected dress into her jeweled fingers.

"Perhaps if you could give me some idea of exactly what sort of dress you are looking for?" the woman responded icily.

"Perhaps you have something in a different phylum?" Jacquie asked sweetly. The woman held out two more dresses with a barely restrained sense of exasperation. Chicago flopped down on one of the puffy pink stools. She had to admit that despite her general disregard for feminine finery, the idea of picking out a dress for a fancy party had been a little exciting. Now it was just trauma.

"Maybe you could give us some time to think," Jacquie suggested. The saleslady nodded her head, an eerie gesture since her skin didn't move, and turned on a haughty heel.

"Whew!"

"Goddamn, this girl shit is hard work!" Chicago sighed.

"And we haven't even started on the shoes and accessories," Jacquie pointed out. She laughed, snatched Chicago's jeans up off the stool, and threw them in her lap.

"Let's get out of here."

The cold fall air felt good. The afternoon was brilliantly clear, and even the K Street business crowd in their suits and khaki topcoats seemed buoyant.

"So, perhaps you could give me some idea of exactly what sort of dress you are looking for?" Jacquie asked in a good imitation of the saleslady's snooty voice.

"How should I know?" Chicago replied in exasperation. "I think the last real dress I had to buy was for my first communion. I just never expected everything to be so—so *stupid* looking! What I want is— Do you ever watch those old movies? You know, where they go to those clubs with the big curved booths and there are those little lamps on the tables and there's like a lady singing into one of those big round microphones . . ." Chicago grappled impatiently with the air as she talked. "And the dresses are all kind of soft and swirly. I want something like an anemone or a moon jellyfish."

Jacquie laughed and grabbed Chicago by the coat sleeve. "Sure, of course! The Cousteau Couture!"

After foraging in a couple of vintage clothing shops and a little work at the sewing machine, Chicago was ready for the dinner. Alex was strangling Finneaus in the front hallway mirror, a 1958 copy of Emily Post's etiquette book open to a diagram of how to tie a bow tie.

"Hold still, I've almost got it."

"Like hell—ouch!" Finneaus jumped back. "You stuck me!"

"I didn't stick you. How could I stick you?"

"A pin—you stuck my neck with a pin! Give me that!" He snatched the bow tie, now gone slightly limp from all the handling, away from Alex and felt around the inside of his collar.

"Ah ha!" He found a pin that had been overlooked in the unwrapping of the new shirt. "Now let me do this. I did it fine once." Finneaus looped the bow tie around the lamp and, carefully following the pictures in the book, successfully tied the bow.

"There!" He waved proudly.

"Great." Alex laughed. "So send the lamp to the ball."

"Don't you have to get ready yourself?" Finneaus suggested, elbowing him out of the way.

"I am ready. I'm just a waiter, I get the clip-on tie."

"Well, get outta my face."

Alex left Finneaus to his formal wear fumblings and ran a comb through his newly black hair. He still half expected the color to come off on his hands, but so far it seemed to be sticking. The first glimpse of his new look had been a jolt. With the dark hair and the mustache that he had let grow since the shooting, he looked very much like the Argentinian he had played for two long years. It was a role he had wanted to forget forever. He slipped the comb back in his pocket and looked up to see how Finneaus was tangling with the tie. Then he saw Chicago.

There should have been bells and trumpets, soft focus, and a choir of cherubs on clouds. If it had been a cartoon, there would have been a view of his heart pounding inside his chest. She was gorgeous. Dark blue satin flowed down Chicago's body and a rope of champagne velvet arched across her shoulders and plunged down her bare back. The dress had a few scrunches and swirls, or whatever they were, and some filmy stuff down the back. It all kind of sparkled and rustled as she moved.

"Wow!" was all Finneaus could say. Alex just stared as Chicago walked down the stairs. She looked half proud, half pleased to have pulled off a big joke.

"Well?" She swept a graceful turn and the silky hem floated up to expose her still bare feet. Alex had never imagined such a transformation. He had always found her beautiful, in an unconventional way, but now, in this wash of glamour, with her hair swept up and the lightest touch of makeup, and this—this softness, he was smitten.

"It's great," Finneaus declared.

"Jacquie did it."

"We both did," Jacquie insisted as she hurried down with Chicago's shoes.

"No, it was mostly her idea. We found this first." She held out the blue satin skirt. "But it had these gross sleeves, so we cut them off, and cut out the back—"

"And made them into gores for the skirt—"

"Then we found this stuff . . ." The two women went on eagerly explaining the transformation of the dress to the men who didn't know a bias from a bulldozer and at the moment didn't care.

"So do you like it?" Chicago asked the still speechless Alex.

"It's great." He stepped close and touched her bare shoulder. "You have the most beautiful collarbones."

"Well, anyway, you guys better get going." Jacquie kissed Finneaus. "Be good. Remember, outside in, the salad fork is the little one."

"I wish you were coming."

"Are you kidding? Some stuffy old affair full of politicians and bankers? No, thank you very much! I've got a date with Humphrey Bogart and Orville Redenbacher."

"I think there's a Sam Adams in there too," Alex offered as they left.

Fifty-Four

HANS GOERBEL BRUSHED the lapels of his tuxedo and checked the cumberbund. He was used to formal wear and it caused him no fuss, but it reminded him that he did not like Vienna. They overdressed for these affairs in general, and in Vienna in particular. They would play that goddamn Strauss all night. They would serve veal in some sort of cream sauce and that damned marzipan. At least with this being an international conference there might be some French wines.

He was about to leave the bathroom when the door opened and Peter Valascheck walked in.

"Well, my goodness, have I turned into such a ghost? You look startled, my friend," Peter greeted him.

"No, it's just that I didn't expect to see you here, Peter. Aren't you taking a risk? There are a lot of people who would know you. The chancellor is here and most of the Austrian cabinet."

"Oh, don't worry. I won't stay long. And anyway, I still have too much invested with the lot of them. They're hardly likely to call in the gendarmes. Oh, that's Paris, isn't it? Hard to remember what country I'm in these days." He looked quickly around the elegant bathroom to make sure they were alone. "I've just come back from Sri Lanka." He turned the water on in the sink and let it run. "Have you kept up with it at all? This whole Tamil separatist thing?" Goerbel gave a slight nod to indicate he was aware.

"Well, it's your routine little protracted insurrection. Guerrillas, separatists, civil war, that sort of thing."

A slow smile crept over Goerbel's face. "You're still drumming up business, Peter?"

"They're in the Dark Ages." Valascheck's laugh was coarse. "They're still just rounding people up and shooting them. Business needs new markets. I thought you would want to know."

He did want to know. Already he was in a better humor as his mind began to work. India produced a lot of chemicals, and the country ran by baksheesh.

"It's worth looking into, but how big a market can there really be? They don't have the oil dollars."

Valascheck shook his head in mock exasperation. "I'm not talking about a market, although I'm sure there is more of one than you think. I'm talking about production and distribution."

Goerbel pulled down a mental map. It would be a good location. One could ship to the Gulf easily from India.

"You're thinking, my friend." Valascheck smiled. "You like the idea?"

"It's worth looking into."

"I thought you might feel that way." He pulled a small envelope out of his jacket pocket. "Here are the people to talk to. You will arrange my usual commission?"

"Which account?"

"Geneva is fine. It will be skiing season soon. I'm thinking about a villa in Saint Moritz." Valascheck turned back to the mirror and straightened his bow tie. "And how is everything else going?" he asked politely.

Goerbel's expression tightened as he was wrenched back from speculation to the immediate problems of the day. "Ruthwilde has offered to try and get the shipment out himself. He says he knows enough people, that he and the senator's aide might be able to pull it off. Until then, Sophie is still at work."

"Ahhh—blissful girl. Has she been of any help?"

"She found Angelica Wattles."

Fifty-Five

For the eighth time Alex hurried down the long corridor and climbed the endless steps with the silver tray balanced on his hand and began to look around for dirty glasses.

"You're walking too fast, amigo," a low voice informed him in Spanish. He glanced over at the other waiter, a stocky man of medium height who looked like the guy in the Colombian coffee commercials. "This your first Corcoran party?" he asked. Alex nodded.

"I thought so. You better slow down. Don't fill your tray so much. This place will kill you."

Alex picked up an empty wineglass and a plate with the shards of pâté on brioche. As he walked by a little conversational huddle of important people, the secretary of labor flung a shrimp tail onto his tray. He hadn't even looked up, just casually flicked it. The tail landed in a smear of hosin sauce, spattering tiny drops on Alex's cuff. Alex smiled at the rudeness. At least he figured his disguise was secure; waiters did seem to be invisible.

It was 8:30 and the gallery was starting to get full. He found Chicago and Finneaus talking with Shana Phillips. He scanned the room. No sign of the senator yet.

"Hey, amigo! Come on, hurry up. We can't let things pile up," a supervisor chastised him. Alex turned and hurried off to the distant kitchen. This wouldn't do. He needed to be doing something that let him stay upstairs longer. On the other side of the drop station waiters were lined up waiting to replenish their hors d'oeuvre trays. Quickly Alex slipped into that line and appropriated a tray of smoked salmon rosettes. Thus armed, he could mingle.

Chicago was still a little overwhelmed by it all. There were at least two hundred people in the great hall. Ladies with drawn-on eyebrows greeted each other with rampaging enthusiasm, while men with gut-strained tuxedo studs rocked on their heels and talked in rumbles. They all seemed expert at snatching up those little decorated canapés. Chicago had not dared to try any; they all looked wobbly and fragile.

"You should have seen the Reagan inaugural balls," Shana whispered to her as they watched two particularly ghoulishly painted matrons brushing cheeks and kissing air. "It was downright spooky."

There was a string orchestra standing in two rows along either side of the grand staircase. There were magnificent floral arrangements everywhere. In one half of the gallery, round tables had blossomed like water lilies: burgundy cloths with brocade overlays, gold plates, and forests of crystal.

"Did you get the seating arranged?" Finneaus asked Shana.

"You're all at table fifteen. Here comes Joe Harland. Wattles loves him right now, because we gave him forty-five seconds on the six o'clock last week. Patting children on the head at the Special Olympics. Nice warm fuzzies. He's one grateful politician." Joe Harland strolled up to their group, a glass of soda water sweating in his hand, a glum expression on his face. Shana introduced them all, then excused herself. "I'm sure the senator will be in a better humor if he doesn't see my nasty self anywhere around!" She winked and melted off into the crowd.

"I hate these things," Harland sulked. "My feet hurt. You better expose the next Iran-Contra for all this."

"Thanks for arranging it." Chicago smiled.

"No problem. I'm still not sure what you expect to find, but I do trust Shana. Mostly," he added honestly and took a sip of his drink. "So the story is you're my niece, moving to Washington, looking for a job on the Hill?" Chicago nodded.

Alex appeared suddenly, a tray of hors d'oeuvres balanced on his palm. "Touch that fish and I'll break your arm," he growled as Finneaus reached for a salmon rosette. "It's two miles to the kitchen."

"Well, get some other kind. Get some of that smeary stuff in the leaves," Finneaus suggested logically as he helped himself to the last rosette on Alex's tray. "No one's eating them."

"Wattles just got here. The smarmy looking guy with him is Darcy Sullevin. I don't know who the kid is."

"Well, then I guess it's time for networking, huh?" Harland smiled. Finneaus offered his arm to Chicago. She glanced nervously at Alex.

"Just pretend it's a lube job," he whispered as he brushed past to gather up some abandoned wineglasses.

Shana caught up to Chicago in the ladies' room. "Girl, you got those men wrapped around your little finger! Where did you learn to flirt like that?" The guests were being ushered toward the tables for dinner.

"But I'm not flirting! I've hardly even been talking to them."

"Well, what do you think flirting is?" Shana laughed. "It's keeping your mouth shut and your big adoring eyes open." She fixed her lipstick and stepped back to check her dress. "You do like that and soon enough they're thinking you are the most wonderful girl in the world because you find them so fascinating and intelligent."

"Is that how it works? Knew I've been doing something wrong all my life."

Shana laughed, then got serious. "Don't screw up now. Here's where you go to work. Wattles has had a few drinks, but Sullevin's stone cold sober. He never drinks at these things. He does, however, look a little besotted by your charms. Keep pouring it on."

"Right," Chicago replied.

"OK, you ready? Remember, focus on Sullevin. Maybe the kid too, though he's just a legislative aide. He might be eager to show off how much he knows."

"Are you at our table?" Chicago asked, suddenly wanting a little more support. She had never felt quite so out of her element.

"Are you kidding? As far as Wattles is concerned I'm the black death! I'll be off behind the Renoir somewhere. Good luck!" she encouraged as she swept out the door.

"Come on, come on; let's go; stay to the right; get your trays." The waiters lined up, as the sweating cooks pulled the platters out of the ovens.

"Sauce, sauce!" the head chef snapped as an overeager young waiter turned away without her sauce. As Alex stepped up for his platter he was suddenly smacked with a rare feeling—panic.

Powers of observation had so far gotten him through the carefully orchestrated duties of a banquet waiter. First course was easy, salad was OK, though there'd been an unfortunate slip with the radiccio, but once he started walking up those stairs with the heavy tray, gravy washing violently from side to side, Alex began to worry.

In his varied undercover escapades he had managed to pull off a number of ruses with reasonable aplomb. He had never, however, had to balance a huge tray piled with ten pounds of stuffed lamb chops, wild rice, sweet potato flan, and sautéed vegetables on one hand, or serve this same repast to a crowded table with a fork and spoon held awkwardly in the other.

Alex was an athlete in excellent shape, but carrying thirty-some pounds of hot food like this was a strain. He could feel the sweat pouring down his body. He approached the table and hesitantly began to serve. Senator Wattles was telling some Capitol Hill anecdote. So far the conversation had been mundane. The only thing that Alex found impressive was Chicago's table manners.

At the start of the meal he had had a moment of worry. He had rarely seen Chicago eat off a table, much less use silverware. Her favorite meal was a can of black olives, eaten out of the can with her fingers. She regularly dined on cream of mushroom soup right out of the can. But here she was, incredibly possessed, flawlessly navigating her way through the various glasses and implements as if she had been dining all her life in Buckingham Palace.

"So you're thinking of moving to Washington, Miss Honeywell?" Darcy Sullevin asked Chicago, alias Kate Honeywell, as he leaned aside to let the waiter serve.

"I'd like to," Chicago answered, her attention caught for a second by the flash of silverware as Alex's utensils clanked awkwardly and sent a lamb chop careening onto Sullevin's plate.

"It's—it's such a beautiful city," she continued briskly, turning on the full beaming smile in hopes that Sullevin would not notice the epic struggle for control of an asparagus spear going on just above his left shoulder.

"And there's just so much going on here! Why even the air seems charged with excitement!"

Senator Wattles laughed. "Now, there's a newcomeh, I do believe," he drawled happily. He was at the placid and rosy stage of intoxication.

"What I mean is"—Chicago glanced at the lady in red at a nearby table. She was copying most of her coquettish moves like a simultaneous interpreter: little dip of the chin, tiny smile, look up through the lashes. "I just want to be part of something that really matters—like you, gentlemen." She leaned aside as Alex came around to serve her now, crouching down to get the tray to the table. French service is particularly awkward for the tall. Chicago was distracted by his presence. She felt blood rush to her cheeks, a mix of sexual excitement and the incredible tension of hoping he wouldn't spill everything. He slid a chop onto her plate with reasonable finesse, but the flan was entirely out of control, and as he battled an unwieldy stalk of sautéed fennel, she noticed the gravy bowl was vibrating dangerously.

Darcy leaned over as soon as Alex had moved on. "With these big affairs they have to drag the bottom for enough waiters sometimes," he whispered in a smugly apologetic way, loud enough for Alex to hear. Chicago did not need to look at Alex to know that his jaw was clenching and a muscle at the back of his right shoulder would be itching right now.

"It is kind of exciting to be here," Willie Wallace broke in. It was his first Washington dinner and he was eager to be fully a part of the conversation. "Once you get used to it. It's kind of hard when you just move here. People are friendly and all, but it's not like back home."

"Oh well, I do have a couple of friends here," Chicago offered casually. She took a deep breath; here was her chance. "Besides Uncle Harland and Finneaus here, I have an old girlfriend in Maryland."

"Oh, that's nice—that's good. Can't beat old friends." Wattles cut a great chunk of lamp chop and began to chew vigorously.

"Yes, well, I haven't exactly seen her yet. She's been working in the Caribbean and isn't back yet." She glanced around quickly but saw no immediate response. "I talked to her parents just today. She's way overdue and they're beginning to worry. But it's only been a couple of weeks so far, and I told them, well, you know how Clara is—that's my friend, Clara Greenway."

Darcy Sullevin's fork missed its trajectory and spilled a blob of sweet potato flan back on his plate.

"She just seems to have disappeared," Chicago went on.

Willie Wallace turned the color of old gum. Wattles didn't register right away. He speared a corner of meat and only as he began to chew did the name hit home. He looked up like a deer caught in the headlights and sucked in a great breath of air.

"Oh, I'm so terribly sorry. Oh, how thoughtless of me." Chicago's heart was beating with excitement. "Oh, Mr. Senator, sir," —it was an Oscar-winning performance—"I didn't even think— that terrible tragedy with your own daughter. Why, I feel just horrible. I can see how me talking about my missing friend Clara Greenway might bring up bad memories."

Willie Wallace looked like he might cry. Darcy Sullevin looked like every cell in his body was trying to send a telegram and the wires were jammed. Senator Wattles was silent. He waved one hand as if about to request silence, then he grabbed his own throat. He was turning purple.

"I think he's choking," Finneaus suggested dispassionately. The senator still clutched the fork that lay like a fallen lance on his plate. His eyes bulged, and a film of saliva rolled over his lower lip as his tongue worked spasmodically.

Chairs scraped. Napkins floated to the floor as Finneaus and Sullevin leapt up. The lady in red at the next table gave a little screech, and a wave of murmurs, cries, and scampers rippled back through the great hall as the crowd became aware that something was happening. Secret Service agents swooped in from the sidelines, their curly little ear wires bobbing.

Alex quickly set his serving tray on the floor, pulled the senator out of his chair, and executed a classic Heimlich just as Finneaus and Sullevin got around the table to help. Two thrusts and out popped a poorly masticated chunk of prime USDA range lamb, no longer glistening with rosemary currant sauce.

Wattles sagged forward, and Alex eased him into a chair. The towering Finneaus was already turning his attention to shooing away the swarm of waiters, guests, and would-be rescuers who had descended on the table.

"It's fine. Everything's OK. Really, he's all right." Finneaus's relaxed charm settled people down. The senator was just fine. He was breathing; his face was turning back from the eggplant blue of suffocation to a florid shade of simple intoxication.

Sullevin was on one knee by his side. "Just catch your breath, Senator," he urged. "Don't talk. Don't even try to talk." This warning was obviously on two levels.

"Willie," he snapped at the aide who had been pushed aside in the commotion like an extra chair. "Go have the car brought around."

"Shall I call an ambulance?" a Secret Service agent asked.

"No, no, thank you. He's fine. I think he just needs some rest. You will excuse us." Sullevin nodded a quick apology to the rest of the table, made a slight wave, and smiled at the nearby tables: damage control, public appearance. Willie hurried to the front door. Sullevin helped the senator up, and was surprised to see Alex solidly supporting the senator's other arm with a grip that went beyond first aid.

"Thank you, uh, thank you very much," he said dismissively.

"I'll help you to the car," Alex offered quietly.

"Oh, that isn't necessary," Sullevin protested. "We're very grateful and impressed. I'll be sure that your supervisor is made aware of your quick action."

"Let's go to the car," Alex repeated softly. Darcy paled a shade grayer with sudden recognition. Alex smiled. "We have lots to talk about."

The two men headed toward the main entrance, each gripping an arm, propping the weakened senator between them. Chicago started after them, but Finneaus caught her arm.

"Sit down and act normal," he whispered.

"But he's going."

"Shhh." He smiled as he glanced around and pulled her back to the table. "You've just met them, nothing's going on. Sit. Eat."

Fifty-Six

THE SENATOR'S LIMO pulled up to the curb as the three men walked down the steps. Willie was waiting by the open door. He looked nervous and confused. Darcy Sullevin glanced quickly up and down the street.

"Before you think about shouting for help," Alex spoke quickly, "there's a thick manila envelope addressed to the *Washington Post* that goes in the mailbox if anything happens to me." They reached the car with no incident and crowded inside. Wattles flopped back against the seat, Sullevin next to him. Willie folded down the two jump seats and with a skittish politeness, offered one to Alex.

"Tell the driver to go," Alex ordered.

Sullevin flicked the intercom and asked the driver to take them to the Capitol.

"OK," Alex said as the car began to roll. "Since we're already on the subject, let's start with Clara Greenway—"

"Oh, my God." Willie's voice was crunched with stress. "That was an accident. Tell him, Darcy—"

"Shut up," Sullevin hissed. Wattles was starting to regain his composure, though he was still having trouble making sense of this rapid sequence of events.

"What is the meaning of all this?" he said, flustered. "Darcy, are we being kidnapped? Is this a terrorist?"

The man was so pathetic Alex decided there was no way he could be the major player. "I'm not a terrorist, Senator," Alex explained simply. "I'm the pilot who flew Clara Greenway's body to Miami where you claimed it was your own daughter. I'm the man someone is trying to kill because of it."

"What do you want?" Sullevin broke in.

"What do I *want*?" Alex regarded him as if he were a particularly obnoxious mosquito. "I want to climb every mountain, forge every stream—what the hell do you think I want, asshole?"

"We had nothing to do with the attempts on your life. In fact"—Sullevin was a fast thinker—"when I found out, I managed to have them stopped. You are, after all, obviously alive."

"I'm alive because I've had the identity of the corpse your people hit by mistake suppressed. Don't shit me, Sullevin."

"That woman—Kate Honeywell—she's working with you?" There was obvious threat in his tone.

"I hired her," Alex answered smoothly. "Central Casting. I knew you preferred blondes, but she was the only one they had available. Now, I don't think I want you to talk anymore. I think Willie here wants to tell me a story." The young man was shaking badly.

"Tell me about Clara, Willie." Willie shook his head. "How did it happen? Who killed her?" Alex added in a gentler tone.

"No! No one killed her," Willie declared in a rush. "She had an accident. Once she was dead we didn't know what to do, so that's when Darcy and Ethan—" Sullevin backhanded the boy viciously across the face. Alex grabbed the satin lapels of Sullevin's tux and slammed him up against the car door so his head gave a solid thud against the window.

"I never liked you much," he growled. "And then you called me a bad waiter!" He dragged Sullevin back to his seat, then offered his handkerchief to Willie, whose lip was bleeding.

"Clara Greenway died accidentally," Sullevin told him tersely. "It was a tragic accident, but we suddenly realized that with the physical resemblance to the senator's daughter, we could fabricate Angelica's death and thereby protect her life."

"Who's trying to hurt Angelica?"

"We don't know. It's under investigation."

Like hell, Alex thought, but decided to let it slide for the moment. "So you cut her head and arm and leg off. Where did you find the sharks?" Alex directed the question at Willie.

"There's a bar in Saint Martin on the beach with a couple of sharks in a pen. For the tourists to look at." He shivered as he remembered the horrible night. Kneeling in the surf, holding the woman's beautiful hair as Grant worked to cut the head off. He could still feel and hear the bones snap apart with a slimy sort of pop. "We had to make it so no one could tell it wasn't Angelica. Then Grant said what about the tattoo, so he—well . . . we had to . . ." Willie's hand made a rolling motion of something out of control.

"But why the arm too?"

Willie shuddered. "It just sort of flopped in. It was a really hard thing to do." There was a pathetic sincerity in his voice. "We had to hold her up and just dangle the parts we wanted to . . . um." Sullevin rubbed a hand across his eyes as if he were listening to a child's embarrassing story. "Um—you know. I half fell in myself and a shark bit me on the leg. It got all infected. I can show you the scar—"

"That's all right." Alex stopped him. "What were you doing down there in the first place?"

"Protecting her," Willie replied.

"The senator was worried about Angelica," Sullevin broke in. "Even before the kidnap threat. We were—it was a fatherly concern. He hired the boys to just stay around and keep an eye on her."

"That's how I met Clara," Willie explained. "Angelica went into this shopping mall place in Saint Martin, and I was following, but from a ways back, and I started following Clara by mistake. They looked so much alike. In the body, I mean. It wasn't until after she went outside and then I saw her better, and saw it wasn't her."

"Then she had an accident and died?" Alex asked skeptically.

"No. Then I asked her to go out. I mean, it was hard to be looking at Angelica all the time, and not—you know. We went out a few times. She was a fun girl. Then Grant started getting interested in her. She didn't like him, but—anyway, the three of us went out drinking one night. Well, she wasn't drinking because she said she had been diving a lot that day and you're not supposed to drink. I forget why. But then Grant got her some of this punch—we were at a party—and it didn't really taste like there was booze in it. They have this pink berry liquor stuff down there; it just tasted like punch. She started drinking it. I passed out for a while. Somehow during the night she must have got up, and didn't know where she was. She fell down the stairs."

"And do you believe that, Willie?" Alex pressed. "That she just stumbled and fell down the stairs?" The young man's eyes widened and he looked horrified at Darcy Sullevin.

"What do you mean? Was it something else?" Darcy sighed and rubbed his temples. Alex saw that Willie was telling the truth as he knew it.

"Just tell me what happened."

"I woke up and Grant was just coming in, and Clara was dead. And I just freaked out. Grant told me what happened. He had just called Darcy in Washington to see what we should do."

"It was all a horrible accident." Sullevin glanced out the window. He had shifted back into his administrative authority voice. "I didn't *order* it, if that's what you're getting at. It was a tragedy, but we saw an opportunity to use the situation to our advantage. It would have been more horrible to let something happen to Angelica. That's all there is."

"No." Alex shook his head sadly. "That's not all there is. Who's trying to blackmail Wattles?"

"That is an FBI matter. I can't talk about it."

"Then let's talk about Ethan Ruthwilde," Alex suggested. "Let's talk about Southstate Chemical and the senator's phony blind trust."

Sullevin's face was a twist of belligerence. "Look," he broke in, his confidence newly flamed by wrong understanding, "if you're on some sort of righteous crusade—I want to tell you, pal, we can survive an ethics inquiry a lot easier than you can a kidnapping charge."

"I have no doubt." Alex paused and looked out the window as they cruised along Independence Avenue. Facing backward this way he could see the Washington Monument, and beyond it, the lights of the Lincoln Memorial.

"What's going on, Darcy?" Wattles asked quietly. He stared at Alex. "What do you want from me? I'm going to retire soon, you know."

"I want to know what Southstate Chemical has been shipping out that requires false manifests. I want to know why a warehouse in Singapore is suddenly buying pesticides from your plant halfway around the world when they can get the same stuff for one tenth of the cost in Malaysia."

"I don't know what you are talking about," Sullevin said quietly.

"Then you should spend more time in the library."

The senator cleared his throat. He looked from Sullevin to Alex and back again as if waiting to be introduced. Then he spoke. "These—um, materials—were sold in the belief that they were going for completely legitimate purposes—"

"Senator," Sullevin spoke sharply and the old man shut up. He closed his eyes and a great belch rumbled out. Sullevin sighed and smiled weakly. He looked out the tinted window and saw the lighted Capitol dome.

"You're working with that reporter, aren't you? Just trying to dish up some scandal for her career?" The car continued on and turned into the staff parking area, where it came to a stop.

"We're willing to discuss this matter," Sullevin offered smoothly, "but I don't think this is the time or the place. Why don't you come to the office tomorrow morning? I'm sure you realize that the only important thing is keeping Angelica safe, and if you have some information that might help us, we will be glad to hear it. . . ." He glanced again out the window.

Alex tensed and leaned forward. Something caught his eye through the tinted glass. "Tell the driver to turn around and head back to the Corcoran," Alex ordered.

Sullevin slowly pushed the intercom button. "Uh, Casey, sorry, we need to go back to the Corcoran." He released the button and looked over at the senator, then past him out the other side window. The limo began to creep forward. Slowly, ever so slowly.

"Tell him to speed it up," Alex ordered, but before he could finish, both rear doors were yanked open and a gun was thrust in his face.

"Sheeet!" Alex heard Willie's exclamation, a mixed twang of fear and cops-and-robbers delight. Before the cop could even speak Alex grabbed his arm. He pulled and twisted and the policeman fell forward into the car where Alex's knee jabbed hard into his chest.

As the car jolted to a stop, Alex fumbled on the dark floor for the officer's gun. Sullevin kicked at his hand and landed a good crushing stomp just as Alex felt the barrel. Alex swore, yanked the weapon free, and reaching over the crumpled body of the cop in his lap, swung a roundhouse blow to the side of Sullevin's head.

Fast, fast. It all comes down to seconds. There was the other cop at the opposite door and the wail of sirens in the background.

"Back off!" Alex shouted as he pointed the gun at the senator.

The second officer hesitated for just a second, then stepped back from the car.

"Drop your gun." The sirens were getting closer. The officer glanced in the direction of help, then sensibly put his gun down gently on the pavement. Alex pushed the first officer up off the floor, shoved him out of the car, and rolled out over him. The man made a lunge for his leg, but Alex kicked him off and spun free. Alex trained the pistol on the man. "Don't move. And don't worry," he added. "I'm not going to kill you, but I'm perfectly willing to go for a flesh wound, if I have to." He glanced to the other officer. "Kick the gun here," he commanded, his voice level but suddenly hoarse. He hated having to do this. The officer kicked the gun under the car. Alex stopped it with his foot. Quickly he pulled out the clip and spun it across the parking lot like he was skipping stones. Then he tossed the pistol in the other direction.

"I'm sorry about all this. I doubt you'll believe me at the moment, but I'm not a bad guy," he addressed them. "Now cuff yourself to the door handle," Alex directed the far officer, still holding the gun on the man at his feet. "Thank you." Once the man was restrained, Alex grabbed the first cop, pulled him up, and leaned him against the trunk of the limo.

"If you ever approach a hostage situation like that again," Alex whispered to him as he cuffed him to the other door handle, "and live to see daylight, you'll be lucky to have a career as a rent-a-cop at a diaper factory."

The first set of headlights strafed the scene as the cruisers screeched into the parking lot. Alex tucked the pistol into his pocket, sprinted across the asphalt, vaulted the low hedge, and took off across the broad lawn toward the Library of Congress.

Fifty-Seven

THE PARTY WAS just breaking up when Alex arrived back at the Corcoran. The coat-check girls looked like they were wrestling bears as they staggered between the racks with armloads of furs. Washington was having another warm spell, with the night temperature now about sixty-five degrees, but over half the female shoulders walking down the canopied steps were draped in pelts.

Alex hung back, watching from the shadows of the giant elms across the street until he saw Finneaus and Chicago finally emerge. He stepped out from between two cars into the light and waited for them to see him. Finneaus grabbed Chicago's arm as she started to break into a run, and escorted her decorously down the stairs and across the street.

"What happened? Are you all right? Where did you go?" Chicago pummeled him with questions. "Did it work? Did you find out anything?" Alex leaned against the hood of a car and smiled. He felt good, that old sense of challenge and danger made him feel incredibly vital, almost high. His knuckles had that good pain only a fistfight can provide. Maybe testosterone was politically incorrect these days, he thought, but it was a hell of a good feeling.

"A little fisticuffs?" Finneaus quizzed as he brushed some dirt off Alex's tux. "Should we be making a getaway?"

"I don't think so. Not anymore." Alex glanced over at the patrol cars parked at either end of the street. "Sullevin must have had some kind of silent alarm in the car. We had a little scuffle in the parking lot, but I sort of doubt they've put out an APB."

"Your hand." Chicago reached for the scraped fingers. Her palm was warm, and Alex found his mind shifting direction.

"Sullevin's foot," he explained simply as he slipped the hand around her satin waist.

"You were brilliant."

"Hey, wait a minute!" Finneaus broke in. "Tell us what the hell happened!"

Alex sketched out the basics. "Can you give Shana a call?" he asked after Finneaus was satisfied. "I'm kind of wound up right now." He glanced at Chicago. "I think we need to take a little walk. Tell Shana I'll tell her the details in the morning." Finneaus looked from Alex to Chicago, read the obvious get-lost vibes, and cheerfully bowed out to hail a cab.

Most of the dinner guests were gone; Washington party goers do not linger. The streets around the Corcoran were empty except for the caterers carrying boxes and tables out to the waiting trucks.

Alex and Chicago walked silently across the grass, the first fallen leaves crunching underfoot. Alex felt restless, his senses jangled and urgent, the adrenaline still sparking in his blood. Chicago's body beside him seemed to give off a trembly sort of heat. He suddenly wanted to throw her down in the grass. What craving was this? The warrior, after battle, returning to sheath his bloodied dagger in the bed of his woman?

He looked up to see the lacy pattern of leaves. City lights reflected off the cloud cover and cast a pearly glow across the sky. They came to a little park with a small memorial plaza. Alex stopped suddenly by the stone base, pulling Chicago toward him. Her lips were soft, her mouth tasted of wine, and her body was so alive. She felt his hands sliding over the satin of her dress, down her leg, under her knees. He scooped her up easily and sat down with her on the stone base. Their bodies were warm, the night air cool. It was heady and exciting, like they were different people, newly met lovers.

Chicago felt light-headed and hot. She braced her palms against the cold granite and kissed him deeply. Alex's hands were like irons, smoothing her flesh, leaving a stinging trail as they slipped along. She buried her face in the side of his neck; he smelled like gravel. She snapped off his tie and felt the cloth tear as she roughly yanked his shirt buttons open.

The satin dress rustled as she moved. At first the only cool spot was on her bare back, then she felt the soft fabric creeping up her leg and the hint of breeze on her ankle. Alex slowly pulled up her skirt; the breeze slipped across her knees, along her thigh.

Alex felt her lips on his neck, then her teeth. He leaned his head back against the memorial, his hand pressing the soft inside of her thigh. Her dress shimmered in the odd light. Alex slipped one finger under the edge of her panties and Chicago arched up in response. With one smooth pull her panties rolled around his hand and he slowly drew them down her legs.

Chicago felt a shiver of delight and grabbed his shoulders. She pushed herself up a little, then slid one leg around so she was straddling him and returning her lips to his, abandoned his shirt and reached for the more essential zipper. Alex flipped the hem of her dress out so they were covered in a tent of blue satin.

"Some walk," she whispered breathlessly into his shoulder when they were finished. She could feel his heart beating fast against her breasts, his arms locked around her, heavy. A sudden noise startled her.

"Don't move," he whispered hoarsely. "It's a *squirrel*!" Chicago laughed, leaned back against his arms, and stretched, arching back and reaching toward the close opalescent sky. Alex kissed the bare skin between her satin-covered breasts. There was another noise and a police car cruised slowly along the street.

Reluctantly she slid off his lap and looked around in the leaves for her panties, her legs still trembling. They sat silently for a few minutes resting against the smooth stone.

"So what did you want to talk about?" she asked lightly.

Alex already felt the weight returning, and tried to push it away. "I wanted to know where you learned your table manners."

Chicago laughed, a soft musty laugh that could have come from a well. She brushed the hair off his forehead and kissed his sweaty brow.

"You handle your utensils so well," he teased.

Her hair had come undone, and she shook it the rest of the way free, so it hung like a blanket down her back. "I told you my father saw to my education." She shook out her dress, and Alex put his jacket around her shoulders.

"When I was around twelve, Dad decided it was time I learned proper manners. Next time we docked in England he hired on a deckhand that once worked as a steward on the *Queen Elizabeth*." She laughed at the memory. "The *QE-1*, that is. He was so old he could barely lift a paintbrush, but he did teach me to eat nicely."

Alex smoothed the dark satin over her leg. She blinked her pale blue eyes in an imitation of the coquettish woman she had been copying all evening. Alex smiled and stared off toward the White House. "Now you want to talk," she said simply.

"I want you to go back to Miami." There was a palpable silence.

"While you do what?"

"I'm not exactly sure—"

"Oh, like hell—" She stopped herself suddenly and glared at him. "Oh, goddamnit, Alex, I promised myself I wouldn't swear in this dress! See what you make me do?"

"Please, just listen to me."

"Alex, don't pull this . . . this . . . lone-ranger business on me now! You have some plan, don't you? And you want to send me off because you're worried?"

"Well, yes. Three people are dead. Maybe I'm missing the bright side, but that kind of worries me."

"I'm not going home now."

"These people are dangerous."

"Life is dangerous! Everything is dangerous!"

"But not everything will get you dead," he pointed out.

Chicago got up and paced anxiously, the heels of her shoes clicking on the stone. This wasn't fair. One minute they had been making love, now they were fighting again. She tried to quell her temper.

"Look," she pleaded, "only one thing is ever going to kill you, and until then nothing else will. So it doesn't matter if you do ten things or a thousand."

Alex stared at her. "There are some gaps in that logic."

"There are gaps in your brain!" She whirled around and her dress seemed to snap with blue fire. "Don't you get it? We're . . . we're . . . we're here and . . . shit." Chicago faltered and stared off toward the trees. "I don't know what we're doing." She traced a stone with her toe. She suddenly felt like running off into the dark and finding shelter among the huge old trees.

"I don't know what to say." Alex felt stupid. "I just don't want anything to happen to you." He knew what they were doing. They were dancing around love like it was a cobra.

"When we were living on the boat together," Chicago spoke in a quiet voice, "there were times when I would wake up and see you and feel—just this sort of—glory. I don't know if that's like . . . love or what. But . . . but . . . it's something." It was the most soul baring Chicago had ever done, and Alex felt like birds were about to fly out of him. He took her hand and pulled it into his lap, curling her fingers under his.

"It is," he whispered. "It is something."

Fifty-Eight

The day after the Corcoran dinner Shana Phillips was at her desk preparing a narrative for that night's broadcast when the phone rang. She answered curtly. They had a temp on the switchboard and she wasn't good at screening calls. When Shana heard the voice she was shocked. Somehow it had never occurred to her that a United States senator actually knew *how* to make his own phone calls, and it had especially never occurred to her that this particular senator would be calling her, or that he would be asking to meet her at his house as soon as possible.

Senator Wattles lived in a small brick house on Capitol Hill. As an old widower he did not do much entertaining, and the furnishings were simple. The personal touches reflected his own interests: mounted trophy fish on the walls, carved duck decoys, a heavy walnut gun case with a display of hunting rifles. The mantel was heavy with photos of Angelica.

He was alone. He seemed nervous and distraught but with a certain self-possession Shana had not seen before.

"Please sit down, Miss Phillips." She sat on a leather chair by the window. It was too soft and she sank awkwardly, her feet nearly off the ground. Wattles sat on the edge of the couch, but then stood again with an apologetic smile.

"Would you like some coffee?"

"Thank you. Yes." She did not want coffee, but she could just imagine how she looked being swallowed by the chair. When Wattles returned he did not seem to notice that she had moved.

"You've been dogging me for some time," he started abruptly, "but that's nothing new. I've been in politics for forty years—there's always somebody." Shana bristled.

"Oh, you're very good," he added, picking up on her reaction. "Persistent. But you have actually been rather polite about it. I appreciate that." He got up and walked over to the window. The glass was original, a hundred years old and ripply.

"I do not consider myself a particularly wise man, Miss Phillips. And I'm not a particularly good man." There was sadness in his tone. "But I am not the devil you imagine me to be. I have done many things in my career that I am proud of. Fewer in recent times. Since my wife died—well, that's not an excuse—I am getting to be a bit of a drunken old fool." This confession seemed surprisingly candid, and Shana felt almost embarrassed. She wasn't sure what to say.

"But there are many more factors at work here than you know about. There are things you don't understand."

"I would like to understand more, Senator," she replied steadily.

"Yes, I'm sure you would." He gave her a sad smile. "I need your help," he explained. "I'd like to offer you an arrangement." Shana waited. "At the dinner last night," Wattles continued, "a man left with me—a waiter. I'm sure you saw it." He was watching her closely. "He knew quite a lot about me, about my situation—and I believe some of this information came from you."

So many layers of strangeness: the very fact of this meeting, the suddenly blusterless figure before her, the mix of excitement and guarded suspicion. Shana realized she had been holding her breath.

"I want to talk to this man. Can you contact him?"

She hesitated. "Yes."

"Will you arrange a meeting?"

"You mentioned an arrangement," Shana parried. This seemed to please Wattles, in a sad way. He looked down on Shana with a regretful, fatherly gaze. He sat down again, but immediately looked restless. "My daughter is not dead. Your friend, the pilot who flew the body to Miami, was the first one to realize this. I assume he's told you what he learned last night?" Shana nodded. Alex had briefed her that morning. "Angelica has been kidnapped. Someone is trying to blackmail me. You have an idea of what's going on, but you don't have the whole story. We have been trying to deal with it alone. I—"

"Wait a minute, Senator," Shana cut in. "I'm sorry, but since we're being honest—well, let's be honest. I know about Angelica's kidnapping, but I also know it was by your own design. Your own people took her away and concocted this elaborate body switch."

Wattles leaned back in the chair in the most defeated posture she had ever seen. His eyes filled with tears. He reached into his jacket pocket and slowly pulled out an envelope.

"Yes. That was all true," he said quietly. "Until this morning." He handed her the envelope. "These came Federal Express."

She opened the envelopes and found two Polaroids. Angelica, petite and pretty, standing on a tropical beach next to a tall woman with long blond hair. In one photo, the blond woman was kissing a puzzled Angelica on the cheek and waving at the camera. In the other they both stared solemnly into the lens. Angelica looked uncomfortable but not scared. Sophie was saluting, and slung over her shoulder was a gun. Shana didn't know much about weapons, but this one looked bad.

"I've been hiding Angelica at my fishing lodge on Ambergris Cay. I don't know how, but they've found her. They found her," he repeated, in a trembling voice.

Shana was afraid the man would break down. "Who is the woman?"

"I don't know, except that she works for the man trying to blackmail me. There was only a short note with the photos. Told me I had three days to comply or they would kill her."

"Comply with what?"

"If you agree to help me, get your friend to help me, I'll give you the whole story."

"What do you want my friend to do?" Shana asked. Her heart was skipping and thudding now.

"Rescue my daughter. Bring her home. Then I'm yours—everything, any way you want it."

"Why do you think he can do this?"

"The way he operates, some things he said, led us to believe he has experience in some sort of—operations. We had some prints checked from the car; we know he once worked for the government."

Shana was burning with excitement. Her first instinct was to bolt and call Alex, but over the years her cannier side had been developed. The senator's guard was down. Later, his confession would be less forthright. She felt a little bad about pressing him at such a time of anxiety, but not bad enough not to do it.

"Tell me some of it first," she asked in a gentle tone. She hoped her voice-activated minicassette recorder was getting all this. Wattles got up and walked to the fireplace. He leaned an elbow on the mantel and stared out the window. "OK. You were right about my blind trust. It was a sham. I've continued to have a direct hand in the operation of Southstate Chemical."

"Excuse me, Senator, but an ethics violation doesn't set off international kidnapping and murder attempts."

"That's all I can tell you right now."

Shana kept her gaze steady, closed her notebook, and with a firm nod of decision, stood up. "Then I'm afraid that's all I can tell you, Senator. Perhaps the FBI can help you with Angelica."

"No, wait!" The senator's voice betrayed his tension. "I can't do that. I can't go to them yet. It's too dangerous. Wait—please." Shana sat back down on the edge of the chair. "I promise I'll give you an exclusive story when it's all over."

"I'll count on that, Senator," she replied evenly. "But for now, why don't you tell me how long Southstate has been exporting precursor chemicals for nerve gas?"

Wattles paled so violently Shana thought he might have a stroke. "How did you know . . . ?" His voice was weak.

"I didn't," Shana admitted quietly, "until just now. But little bits all over the place finally began to add up."

Wattles shook his head, ran a hand over his face and neck, and gripped the back of a chair. "I don't believe this . . . I don't believe this."

"How did it start?"

"I never intended to get involved with this," he stammered. "I swear to you. Then I tried to stop." She waited patiently. Wattles continued in a slow monotone. "Last year, spring of Eighty-nine, the Pentagon was looking for a supplier for a chemical called thionyl chloride. There were only two U.S. producers who could supply the quantities they needed, and neither of them wanted to do it. Our government needed it—for defense."

"To produce methylphosphonic dichloride," Shana prompted when he seemed to stall, "for the nerve gas Sarin."

Wattles nodded "It was for production of our own binary chemical weapons. No one wanted to supply it. I saw an opportunity to help my country and, yes, to get a very lucrative contract. I quietly had two of our obsolete plants retooled to produce the stuff in the quantities they needed."

"How much was that, sir?"

"About eight tons. The Pentagon needed it by June, or they would lose the funds for production." He stared at her, anticipating her next question. "That was forty-seven million dollars." Shana felt a hard pain in her stomach.

"In September, the Pentagon sent purchase orders to the other two companies, but they refused to supply. A few days later, Southstate Chemical made a quiet bid."

Wattles took a big breath and spoke faster now, with a fatalistic air. "We produced five tons, but the army wasn't convinced we could deliver fast enough for the deadline. Then some hotheads in the Pentagon decided they didn't like getting pushed around by the chemical companies. They decided to try and force the other companies to produce under the Defense Production Act. Things got noisy, and Southstate got squeezed out in the shuffle."

"So you had five tons of thionyl chloride on your hands."

"Not to mention the expense of refitting the plants! God, I was about to lose millions." He stopped as if this explained everything.

"So you just shopped around for a foreign despot to take it off your hands?" Shana could barely restrain her anger. "How does one go about that, Senator? Is there a yellow pages or something? What do you look under—*P* for poison gas?"

"Thionyl chloride has many commercial uses," he interrupted. "Pesticides, plastics . . ."

"Yes, of course," Shana replied coolly.

"I don't need your moralizing, Ms. Phillips. It was a business deal. I saw an opportunity to help my country and make a profit at the same time. There is nothing wrong with that. You asked me how it started. I've told you."

"And the people who bought the chemicals from you are blackmailing you for more?"

Wattles nodded. "I don't know how they traced it to me. It was all done very carefully, but somehow they found out. After the very first shipment they realized they had me over a barrel." He snorted at the accidental pun. "So to speak. They asked for more. We were afraid— Oh, don't look so aghast. You have to understand business. These people were going to get it from somewhere."

Shana nodded weakly. She reached into her purse and almost frantically felt around for the packet of letters. She had started carrying her brother's letters from the Gulf around all the time as if they were in some way a talisman against danger. The thin airmail notes made a flimsy stack. When her fingers touched the worn paper she relaxed.

"Why do they want it from you, Senator? There are lots of chemical producers around."

"After the Kurds and the UN investigations, everyone has tightened up controls. All the German plants are being monitored."

"So you continued to supply the chemicals?"

"Three other shipments."

"Then you had a change of conscience?"

Wattles nodded. "This Iraq thing! Why I'd be crucified . . . I mean—I *didn't even know* at first. I had no idea who was buying the stuff. I just wanted to get rid of it. Look, it's over now. Whatever happens, it's going to come out. I'm finished." He had tears in his eyes as he scanned the wall of photographs that illustrated his years in the Senate. "I can accept that. I'll go public. I'll tell you everything when Angelica is safe." He had no bluster left. He was a tired old man. "Help me bring her home. I'll . . . I'll resign live on the six o'clock news if you want."

Shana walked steadily until she turned the corner, then she broke into a run. Two blocks, there was a restaurant. She dashed inside and found the pay phone. She dialed Finneaus's number at EPA.

"Oh, God, Finneaus, you're not going to believe this. Where's Alex? I got to talk to him right away."

"He's gone. We left you a message."

"Gone!" Shana screamed. "Gone—when? Where?"

"About an hour ago. They're off to Belize."

Fifty-Nine

PHILIP GREENWAY HAD a plane chartered and waiting for Alex in New Orleans. Since they'd taken a commercial flight from D.C., Alex waited until they got to Louisiana to pick up the weapons.

"What's wrong?" Alex asked, noticing Chicago's sudden silence.

"I don't know." She had a sick feeling in the pit of her stomach. "I didn't think about guns."

"Have you ever handled one?" he asked. "You must have had some weapons on your father's ships."

"Not like those." She stared at the evil-looking guns and shook her head. "We had shotguns, a couple of pistols, but you know, regular ones. These are like . . . like movie guns."

He smiled and wished again he could somehow talk her into staying behind. "Hopefully we won't even need them. But you can't be afraid of them either. Here"—he handed her the unloaded pistol, a nine millimeter Parabellum—"this is yours. It's not the lightest around, but it's good for a smaller hand," he explained. She took it reluctantly and held it gingerly. Alex looked at her hands and remembered how graceful they were underwater. This seemed almost sordid, but there was no way around it.

"This is a short range, defensive weapon," he explained in a cool, professional tone. "There are eight bullets in a clip, plus one in the chamber. This is a shotgun." He opened another bag. "Just like you're used to, but with assault grips." Chicago nodded blankly. "And that's an Uzi." He pointed at the third bag but did not open it. "I'll teach you to use them once we get to Belize. Meanwhile, we've got to stow them someplace discreet. We still have to go through customs in Belize City."

The mood was heavy as they took off, the seriousness of their quest suddenly too real. It was about a three-hour flight to Belize City.

"You want to fly it?" Alex asked once they were out over the sea.

"Can I?" Chicago's eyes shone with excitement.

"Sure." Alex laughed. "Flying's easy. It's just the takeoff and landing that's tricky." She tentatively took the yoke.

"Push in, you go down," Alex explained. "Pull back, you go up. Then just steer like a car." The sense of apprehension lifted as Chicago played with the plane. Alex let her fly for a little while, until her erratic steering threatened to get them too far off course, then he set the autopilot.

Once they cleared customs it was only a fifteen-minute flight over the reefs and shallow lagoons to the landing strip on Ambergris Cay. Chicago pressed her nose to the window in delight. She was entranced by this new view of the world. She knew the coral reefs from a fish's point of view, now she could see them as a bird.

It was like some wonderful painting, a swirl of colors: pale greens and turquoise in the shallow water, then darker blues out beyond the barrier reef. She saw the vivid dark greens of mangrove swamps and the paler greens of the palm-covered cays. Alex dipped the plane and flew lower, scaring her with some minor maneuvers and a steep swoop, almost skimming the water. He banked the plane to the left and pointed to a section of reef where dozens of huge stingrays could be seen swimming gracefully in the water below.

"Wow! I can't believe you can see them from here!" It was an entirely new perspective on undersea life. "Too bad we won't have time to dive while we're here." Chicago sighed. "It would be great if we could do the Blue Hole."

Alex nodded absently as he prepared for landing. "What's that?"

"It's amazing. It was a cave once on dry land some millions of years ago, a limestone cave with stalagmites and stalactites. Then the seas rose and now it's one hundred fifty feet below the surface!"

She spoke in wonder, as if actively watching the geological sweep of eras. "Eventually the roof of the cave collapsed. Now there's this perfect circle of deep blue. You swim down and you're in this soft, twilight tunnel. There aren't many fish, it's just a long chute. But there's this incredible *feeling* the water is so absolutely still and clear. It's like you're swimming to the center of the earth. And then you get down to the stalactites and you only have five minutes and you have to turn around!" She laughed as if this were some particularly rich design of nature. A diver's stay underwater is limited by depth. The deeper you go, the less time you can stay. If you overstay, you risk developing nitrogen narcosis, or the bends.

The landing strip came into view, and the little plane dropped neatly. A few dogs roused from their sunbathing and loped off the tarmac as Alex landed.

Ambergris Cay is a long narrow island, and the town of San Pedro is a long narrow town. There are three main streets, Front, Middle, and Back streets. The pace of life is slow and easy. The streets are sand and almost no one wears shoes. They got a room at Ruby's Guest House on Front Street in the center of the town. It was an old two-story wooden building where the rooms started at ten dollars a night, and where deluxe meant you got your own bathroom and a ruffled bedspread. On Greenway's generous expense account, they could have stayed anywhere, but Ruby's was the shabby sort of comfort they were used to. It also gave them a fine position in the middle of town, with views toward both water and land.

They did, however, get a "deluxe" room facing the water, with two windows opening on the balcony. An ancient black metal fan sat on a stool. The floorboards were scoured to a silvery smoothness, and the window frames had been recently painted a bright blue. They had a ruffled bedspread. In a very little while, the fan was on high and the spread was on the floor.

Sixty

"TELL ME YOU didn't. Just tell me this is all a bad joke." Darcy Sullevin's voice was choked. It seemed the walls of the senator's office were closing in on him. He stalked into the bathroom and ripped the cap off a new bottle of aspirin. When he emerged again, the senator was gazing at him with a new sense of tranquillity, one that went beyond the peaceful haze of alcohol, in which he was nonetheless firmly entrenched. Sullevin recognized it as a dangerous repose, the senseless silly glee one sees in a man who has resigned himself to freezing to death and is now enjoying the last demented sensation of warmth.

"You will learn, Darcy," Wattles offered with an insipid sagacity. "Someday, you will learn what really matters . . . in this life."

"Your life! Your *old . . . overblown,* life!" Sullevin spit the words out. Ethan Ruthwilde sat very still. He had moved very little since Wattles had announced his bombshell, but his mind was off in four directions and three different countries, examining their options now. He was not as surprised as Sullevin. His own fury was directed toward Goerbel. The man was a fool to have sent Sophie in the first place; she was too impetuous. He glanced again at the Polaroids of Sophie and Angelica on the edge of Wattles's desk.

"What about *my* life? Huh?" Sullevin continued, ranting now. "Priority, my ass. My career *is* my priority!" He pounded the desk.

Wattles looked like he wanted to say something, but Sullevin didn't give him a chance. "You can't do this to me now!" He paced the office; his chest felt tight; his head pounded. Crowding the fringes of his mind were images of prison jumpsuits and handcuffs, crowds of photographers, headlines: THE MAN WHO SOLD POISON GAS TO SADDAM HUSSEIN!

Maybe there won't be a war in Kuwait, he thought desperately. It could all blow over. Chemical warfare would go back to being an obscure threat against far-off people who didn't matter. But what to do now? If it was just the blind trust and the government contract business, he would be OK. He had nothing to do with the murder attempts. Ruthwilde had arranged all that. Sullevin began to speculate. He would be remembered in the right circles, he would have to lie low for a while, but he could come back. But, oh, God! If the war really did happen, if even one canister of mustard gas was used against U.S. troops in Kuwait . . .

"Darcy." Ruthwilde's voice startled him. He had almost forgotten the man was there. "Let's think this through. . . ."

"Think it through!" Sullevin let out a bitter laugh. "That's what got us into this whole fucking thing—you thinking things through!"

"This Sanders fellow can't just cruise in and land on Turtle Island and snatch Angelica away," Ruthwilde pointed out calmly. "Sophie is an accomplished and experienced—uh—operator, and he doesn't expect her to be there!" They were ignoring the senator by now, speaking of his daughter's captor as if she were on their own team now.

"Damn it, Ethan, I don't care if she's James Bond in drag. This Sanders guy has been a step ahead of us since the beginning. Now we find out he's some kind of special agent!"

"But he thinks he's going in against Wattles's own people—he's not expecting this. He's working for Philip Greenway. He left before the senator could talk to him." The irony of both fathers soliciting Alex's help was not wasted on Ruthwilde.

"If he brings Angelica out now, it's over—we're dead," Sullevin told him simply.

"And if you do anything to interfere"—the senator stirred from his bleary repose—"if anything happens to my daughter . . . I have nothing to lose now. Corruption, murder." He shrugged. "If I lose Angelica, I don't care what happens."

"Look"—Ruthwilde pulled himself erect with the austere air of a playground monitor trying to break up two scrapping boys—"we still have some options. Senator—"

"Don't interfere, Ruthwilde." Wattles's threat sounded feeble, couched in fear.

"We won't risk Angelica, but we don't have to give up and put your head on the block yet either," Ruthwilde continued in measured tones. "There is still a very good chance that we can salvage the whole thing."

Sixty-One

SCHOOL WAS OUT in San Pedro. Front Street erupted in noise and laughter as the children burst out in a happy mob. They jumped and jostled and wrestled each other. A class of little girls had made art projects with seashells stuck to cardboard. They carried them like treasures, balancing the wobbly cardboard like trays full of jewels. The older girls walked in groups, their heads tucked together in talk, long-legged and accidentally beautiful in their blue plaid uniform skirts. Little boys, shirttails flying, dashed into the shops to buy penny sweets. Their physical exuberance was like a wave rippling through the pokey afternoon.

Chicago watched them swirling through the street as she bit into an orange. The scene brought back long distant memories of her own childhood. The freedom, the security, the sense of belonging to a place so totally. How perfect to grow up on an island. She watched Alex walking barefoot down the sand street, coming to meet her.

"What are you thinking about?" he asked as he accepted the other half of her orange. The rind was peeled off leaving just the white pith, then the fruit was cut in two and sprinkled with salt and hot peppers.

Chicago smiled. "It makes me a little homesick. In the good way, you know? Island life. I used to think our island was all of the world. Well, Trinidad was the big world, and Tobago, where we lived was the little world. There was the sea all around. It made the horizons sort of . . . cozy?" She didn't know if that made much sense, but Alex smiled. "It was like the sky was a bowl over the world, and all the people inside belonged to me." She sucked on her orange. "Anyway, what did you find out?" she quizzed.

Alex rested his elbows on the railing. "Turtle Island is at the far north of the cay. It's really a fragment of the cay, but it's separated from the mainland by mangrove swamp. Ironically enough, way before the good senator bought it, it had another name—Point Deception."

Chicago laughed. "I can see why a politician might want to rename that."

"Apparently, the place looks beautiful from sea," Alex explained. "Ships would go through the cut, thinking they could get to the mainland. Once inside they found out they were cut off from the rest of the cay by the swamps, and then had trouble getting back outside the reef. Apparently, the bay inside the reef is pretty shallow, and you get bad tidal surges."

"Plus there are shoals around the tip and bad eddies." Alex looked at her quizzically. "I checked the navigational charts." She shrugged. "But go on."

"The whole place is about one square kilometer. Wattles owns the northern tip. He bought it fifteen years ago and built his fishing lodge. It's supposedly quite a place, cost a couple of million. He brings whole groups of his cronies down for bonefishing. And the only access is by sea or helicopter." Alex looked tense. "If Angelica really is there, she's not going to be easy to get to."

"She's there," Chicago replied casually, taking another bite of her orange.

"How do you know?" Alex asked eagerly.

"Glamour, Mademoiselle, Cosmo, Elle, and *Vogue."*

"Oh great; I'm out working hard all day and you're sitting around reading magazines?" he teased.

"I don't read them." She smiled. "And I doubt that the maintenance guy from Turtle Island lodge does either, but he buys them all at the newsstand whenever he comes to town."

Alex's eyes widened like a dog thrown a juicy bone. "How did you find that out?"

Chicago considered boasting some extreme cleverness but didn't. "I was just poking around, and the clerk asked me if I wanted to buy some magazines. Said this guy hadn't come in to pick them up lately."

Alex frowned. "That doesn't sound good."

"You think something might have already happened to Angelica?"

"I think we better find out real soon," Alex replied as they started walking down the street. "The main problem is getting to the island. It's ringed with breaking reef, and there's only one channel leading right to their dock. According to the locals, you can't get over the reef anyplace else."

"Even with an inflatable at high tide?" she suggested.

"The hurricane a couple of years ago piled up three or four feet of broken coral and debris. Even at highest tides, too much reef is above water. It's like a fortress."

"So we just have to come up with some kind of reason for them to let us visit. Can we arrange—oh, a friend of a friend or something?"

"Maybe."

Chicago glanced across the street and saw the window of the realty office, full of Polaroid snapshots of property for sale. "How about we're interested in buying land? The backside of the island?"

"Good thought, but the rest of the land is tidal flats and scrub." They fell quiet. The children had dispersed, and the afternoon street seemed deserted. Most of the tourists would be diving or napping. Alex wiped his sticky hands on his shorts, and leaned over with a sweet, salty, peppered kiss. Chicago's hair had come loose from her braid and frizzed gently around her face.

"Hmm. Maybe tomorrow we'll just play tourist. We could rent Ruby's boat and go out fishing; pack a little picnic, go for the whole day. We could explore the north end of the cay. That boat's kind of old, though, it might just break down or something." Chicago smiled. "Or run out of gas."

Finneaus fumbled with the keys. The phone had just stopped ringing, and he knew the machine had switched on. First the iron grille, next the deadbolt—damn, wrong key. It was Tuesday, Jacquie wouldn't be home—she coached the girl's swim team after school. Damn this city life with its piles of keys! Faintly, through the door, he could hear the tone on the answering machine. The lock was old and getting sticky; ah there. Now the bottom lock. Finally. He swung the door open, sprinted through the foyer, tripped over Mittens, and snatched up the receiver just in time to hear the final click.

Alex hung up the phone and leaned against the wall.

"They're not home, but I left a message."

Chicago yawned. It had been a long day. She usually followed the tropical notion of siestas in the afternoon, but the day had been too full. "Maybe we should call Shana. She might have found out something new."

"Yeah." Alex was clearly not eager to spend another fifteen minutes trying to get through to the U.S. "But I'm sure Finn will tell her we called. We'll try again tomorrow night. By then we might have some new news for them."

"No, they didn't call here," Shana reported when Finneaus called. "What did he say?"

"Just that they got there all right, everything was fine, they have a definite fix on Angelica, and they're going to snoop it out tomorrow."

"Damn." Shana sighed. "So they have no idea about Sophie. We need to warn them. Did they say where they were staying? Leave a number?"

"A place called Ruby's Guest House. It doesn't have a telephone."

Sixty-Two

ANGELICA WAS SITTING on the porch painting her toenails and thinking about the new developments. Was Daddy really in big trouble? Although she was terribly worried and concerned for her father, Angelica was also a little thrilled to be in the center of such a drama. Something must really be brewing or her father wouldn't have felt she needed two new bodyguards.

It was certainly nice to have new people on Turtle Island, she thought as she wiped a smudge from the corner of her toe. Grant Darlington was cute. He was shallow and arrogant, but cute. Hell, on a desert island a girl couldn't exactly be choosy. She had known Grant slightly since high school, although they had never moved in the same social circles. She hadn't known he was working so seriously for her father. To think that he had been her invisible bodyguard for two months! It was romantic, and even though he had never actually had to rescue her from anything, rather heroic.

Angelica capped the bottle and rested her feet on the railing to dry. This Sophie, on the other hand, she was kind of creepy. Where did Daddy ever find her? Angelica wished he would call and explain, but the phone lines to town had been out for three days, and he wouldn't risk radio contact. Once Sophie and Grant had arrived, security had really gotten tight. Tobo hadn't been allowed to go to town, and Buster had been put on all-night patrols. Angelica felt a little thrill of excitement.

A noise suddenly caught her attention. It was the sound of a motor. She glanced over at their own dock and saw that all the boats were still there. So this would be someone new—but friend or foe? A small boat came around the curve of the island. She saw a man and a woman in a little rented skiff. Every now and then tourists came up this far, not knowing that the island was private. She was about to run down to the dock and see the visitors when she felt a large hand on her shoulder.

"Go inside, sweetheart," Sophie suggested.

"Oh, look, they're just tourists."

Sophie shook her head and patted the girl like a nanny. "Go now, we have to suppose everyone is danger."

Grant came running from the back of the house. He had been working out, probably the first time her father's Nautilus machine had ever creaked into use, and his body was shiny with sweat.

"Visitors, darling. Let's make them welcome." Sophie nodded toward the dock.

"I want to see them!" Angelica whined. Grant slung her a contemptuous look. "Get inside."

Angelica stomped inside and slammed the door behind her. The people were clearly tourists; why couldn't she just *talk* to them. She hadn't talked to anyone besides the Belizian staff in three weeks! The only white person around was Buster, and he was nearly fifty and sociable as a hermit crab. In fact now that he was patrolling all night Angelica hadn't even seen him in two or three days.

Daddy, you are really going to have to make this up to me, Angelica thought as she dragged her sorry self into the kitchen. A big party, a really huge party, she thought as she rummaged through the pantry looking for something to eat. Maybe a trip to

Europe. She looked forlornly out the kitchen window. The couple in the boat had come in to the dock. The man was holding up a red gas can and pointing at the outboard. Grant jumped down in the boat and pulled the starter cord. Angelica sighed and ambled over to the refrigerator.

"I didn't even think to check the second gas tank," Alex explained apologetically as Sophie stood stone faced on the dock. It was a nice dock, with a good-sized boathouse. Chicago looked inside and saw neatly hung life preservers, fishing gear, several sets of new scuba gear, a compressor. A row of brand-new scuba tanks were lined up in a rack outside. Maybe I should consider a life of crime, she thought jealously.

Angelica stood at the open freezer door, spooning out the last little scrapes of ice cream in the carton. The isolation had forced her into a terrible snacking state. She rummaged around but did not find another carton.

"Marion," she called. "Marion, didn't you bring up more ice cream?" The cook didn't answer. "Oh, blast, I'll just go get it myself."

"We thought we'd just go all the way around the top of the island and check out the other side," Chicago explained.

"We had no idea it was this far," Alex added.

"It was a lot farther than we expected," Chicago agreed cheerfully, in a tone that was hopefully naive. There was an all-around lull as Grant filled the gas tank.

"What a lovely home," Chicago offered. "Do you live here all the time?"

"It's a vacation home," Sophie replied tersely.

Chicago refused the discouragement. "I'll bet it's beautiful inside too."

"We're still working on it." Sophie ignored the hint.

"There you go." Grant handed the tank to Alex in the boat, Alex set it down and began to fumble with the connections.

"Now, this hose goes somewhere here doesn't it?" he asked, still stalling for time.

Chicago was carefully scanning every detail of the house and shoreline.

Angelica walked through the back of the kitchen to the side veranda and down the wooden stairs to the little storage area on the ground floor. There had to be more ice cream in the freezer. Tobo had gone to town in the big boat a week ago to pick up all sorts of specially ordered provisions. At least Daddy wasn't failing in that department.

"Marion! I don't believe this, you are such a bitch!" Angelica cursed the pettiness of the cook for putting a lock on the freezer. Suddenly this small insult was just too much. Angelica burst into tears and pounded her fists on the freezer, laid down her head, and sobbed.

With noticeable irritation, Grant climbed down to the little skiff, connected the gas line, pumped the priming bulb, pulled out the choke, and yanked the starter cord. The outboard roared to life.

"Oh, hooray!" Sophie gazed at Chicago with heavy-lidded eyes. "Now you'll be able to finish your little trip."

"Hey, let me at least pay you for the gas . . ." Alex stepped onto the dock.

"That isn't necessary." Grant waved him off. "Just trying to help you get on your way."

Alex ignored the suggestion. "Say, what's the fishing like out this way? Any good?"

"We don't fish," Grant answered coolly.

"How about diving?" Chicago tossed out. "I see you have lots of gear."

No, damn you. Angelica sniffled. I'll show you. I'm not going to just sit here and cry. I want my ice cream and I'm going to *get* my ice cream! Furiously, she scanned the little room and saw the tools on Tobo's workbench. First she grabbed a crowbar, but she hadn't the strength or size to get enough leverage. In her frustration she kicked the freezer, then looked for a new weapon. She spied a sledgehammer, picked it up and began to smash away.

The lock held, but the latch gave. It ripped clean out of the freezer lid and fell to the sandy ground. Angelica had a moment of surprise and joy at her own strength. Then she lifted the lid. She screamed. There, between the neatly labeled parcels of beef and chickens, laid out on top of eight half-gallon cartons of assorted flavored ice cream, with his head on a frozen pizza, was Buster Cray.

All heads turned suddenly to see Angelica running toward the dock, screaming hysterically. Grant looked to Sophie, but Sophie looked automatically to their visitors. She saw Chicago's eyes widen as she turned to Alex, mouth open but sound cut off at the last second. Sophie saw Alex's too-guarded response, a warning look in his eye, the tiniest shake of his head.

Sophie shouted, crouched, and swung one powerful leg up into a karate kick, landing the edge of her foot about two inches above Alex's groin with enough force to send him sprawling. He did a back tumble and rolled to his feet. Sophie was coming at him like a runaway train. He threw himself in a sort of kicking handspring and landed a blow to her ribs. She was surprisingly nimble and ducked most of the force.

Alex heard cursing, the solid thunk of a fist against bone, then a great splash. He glanced up and saw Chicago in the water and Grant rubbing his head in pain. Then Sophie launched herself with a banshee cry and landed full force on top of Alex. Grant ducked into the boathouse and came back out with a pistol. He pointed it at Alex first, but Sophie seemed to be having too much fun with the full body clinch to let him surrender even if he wanted to, so Grant instead pointed it at Chicago, who was now pulling herself up the ladder. Angelica had stopped at the end of the dock, frozen by the sudden events.

"Get back!" Grant yelled at her. "Go! These people are trying to kidnap you!"

"No, we're not!" Chicago shouted. Grant jumped on her, threw his arm around her neck, and jabbed the gun in her side. "Get out of here! Go to the house!"

"But Buster is dead!" Angelica screamed hysterically. "He's in the freezer! What's happening!"

"Go!" Grant ordered. He glanced over his shoulder to where Sophie and Alex were still wrestling. "Someone got on the island last night. He came through the mangrove swamp and killed Buster." Grant lied fast and well. "Get out of here! These people came to pick him up. It's OK, just go back to the house." His voice was sincere and soothing.

"It a l—" Chicago's warning was stifled as Grant twisted her head around and threw her to the dock. Angelica turned and sprinted back toward the house.

Alex was not used to fighting women, even a woman bigger than himself, and this dampened his instincts at first, but Sophie was the kind of gal you get to know pretty quick and don't mind punching at all once you do. Alex threw her off, flattened her with a good knee jab, and was twisting one of her shot-putting arms behind her back when he heard the gunshot.

He felt Sophie tense beneath him. He looked up and saw Grant with a vicious hold of Chicago's neck and the gun pointed at her side.

"You know I'll do it," Grant informed him with a sinister blandness. Alex slowly raised his hands. Sophie wiggled out from under him. She was breathing hard and grinning like a kid just finishing life's best sledding run.

"Grant, baby, you're always ruining my fun." She smoothed out her shirt and brushed her hair back from her face. Chicago, quick as a cat, suddenly twisted and wrenched away, trusting somehow that Alex would be in motion. He was, and with a flying leap, Alex kicked Grant's gun arm. The pistol spun across the bleached boards and fell into the water. Alex threw Grant to the dock. Grant bridged on his neck and twisted, almost managing a classic wrestling escape. Alex could hear Chicago shouting to Angelica. Then he felt the boards vibrate. He gave Grant's head a hard smack against the dock and swung around to meet Sophie, but all he saw was a flash of yellow. Sophie had picked up a scuba tank in one powerful arm, and swung it like a baseball bat against his skull.

Sixty-Three

"MR. RUTHWILDE, I'M beginning to think you Americans are hopelessly incompetent." Hans Goerbel rested the phone on his shoulder as he scanned the latest international exchange rates. "Did I ask that much of you? Simply to control Wattles?" He felt annoyed as much as threatened by the new developments.

"I can't see much of a future for us if you are constantly running to me like a big brother to take care of all your bullies."

"Bullies?" Ruthwilde barely squelched his fury. "You want to talk about *bullies*? What the hell were you thinking about when you threw that damn Valkyrie into the middle of this? And I wouldn't exactly classify your efforts with the pilot as 'taking care of' anything. All you did was get him mad and set him on our heels."

"I am sorry about that. I really am." Goerbel pulled a small notebook out of a locked drawer and began to flip through it. "Good hit men are getting so hard to find, especially in Miami. The good ones are booked way in advance. But trust me, if this fellow shows up on Turtle Island, Sophie will take care of him."

"Fine," Ruthwilde's tone was short. "But you screwed us up with Wattles. You pushed him too far. He's ready to spill his guts, and this reporter is going to lap them up."

"What has he told her so far?"

"I'm not sure, but she had already dug up a lot. And it won't take much more digging to get to you." For all his comportment on the telephone, Goerbel was starting to feel tense. He couldn't afford this now. He was cultivating new clients. In another six months, if things in India came through, he could be out of Germany altogether.

"All right," he sighed. "Get together as much information on her as you can. Address, car, boyfriend, how she goes to work, everything." Goerbel looked at the clock. "What's that nice hotel by the White House? The Adams something?"

"Hay Adams," Ruthwilde offered. He had an odd, sick feeling in his stomach.

"Wait there in the lobby between four and five this afternoon. Someone will contact you."

"Wait." Ruthwilde's mind was spinning through options. *Think the thing through.* "I'm not sure it would be a good idea to actually kill her—"

"Mr. Ruthwilde, I'm a very busy man. I've gone out of my way to accommodate you in this, but I'm not interested in the details. You may discuss them at your meeting. Good-bye." The line went dead.

Sixty-Four

CHICAGO NURSED HER anger like a freezing man stoking his fire. She was most immediately mad at Sophie, then she was mad at Senator Wattles and Ethan Ruthwilde—greedy, pestilential slimeballs. And she was furious at Angelica Wattles, the stupid little twit. Finally she was mad at Alex because he'd gotten knocked out and didn't have to think about their fate for the moment. She felt her eyes growing hot with tears again, and prayed that he would be all right. Chicago wasn't sure she believed in God, but she had never met a sailor who didn't pray sometimes.

She glared out over the water as the fast-moving boat skimmed the waves. She had to stay angry; it was the only emotion that could displace the terror. She squeezed her eyes shut and took a deep breath, trying to clear her mind. Think, think, was there *any* way out of it now? What she really wanted was to cry, to have Alex wake up and be all right, to be home and have this whole thing over with.

Alex woke to the unique queasiness of seasickness, the rough deck of the boat hard against his cheek. He tried to move, found his hands tied, and remembered suddenly what had happened. He jerked around frantically, and his body relaxed when he saw Chicago, tied up but unharmed, close by.

"You all right?" His throat was dry.

Her eyes flew open and she gasped in relief. She nodded. "Are you?"

"Yeah." He slowly pulled himself up. "Except I feel like I was hit in the head with a scuba tank."

"Funny thing."

Alex stared at their captors. "Have you met our friends yet?"

"The woman's name is Sophie, she's German; then there's Grant. The guy driving the boat is Belizian."

"Hmm," Alex mused as he looked over the diverse group. "Maybe we just stumbled into a weird Benetton ad."

Chicago smiled in spite of her fear. "The Belizian guy's name is Tobo, and he thinks Sophie and Grant are the good guys. They've convinced Angelica that they were sent to protect her from people like us."

"Any idea where we're going?"

"Yeah," she responded blankly. "The Blue Hole."

Alex leaned his head back against the gunwale and was silent for a minute. "You should be more careful what you wish for."

Maybe there would be other dive boats at the Blue Hole, he thought to himself. Sophie was probably planning to make it look like an accident, but the Blue Hole seemed like overkill for a diving accident. That meant she had a flair for drama. That was good. A creative scheme left lots more chance for escape then, say, a bullet in the back of the head. His grandmother used to love to watch "Batman" on TV but she went crazy over the villains' evil schemes. "Shoot them, damnit! Why doesn't he just shoot them?" she would shout as the Penguin left the dynamic duo hovering over a freezing vat of liquid nitrogen or something. Tune in next week . . . !

Perhaps Sophie just wanted to enjoy seeing them squirm. As they reached the Blue Hole the engine slowed to an idle. Alex craned his neck for a look around. He saw only empty flat water. November was a slow tourist month, and there were no other dive boats to be seen.

"Listen," Alex whispered urgently while the engine noise still gave them cover, "we're gonna get out of this."

"Yeah?" Chicago snapped. "I'd click my heels together three times, but the goddamn ropes are too tight!"

Alex smiled but ignored her sarcasm. "Once they drop us in we've got to stay together. We can get up against the wall and grab hold of something."

"Alex, there's nothing to grab! I told you—it's sheer as shit."

"It can't be that sheer—it's rock."

"It's covered with silt and algae—it's slick—"

"Just shut up and listen!" He caught himself. "Sorry. There has to be some way to do this." Heavy footsteps stopped him. Sophie stood over them, her broad shoulders blocking the sunlight, the edges of her yellow hair rimmed like fire.

"Well, little buddies, ride's over, jah? Time for swimming." She grabbed Chicago with one hand under the arm and pulled her to her feet as if doing curls. Chicago ducked her head and butted the woman as hard as she could. Alex winced. He couldn't help respecting her guts, but she did need work in certain areas of finesse. It was a good hit, right below the sternum, and Sophie staggered back a step, surprised but barely winded. She raised her hand as if to smack Chicago but instead grabbed her by the throat.

"If you weren't such a skinny little bitch and about to die anyway I would make you hurt for that!" she hissed.

Sophie dropped Chicago and kicked Alex's foot. "Get up." She grabbed a fistful of his T-shirt and pulled. The shirt ripped. Alex stood up slowly, looking her steadily in the eye. Sophie made an appreciative little sound as she gazed at his chest. Slowly she tore the rip bigger until she snapped through the neck and hem. She smiled. She stood back and looked at Alex in his swim trunks and shredded T-shirt.

"Ooh, it's always hard to throw away such a nice body."

She walked around him, gazing appreciatively. "We could spritz a little mist on your chest and you'd look like a calendar boy!" she sneered. She ran one fingertip lightly down the side of his chest leaving a trail of goosebumps in its wake.

Alex shrugged. "Look, there's no need to kill us. I'm just a hired hand. The real dead girl's father wants me to find Angelica so he can prove his own daughter is dead, that's all. It's just a job." He shrugged and dropped his voice a tone. "I could just as easily work for you."

To Chicago his offer sounded pretty hokey, but Sophie seemed at least flattered by the idea. She patted his cheek.

"Nice try, baby, but I don't believe you. Your smart-ass little girlfriend here doesn't make sense."

She pulled out a dive knife. "So let's get on with it. Tobo! Grant! Get their gear ready," Sophie commanded. Grant set up two scuba tanks while Tobo strung lead weights on two pieces of rope. "It's interesting stuff, this." Sophie handed the tail of the rope to Alex. "It is very strong, but will start to dissolve after about an hour. The weights will fall off, and your dead bodies will float up. Some boat comes along, finds two poor divers dead in the water. What a tragedy."

Sophie cut the ropes holding Chicago's hands. Grant slipped the tank on her, then began to retie her hands with the special rope.

"Wait! I—I have to hold my nose!" Chicago pleaded quickly. She didn't actually have to hold her nose to equalize, but she figured that any escape would be easier with their hands in front.

"What for?" Grant sneered.

"So my ears don't hurt when I go down."

"You're going to die, stupid. What the hell does that matter?"

"Oh, please?" She was trying for a little feminine charm again; that stuff sure could come in handy.

"What is this now?" Sophie looked up crossly as she was helping Tobo get Alex suited up.

"Oh, I wish I had a chance to take you diving, Sophie." Alex quickly smiled. "I'll bet you look great underwater."

"Cut the crap. What do you want with holding your nose?"

"When you go down underwater you have to hold your nose and blow a little or your eardrums pop. It hurts like hell." He gave her his sweetest smile. "I'm so bad with pain."

Sophie pushed Alex into a sitting position on a gear box and stood over him, her legs astraddle his.

"I bet you are," she taunted. She felt an animal urge stirring. She considered throwing just the bitch overboard and adopting this one. Maybe he could be retrained. She was seriously thinking of at least taking him below deck and giving those thighs one last workout first, when she heard the distant sound of a boat engine. Tobo looked up and squinted into the distance.

"Look like Turneffe dive boat coming." Sophie jumped up. She shook her head sadly and made little tsk-tsk sounds, then she planted her mouth on Alex's and ground out a kiss.

"Sorry, sweetie."

"My hands?" Alex reminded her.

"Forget it. No way your hands in front."

Chicago felt a shaft opening in her stomach, like an iron pipe had been thrust into her. It was really going to happen. She felt her legs trembling. She squeezed her eyes shut and tried to concentrate on the feeling of wind on her face. The last time she would feel it. Grant tied her feet together with the weighted rope. It felt like thirty pounds. They would sink fast.

Sophie hoisted Alex's tank up with one hand.

"My hands?" Alex reminded her.

"Damnit, man, shut the hell up. Grant!" she shouted. "Look around in that box. I saw Angelica with nose plugs once, see if they're in there." Alex began to rack his brain for a new ruse. "Leave the bitch the way she is," Sophie commanded as she fitted the nose clip on Alex. "She seems to like pain OK."

The other dive boat was fast approaching. Grant and Sophie shoved the captives over to the side while Tobo started the engine.

Chicago glanced at Alex. His face was composed, concentrated. He smiled at her, started to say something, but Sophie turned his head away. With no ceremony, and no time for good-byes, Grant shoved her regulator in Chicago's mouth, pulled her mask down over her eyes, and pushed her in.

Sixty-Five

THE FIRST TEN seconds were hell and terror. They were dropping like cannonballs, in a swirl of bubbles and foam. Chicago swallowed to clear her ears. She was tense with fear. She tried to kick, but her legs were bound too tightly. She couldn't see Alex. She moved her body in a dolphin kick, frantically twisting in the water. Stop, she told herself. Stop, breathe, think, act. She arched her back, trying to flare out her body as much as she could and began to look for the closest wall. Get up against the wall. That was the plan. She was dizzy from the rapid descent. It was impossible to orient on anything; the smooth gray walls all looked the same. Only the blue sky, receding far above them showed how fast they were falling.

Chicago took a big breath and held it. This would slow her a little. Where was Alex? She looked up, then down, then in sweeping glances to both sides. There he was, maybe ten feet away, a little above her, moving his whole body in a dolphin kick, straining against the weight on his feet, but making some progress.

Stay together and get up against the wall. They had a plan. They had a chance. They could keep living. They had full tanks of air. But they had four hundred and some feet to fall. Her mind was racing between panic and hope. What if they could ride it out all the way to the bottom? Regular air became toxic to breathe at three hundred feet. How long would they have to escape? Even if they got the weights off at that depth could they swim through the incredible weight of water? They had to stop before they hit bottom. She began to kick toward Alex. No need to equalize now,

Chicago noticed; they must be about ninety feet down, the greatest pressure change was over. Suddenly she brushed against Alex and they hit the wall. She felt his body against hers, his knees pressing against hers. Alex grunted into his regulator, and caught her knee between his.

They slid down the wall, frantically hoping to snag on something, but it was, as Chicago remembered, thickly covered with slippery growth. There was no friction, no stopping. It was like a nightmare water slide. They would plunge to the cold, far bottom. She would finally get to see the very end of this wonder of the world.

Then something snagged. Chicago felt her feet catch on something. She squeezed Alex's knee as hard as she could. Her weights had caught on something. She felt the ropes tug her ankles. She felt Alex holding on with an iron grip. Their bodies tumbled around the point of resistance and bumped gently against the slimy wall, until they hung upside down. Stopped. They stayed very still. What now? They hung for what seemed like hours, but might have been fifteen seconds.

Chicago could feel their bubbles, mixing together and rushing upward, tickling up along their bodies. Bubbles, a great weight of bubbles, pushing skyward, bubbles collecting in a rush, a push powerful enough to loosen the tenuous snag.

A cloud of muck enveloped them as her feet were knocked loose, and they began to plummet once again. They lost hold of each other. There was a cloud of silt below, another thermocline. They plunged through it into colder water, their fall accelerating all the time now the deeper they went. There was only one chance now, Chicago thought. There was a shallow bowl of the original cave back behind the stalagmites at about a hundred and fifty feet. They would have to get to it. Chicago had a bizarre image of them landing like ballerinas *en pointe* atop the stalagmites.

There it was now, the cave. Poking up and down from the ancient rim were the limestone pillars looking now like giant's teeth. With all her strength, Chicago began to wiggle her body toward the cave. The weights dragged on her legs; one began to cramp. Still she struggled. The cramp got worse. She saw Alex kicking beside her. She closed her eyes and suddenly felt Alex in her mind, pulling the both of them into the bowl of the cave.

Suddenly, with a little thud like an elevator settling, they came to a stop. Muck swirled up around their legs. Alex felt a wave of nausea. Chicago saw stars swarming in front of her eyes and took a deep breath. The ride was over.

Chicago opened her eyes. The light was dim. They were in the back of the cave looking out through huge mossy teeth. It was eerie and beautiful and very, very cold. They were now about to die, she thought, but she felt very calm. At depth, the nitrogen in the compressed air can make a diver feel drunk. Chicago knew it was the nitrogen narcosis working its numbing effect, but that was OK: calm was calm. She looked for Alex. He had landed some ten feet away.

Alex looked around for a few seconds. His mind felt thick and drugged. Was this real? It was the strangest place he could imagine. His thoughts felt slow, yet marvelously crystalline. Each thing he saw—the giant pillars, the soft swirling clouds, the curve of Chicago's collarbone, and the way her hair floated around her—everything seemed equally marvelous and rare.

But that couldn't be, he reminded himself; this was a bad place. But how beautiful Chicago's hair was swirling around her face. She was a mermaid. They could just stay here; it was so peaceful. But no. Alex forced his mind into concrete thought. The ideas were simplistic but clear. Get to the good place. The ropes. Cut the ropes, get my hands free. It was a complicated thought in this drugged condition, but he acted on it. He dragged himself over to one of the stalagmites and began to rub his ropes against it.

Chicago felt a wave of despair as she watched. His movements were slow and clumsy; this would take forever. How long did Sophie say? The ropes would loosen in about an hour. Could they hold out that long? She concentrated on her breathing, slowly, slowly. There was no way; they were too deep. If they were very lucky and very efficient, the air might last a half hour. But they had already lost so much in the hard-breathing struggle.

They had to get free. She saw Alex still rubbing the ropes. They needed something sharp. What was sharp? She closed her eyes and fought the narcosis fog. A shark—that was a good idea, a shark could come along and bite through the ropes. Or a moray eel. She could wiggle her fingers, and he would think it was a fish and bite it. A sea turtle would do. Maybe the edge of its shell. Stop it! Think straight! What is sharp? She mentally reviewed every piece of dive equipment. What had a sharp edge? Of course!

She felt a surge of strength at the new hope. Chicago scooted over to Alex and squealed into her regulator to get his attention.

She shook her head, then rubbing against his shoulder, Chicago pushed her mask off.

Alex first felt a jolt of worry. Was she narced and flipping out? Was she giving up? Ready to get it over with? His thoughts were thick. He watched the mask tumble slowly to the cave floor. Why would she want to lose a good mask? It might break. It might *break.* Of course. Chicago was trying to grope around behind her now and find the mask. Alex grunted, laboriously swung his legs around. He gently pushed her away with his feet.

She rolled around and glared at him. Didn't he know what she was trying to do? Without her mask he was just a blur. The silvery streak in his hair had come back as the dye wore off and looked like a little waving garden eel.

Alex slowly raised his weighted legs, straining every cold, weary muscle, and let them fall over the mask. The lead landed in the silt a few inches away, sending up a sand storm that almost buried the mask. He tried again. This time he hit the strap and a corner of the silicone skirt so that the mask flipped over. It still did not break. A cramp seized his right leg and he had to pause, relax it, will it to release.

Chicago could only see clouds of muck as he worked. Breathing without a mask required more concentration, and she was suddenly so tired. Again and again, Alex strained to lift his legs, aiming the weights over the glass, letting them fall, missing, missing again. One hit, a chip. The glass was tempered and difficult to crack. He could barely raise his feet anymore. He rested. He looked out through the stalagmites and saw them as prison bars. He tried to remember the light. He wrenched himself back to the task. Another try, a glancing blow. He closed his eyes, relaxed everything—control, find the center, the balance point. One clean hit and the glass shattered. He turned around and felt around in the muck for a piece of glass, then scooted over to Chicago and began to cut her ropes. It seemed like hours. He cut his fingers on the glass. Once he freed Chicago's hands she took the shard and cut him loose, then they went to work on the ropes that bound their feet.

Alex grabbed her arms as if he had never touched flesh before. Indeed, in the warm peaceful swirl of narcosis, the touch did feel surreal. He had trouble thinking now. Get to the good place. The good place is up. But where was up? Alex looked around at the cave, out at the massive limestone teeth, looked up and saw only more stone. Where were they?

Chicago felt disoriented, but instinctively looked for her bubbles. They would always point up. They could get out of this. She gripped his hand, and they began to swim up. The pressure one hundred and fifty feet underwater is about five times that of the surface. Even with no weights it was hard to swim without fins. Chicago steered them close to the wall so she could see if they were actually making progress or simply treading in place. Slowly they made their ascent. By one hundred feet, Chicago's head began to clear. By eighty she was thinking fast. The danger wasn't over yet.

As his head began to clear, Alex looked at his air-pressure gauge. He had eight hundred pounds of air left. Chicago had a little more. Less than ideal, but not bad, certainly enough to get to the surface, but they had to do a decompression stop. There was still the problem of the bends. How long had they been down?

Ten or fifteen minutes at a hundred and fifty feet. Chicago tried to remember the special deep-diving tables she had used in the past. Her thoughts were scattered. She could picture the book the tables were in; she could even remember the page and how the chart looked. She could not, however, remember any of the actual numbers in the chart.

As they rose up through the Blue Hole, the water got lighter, warmer, easier to swim through. It was like emerging from hell into paradise. Alex checked his depth gauge—sixty feet, fifty, forty. The water was warmer up here, but they were both shivering. There were fish again, like choirs of angels.

Now that the first rush for escape was over Alex realized that Chicago was still swimming without a mask. They had to spend some time decompressing; the least he could do was let her watch the fish. With only a second's pause, while he remembered her many previous fiery refusals of chivalry, Alex pulled his own mask off and pressed it into her hand.

She did not protest. Eagerly she pulled the mask on, cleared the water out, and blinked her stinging eyes. Here they were again, in the lovely world. Near the top of the Blue Hole there were once again beautiful fish and corals. Everything was so lovely. Chicago felt like flowers were growing on her bones. She fixed her attention on a little blue damselfish, watching it transfixed, afraid to take her eyes off this little flickering life.

But she had to plan their decompression. She looked at her watch, and decided they should stay at thirty feet for three minutes, then at twenty feet for five. Fifteen feet was the critical depth. They should probably hover there for ten or fifteen minutes at least, but they would be limited by air. After about eight minutes Alex ran out of air. He was expecting it, and not surprised. He took Chicago's backup regulator and they both shared her dwindling supply for another couple of minutes. When her gauge showed almost empty, they slowly swam the remaining few feet.

Sixty-Six

ALEX AND CHICAGO rested on the surface. The dive boat from Turneffe reef was idling just outside the coral ring that guarded the Blue Hole. There were six divers on the rear deck—four men and two women—all laughing and talking excitedly as they geared up for the dive. Their voices carried over the calm water. One of the women pulled on a bright yellow wet suit. The other was easing a video camera into its housing. A man spit in his mask, rubbed it around and rinsed it. The ordinariness of the scene made Chicago shudder. She felt so strange—displaced. How warm the sun was, how beautiful the sky, how light their bodies were now. There should be music.

"We need a story," Alex whispered, interrupting her rapture. Chicago looked at him blankly. "We have to tell them something." She could not believe even Alex was this calm and rational after their ordeal. "You know, what are we doing out here alone? How did we get here?" he continued as he watched the dive boat. He rubbed his eyes, noticed the cuts on his hands and splashed them to rinse off the blood. "We've got to tell them something."

"Right." Chicago nodded. "We could tell them someone tried to kill us. How about that? That's a pretty good story."

The divers on the boat were surprised to see them, but once they heard the story they were sympathetic to their plight. Two yachties anchor their boat at nearby Half Moon Cay and decide to go out in their inflatable Zodiac to dive the Blue Hole. They hit the coral trying to anchor inside the ring, and the dinghy sinks. A sailor all her life, Chicago felt embarrassed to have behaved so stupidly, even if it was just a story.

The Turneffe skipper agreed to drop them off on Half Moon after his party finished their dive. Chicago sat huddled in a towel, while Alex talked easily with the skipper about sailing and fishing around the cays. The divers soon returned from the Blue Hole. Some were awed, some were disappointed.

"There wasn't anything to see," one man complained in a thick Louisiana drawl. "Warn't no fish or anything, just this big ol' hole."

"Well, it was your idea to come out here!" his wife reminded him.

"I loved it. I couldn't believe it was all up on dry land once!"

"And you could see it was a real cave . . ."

"Yeah, like, what's those caverns we went to in Virginia?"

The talk seemed so . . . normal. Chicago couldn't stop shivering. The boat up-anchored and detoured by Half Moon Cay to drop them off. As they neared the island she had a sudden new worry.

"Alex, how are we going to get *off* again?" she whispered fiercely. "Unless there really are some boats in the anchorage we'll be stuck here. It's a goddamn *bird sanctuary.* I'm not sure anyone even lives here."

"Someone does," Alex replied calmly. "Look, there are houses and a couple of boats." The dive boat eased up beside the old dock and Alex cheerfully thanked the skipper and helped Chicago jump off. The divers handed off their gear and waved as they motored off. A great flock of boobies, bothered by the commotion, wheeled out of the trees and circled out over the shallow water.

"OK, Mister big plan. Great idea!" Chicago stormed up the dock and whirled around. The terror was threatening to overtake her again, and she groped for anger instead. "Now it's just us and eight hundred boobies. What are we . . ." She looked at Alex and stopped. He stood stiffly, half leaning on a pylon. He seemed to have shrunk a little, the color drained from his face. There was a quiver in one muscle right above his knee, and his hands seemed too heavy to lift. He looked at her as if he didn't quite recognize her.

"Alex?" Thick tears suddenly blurred her vision. She ran back the few steps. He reached for her as if it took all his strength, and she fell into his arms. They half sat, half crumpled together to the dock.

Sixty-Seven

"Move in just a little, Shana. I want to get the Christmas tree over your shoulder." Shana was standing in front of a rack of cards in a Metro center Hallmark shop. She shifted a little to the left until Sam, her cameraman, signaled an OK. The lights came on and she blinked.

"Whenever you're ready."

She gave a terse nod, stared into the lens for a slow five count, then began her lead-in. "This year, for the first time, consumers are glad to see the early displays of Christmas merchandise—"

"Hold it, hold it."

Shana lowered her microphone and glared at him. "What's wrong?" she snapped.

"Shana, dear, what's the matter?" He cut the bright light. "Come on," he said quietly, not wanting to correct her in front of the crowd of shoppers watching the broadcast. "We're talking Santa and mistletoe here, not murder in the street. Lighten up!"

Shana opened her mouth, quashed the retort, and turned away. "I'm sorry. You're right." She tugged at her jacket, touched her hair.

Sam was surprised. Shana was usually so easy to work with. Maybe it was a bad case of PMS. He fussed with the cables for a few minutes, letting her have time.

"OK, let's shoot it." She took her position again.

"Just relax. It's elves; it's fruitcake; it's candy canes and eggnog!" Sam joked.

"I hate eggnog." Shana scowled.

Sam laughed. "Go when you're ready," he directed.

"This year, for the first time," Shana repeated in a lighter tone, "consumers are glad to see the Christmas merchandise on display so early. The Postal Service reminds family and friends of service personnel in the Gulf that tomorrow, November sixth, is the last day to send mail in time to reach our troops for Christmas. Mail call has always been an important time of day for soldiers serving overseas. To our troops in Saudi Arabia, that card or letter is often the only thing breaking up the loneliness of months in the desert . . ."

They finished the taping, and Shana handed the microphone to Sam who was packing the camera up.

"I'm sorry."

"Don't worry about it. On your worst days I still get better stuff from you—"

"Did you say stuff or fluff?" she retorted with a trace of bitterness. "Oh forget it, Sam," she added quickly as he gave her a surprised look. "I'm just . . . look, I need a minute here while you pack up the gear, OK?" She looked over the racks of gaily colored greeting cards. "I guess I should follow my own advice and pick up a card for my brother."

Two teenaged black girls in giant Nefertiti earrings were waiting for her autograph. A few shoppers wanted to tell her how nice they thought she was, then Shana managed to escape the crowd and scan the racks. She pulled out one card—a flock of bluebirds decorating a tree—too cute. Another had Rudolph dancing with Ms. Claus. They all seemed so silly. She pictured the rows of cards they used to hang on the window blinds as children. Was there anyplace to hang cards inside a tank?

Another card had a flock of angels hovering around the baby in the manger. There was the madonna with her blue eyes and blond hair, kneeling next to a creamy white baby Jesus. Shana thought of the TV footage from the Middle East, of dark-skinned mothers and their babies waiting for war. She thought of dead Kurdish babies, still clutched in their mother's arms where they fell in the street. She slipped the card back in the rack. Christmas seemed uniquely absurd this year.

"Miss Phillips?" She turned wearily, expecting another shopper and was surprised to see Darcy Sullevin.

"Miss Phillips, your station said I would find you here. I need to speak with you." She shook her head, too surprised to speak at first. "Please—it's very important." He took her arm.

"I'm not going anywhere with you." She yanked her arm away.

He raised his hands in a gesture of surrender. "I'm hardly about to kidnap you in broad daylight. Can we walk, then?"

"I don't know what you want from me, Mr. Sullevin, but—"

"Please. I just want to talk." They left the store and started walking down F Street. The lunch hour shoppers had returned to work and the crowd was thin.

"The senator has told me everything," Sullevin explained. "I must say, I'm still getting over the shock of it." His tone was smooth, professional, decorated with a twinge of regret, almost convincing.

"Yes, I can imagine you are," Shana replied coolly.

"I feel bad about everything. When he first asked me for assistance—after the kidnap threats—I had no idea what we were involved in. We had to act fast, and I'm afraid we didn't stop to think things through very well. I should have insisted we go right to the FBI; but my first concern, after insuring Angelica's safety, of course, was naturally to consider the senator's position—"

"Oh, Sullevin—cut the crap." Shana stopped him abruptly. "I don't have time for this. It's over." She felt particularly triumphant to be standing here knowing he had to be shaking in his shoes. "Unless they drop bombs on Baghdad in the next week or so, this is going to be the lead story for a long time. I've got my dress picked out—I bought some Diane Sawyer jewelry for the interview." Shana was rarely so snide, but she was enjoying it.

Sullevin's eyes narrowed. He looked up and down the block, then glanced up the wall of an old department store, hoping perhaps a cornice might fall.

"Listen to me. I haven't gotten this far in politics by making stupid mistakes. And I haven't gotten this far to let some two-bit greeting card reporter ruin me."

"We have nothing to talk about, Mr. Sullevin." Shana turned away and began walking quickly up the street. Sullevin grabbed her arm and yanked her into a doorway, pushing her roughly against the bricks.

"That's assault, Mr. Sullevin," Shana snapped.

"Shut up." He let go of her. "Just listen. You've worked for months to screw the senator—you don't want to lose your story now, do you?" Shana looked at him suspiciously.

"I won't be dragged into this," Sullevin continued in an urgent tone. "I'm ready to go to channel seven right now with the whole story. Look"—he waved his tie at her mockingly—"navy suit, red tie, good colors for TV, don't you think?"

Shana held her breath. Was he bluffing? She felt sick.

"Can you picture it? Your rival Marcy DeLour from channel five up there with her crispy hair, with the biggest scoop of the year? Darcy Sullevin, administrative aide to Louisiana Senator Robert J. Wattles has just come forth with the shocking news that . . . Well, you know how it goes." Sullevin smiled and stepped back. He straightened the lapels of her coat in a patronizing way. Shana slapped his hand away.

"You won't come out unblemished."

"Blemishes fade."

Shana's mind was racing. "What if I promise to leave you out? You're going to take my word on that?" she asked suspiciously. Sullevin's threat to scoop her story would be useless once she actually broke it. He had to have something more to threaten her with.

"I guess I'll pretty much have to. But then again, there's always this." He reached into his jacket pocket and handed her an envelope. Shana opened it and saw the legal papers.

"It's a temporary restraining order. I had a few meetings this morning: FBI, ICC. The whole affair is now an official investigation. You breathe a word now and you're interfering. In fact, a few people are already talking about obstruction of justice. You've been holding back information of important national interest." He sneered. He looked at his watch. "Whoops—gotta run. Don't want to keep the State Department waiting. This poison gas business is nasty stuff; got a lot of people concerned." Shana leaned against the cold bricks and stared silently as Darcy Sullevin touched his head in a cocky salute, sprinted across the sidewalk, and hailed a taxi.

Sixty-Eight

ON HALF MOON Cay the only man-made structures besides the lighthouse were a couple of ramshackle houses, two picnic tables, a fish-drying rack, and an observation tower in the bird sanctuary.

In the busy season there were usually a few yachts anchored on the lee side, but today the bay was empty.

Alex and Chicago walked over to the house. It seemed no one was home. A couple of chickens scratched in the dirt by the doorway. A long-bodied old dog lifted his head off his paws and regarded them with his one good eye. The screen door hung open, and they went inside. The house was sparsely furnished, but did appear to be lived in. The tinned food was recent—the salt air and heat had not yet curled the labels. They found plastic jugs of water and a fresh loaf of white bread. They reluctantly passed over the bottle of rum. So far they both had no symptoms of decompression sickness, but it wasn't a good idea to drink now.

When the old man found them, they had dozed off, nestled together on a sandy patch in the warm sun. Chicago woke slowly, reluctant to pull out of the sweet warm peace. She saw the old man smiling at her and thought at first he was part of her dream. Then she woke fully and sat up. The movement woke Alex, who lurched awake and sprang to his feet.

"Relax, relax." The old man laughed. "I don' mean to be scarin' you."

"Sorry—sorry, you just surprised us," Chicago explained breathlessly.

"I be de cahtaker." He nodded in the direction of the house. His accent was thick, with an undiluted old Caribbean rhythm.

"We—ah, we went in your house," Chicago explained. "We needed some water; we were very thirsty—"

"We had an accident," Alex said calmly now. "Our boat sank on the reef. We swam to shore."

"Out here you wreck? Dis reef?" The man's face showed surprise as he waved toward the lagoon.

"We came out from the mainland," Chicago explained, trying to formulate a plausible story. "I guess we were going too fast and didn't really pay attention. The boat broke up and sank."

He nodded and stared out to the reef. She could see now that he probably wasn't all that old, maybe fifty. He was compact and wiry, a little concave in the chest. His eyes were clear and dark as ink. His fingers were long and expressive. He reminded her of a Balinese dancer.

"I'm sorry. My name is Chicago. This is Alex." The man took her hand, his palm was rough and calloused.

"My name Bird." He smiled. "Me Christen name Sebastian, but I take care the birds here." He waved again toward the bird sanctuary at the other end of the island. The gesture was eloquent, the palm turned in a little caressing motion as if petting one of the birds.

"Yes." Alex brushed the sand off his shorts. "We wanted to see the birds."

"And you wreck your boat." Bird shook his head in sympathy. "You need some clothes. I got plenty water to shower you too." He got up and started toward the house. "Catch it from de roof dere." He pointed to his rain catcher, a clever patchwork of corrugated fiberglass and tin. "Den we talk 'bout raise up de boat. Me sons come out tomorrow or next day. Or I get dem on de radio. We bring up your boat."

"I don't know," Alex stalled. "It broke up pretty bad."

"Always something can be salvage," Bird replied cheerfully. As they walked back through his little compound they saw that he was indeed, a salvager. Chicken coops were made of driftwood, wind chimes from bits of wave-worn glass bottles. "Least we get up de motor," Bird went on nonchalantly. "Motor be broke down, dry out, and good as new." He smiled and looked at them as if enjoying some kind of joke. "And dis must be some kind of motor go so fast to crack up a whole boat! And so quiet too!" He gave a conspiratorial laugh. "Why I been 'round here all the day, and I never even hear your motor noise." Bird didn't pursue their obvious lie. He waved toward the end of the house where a bucket was rigged to serve as a shower. "Go on now. I go find you some clothes." The old man's face was impassive, but there was a sparkle of challenge in his eyes.

They told him the real story that evening as Bird cleaned and cooked a fish for dinner. He let them tell it straight through. Telling it like this, sitting around a little fire on the beach so far from danger, it seemed like someone else's story, Chicago thought. For they were telling only the barest facts, not the emotions. Bird thought for a few minutes in silence.

"So now you need go onto that place—Point Deception—what they callin' Turtle Island now?"

"Yes," Alex replied patiently.

"Used be big nesting place for de frigates dere long time back."

"That's appropriate," Chicago noted wryly.

"How's that?" Alex asked.

"Frigate birds are pirates. They like to swoop down on other birds and steal their catch."

Bird sucked noisily on the fish head, then threw the bone into the fire. He squatted back on his heels to think. "You want to go dere?"

"Do you know a way over the reef?" Alex asked. Chicago saw a new zeal in his eyes.

Bird licked his fingers and shook his head. "No, can't go over." He shook his head. "But"—his calloused palm made a leaping gesture—"you might go troo." The hand swooped down and imitated a wiggling fish. He watched their faces open in surprise, then tipped his head back and gave a great delighted laugh.

"You know a way *through* the reef?" Chicago pressed. She wasn't exactly sure if she wanted there to be one.

"Been years since I go dere—but I used to be dive guide. Dere some tunnels troo de reef. We call 'em de Love Tunnels." He chuckled. "Mebe I still find dem."

Sixty-Nine

SENATOR WATTLES WAS sunk in his chair watching the evening news. On channel four Secretary Baker was campaigning for a UN resolution to approve the use of force in Kuwait. Wattles switched to nine.

"Bush announced today he will visit the troops in Saudi Arabia for Thanksgiving . . ." Dan Rather intoned. Wattles blipped impatiently back to four. He desperately wanted another drink, but he was staying as sober as possible these days. Tom Brokaw was on split screen with a talking head from the Pentagon.

"Tom, there are two types of chemical warfare agents our soldiers in the Gulf could face. Mustard gas is a blistering agent . . ." Wattles dropped the remote in his haste to change the channel. The voice went on as he fumbled for the buttons. "Saddam Hussein is believed to have enormous stockpiles, and has already used it against the Kurds . . ." Wattles's hand was shaking, and he hit the color adjustment and the automatic timer before the picture finally flickered away. He stared at the blank screen.

Finneaus swooped his wiggling piece of injera over a morsel of dora alecha and expertly navigated it toward his mouth.

"I think the best part about Ethiopian food is that you get to eat with your fingers." He sighed happily. They were dining at the Red Sea, their favorite neighborhood restaurant.

"Look, there's Shana." Jacquie pointed over Finneaus's shoulder.

"Uh-uh." He smiled as he chewed. "You can't pull that old trick on me, I know you want that last bite."

"Really, Finn—on the news." He turned in his chair to see the TV over the bar. "Where is that?" Jacquie asked, squinting to see better.

"Looks like Sunny's Surplus on H Street. They sell old military stuff." Shana was holding a microphone to someone's mouth and nodding her head. Then the scene cut to a close-up of a hand holding the strap of a gas mask. "Can you hear any of it?"

Jacquie shook her head. "It looks like another of those man-on-the-street interviews she hates so much."

"Well, once she breaks this Wattles affair, she won't have to be doing them anymore," Finneaus whispered.

"I talked to her this afternoon." Jacquie's voice was worried. "She hasn't heard from Alex either. Do you think something might have happened?"

An old man at the bar began shouting, interrupting the conversation. Finneaus turned back around and recognized the man. He was there most nights, just a lonely old Ethiopian man who came to talk to his friends and smile at the beautiful waitresses. He was hardly a drunk. Unless someone bought him a beer he could sit there with the same bottle all night, but now he was acting crazy or drunk or something. He pounded on the bar, and his voice was almost a wail. Two waitresses hurried to the man; one put her hand on his arm and they talked to him in low voices. The man began to sob. The bartender slipped out under the bar and helped steer him toward the back room.

"I'm so sorry," their waitress apologized when she came by their table a minute later.

"Is he all right?" Jacquie asked.

The woman nodded. She looked sad. "He is very old. Now, with all the talk of the war he gets very sad. I think it makes him a little crazy. The news lady was talking about gas. They say he lost his family from the gas. Now all this makes him remember."

Jacquie looked puzzled. "You mean in the war? He was a soldier?"

"No, no." The woman shook her head. "When Mussolini came, in 1936. He was a little boy. Mussolini put the mustard gas on many villages. He killed many of the people—thousands."

"I think I do remember reading about that once." Jacquie stared at the man's empty stool. "What happened?"

"What do you mean?" The waitress looked puzzled.

"What did people do about it?" Finneaus asked. "I mean the rest of the world?"

She shrugged. "Nothing. We were just a poor country." There was not even bitterness in her voice, just the weariness of long living with the cruel way of the world. "Ethiopia is very far away, and my country had no oil."

Seventy

CHICAGO WAS SWIMMING through a long tunnel. There were stars along the sides. She tried to touch them, but the sides of the tunnel began to move, and she was in the lung of a huge fish. She was alone, and very small. She tried to grab the stars, but they kept moving away. Suddenly she was sliding down the tunnel; she tried to grab on to something, but it was slippery. She was falling. There was nothing to hold on to; she was being swallowed. Something was shaking the tunnel, beating on the sides. The stars started falling in a shower, hitting on her bare arms and legs, stinging her like sand.

She came awake, opened her eyes to a sky thick with stars. Alex was thrashing, his arms kicking up a shower of sand. Chicago grabbed him, afraid of the violence of his dream. He bolted upright.

"Alex! Alex, wake up. It's OK." His body was drenched with

sweat. "Alex, it's a dream—you're dreaming." He jerked away and sprang up off the mat and was on his feet, slipping in the loose sand, breathing hard.

The sky was creeping through the first subtle shades before dawn. Chicago could only see Alex in silhouette. She pulled herself up off their pallet. She still felt heavy from an exhausted sleep. Her body ached. When she stood she had to find her balance. "Alex?" She groped for him in the dark, found him leaning against a palm tree.

"You were dreaming. It's OK now. We're OK. It was just the dream," she assured him.

"I know." His voice was tight. She stood with him quietly, leaning against the tree with one hand on his arm, as if too much touch would be unbearable. Her own nightmare had been simple; but his did not come from the day's event. It was the regular horror, something from long ago. She did not know the content. He did not offer and she did not ask. The sky lightened another shade, a morning glory blue. Frigate birds made spiky outlines against the clouds.

"I'm going for a run," Alex said. He seemed weary but agitated at the same time. He would not meet her gaze. "I'll be back soon." He took off along the beach, a gray shadow blending into the slate sea and turning sky.

The sky grew lighter, and Alex didn't return. Clouds thickened the sky, and the sun slipped up unremarked. Chicago waited on the beach by the lighthouse, walked out among the tide pools on the rocky flat, then finally decided to go look for him. She followed the little path through the underbrush to the northern end of the island where the bird sanctuary was. She could hear the cacophony before she came out of the thick forest. Every tree was thick with the birds. The branches rustled and swayed with their movement, and the sky above was dotted with the black-and-white shapes.

There was a wooden platform built up in the middle of the trees, and there she found Alex. He was standing on one hand, the other held out to the side, his torso curved, his legs slowly rotating. He couldn't hold it long. He dropped the other arm, established his balance, sprang up again. His body was shiny with sweat, and he was breathing steadily but hard. His face was almost trancelike with concentration. She watched silently as he repeated the Capoeria exercise. This unique Brazilian martial art looked like a blend of gymnastics, dance, and karate.

Chicago watched from afar. It was a beautiful, mysterious place, with an odd sort of tranquillity. There was a ceaseless squawking as the birds cried out their territory, aggression, triumph, and scolding; but there was a rightness to the sound, a succinct peace. In this place Alex looked solid and primitive—perfectly made, but caged, as if only here on this platform in the trees was he whole. Here the sweat on his skin was clothing, the clouds his shelter, and the noise of the birds a barrier. She could leave him here this way, or she could bring him back out, and someday he would die.

When he finally stopped, she rustled through the trees and climbed to the platform. Here they were, alone in the bird morning. Alex smiled warily. They stood together silently a few minutes, just watching the birds.

"What *is* it? What is so horrible?" Chicago asked quietly.

Alex stared at the frigate birds, a strange look of hardness in his eyes. "Maybe I am," he finally said. Her silence asked more than a simple why. "I like this stuff, Chicago. I mean, I hate it— God, but, it makes me feel so . . . right." Alex moved away restlessly. "Oh, shit, I don't know what I mean. I can't explain it. I do wish nobody would ever get hurt and killed, and there was peace in the world and all that . . . believe me. . . ." His voice trailed off.

"But you like the excitement?" she prompted quietly. "The challenge?"

"Something like that. I don't know. This business was my whole life. And it almost destroyed me. There was so much ugliness, deception . . . but—I did some good things. I miss it. . . ."

Chicago picked up his hand and kissed his palm. "Tell me about Colombia," she finally said quietly.

Alex leaned back and let out a breath. "Whoa, where did that come from?"

A frigate swooped on a booby and tried to make it drop the fish it had just caught. Chicago waited. "The dreams." She felt scared to go on, but more scared not to. "I know some of it. Wonton found out a lot after you left."

Alex crossed his arms and stared at the trees. They were silent a long time, standing some few feet apart watching the birds wheel against a thick gray sky. Finally they looked at each other, as if now there should be something different.

"In Colombia." Alex spoke in an even tone, a recitation of facts. "Things went wrong and I was caught. They kept me there a while. I was hurt." He still could not say "tortured." "They—hurt the two guys I went in after. They killed one. I had to watch."

Chicago felt a cold chill.

"They wanted information about U.S. agents in the country," Alex continued evenly. "They didn't believe I didn't know. So, they began to hurt other people. They burned a village; there was nothing I could do." Alex looked away. "I had been in the business a long time. You see a lot of shit. But then suddenly it all gets too crazy. They thought I would tell them rather than see innocent people get killed." His voice cracked for the first time. "And they were right. I would have told them anything. I *did* tell them everything. I just didn't know anything of interest. I purposefully kept it that way. But it took them a while to realize that."

Alex looked away into the bird world and took a deep breath, wishing he could just soar with the rest of them. "A lot of people were hurt."

"Someone you cared about?" she pressed gently. Alex shrugged, but Chicago saw that this was close to the root of his pain.

"A girl. I didn't know her. She was twelve or thirteen. They kidnapped her from a village." It had been OK up to that part. Up to the girl. He couldn't tell that part to anyone, especially Chicago. It was just too cruel an image. Something to stay and burn in your mind forever. He looked at her again. "I have dealt with it." His voice was clear—sad but steady. "It fades. It just—it just doesn't really ever vanish."

A light rain had started, warm heavy drops that smacked and turned to stars on the dry boards of the platform. The boobies began to squawk and fuss, and a steamy rank smell rose out of the sanctuary. She ran her hand down Alex's arm, the rain and sweat mixing, the skin warm.

"This feels like yesterday," Chicago finally said. "After we came up."

Alex smiled. "Yeah. It does kind of."

Seventy-One

It was a long slow trip from Half Moon to Ambergris Cay in Bird's old skiff, but they finally got there just after sundown. Alex and Chicago left the scuba gear in the boat, and went to pick up the rest of their things from Ruby's. They made a quick trip to the market for some food and bottled water, then loaded everything on the plane. Alex opened a storage compartment in the back of the plane and pulled out the guns. He wrapped the pistol and the Uzi carefully in plastic, then loaded the shotgun and slipped it under the seat out of sight. They hadn't had time for Chicago's shooting lessons, but he was hoping it wouldn't come to that. If everything worked well, they would spirit Angelica off the island before anyone even woke up.

After dark they snuck back to Bird's skiff. They motored north along outside the reef, until they got near Turtle Island, then Bird killed the engine, and they paddled the rest of the way. He began to scan the shore. Things had changed a lot. The birds were still nesting here back then, and the lodge was only piles of blocks and beams. Years ago when he used to bring divers here, Bird would line up a certain coconut palm on the beach with a casuarina on the hill and that would tell him where the tunnels were. But last year's hurricane had knocked down trees and rearranged the shoreline, and the hill had been cleared for Wattles's grand lodge. Bird stared for a long time, then handed the binoculars to Alex and without comment, began to watch the water. For almost ten minutes he simply stared into the sea. He's looking for patterns in the currents, Chicago realized. Some difference in the way the waves formed that would tell him something about the shape of the reef below.

Meanwhile, Alex watched the island. There were bright security lights around the lodge itself and all along the dock, but the heliport was almost dark. Alex could see the chopper. It would take him only a few minutes to disable it. They hoped to be able to steal Angelica away with no one noticing until morning, but he wanted to make sure there was no chance of quick pursuit if something went wrong.

Bird picked up his paddle and turned the skiff in a wide circle. He stopped again, stared at the island, looked down into the reef, then nodding his head he held his palms down over the water in a gesture of finality.

"Heh. Around heh."

Quickly, Alex and Chicago slipped into their black spandex skin suits and pulled on their scuba gear. They each wore four extra pounds of weight, and Chicago tied a mesh bag with the extra skin suit, mask, and fins to the strap of her vest. Alex slipped a handful of cylume sticks into his pocket and handed out the tiny flashlights. Bird's gear was ancient. His tank was fastened to a homemade backpack built of wood and canvas strips. He wore no BC, and his mask was black rubber. His fins were the kind you might buy in the five-and-ten for a child to use splashing around in the backyard pool. But he had been swimming since he was born, and the equipment served well enough.

He dropped the little anchor and tugged on the rope to set it. Alex strapped one compass on his wrist and handed another to Chicago. She took it, feeling a wave of guilt. She wondered if now was the time to mention that she was terrible at compass navigation. There was something about magnetic north that she didn't quite believe in.

"Why don't you lead and I'll keep our depth?" she suggested casually. Alex nodded and smiled but didn't say anything. His face was drawn with concentration as he went over every detail to see if anything had been overlooked. Bird waited patiently. The moonless night was so dark that the lights from the lodge reflected deep into the sky. Finally they were ready. Chicago checked both her regulators and pulled her mask on.

The three slipped into the dark water with barely a ripple and dropped silently below the surface. It was only about thirty feet deep. Alex checked the anchor then cracked two cylume sticks. As the chemicals mixed they gave off a yellow glow that would last a few hours. He tied the cylume sticks to the anchor line about ten feet apart, then rejoined the others. The water was warm and clear. The thin beams from the flashlights showed the bright coral colors as Bird led them along the reef.

The reef at night is a magical place, so different from the sunlight world of day. Crayon-bright parrot fish are wrapped up in cocoons, sleeping in crevices. Crabs and lobsters scuttle boldly in the open. Eels swim free, and delicate shrimps tiptoe over the coral. Bird swam slowly, strafing the reef with his light, looking for the opening. The tiny beam exposed orange sponges and corals in vivid blues and greens. They could not risk brighter lights, which could be seen by anyone standing on the hill.

There were holes and crevices, but so far nothing that looked like a way through. Alex looked at his watch: ten minutes. He stared at the craggy reef, as if he could bore a way through with his eyes. An octopus ruffled its skin into a flare of orange, picked up its legs like a skirt, and side-slunk away.

Chicago shivered. The lycra suit didn't provide much warmth, and this slow swimming made her chilly. A spotted eel poked its head out of a crevice, and she waved to it. He was a lovely little fellow. She felt a sensation of being watched and turned slowly to find a little school of cuttlefish, hovering in formation like a curious choir. Their big eyes looked lustrous, and their delicate mantles rippled to keep them in place.

Then she heard a metallic tap as Bird rapped on his tank. Alex and Chicago swam quickly up to his side. Bird waved his hands toward the reef and pointed the thin beam of light into the opening of the tunnel. Alex glanced at Chicago. She nodded. Alex tied a cylume stick at the entrance, and Bird led them in.

It was not a tunnel exactly, but a series of cracks and gaps in the reef. There was only one real tunnel, a claustrophobic space about eight feet long. There was a small nurse shark resting under an overhang at the entrance. It didn't even move as the trio slipped past. They had to move carefully in the narrow passage so as not to stir up the sand. The tunnel opened into a wide rock basin, like the bottom of a well. Bird ran his light over the walls until he found the opening some ten feet above. They swam up into the crack and continued on through the reef.

In the daytime, it would be a fun place to explore. There was probably lots of light, and unlike a real cavern, one couldn't actually get trapped. At night, however, it was a confusing maze of up and down and twisty turns. Bird made one false turn and had to backtrack, but essentially the passage hadn't changed much, and he found the way easily. At every bend or confusing place, Alex tied a glowing cylume stick to mark their way back. Chicago frequently turned and memorized details of the reef, so she would recognize it visually as a backup. In a little over a minute Bird had led them through to the other side of the reef.

The old man turned and swam back through the reef to wait with the boat. Alex and Chicago slowly ascended. Alex looked back to see if the skiff was noticeable, but the rubble on top of the reef obscured his view. They would just have to hope no one in the lodge was gazing out to sea. He looked toward the shore, found two fallen coconut trees, their trunks crossed, lying on the beach.

"There—see those two trees?" he whispered as he pointed. They both took a compass reading on the trees, then they began to swim silently to shore.

Seventy-Two

Angelica brushed past Tobo in her most dramatic, wounded huff and yanked open the refrigerator door. She pulled out one of the last Diet Cokes and whirled around to face Marion at the table.

"Ah you awareh that there is only one Diet Coke left?" she whined indignantly. Marion ignored her and turned a page.

"I just need to fetch in another case," Tobo assured her gently. He was still shaken by the previous day's events and was, at the moment, fairly drunk. Killing people like that—that wasn't supposed to be part of it. He was loyal to the senator, but this was getting to be too much. Couldn't they have tied him up somewhere until it was all over? And how could someone have come through that mangrove swamp at night to kill Buster? He imagined a sinister figure, swimming and climbing over the gnarled tree roots.

"I'll have y'all fired when this is all ovah!" Angelica declared as she stomped out the swinging door. Tobo listened to her footsteps on the marble of the long hallway.

Alex and Chicago swam ashore as far south of the senator's compound as they could. They stowed their gear high up on the beach.

"OK, here we go," Alex whispered. "Give me ten minutes with the helicopter, then meet me up there by that tree. Then we'll find Angelica's room." Alex was hoping that the sight of a strange woman wouldn't scare Angelica as much as if he turned up alone in her room at night. "You ready?" Her heart beat fast, but her head felt astoundingly clear. She was scared, but in a delicious sort of way. Alex seemed so in control of everything, it was hard to imagine anything going wrong. She nodded. Alex kissed her, paused as if to say something else, kissed her again, then sprinted off toward the helicopter.

The magazines just made it worse. Each one was full of beautiful clothes Angelica should have been wearing, pictures of parties she should have been going to, and gorgeous young men she should have been dating. She was moping and feeling supremely sorry for herself. Finding Buster's body in the freezer had been a tremendous shock, but no one seemed to care about her emotional trauma. Sophie and Grant had returned late and wouldn't speak to her. Nothing made sense. Who should she trust? What was really going on? And how could she find out? Angelica jumped off the bed and looked out the window. Everyone in the house had already gone to bed, but she could see a light on in Grant's room.

Well, I'll just have to use my own wits, she thought with new determination. She hurried into her bathroom, bent her head, brushed her hair upside down, flipped it back so it tumbled around her shoulders, pulled on a bright pink minidress, checked herself in the mirror, hesitated over the little bulge around the thighs, decided it was OK since it was dark out, put on some lipstick, and opened the door.

Fifteen minutes had passed. It seemed like all night. Chicago restlessly dug her toes around in the sand, glancing between the house and where Alex ought to appear from. Suddenly she heard voices. Her heart stopped. She held her breath. There was a woman's voice, light and musical, followed by a man's voice. She couldn't hear the words, but she recognized the flatness and cadence as American, not Belizian. She ducked back in the brush and peeked out. Two people came into view. Angelica and Grant!

Angelica in a tight pink dress. Tight, hell, it looked like a coating of Pepto Bismol. They were holding hands, strolling the beach like lovers. Christ, what do I do now? Chicago thought desperately as they approached.

The pair stopped about twenty feet away. Chicago watched with a growing sense of desperation and embarrassment as the two began to kiss. Christ! Alex, what's taking you so long? They weren't shy. In no time Grant's hands were caressing their way down Angelica's back and rounding their way around her curvy little bottom, apparently unbothered by the five extra pounds.

Angelica began to rub her body up against his. She tossed her head back, and he began to kiss his way down her neck. The little pink dress didn't have far to slide up, but Angelica didn't seem concerned about keeping it down. Chicago looked once again to the spot where Alex should appear. He still wasn't there; back to the torrid pair.

Oooops. Grant had steered Angelica up against a palm tree. Well, actually, Chicago wasn't so sure about who was steering whom. Angelica had one knee up and her leg wrapped around his. He had one hand on the entwined thigh, the other under her skirt and his face buried in her cleavage. Angelica giggled and pushed him coyly away. Chicago couldn't hear what they were saying.

Alex, where are you? What should I do? Would someone in the house notice Angelica was gone and come looking? Was Grant planning to seduce her? Shit, Chicago decided. She looked around and picked up a coconut.

Chicago had never tried to knock anyone out before with a coconut or anything else. How hard do you hit? And where exactly? It always looked easy in the movies, but what if it doesn't work the first time—do you just bonk them again? She had had to knock lots of rats on the head to feed her snake, but there it didn't matter if she messed up. She crept silently along the edge of the brush until she was behind the palm tree. She took a deep breath and raised the coconut.

Grant's plunge into unconsciousness was a blissful one, his head falling into the cushion of Angelica's breasts. Angelica was too startled to scream at first. She looked up and there was a tall wet woman in a black cat suit standing in front of her holding a coconut.

"Don't scream. I've come to rescue you," Chicago blurted out. She was immediately embarrassed. That sounded like the Royal Canadian Mounted Police or something.

"I mean, I mean—something has happened." Nervously Chicago dropped the coconut.

"What have you done?" Angelica dropped to the sand and rolled the unconscious Grant over. He was breathing easily, but there was a lump rising on the top of his head.

"Your father sent us to rescue you. We have to take you away. Grant and Sophie are not your friends."

Angelica looked doubtful and suspicious, then her eyes widened with sudden recognition.

"You were here the other day! You're the spies!"

Oh, please don't scream, Chicago thought. She looked up once more with a sigh of relief to see Alex running toward them. Angelica took this moment to bolt. She darted back toward the house. Chicago reached for her, but only brushed the fabric of her pink dress.

Angelica was fast, but Chicago was faster. In only a few strides she tackled Angelica, and the two fell to the beach, grappling. Chicago tried to pin her arms, but Angelica got one hand free and raked Chicago's arm with her fingernails. Chicago jumped back in surprise. She had never fought a girl before. She didn't think about fingernails. It didn't seem fair. But fair is a short-lived concept in a struggle, and when Angelica opened her mouth to scream, Chicago threw a handful of sand in her face.

Alex reached the two women a second later as Angelica was spitting and punching, and Chicago was sincerely trying to apologize and duck. Alex caught hold of Angelica, pinned her arms, picked her up, and carried her the few feet to the water where he dunked her.

"All right, quiet down." His voice was gentle but commanding. Angelica was wiping the water off her face and sobbing. He looked quizzically at Chicago.

"Don't look at me! What the hell took you so long?"

"What happened to Grant?"

"Who *are* you?" Angelica broke in. "What is going on! I hate this!"

"I explained it to her." Chicago rolled her eyes in exasperation.

"I don't believe you," Angelica said angrily. "Daddy's already had me rescued once and hid me heah, so why in the world would he want to go and rescue me from the rescue place?"

"We'll explain it later," Alex interrupted. "We've got to get out of here. Don't scream," he warned her. "They've already landed on the other side of the island. Six mercenaries with AK forty-sevens." He winked at Chicago as Angelica's eyes grew wide.

"Really!"

"They looked like KGB," he added as he grabbed her arm and steered her down the beach toward the waiting scuba gear.

"Russians? After lil' ol' me? Is *that* what this is all about? What would my father do to get in trouble with the Russians?" Fortunately, Alex thought, Angelica wasn't up on *perestroika* and *glasnost.*

"We'll explain everything once we get you out of here," Alex soothed.

"But how ah we going to get off this island? You can't get off in a boat, you know." She yanked back on her arm and planted her feet. "And I will not under any circumstances go through that nasty ol' horrible swamp."

"Done any scuba diving?" Alex asked as he hurried her along.

"Whe-yl, I dated a boy for a little while who did that. He let me try it one day." They reached the pile of scuba gear. "Oh but surely you have got to be kidding!" Angelica took a bossy stance, hands on hips, as if she were refusing to get in a boyfriend's beat-up old car. "It's night out!"

"Damn, she's smart," Chicago snapped as she began to slide the extra weights on a belt for Angelica.

"Put this on." Alex handed her the lycra skin suit. "And don't make trouble." He caught hold of both her arms and looked sincerely into her eyes. "I've come up against these people before"—a catch in his throat, a meaningful pause—"I know what they can do." Chicago recognized the effectiveness of his melodrama, but had to stifle a laugh.

"I've got to take care of Grant so he can't warn the others." His voice was cold, and suddenly Chicago was worried. She had never seen this side of Alex. Grant had tried to kill them. What kind of "take care of" was Alex thinking of? She did not ask.

When he returned, Chicago had her gear on and was standing in the shallow water with Angelica. They had no tank for her, it would be easier with her breathing off Chicago's octopus. Alex tossed his tank on, grabbed his mask and fins, and waded out to meet them.

"It will feel a little weird, but just relax," Chicago coached her. Angelica saw Alex approaching out of the corner of her eye and sucked in her tummy a little. She knew the black suit had to be flattering.

Alex ignored her. "I tied him up and hid him. You ready?" he asked.

Chicago nodded. She checked the buckle on her weight belt, then handed Angelica the mask.

"Hey, how come I have to go with her?" Angelica batted disappointed eyes at Alex. "She threw sand in my face. Why can't I go with you? I'd feel eveh so much more comfortable."

"Because," Alex said as he twisted the bezel on his underwater compass 180 degrees. "She's the pro." As he passed by Chicago he added in a whisper. "And she can't navigate!"

Chicago glared at him. He gave her his most dashing grin, with that little curl at the edges, and pulled his mask on. Chicago turned her attention back to Angelica. Angelica Wattles was the sort of woman Chicago always cringed to see show up in a dive class. They usually came attached to a big strong boyfriend or husband and took advantage of every chance to be scared and helpless. They carried huge tote bags with full-sized cans of hair spray and wore heels that made noise. They gave pet names to everything.

Chicago had learned how to deal with them, but right now she was having trouble summoning the energy necessary to coddle this pampered ditz along anymore.

"OK, just breathe normally, and don't ever hold your breath."

Angelica looked at the regulator mouthpiece as if it tasted bad. "Ah know that. I told you ah've done this. We went to the pool at the country club," she sniped haughtily. She put the mouthpiece in, turning away because she thought people looked stupid with these things in and she didn't want Alex to see her.

"Good—now just take a few breaths." Chicago gritted her teeth. Angelica took two breaths then spit the regulator out.

"If y'all are going to kidnap me, why don't you just get on with it!"

"I'll have hold of you all the time," Chicago continued civilly, wishing she could have this hold around the girl's throat. Alex stayed silent, but was clearly eager to leave. He watched the house intently, waiting for any signs of discovery. Grant's involvement made everything stickier.

"Try not to squinch your face around, that will get water in your mask. If you do get some in, try to live with it. If it's bad just stop me and we'll clear it like I showed you."

"I know how to clear my mask!" Angelica snapped indignantly. "I told you I had a boyfriend that did this."

"Good." Chicago controlled her temper. "But once we start swimming it's best not to stop. We're following a compass course," she explained. She checked Angelica's weight belt, helped her get the fins on, then looped the tether line around her waist and clipped it to her own BC. They knelt in the sand. Angelica was so much shorter that the tiny wave ripples that washed against Chicago's shoulders were licking at her chin.

"You ready?"

"Ooooh—I don't like this. I don't want to do this." She tried to stand up and floundered over the fins. Chicago caught her.

"Shut up and breathe." She stuck the regulator in Angelica's whining mouth, and nodded at Alex. So far so good. Time to swim.

Seventy-Three

"It's been four days, Shana. Maybe we should go to the authorities," Finneaus suggested tentatively. "I mean—we haven't heard a word. Not you, not me, not Philip Greenway. Belize isn't that cut off that he couldn't phone or get some kind of message to one of us."

"Alex said he wanted time," Shana pressed. "You know him better than I do. Can't you trust him?"

Finneaus shrugged. "No one knows Alex very well." He spun his empty beer mug between his hands. They were huddled in one of the dimly lit rear booths at Millie and Al's. It was four in the afternoon, and the bar wasn't crowded. It wasn't a happy hour sort of place. It was the sort of place where your feet stick to the floor and the waitresses have no grand aspirations.

"Hell, I knew him for six months before I had any idea what his real life was all about. And I still don't know much."

"Well, Wattles found out enough to want to trust him with mission impossible. Why can't we?" Finneaus started to protest, but Shana hurried on. "You think this is just about my story, don't you? You think I don't want to lose the scoop?"

"I think you've worked for months on this, and now it's all on the edge."

"This"—she slapped angrily at the temporary restraining order —"this is garbage. I'll defy this. I don't care what happens. But I wouldn't risk Alex or Chicago . . . or even Angelica Wattles."

"I know." Finneaus smiled. "I just have a bad feeling."

"What can the FBI do, anyway? They can't just ride in with the posse—Belize is a foreign country."

"What are they going to do with Sullevin's information?"

Shana slumped back in her seat. "How do we know that he really told them anything? He might be bluffing."

"He'd have a hard time getting the restraining order without telling them something."

"Look"—Shana leaned forward over the checkered oilcloth—"I could break my story tomorrow. I have enough on paper to show that Wattles is still involved with Southstate, that he tried to use insider knowledge to get the government bid for the dichlor, and that he then sold the stuff overseas. Add the UN stuff Allen Dray sent me, and we can raise a lot of suspicion, but then what?" She shrugged. "It *looks* like Wattles is connected to some German guy named Goerbel, who is probably connected to this big fugitive guy Valascheck—but we can't *prove* it. It *looks* like Wattles's shipments wound up in Iraq, but again, we can't prove it. What about Clara's death, the cover-ups, the attempts by this Sophie person—" With each name Shana slapped the table like she was squashing bugs. "We have to get *all* of them!"

"*You* don't have to *get* anyone, Shana," Finneaus reminded her gently. "You're a reporter. Do the story. Let the feds sort out the details. I guarantee you're still good for at least the cover of *Time*. Maybe even a movie of the week!"

"Finn, I'm not trying to get famous—"

"So what's wrong with a little fame?"

"True." Shana laughed. "But if Alex and Chicago bring Angelica Wattles back, the senator spills all. To *me,* exclusive; I want that! Then they can have it. State Department, FBI, Interpol, I don't care. I want it first, and I want it solid." She picked up a spoon and spoke into it like it was a microphone. "As chemical warfare continues to be a threat to our troops in the Gulf, channel seven has shocking new evidence that some of the chemicals that went into making Iraq's mustard gas may have been supplied by a United States senator . . ." Shana whispered in her broadcasting voice.

"And if something's gone wrong down there?" Finneaus reminded her.

Shana hesitated. "I don't know."

Seventy-Four

ANGELICA WAS A floater. For the first few minutes it was all Chicago could do to keep her under. Beginners tend to float anyway, and Angelica's body did not boast much muscle mass. Chicago struggled and cursed as she tried to steer her charge along. Once they got down to about twenty feet, it was easier, but Angelica was still awkward as most beginners, bicycling her legs and churning her arms. Guiding her through the water was like ice dancing with a cow.

Inside the reef, the sea floor was mostly sand and clumps of eel grass. Even in the dark, Angelica could see the clear bottom, and began to relax a little. Alex swam slowly, his eyes on the compass, counting his kicks. There were no currents; visibility was good; he began to feel the first tingling of success. As they neared the reef the bottom composition began to change. There were small coral heads and more reef fish—black durgons and triggerfish, a goofy-looking spotted trunkfish, with eyes like a labrador retriever. Just before he counted off the last kick cycle Alex saw the reef. They were almost perfectly on course. There was the cylume stick marking the entrance to the passage about ten feet to the right and a little above them. He turned to check on Chicago and Angelica.

Chicago was breathing harder than usual, obviously struggling to tow and support Angelica. He paused to let them catch up. Alex pointed toward the hole, but Chicago held her palm up in a signal to wait. Angelica had some water in her mask.

Mask clearing was the most likely time for a novice to bolt, and it was better to clear it now. Chicago shined her light on her own face and showed Angelica again how to clear her mask. Angelica gave it a tentative effort, didn't quite get it, and wound up with her mask half flooded. She squealed in fright and lunged toward the surface, struggling to get free. Alex caught her shoulders and held her down. The flashlights spun crazily, throwing jerky beams around as Chicago caught the panicky girl. She held her arms, gently squeezing, holding her steady until Angelica was ready to try again.

The second try got most of the water out, then one more blow and the mask was dry. Chicago breathed a sigh of relief. Alex tapped his watch and pointed to the reef. Chicago signaled OK, cupped her palm around the light, and followed his lead. She could feel Angelica trembling beside her as they slipped through the crack between the coral towers.

Angelica had grown up with manicured lawns and docile flower beds. The wildest thing she had ever encountered before was an occasional daddy longlegs. She did not like creepy crawly slimy bug things. She did not like tentacles. She did not like eyeballs. She did not really even like fish unless they were sushi, and only then because it was sophisticated. She did not like anything she was seeing as they wound their way through the coral labyrinth, and she liked it even less in the dark. All kinds of things were touching her, slimy, nasty things, octopuses and snakes and giant jellyfish. She jumped around like the walls were electrified, scraping them both more than once into the coral.

To Chicago, the passage back seemed much shorter, almost a game as they followed one cylume stick after another. It wasn't much fun getting kicked and banged into the coral, but she couldn't really blame Angelica. It was a foreign world to her. Where Chicago saw a harmless little brittle star, Angelica saw a hairy-armed spider. Where Chicago saw a cluster of feather duster worms, Angelica saw poisonous stingers. Chicago saw a spotted snake eel calmly snuffling along a sandy patch of bottom and prayed to God that Angelica wouldn't see *that* at all.

Finally they came upon the little open space before the tunnel. Alex hovered easily and watched amused as Angelica brushed her arms and dragged her fingers through her hair as if she were covered with spiderwebs. Chicago looked exasperated. He checked his watch. It was quarter after twelve, a little over an hour since they had first dropped anchor. He was anxious to get on with it.

The tunnel would be tricky. It was narrow, and they would have to go through single file. Chicago unbuckled her BC, took off her tank, and strapped it on Angelica, who looked surprised and not at all happy. Chicago pointed to the tunnel, brought her palms together to indicate it was narrow, then trailed one hand after the other to show Angelica they had to go single file. Alex was always impressed with the eloquence of Chicago's underwater language and the grace of her hands. With just the small flashlight shining on them they looked like pale birds.

Chicago led Angelica to the mouth of the tunnel. It was only eight feet long. Chicago would take a breath and swim through first, then Angelica, then Alex. As soon as Angelica was through, Chicago could pick up the second regulator and get to her air again. She could hold her breath for at least a minute, so she wasn't worried.

Angelica took one look at the small tunnel entrance and balked. She clung to Alex, knocking his light so that the beam bounced around like a searchlight. Finally, however, she realized this was the only way out. Holding tightly to Alex's hand, managing somehow to look like a helpless belle even underwater, she let him lead her to the entrance. Chicago took a deep breath, took out the regulator, and slipped into the tunnel. She glided smoothly and did not kick, pulling herself along on the walls so as not to stir up the sand. As soon as her fins disappeared, Alex steered Angelica into the tunnel, resisting an urge to just stuff her in.

Chicago slipped out the other side and turned to wait for Angelica, shining her light down on the sand as a beacon. In the edge of the little circle of light she saw the nurse shark. Oh shit! she realized. Angelica will freak out if she sees this! The nurse shark was still lying in the same little nook, as uninterested in the human visitors as the man in the moon. It was a sweet little shark. A docile little shark.

It was a shark! Angelica screeched into her regulator and tried to back into the tunnel. Her screams made a squeezed, tinny sound coming through the regulator. She thrashed and kicked and slapped at Chicago's hands. Right behind her, Alex was lost in the cloud of sand. She kicked him in the face, crashing his nose and flooding his mask. He found one of her fins in the murk and grabbed it, worked his way up to her ankle, held it tight, and shoved her forward. The nurse shark cowered deeper in its hole.

Angelica popped out of the hole and a mean and ragged Alex followed. That was enough for the little shark. Like a shadow he slipped past the flailing limbs, flattened himself under his own secret passageway, and escaped to the safety of the outside reef, as the two women sorted out their regulators and settled down to breathing.

Three more cylume sticks and they were all the way through the reef. Alex spied the glowing markers on the anchor line, then saw them moving up toward the surface. Bird had seen them coming and was pulling up the anchor.

"I hate you. Y'all tried to kill me!" Angelica was spitting and slapping the water as soon as they hit the surface. "My daddy would nevah send anyone as mean as you to rescue me from anything! Why, I—" Her indignant tirade was stifled by Alex's palm across her mouth.

"Shut up," he hissed. "You make one sound now and I'll drown you myself."

"Man walking around de house," Bird said quietly. "Just a few minutes ago come out."

Chicago silently handed her weight belt up to Bird, then pulled herself quickly into the skiff. Bird stowed the anchor as Chicago hauled Alex's gear up. They worked fast and efficiently. The trauma of the underwater night adventure had so debilitated Angelica that she could not climb into the boat and didn't even care how undignified she looked getting pushed and pulled aboard. She collapsed in a sobbing, snuffling heap in the bottom.

As soon as Alex climbed on, Bird started the outboard and turned them around. Alex grabbed the binoculars and watched lights coming on all over the lodge. People were running around; the dogs were barking. As they roared off, a bright spotlight began to sweep the water.

Alex began to figure their odds. They had a slight head start, but far less horsepower; Bird's knowledge of the reef, but an overloaded boat. He had the 9 millimeter pistol and the Uzi against an arsenal of weapons he didn't even want to imagine. Bird stood calmly in the stern, his hand on the throttle, not even squinting against the wind as they raced for San Pedro and the airport.

Once south of Turtle Island the old boatman steered them through a cut to the inside of the reef. One more advantage: the water here was smoother and they could move faster. Alex didn't think Sophie would know about the cut, or risk it if she did, but she didn't really have to. She would be slowed by the ocean chop out there, but her boat was still twice as fast.

In the moonless night, the shore passed in a scratchy black blur. They could see the faint glow of San Pedro in the distance. Think: what else could they do? Swing into shore along here and jump off? Hide out in the mangroves until they could make their way down to the airport? No, the cay was too narrow, too populated.

Even if they could make it that far under cover of darkness, which was doubtful with Angelica in tow, it would be too easy for Sophie or Wattles's men to spread out and cover the airport. He felt Chicago slide up next to him on the seat. Tendrils of hair whipped around her face. She touched his arm. Alex looked at her hand and remembered the way it looked underwater.

"What about Bird?" she asked simply. She was shivering, and he put his arm around her.

"We'll take him in the plane with us. We'll get him back home later." They rode in silence for several minutes. Angelica was curled up in the bottom of the skiff, wrapped in all the available towels, suffering grandly.

"If it's dark, and we're running fast," Chicago asked hopefully. "Well, they can't really *aim* that well, can they?" The logic was oddly childlike. Alex smiled and shook his head. He didn't want to tell her how a spray of automatic gunfire didn't really need much aim.

They zoomed past the Royal Belizian. Five more minutes to San Pedro. The closest dock to the airport was just to the south of town near the package store. As Alex sidled back next to Bird to discuss their plan, Chicago pulled on her sneakers and gave the extra pair they had brought to Angelica.

"Put them on. I hope you run better than you swim."

"You don't have to be so uppity about everything!" Angelica snapped. Chicago felt a pang of remorse. She had never hung out with girls much, not this kind anyway. Angelica was as alien to her as a sea squirt. Besides, she was only a kid.

"We have clothes for you in the plane," Chicago added with an effort at gentleness. Alex came back and crouched down between her knees so she could hear him.

"Bird says he knows where to go—has his own escape plan. I can't change his mind."

Chicago looked at the man and started to protest, but Bird just smiled, tipped his head up once in assurance, curled his fingers into a ball, then popped his palm open, showing her how he would vanish. She looked past Bird's sharp profile and could see the pursuing boat, still outside the reef, but gaining fast. Sophie was visible at the helm, her long blond hair streaming out behind her. Another minute and they would be alongside; soon after that they would reach the main cut to San Pedro, dart through to the inside of the reef and . . .

There were the lights of the Tackle Box bar, then the yellow glow of Ruby's Guest House. How Chicago longed for the cozy room right now!

"Get down," Alex commanded as the first shots rang out. They dove for the bottom of the boat. "Shit!" Alex grinned and almost whistled with surprise. "Sounds like a fucking shotgun!" Chicago stared at him. "You're happy about that?"

"Sure," he said as he carefully peeked up over the side. "They're still out of range for—" But even as he spoke, a second gunshot cracked the night, this time with the violent report of an AK47. Angelica screamed. They heard the metallic *zing* as a bullet hit the outboard. Bird, steering from the lobster hold, cranked up the throttle and turned them sharply toward the dock.

"Bird's going to run right under the dock." Alex was loading the Uzi as he talked; the pistol was tucked in the back of his shorts. His eyes burned, but his voice, steady and clear, gave Chicago a certain thrill of confidence. This was what he was talking about on Half Moon Cay. This was his element. "Jump out fast. Stay low and run like hell. Straight to the plane. I'll distract them a few seconds."

The dock was rushing up on them. Alex lifted his head and glanced over the stern just in time to see the other boat whirl around in an arc of spray. They had missed the cut! That gave them a good extra ten, maybe twenty, seconds. Bird cut the throttle and turned the skiff around so the beam was sliding toward the dock. They were still going fast, and they hit with a jolt.

"Go!" Alex shouted. Chicago sprang up and Alex gave Angelica a shove to the dock, then threw one leg up and rolled up himself.

"Run! Keep low!" He pulled the Uzi up and fired toward Sophie's boat, then rolled a few more times until he was behind a pylon. Alex heard the roar of the motor as Bird jammed the throttle up and fired again to direct Sophie's attention away from Bird. He saw the skiff out of the corner of his eye as it roared back out toward the reef.

Chicago and Angelica sprinted down the dock onto the sand. In slowed time Chicago felt her senses wide open. Everything was louder, sharper: the feel of wet sand under her feet, the thick tropical air in her lungs and on her skin, the strange glow of Coke bottles stacked under a yellow light, the sharp shadows of palm trees against the night sky, a hermit crab—oh, God, would that scare Angelica? Chicago felt the burn of terror. This was out of control. Bullets were solid and small. She thought about childhood rock fights and the sting of zipping pebbles. How much harder would a bullet feel? She saw Brian's body flying across the boat. His sturdy body lifted like a rag doll.

She turned to see if Alex was coming yet, saw flashes from the muzzle of his gun. She grabbed Angelica's arm and pulled her along. There was the tarmac. Flat and wide and still hot from the day. Easier to run now. Loud foot slaps, loud breaths. Fear tasting sharp in the back of her mouth. Gunfire snapping up the air. There was their plane on the far side of the field.

Chicago ran around to the passenger side, yanked open the door, and pulled the seat forward. Through the windows she could see Alex just bursting out of the trees onto the landing strip. No cover now. He stopped and fired back into the trees, then sprinted toward the plane.

"Get in, goddamnit!" she shouted at Angelica, who tumbled in the back. Chicago slammed the seat back down and jumped in. She looked for Alex through the pilot's side window, her eyes stinging. She saw him running hard. What could she do? She remembered the shotgun under the seat and bent down to find it. Then the glass shattered. A bullet flew over her head and slammed in the metal of the door. Angelica screamed. Chicago looked up and stared at the broken window. She felt like she was watching some horrible event from far away. "Get down!" she whispered to Angelica. Why was she whispering? "Get on the floor." She peeked out the window and looked for Alex, but all she saw was a blank open runway, a hundred miles wide it seemed. "Alex—oh, my God . . ." Desperately, she grabbed the shotgun and pushed open the door. "Alex!" she screamed into the night.

There was silence, then suddenly he was there, scrambling up off the runway and dashing the last few feet to the plane. There was a row of fire flashes from the trees. Then Alex vaulted into the seat.

Chicago felt paralyzed. She stared at him as if he were a ghost. His hands and feet were moving all over the controls, sure quick motions. There was a roar, and the propeller began to spin. The plane began to shake. Alex was doing things. Of course, he was going to fly the plane. He was shouting at her. What was he saying? His forehead was bleeding. Something was thudding against the back of her seat—Angelica, screaming and kicking. Chicago couldn't hear anything.

Alex was bleeding, but he couldn't have been shot in the head. Wouldn't that make him dead? Where was the flashlight? He could have scraped his head on some coral. Where was the flash-light?

"Illy, Illy, talk to me damnit! Are you all right?" His eyes were wide and his face green in the glow of the instruments. The plane was bouncing down the runway.

"Chicago!" He was shouting at her. Why was he shouting? Alex revved the engine, glanced over his shoulder to where Angelica was having hysterics in the rear seat.

"Shut up!" he yelled. A spasm of pain shot over his face as he turned back to the controls. "Baby, please talk to me," he pleaded. Suddenly the ground fell away beneath them. They were in the air. The lights of Ambergris Cay grew tiny and faint. They were flying. Her head began to clear; the world was funneling back to reality.

"Baby, are you with me?"

"Your head is bleeding. I can't find the flashlight." She was shaking uncontrollably.

"I hit it on the plane." His voice was tight now and sounded odd. He shook his head and rubbed some blood out of his eye. "It's just a scratch. Are you both all right?"

Chicago leaned over and wiped the wound with the cuff of her skin suit; his face was cold and sweaty. It was hard to see in the dim light from the instrument panel. Alex pulled his head away.

"Wait a minute." He flipped some switches on the panel. "I have to set the autopilot." He blinked and shook his head; he seemed to be having trouble. Finally he adjusted the dials and sank back against the seat.

"I'm sorry, Alex—"

"Don't"—he coughed—"don't worry. You did great. You too, Angelica. Now listen—shit." His eyes closed and his head fell back against the seat.

"Alex, what's wrong?" There was new alarm in Chicago's voice. She cupped her hand under his face and lifted it. He opened his eyes.

"I don't guess . . . you know how to fly a plane, do you?" he asked feebly. Chicago felt her heart stop.

"Don't joke," she sobbed even as she knew it was no joke. Frantically she ran her hands down his chest. "Please don't joke."

He tried to push her hands away, then he cringed in pain.

"Did they shoot you?" Chicago almost screamed. "Goddamnit, where's the flashlight?" Just under his ribs on the right side she felt blood, sticky and warm.

"Oh, my God—Alex." There was already a pool of blood on the

seat. "Angie, help me! Give me something—get that bag!" Angelica's crying was fading out. "Hand me that bag now! Alex has been shot!" Angelica snapped out of her fear and snuffling and grabbed the bag. She turned out the contents and handed up a T-shirt. Chicago pressed it against the wound.

"Something bigger!"

"I'm looking," Angelica cried.

"I think there's . . . my leg too," Alex informed her with an infuriating calm, as if he were pointing out spots to the dry cleaners.

"Shit," Chicago swore as she felt his thigh for the bullet hole. Alex jumped when she hit it.

"Just relax, just relax, and—and hold your blood in," Chicago ordered stupidly as she worked to staunch the wounds. "Like those mystics and swami guys—like walking on hot coals." She stopped to wipe her eyes with the back of her hand. The smell of his blood on her hands was sharp.

"Chicago . . . I think it's . . ." What was it? He was having trouble thinking of the right words.

"Don't talk!" she snapped angrily. "If you die, Alex—you bastard—I swear I'll kill you!" She pressed on the wound.

Angelica stared at the blood seeping through the cloth. "Oh, my God—do we need a tourniquet or something?"

Alex smiled. "Look . . ." His voice was weak. What could he tell her? The two-minute flying lesson? "I set . . . the autopilot for Mérida—Mexico. . . . It's about an hour flight. . . ." The effort of a whole sentence made him faint. He felt like the whole middle of his body had caved in.

"Alex, Alex wake up!" Cool hands on his face. Chicago's pale blue eyes.

"We're going to crash," Angelica sobbed from the back.

"You might try . . . to land in the water. . . ." He lunged upright. There was a vague delirious glint in his eyes. "Look . . . remember? Push for down . . . pull for up . . ." Alex collapsed. He fell against the console, and the weight of his body pushed the wheel in, hurling the plane into a dive.

Chicago cried out and grabbed Alex. She pulled him back against the seat. Her hands were covered in his blood. The plane was diving toward the sea. Suddenly Angelica reached from the backseat and grabbed the wheel. Their arms tangled for a moment. Chicago struggled to hold Alex's body back against the seat.

Angelica pulled hard on the wheel, easing the nose of the plane back up. Chicago looked at her in astonishment.

"Can you fucking *fly*?" she screamed.

Seventy-Five

FINNEAUS AND SHANA walked home from Millie and Al's, talking little now, their thoughts subdued by the discussion and the cold wind.

"Why don't you stay for dinner?" Finneaus asked when they got to his house.

"No thanks. It's been a long day and I think I need a little solitude." She smiled and tossed her scarf back over her shoulder. "I'll talk to you tomorrow. Call if you hear anything," she added as she turned the corner to Eighteenth Street.

Finneaus stopped to pick up some beer bottles from the little patch of grass by the sidewalk. Mittens streaked out from under the porch and meowed, eager to be let in. He picked her up and petted her. He had barely gotten his key in the lock when Jacquie flung the door open.

"Oh, Finn! Phil Greenway just called. Alex called him from Belize a few hours ago." She wasn't crying so no one was dead, but there was a tenseness to her face.

"What's going on?"

"I'm still not sure, but they found Angelica. They were going to try to get her off the island tonight and fly her out. There's been no word since then. I left a message with Shana."

"She just left." Finneaus pointed toward the corner. "I can go get her. But what did he say? Was everything all right? Nothing happened with Sophie?"

"Apparently they had some trouble but got out of it. Alex didn't elaborate."

"Damn—"

"This is so crazy! Finneaus, what do we do?"

"I don't know. Is Greenway going to the police yet?"

"Alex told him to wait until tomorrow night. If they get her out they could be back by then, or at least someplace they can call from. If not, they're in trouble."

"What about Wattles?" Finneaus pressed. "Was Greenway going to tell him?"

Jacquie shook her head. "Alex told him not to. I don't know why. Couldn't he help get them out?"

"Or double-cross them." Finneaus looked worried. "Shana doesn't want to go to anyone yet either." He glanced at his watch. "Give her ten minutes to get home. I'll call her again."

As soon as Shana unlocked the door she could see the blinking light on her answering machine. She kicked aside the stack of mail that lay on the floor, set her briefcase down on the radiator, and hurried to the machine. The first message was a computerized sales call. Impatiently she fast-forwarded. Her cat scampered in from the kitchen.

"Hey there, kitty," she coaxed absently as she listened to a long message from her mother, chastising her for not calling in so long. Shana was eager to listen for the important messages, but felt guilty about fast-forwarding through her own mother. The little cat rubbed against her ankles. Shana shrugged off her coat and picked the cat up. Finally the voice of Mom clicked off, and Jacquie's urgent message came on the tape. Shana dropped the cat and hurriedly punched Finneaus's number.

"Finn, what's going on? I just got Jacquie's message."

The little cat, oblivious of the world drama unfolding around her, knew only that she was being neglected, raised her tail, and stalked off in a huff. Shana sat on the edge of the couch, nodding and scribbling notes as Finneaus briefed her.

"What time was that? And Belize is one or two hours behind us?"

The cat walked deliberately over Shana's coat and took its wounded pride into the foyer.

"So they could be back as soon as tomorrow?" Shana was getting excited. "I know . . . of course. It's just good to have a little lead time. . . ." With one smooth motion the cat jumped up on the radiator, and began to exercise her little claws on the edge of Shana's very expensive leather briefcase.

"Psssssst!" Shana hissed at the cat, grabbed a magazine off the

couch, and pitched it toward the unruly animal. The cat sprang, the briefcase tipped, then case and cat crashed to the floor on top of the overlooked mail. There was an explosion.

Seventy-Six

"CAN YOU FLY?" Chicago shouted to the trembling girl. "Tell me, goddamnit! Can you fly this plane?"

Angelica choked a little. "Well, I . . . I dated this boy who was a pilot for a while." She sniffed through her tears. "And he was giving me lessons, but then he met this girl, she was a friend of the sisteh of my very best friend—"

"Shut the hell up!" Chicago felt her head might fly apart. "Can you fly this thing or not?"

"Well, a little . . . but—"

"Come on then." Chicago was already up and kneeling on the seat. There was no more time for emotion, no time for trembling. "Help me get him back there." The two women struggled to lift and pull Alex out of his seat and stretch him out in the back.

"Go start remembering," Chicago ordered. "I'm going to fix him up."

Angelica slipped into the pilot's seat and began to look over the array of dials and instruments.

Chicago opened the first aid kit, held the flashlight under her chin, and carefully pulled the blood-soaked T-shirt away from the wound. She choked and the light wobbled crazy waves over Alex's body. The wound looked messy, but the bleeding seemed to be stopping. She carefully felt his back and found the entrance wound. So the bullet had gone straight through. That was good, wasn't it? She had heard stories of people getting shot and the bullet missing everything important. She pictured the arrangement of organs from a long-ago biology textbook. It seemed crowded.

She piled two trauma dressings over the wounds, and wrapped it up as tight as she could. The leg wound was much neater, a single shot about an inch in from the outside of his thigh. Once Alex was properly bandaged Chicago felt faint. Her stomach heaved and contracted. She stumbled to the far end of the plane and threw up in a box. When she recovered she crawled back up and spent a few minutes wedging the bags of clothes and life jackets in around Alex and tying him down. She climbed back to the copilot's seat.

"Is he alive?" Angelica asked tensely. Chicago nodded.

"Do you think, maybe he'll wake up in a little while?"

Chicago felt her eyes flood with fresh tears. "No."

"Oh, dear." They rode in silence, the plane's vibrations were almost soothing. "Is he your boyfriend?"

Chicago looked at her startled. Her boyfriend? "I—I don't know."

Angelica looked puzzled. "What do you mean? How can you not know?"

"Well—we—we're—I guess we're kind of something."

Angelica looked over the instrument panel and bit her lower lip. "Well, y'know I'm sorry I was fussing at y'all and everything. . . ."

"That's OK. I guess I'm sorry too."

"Well, there now, we can be friends." Angelica smiled.

Chicago saw that she was sincere, but felt fairly lost as to how to go about this being-friends business. She's just a kid, Chicago reminded herself, a rich kid.

"Now, Chicago—is that really your name?"

"Yes." There was a pause.

"You don't have many conversations, do you?" Angelica asked with all sincerity and a note of sympathy.

"I guess not." Chicago tried to concentrate on this, but her mind was full of Alex.

"Well, what I mean is *why* are you named after a city? I think it's really cute."

Chicago almost smiled. Oh OK; conversation, we are having a conversation. It seemed bizarre and funny at the same time. They had to almost shout to be heard over the noisy engine.

"My mother was from the Caribbean, from Tobago," Chicago explained. "She hadn't really been anywhere else, and she had an old *National Geographic* magazine with pictures of Chicago. She thought it was this perfect, romantic, beautiful city."

Angelica smiled as if she had just won a prize. "That's really sweet. That is. It's just really sweet. I'm just named after angels." She said, "Angels in general, not any one in particular." There was another long pause.

"That's, uh, that's nice," Chicago offered lamely.

"Now, Chicago"—Angelica smiled as she turned back to the control panel.

"Yes?"

"Well, you see—I don't really remember much of this."

"OK." Chicago tried to keep her voice calm. She looked over the confusing array of switches and lights and dials on the console, then back to the chatty little woman who suddenly held their lives in her manicured hands. Chicago took a deep breath and patted Angelica on the arm. It seemed the right kind of gesture.

"OK—but you have flown before?"

"Yes." Angelica sniffed.

"That's great."

"Five times."

"Oh—oh, that's plenty!" Chicago forced encouragement. "And so you've seen a lot of landings right? I mean, it was part of your lesson, right? You were probably going to try it yourself the next time."

Angelica shook her head. "I was scared. Landing is really scary." She snuffled. "And Lenny—that was my boyfriend—he always looked so cute when he was landing. He would get all concentrating, and he would just distract me."

"But—but you watched him, right?" Chicago tried to control a mounting anxiety. "Try to just relax and imagine what he used to do. . . ."

Angelica was shaking her head. Big tears filled her blue eyes. "Oh, you just don't understand anything! I told you—I was in love with this boy and he flew planes." As if that explained everything. "And then he jilted me. What would I evah want to fly a plane myself for?" She burst into tears.

"Stop it!" Chicago grabbed her arm and shook her. "We didn't come all this way to crash and burn in the middle of Mexico!"

"Oh, you stop it! Let go of me!"

"You've got a brain in there somewhere, so use it, goddamnit!"

Angelica started sobbing into her hands. "You are so hateful!"

"Shit! I'm sorry! I'm trying to be nice, OK! I haven't had much practice!" Chicago sat back in her seat and waited for Angelica's crying to stop. How long had they been flying? Shouldn't she at least be paying attention. "Look," she said when the sobs had stopped, "I'm just as scared as you are, and I'm sorry I'm yelling, but I don't know anything about flying. You relax, and I'll try to get someone on the radio to help us."

Chicago flipped the radio on and began to twist through the frequencies. A cold wind was blowing in the broken window. "We're going to wind up on the ground one way or another, so we might as well try to get it right."

Angelica's eyes grew wide. "Ooooh—I saw that on TV once. On one of those real-life rescue shows. I mean, it was a reenactment and all, but it did actually happen."

"Mayday—Mayday—Mayday!" Chicago ignored her. "Aircraft in distress." She paused, turned the squelch knob, listened. For the next few minutes she ignored the pouting Angelica while she broadcast their distress alternately in Spanish and English.

Gabriel Jimenez had just picked up a thirteen-year-old Mexican boy with acute appendicitis in Bacalar, and was flying him to the hospital in Mérida. He was in the middle of the Yucatán peninsula, about a half hour south of the Mérida airport when the Mayday call crackled in over his radio. Gabriel had been a volunteer pilot for Wings of Hope air ambulance service for three years, taking two shifts a month between his regular job as a commercial pilot for Taca. He was cool in a crisis.

He snapped up the radio and acknowledged the call.

"Nos puede ayudar por favor!" Chicago cried in Spanish. "We're in a small plane and our pilot has been injured."

"You are not a pilot?"

"No. He is—" What was the Spanish for "unconscious"? *"Se ha caido, se ha dormido,"* she fumbled for the words. "He is hurt. Will you please tell me how to land?"

"Tell you how to land?" Gabriel heard the fear in her voice. "Do you know how to fly?"

"No—but my friend does a little. She only speaks English, but if you tell me, I can translate."

"OK, calm down. Who is flying right now, amiga?"

Chicago closed her eyes and took a deep breath. "We are on autopilot for Mérida. We took off from Ambergris Cay in Belize about twenty minutes ago. . . ."

Gabriel stared at his own instrument panel, crossed himself, and made a quick request to Saint Christopher, who, desainted or not, had still managed to come up with a miracle now and then, and began to guide the women through the essentials. Gabriel spoke some English, but he flew in Spanish. He did not know the English names for such things as vertical velocity indicator, or transponder.

"Angie"—Chicago pulled the earphones away—"do you know some kind of wheel? Something you have to turn to adjust the handle here?" Chicago tapped the yoke.

Angelica thought about it, then her face brightened. "The trim wheel." She smiled with the first hint of confidence Chicago had seen, and pointed it out.

"OK, we found it," Chicago informed Gabriel. "Don't touch it yet? OK—OK—"

"What's he saying?"

"I don't know—actitud? Check my *attitude*?" Chicago looked puzzled. "We're about to crash a plane—what the hell kind of attitude should I have!"

"Attitude? Check your. . . . Attitudinal!"—Angelica cried triumphantly. "This thing"—she pointed to the dial—"it shows if your wings are level. Tell him we're level." Chicago translated the information.

"And—and tell him our vertical velocity is OK too," Angelica added. Chicago grinned at her; Angelica smiled back. She was sitting up straight now, concentrating on the instruments. They were suddenly looking more familiar to her. Maybe they *could* do this!

"OK. Do you have your outside lights on?" Chicago asked. Angelica glanced out the window, shook her head, and found the switch. They saw the wing lights come on, then Chicago began talking to Gabriel again in Spanish, nodding her head.

"Chicago," Angelica interrupted. "Chicago!" she shouted with a little screech. "Oh, my God, look!" She pointed out the window. Chicago stared. She thought she knew what she was looking at, but she didn't want it to be true.

"That spray," Angelica whimpered. With the outside wing lights on, they could now see a plume of liquid spraying out of a gaping hole in the wing. Chicago didn't know much about airplanes, but she did know where the fuel went. Angelica looked quickly at the gauge. It was a little above empty.

"Tell him we have to land real soon," she instructed.

Gabriel fired off another quick prayer, then quickly explained how to turn on the transponder and "squawk."

"It's a little box—a dial—with numbers you can adjust," Chicago translated.

"Right—I have it."

"He says to turn it on. It's going to indicate our position. OK, now we take it off autopilot and we look for someplace to land."

Gabriel thought hard. There was no way to tell what part of this vast and dark sky was holding them. The Yucatán ranged from thick rain forest to flat plains covered with scrub. Where could they land?

"He says to look for lights, for a road—or any flat clear ground. Do you see anything—" Chicago's words were cut off as she was hurled back suddenly against the seat. Angelica had switched off the autopilot. The plane nosed up and tipped wildly to one side, then started to dive. Angelica alternately pulled and pushed on the yoke while the plane jerked around like a dying fish. They plummeted, wobbled, and soared. For a tiny woman, Angelica had the touch of a stevedore. Chicago gripped her seat and held her breath until Angelica finally managed to get the plane under control.

"Are you all right? Please respond." Gabriel waited for what seemed like an hour, then heard Chicago's rattled voice.

"We—uh, took it off the autopilot," she explained. She listened, then turned back to Angelica. "*Now* is when you do the trim wheel," she explained urgently. "That makes it easier to *steer.*"

"Whooops!" Angelica grinned sheepishly as she made the adjustment. "I should have remembered that part."

Chicago concentrated on their next set of instructions.

"OK, now we set up for a glide—airspeed one sixty-five kilometers—"

"That's metric! I don't know metric. . . ."

"About seventy-five," Chicago shouted, her own fear again rising. She's just a kid, she reminded herself. Our lives are in her hands. "Now we fly slow curves and check for a clear place to land."

Gabriel thought hard. If the plane had been set on a straight course, they should be flying fairly near the main highway. But there was an easterly wind, which had probably blown them off course.

"Gabriel says . . . we should steer east and look for a road." Chicago pulled off the headphones. "And move away everything that could knock around the cabin when we land. I'm going to check Alex." She slipped back and wedged the sleeping bags tighter around his body. His pulse was weak and his skin clammy, but he did not seem to be any worse. She shone the flashlight on the bandage and was glad to see no blood had seeped through.

Angelica was steering the plane fairly well now, flying low, sweeping gently back and forth, looking for a place to land. They had still not seen any lights; the ground was just a hard black place below them.

Chicago climbed back in the copilot's seat and got their next instructions. "Electric off, fuel pumps off—landing lights on." Chicago passed on Gabriel's directions.

"Look! Look over theah!" Angelica pointed out the front window. "Could that be something?" There was a low, flat-topped hill in the near distance. It was barely visible in the dark, but it had a squareness that seemed man-made.

"Ruins," Chicago guessed. "The Yucatán is covered with Mayan ruins." She told Gabriel what they had found. "He says circle around it. There may be a road."

Angelica flew lower and steered an arc halfway around the hill. "There—what's that?" She turned them around and passed it again.

"Maybe," Chicago offered doubtfully. "But it sure as hell isn't much."

Gabriel thought hard; there were several uncovered sites in the western part of the state that they could be seeing. The road was probably just a dirt track to get the occasional archaeologist in for a visit. But they had to get in from somewhere, right?

"He says follow the little road east," Chicago translated.

"Oh, my God, oh, my God!" A red light had blinked on above the fuel gauge. "What do we do? We're going to crash. Oh, my God, this is a jungle."

Chicago gulped down her own panic. "Angie, look, you're doing just fine. We'll get out of this."

"No! No, we can't *do* this!" Angelica was getting hysterical again. "We can't land down there! It's a jungle. It'll be full of snakes!"

"Angelica, I guarantee you—you just land this plane and I'll take care of the snakes," Chicago promised.

"OK, *ninas.*" Gabriel's voice was reassuring. "You have to prepare to land." Chicago listened intently. The plane was noisy, and the radio contact scratchy.

"This is our approach," she translated carefully. "We're going to land on the road."

"It's *not* a road!" Angelica screamed. "It's not a road!"

"It's a road!" Chicago shouted back.

"It's not a road!"

"It's a road, damnit! Right now a road is a road is a road!"

Angelica stared at her, then suddenly giggled. "That's a poem!" she said, giggling almost uncontrollably now. "That's in a *poem*!"

"Shut up! *Nose—up.*" Chicago bit off each word, praying Angelica wasn't going hysterical now. The plane bucked up. *"Gradually!"* Angelica smoothed it out.

"Now your airspeed indicator should be dropping . . ." Chicago said. "Don't let it go below fifty or we—" The cockpit suddenly blared with noise. "Stall!"

"Oh, my God! What's that? What do I do?" Angelica screamed. Gabriel heard the stall-warning alarm over the radio.

"Push in, drop the nose. Increase airspeed," he shouted, his own hands tense on the stick, his heart beating faster for the distant danger. Chicago in her fear, repeated the Spanish. When Angelica didn't respond, Chicago grabbed the yoke herself and pushed in, sending the plane into a sudden plunge. They picked up the necessary speed and escaped the stall, but now they were speeding toward the ground. Angelica screamed and pulled back. They nosed up again and stalled again.

"Cut it out! He said push in!"

"I can't! We'll crash!"

"Push in or we stall!"

Angelica closed her eyes and eased the yoke forward. The plane picked up speed.

"I can't do this!" she shrieked. The ground was suddenly too close. She could feel it: a great hard mass sucking them into it. She jerked back on the stick, wanting the sky again, the safety of soft air, but the stall horn sounded again.

"Do it!" Chicago shouted, but before Angelica could avoid the stall, the engine sputtered and died. They had run out of gas.

"Amiga! Amiga!" Gabriel felt the sweat on his own brow drip into his eyes. "What's happening?"

"We're out of gas." They could see the brush coming closer, a thick low tangle of branches.

"Pull back now—pull up easy. . . ." In the landing lights was the sudden fact of earth. "Bring the nose up now . . . all the way back . . . nose up . . ." The wings began cracking off the tops of the low trees with a sound like machine-gun fire. Angelica screamed, lost her grip, and the plane bounced back up.

"Nose down—down, Angie—land it!" They hit the trees again; the cockpit was rattling from the smack of branches. For long, terrible moments, they jolted and bounced, dirt and rocks hitting the windshield, then somehow, the wheels hit the narrow road.

"Brake! Brake!" Gabriel's voice was steady in her ear, but Chicago was screaming by now. "Where's the fucking brake?"

Angelica remembered the pedals. Her legs were shaking. She stomped down, and they veered to the right straight into the thicket. She hit the other pedal, and there was a screech of brakes. The plane turned, tipped; the wheel hit a rock; one wing jerked up and the other crunched against the more solid base of the trees.

Angelica screamed. The plane began a crazy pivot like some fractured ice skater. Something hit the windshield. There was a loud metallic grating sound, then the dragging wing tip snapped off. The plane bounced back up to two wheels, tilted perilously the other way, then came to a shuddering stop, two wheels finally on the ground.

Seventy-Seven

GRANT FELT THE sand grinding into his teeth, splitting his lips and tearing into his gums. He squeezed his eyes shut as tightly as he could, but feared he might already be blinded. His lungs burned, and when the bright stars started hammering his skull again he prayed that this time he would slip into unconsciousness. But as soon as he started falling into that sweet state, he felt the yank on his hair, and Sophie pulled his head out of the surf.

He gasped and coughed, his whole body racked with the need for air. She held him with an iron grip, only inches from the water as he tried to fill his lungs before the next plunge. A small wave splashed him, and he choked on the salt water. It was like breathing hot coals.

"Enough." With a bitter laugh, Sophie dragged him up by the hair and let him fall on the beach. Desperately, Grant struggled to escape, clawing in the sand, but she stepped on his hand. "Have you learned not to be such a stupid boy?" she sneered. He nodded, still unable to lift his head from the sand, trembling in the first real fear of his young life. Sophie laughed, and Grant felt he knew what hell was really like. "When you feel better, *schatze,* I suggest you crawl off to your nice bed in the house. We must make an early start tomorrow." She twisted her foot, grinding his wrist painfully into the sand.

When he tried to pull away Sophie kicked him viciously in the stomach. The pain was overwhelming. He gagged and began to retch. "You are lucky that I still need you, sweetheart," Sophie crooned as she turned away. "Otherwise, I might have hurt you."

As soon as Gabriel Jimenez delivered his patient to the waiting ambulance in Mérida, he sprinted upstairs to the air traffic control tower to see if they had a fix on the downed plane.

"We had it to about a twenty-mile radius," they explained. "Then we lost it. Either a malfunction, or she knocked the switch off by mistake."

"Shit," Gabriel swore. "Do you know that area? Any towns?"

"A few villages. The terrain is low scrub, so even if she really botched the landing there is a good chance of surviving."

"How about ruins? She said they were near a low square hill. I thought it might be ruins."

"I don't know of any around there, but we can find out. Could be that they were farther north, too; lot of little hills there." Gabriel stared at the map.

"We've put out a general alert," the controller told him. "And we'll start a search in the morning. But there's not much we can do now. No one's going to be flying over the Yucatán at night except drug dealers."

And vultures, Gabriel thought.

The silence of disaster is as heavy and cold as cement, a pounding silence punctuated by creaks and snaps and a sort of rushing noise that is the miracle of your own blood still flowing. Chicago and Angelica sat for a minute listening to the silence. They were alive. Chicago pushed open her door, and branches fell into the cabin. Her head swam, and she had to bend over and breathe deeply. Somewhere far behind her, she could hear Angelica murmuring, "Oh dear Jesus" over and over in a small, amazed voice. Chicago leaned against the plane. Her skin suit was still slightly damp and felt crawly against her skin. She tugged at the neck. There were no lights anywhere, no glow over any distant horizon. There was no moon, and she could not see far, but they were definitely on solid ground.

"Shana! Shana!" Finneaus shouted into the phone. "Shana, are you all right?"

"What happened?" Jacquie ran over.

"I don't know. An explosion. Call nine one one." Finneaus handed her the phone. "It's Newton Street," he shouted as he pulled on his coat and grabbed the keys. "I don't know the number. It's a few houses in from Eighteenth."

"Finn, be careful!"

He slammed the old Impala to a stop, double-parking in front of Shana's house, and sprinted through the gathering crowd. The door had been shattered, and smoke still hung in the air. He heard sirens approaching.

"Shana?" Finneaus paused at the doorway. "Shana, are you all right?" He stepped tentatively inside. The foyer was filled with rubble; the radiator was mangled and hissing steam. Finneaus ducked through it and ran into the living room. There were bits of plaster and debris all over. He heard the sirens stopping outside, heard footsteps on the steps.

"Shana?" Finneaus saw her coat on the floor, the telephone lying tangled beside it. He pulled away the toppled coffee table and found Shana lying beneath it.

Seventy-Eight

By nine o'clock in the morning the fierce Yucatán sun was beating down on the plane. Chicago was suffocating. In her heavy, exhausted dream state she thought there were goats sitting all over her. She kicked at one. There was a low groan. Slowly her mind clambered toward consciousness. She was horribly hot. She felt jittery and disoriented. There was movement next to her, and suddenly she broke awake, realizing it was Alex she had been kicking in her overheated sleep. She sat up and flung back the sleeping bag.

"Alex? Alex, can you hear me?" His eyelids flickered. His shoulders heaved, and one hand scuttled out to the side as if trying to find leverage to lift his elbow. She caught it and pulled it back to his side. His body felt so hot. She pulled the sleeping bag all the way off.

"Alex, it's OK. Don't move." She touched his face. Angelica began to rouse, also stirred by the pounding heat. She ripped her way out of the sleeping bag, sat up, and blinked. She rubbed her eyes, scratched her head.

"Gawd, my hair feels like a horse's tail," she moaned.

"Can you get these windows open for some air and pass me that water jug?" Chicago asked distractedly. "I think Alex might be waking up."

"Can you please not ordah me around first thing in the morning!" Angelica snapped. "These are very traumatic circumstances to wake up in!"

"I'm sorry, Angie." Her apology was genuine, but she was too tired and beaten to expend much sympathy. Chicago stepped over Alex and got the water jug herself. She poured a little water out in a cup and lifted Alex's head into her lap.

"Alex, wake up." She rubbed some water on his lips with her finger.

Angelica got up and slid open the windows, then knelt down beside Chicago. "I think he looks so much bettah."

"Oh wait—don't tell me—you once dated a doctor."

"Weyll, yes, I did, as a matteh of fact. . . ." Angelica replied before she realized the sarcasm. "Oh, you—you!" She sat back in a huff. "I think you must sit around and concentrate on ways to be so mean about everything. I was just trying to give you a little comfort and encouragement."

Chicago stared blankly at the disheveled debutante and realized this was true.

"That's what girls are *supposed* to do," Angelica went on, almost scolding. "Give each other encouragement like those girls in *Steel Magnolias.* I was a volunteeh at the county hospital with the junior auxiliary and I have seen many gravely ill people and I was very good at bringing solace to their loved ones," she rattled on in a huff. "But if you don't want any solace, that's fine!" Her voice faded as she climbed to the front of the plane and shoved the door open.

Alex fought his way out of the fog. His senses were rattled and numb; sounds and images sifted in muffled, as if coming in through a long tunnel. Voices. Heat. Confusion.

"Alex—Alex, stay awake. Come on . . ." Chicago rubbed her fist on his chest.

The sky was blue. A small square of blue. A window. A familiar sort of window. Plane window. Each realization brought Alex a small pang of triumph. He shut his eyes again, tried to focus on the sounds—words, a good voice . . . he should say something . . .

Chicago leaned back on her heels and stared out the window, her vision blurred with tears. "Damnit, Alex—I don't know about this stuff! This . . . this I don't know!" She took a deep, wobbly breath, glad he couldn't hear her rambling confession of doubt. Chicago wiped her tears away. The skin on her face felt thick from the salt and grime.

"Oh, my gawd," Angelica announced dramatically. "I have nevah seen so much nothing."

Seventy-Nine

Shortly after dawn an advisory was issued to all airports in the region to be on the alert for a small plane crashed in the Yucatán. The news traveled quickly, but by the time it reached the tiny office of the San Pedro Airport, Sophie and Grant were already on the runway. They had chartered the plane that usually took tourists on day trips to the Mayan ruins in Ticul.

"What's taking you so long?" Sophie snapped.

"Just another couple of minutes," the pilot explained. He hoped she wasn't going to be one of those demanding, imperious tourists. "Another plane is cleared to land before we take off. Here it comes now." He pointed. Sophie leaned back irately and folded her arms. She did not wait gracefully. The other plane landed, taxied past them. She punched the pilot urgently.

"Go now! We're paying you to fly, not sit!" Sophie did not like to lose. She was feeling cheated and predatory. Grant cowered in the seat beside her, staring out the window, trying to be invisible. He watched the other plane, but he could not see more than a glimpse of the passenger as the plane taxied past them. They were taking off by the time the other plane discharged its passenger, and neither Sophie nor Grant noticed Ethan Ruthwilde getting off.

"Dust! I see dust!" Chicago scrambled up on the wing of the plane, then up to the roof of the cabin to get a better view. "There has to be a road over there."

"How far?"

"I can't tell. But it can't be more than five or six miles." She jumped down off the plane, climbed back inside, and began to stuff the knapsack.

"What are you doing?" Angelica shrilled in alarm.

"What does it look like I'm doing?"

"You can't leave me here all alone!"

"Look, this track has to go somewhere. Most likely to a real road. One of us has to go for help, and I kind of don't get the feeling it's going to be you."

"Why can't we just wait here until they rescue us? They know we're out here."

"Right." Chicago waved her arm in a circle toward the empty landscape. "They know we're out here somewhere. The radio's dead, and Alex is going to die if we can't get him to a doctor. I'm going to the road. I'll stop a car. We'll come back and get you." Sounds simple enough, she told herself.

"Well, they must have search parties out by now. They'll have airplanes looking for us. Why don't we just wait until someone comes?"

"Someone like who?" Chicago reminded her gently.

"Oh, my God . . . the KGB . . . I forgot. You really think they will come looking for us?"

Chicago quashed a sarcastic retort, reminding herself again that Angelica was young, inexperienced, afraid. Yeah, like I'm really an expert at this, she thought to herself. She took one of the water bottles and stuffed it in the knapsack. "While I'm gone, pick up all these broken branches and stuff and cover the plane as much as you can."

"You're crazy! How will anyone find us if we hide the plane?"

"If they don't find us, they can't kill us."

"I'm not staying here alone!" With her dirty hair and pouting face Angelica looked like an especially grumpy little dog.

Chicago ignored her petulance. "I'll be back as soon as I can." Chicago zipped the bag, then carefully reached under the seat where Alex had tossed the guns. She was pretty sure the Uzi was empty. There was no clip or magazine or whatever it was that the bullets were stored in. Alex probably shot the whole thing during their escape. The nine millimeter, however, had been tucked into the back of his shorts, unfired. She laid the pistol gingerly on the cabin floor, the muzzle carefully pointing out to the trees, then unzipped the case with the shotgun.

"Did you ever date a soldier of fortune by chance?" Chicago asked hopefully. "Anyone who might have shown you how to work one of these?"

Angelica looked at her skeptically. "My daddy showed me how to shoot his bird gun, but I never went hunting."

"Good." Chicago smiled. "What about the pistol?"

"On TV they slam up on the bottom and then kind of pull back on something on the top," Angelica suggested. Chicago examined the pistol. "Isn't there usually a safety?" The two women crouched behind the gun as if it might come alive. "Try that." Angelica pointed to a little button. Carefully, Chicago picked up the pistol and pushed the button. The clip fell out.

"Well, at least it's unloaded now," Angelica offered. "Try the trigger." Chicago held her breath and squeezed the trigger. Nothing happened. "What about this?" Angelica pointed to a small lever, and Chicago slipped it down. "Try it now," Angelica suggested, "while it's still empty." Chicago pulled the trigger and the gunshot cracked across the empty landscape. Angelica screamed and almost fell over backward.

Chicago's hand jerked up with the force. "Shit!" she cried as the hot metal casing landed in her lap. There was a sharp smell. Her heart was racing and her ears throbbed from the noise. "Shit!" she repeated as she remembered Alex telling her, "Eight in the clip, plus *one in the chamber.*"

Angelica stared at her as if Chicago had shot her own mother. "How come you're on this mission and you don't even know how to shoot a gun?" Angelica's voice was taking on a shrill pitch. "I don't know why my father would ever pick someone like you to rescue me from the KGB, but you can just believe—"

"Shut up," Chicago broke in. She was rattled. "There is no fucking KGB." She grabbed up the bag, stuffed the pistol in, put the clip in her pocket, and hoped her knees would quit shaking soon. "Your father is being blackmailed. Sophie and Grant work for the blackmailers and—" She stopped. Angelica would find out the truth soon enough. "And I don't have time to explain it all now."

Angelica looked stunned and a little disappointed. "But Alex said—"

"He said that to shut you up." Chicago felt a wave of compassion for the girl. "Look, I'm sorry. I have been mean to you. But . . . well, I'm sorry." She felt so drained, it was all she could do to keep herself together right now. "It shouldn't be more than two hours to the road. It's nine-thirty now. If I'm not back by two o'clock, uncover the plane and . . . hope someone friendly comes along. Keep Alex quiet. He was moving around a little and he opened his eyes a couple of times. If he wakes up try to get him to drink. I'll take the pistol, you keep the shotgun. If any bad guys show up, shoot 'em."

Eighty

"WELL, GOOD MORNING. Can you hear me yet?" Finneaus looked up as Shana came into the kitchen. She was wearing Jacquie's robe, which she had to lift to keep from dragging on the floor.

"What did you say?" she answered, then laughed. "Yeah, I can hear you. You and about fifty big brass bells." She slipped into a chair.

"The cops called. They want to talk to you as soon as you wake up. Want some juice?"

"Hey, thanks for bringing me home last night. I really didn't want to stay in the hospital."

"No sweat." Finneaus looked her over. "You sure you're feeling OK?"

"Yeah—really. Just a headache. Did you talk to Phil Greenway?"

"About an hour ago. He'll let us know as soon as he hears anything." She nodded.

"Shana—"

"Don't say it."

"We have to go to the FBI."

"You're right." Shana nodded. "You're absolutely right."

"Today."

"No." Finneaus started to protest but Shana stopped him. "Just listen a minute. I've been thinking all night."

"Shana, you were unconscious half the night."

"OK. I was thinking the other half. Look, Alex and Chicago might be on their way home right this minute with Angelica."

"We don't know that—"

"Well, we will know by this afternoon. And if they are, then I get my story today. Maybe for the six o'clock news."

"And if they aren't?"

"Then something has happened and we get them some help."

"Meanwhile, what if they try to kill you again?"

"That's the thing, Finn." Shana's face was serious. "I don't think the letter bomb was meant to kill me."

"What—did it have a Love stamp on the envelope or something?"

"It just doesn't make sense. Think about it. What's the purpose of killing me?"

"To prevent you from exposing the story."

Shana shook her head triumphantly. "Naw—you see, that's just it. These people are smart. They knew if I were dead someone else would still break it open—only worse. I think they were trying to scare me. Stall for time."

"Well, they should have accomplished that!" Finneaus pointed out. "But if all they want is to stop your story, why wouldn't they just try to destroy your evidence—steal your notes?"

"How? This is the computer age, Finn. It's not like I have the secret documents. I have everything in triplicate on disk. Harland's got a set, I have a set, and I even have a copy in a safety deposit box. They would have to be stupid to think that killing me would end the investigation. If anything, it would just make it worse."

"So you think they figured on just intimidating you out of the way?"

"Yes." She nodded.

"Well, I for one vote that you accept their efforts."

Eighty-One

ANGELICA DRAGGED ANOTHER branch up on the wing of the plane. She was not a particularly inspired worker, and so it was not a particularly thick cover. It was almost noon, and she was hot and tired. She tossed the brush up on the pile, then plopped down in the open doorway for a rest. A rustling noise startled her. She shrieked and pulled her knees up, searching the underbrush for snakes before she realized the noise came from inside the plane. Angelica turned and saw Alex had wakened and was trying to sit up.

"Oh, honey, don't move."

"What's . . . happened? Where are we?"

"Now don't you get all worried." She clucked as she rushed to his side. "Everything is just fine. I landed the plane and Chicago has gone to get help, and you're going to be just fine. Do you hurt?"

"Where are we?" His head was heavy, and the link to consciousness tenuous.

"We are in the Yucatán peninsula," she answered as if reciting in geography class. "Last night we did that terrible escape. Do you remembah that? And that horrible woman shot you. And she shot the plane and we were losing fuel. It was all just so awful. Here now." She suddenly remembered and grabbed the water bottle. "You have to drink."

She pushed a sweatshirt under his head and held the bottle to his lips. Alex drank and the simple effort exhausted him. He tried to relax, to focus away the pain.

"Where's Chicago? Is she all right?" he gasped.

"I told you she's fine. She went to the road. But I have to tell you, Alex, I'm not at all sure she knows what she's doing. I mean, I know she's your girlfriend and all, but really—do you think she knows what she's doing? Why, she didn't even know how to work your guns! I'm not being prejudiced or anything—I know there are ladies in the army and everything—but I simply don't have that much confidence in her to tell you the truth. . . ."

"Slow down." Alex blinked and tried to concentrate, tried to sort out her rush of words. Sketchy images of last night began to come clear. He tried to pull himself up, but his head swam and the black cloud threatened to engulf him again.

"Where did she go?"

"Well, we're on a road, but it's not hardly a road. It's just tracks to these ruins—but far off there's a regular road. Oh, I don't know! What do we do?"

"Shhhh!" Alex pulled himself up on one elbow, the cabin began to spin. "Do you hear something?"

Angelica sprang to the window and craned her neck to see. A small plane was approaching from the north. "Oh, dear! . . . Oh, dear, oh, dear . . ." She crouched back by Alex and rested her hand on his chest.

"Oh, please, there's a plane out there, but that's what I mean. Chicago said not to let them see us! She said it might be Sophie, but Alex, I don't think she really knows what she's doing!"

"Stay. Don't do anything yet." Alex's reply was drowned by the approaching plane. Angelica ran back to the open door. She could see the plane almost overhead.

"Shit!" Chicago leaned her head out the truck window and saw the plane circling. *"Pronto! Pronto por favor!"* she pleaded.

"Señorita, lo siento muchisimo," the farmer replied. "The road is bad and this is an old truck. It does not go like the race car."

"Damn—goddamn." Chicago leaned far out the window. She could see the small plane circling like a hawk. Good guys come to the rescue? Or bad guys come for the kill? She pulled herself up so she was sitting half out the window, the hot steamy air stinging her face. What should she do? She slid back into the seat, opened the knapsack, and pulled out the gun. The farmer stared at it with panic.

"I'm sorry," Chicago explained quickly in Spanish as she shoved the clip into the pistol. "I'm not an outlaw; you've got to believe me. Keep driving." Even if it was a rescue plane, they couldn't land here. They would have to send help by the road. She was already here with a vehicle to take Alex out. What did they have to lose? She held the gun out the window and pulled back the slide, feeling a strange thrill to hear the cartridge click into place. She slipped off the safety, leaned far out the window, braced her knees against the door, and fired at the plane.

Angelica saw the dust of the approaching truck, heard Chicago's shots. "Oh, God! What do I do?" she screamed at Alex. The plane had clearly seen them; it was circling closer. Angelica peeked out the window and watched the truck speeding toward them, saw Chicago hanging out the window shooting at the plane.

"What do I do?" she whimpered.

"Give me the gun." Alex pulled himself over to the door. Angelica handed him the shotgun, but the exertion was too much. He got it loaded and cocked, but as he struggled to brace himself in the doorway, he passed out again.

"Alex!" Angelica caught him before he tumbled out the door. "Oh, damn you, Chicago! If these aren't the bad guys . . ." She swore under her breath as she fumbled for the gun. Shaking with fright and panic, Angelica ducked out of their shelter, crouched under the wing of the plane, and pointed the gun toward the sky. She took a deep breath, shut her eyes, and squeezed the trigger.

"Santa Maria, madre deo!" Gabriel Jimenez pulled back on the yoke and steered his plane back toward the sky. He glanced quickly at his gauges, then out the window for damage as he veered up and steered away.

"Mérida airport, Mérida airport," he radioed in. "I'm getting shot at. There is a plane down, but it sure as hell don't want to be rescued by me anyway! They're shooting, man!" He looked down once more and saw the truck speeding toward the site.

He had been searching since sunrise, flying an orderly grid over the vast empty territory where they suspected the plane would be. When nothing had turned up, he had gradually expanded his circles. This place was far west of anywhere they had expected, and there were no ruins marked on any maps, but when he had spied the little track through the trees, he had decided to follow it.

He saw the plane, and noticed the attempt to disguise it. Now he saw the truck speeding toward it, and figured it was a drug pickup. If he still had any doubts, the shooting clinched it. Had he decided to circle back for a better look, he might have wondered why drug dealers would be using such a beatup old farm truck to pick up their contraband. He might have seen that the gunman in the plane was actually a blond-haired woman who was now crying in the dust over the pain in her shoulder from the kick of the gun.

But Gabriel was a wise man. No one buries a plane under piles of brush unless they're hiding out from something. Why circle back and let drug runners get another shot at him?

Eighty-Two

DARCY SULLEVIN ESCAPED into Senator Wattles's office and shut the door. So far it had been a successful morning. The senator's two-day absence was starting to worry some of the staff, and a small-business group visiting from Louisiana was disappointed that he could not meet with them, but things were still under control. He checked the schedule. Wattles had a committee meeting at two, important but not vital, but there might be a vote later that afternoon. Damn old sot, he thought tensely. The phone gave its polite little bleep, and Sullevin picked it up.

"Shana Phillips on line two, Mr. Sullevin."

"I'm not talking to any reporters. Tell her the senator has the flu and will probably be back tomorrow."

"She said it's urgent, sir."

"Tell her to—" He controlled himself. "Tell her we're busy; we'll call her back later. Take a message," he added in a forced voice. He hung up the receiver and felt around in his pockets for some Rolaids. A minute later the phone blipped again.

"I'm sorry, sir. I know it sounds odd, but she just said to tell you she's healthy and feeling fine and to thank you for your concern." Sullevin felt a strange creeping sensation on the back of his neck.

"OK," he answered lamely. "Thanks, Nancy." What the hell was *that* all about? He saw the light start flashing on the senator's private line. "And hold my calls, please. I've—ah—got to look over the senator's briefing papers before the committee meeting." He hung up and stabbed at the button on the other phone. "Yes?"

The sound was clear, but Ethan Ruthwilde's voice was faint and tinny. "Darcy? Darcy, is Wattles there?"

Sullevin sat up alertly. "No. Where are you?"

"Belize—San Pedro. I flew in this morning and I've got a plane waiting. Look, everyone is gone. The house staff doesn't know what happened, but Sophie rented a plane early this morning and it looks like she went to Mérida."

"With Angelica?"

"I don't think so. I can't piece it all together, but Alex might have her."

"Listen, I just had a strange call from Shana Phillips."

"Phillips?" Ruthwilde couldn't hide the surprise in his voice. "When?"

"Just two minutes ago," Sullevin told him. "She left a message that she was fine and healthy and to thank us for our concern. Does that mean anything to you?"

"Shit." Ruthwilde leaned against the wall and watched his plane taxi up. "Darcy, call Goerbel, tell him what you just told me—"

"Call who?" Sullevin smiled to himself.

"Goerbel—*Goerbel*—" Ruthwilde repeated, thinking it was the bad connection that kept Darcy from understanding.

"What's going on? I don't understand." Sullevin pressed. "Did you try something? Did you threaten that reporter? We warned you to back off, Ruthwilde—"

"Sullevin, I don't have time for this. I have a plane waiting. I'll call you from Mérida." Still vaguely worried about Darcy's response, and thoroughly worried that Shana was still in action, Ruthwilde slammed the receiver down.

Darcy Sullevin hung up gently, smiled to himself, leaned back in the senator's leather chair, and watched the reels on the tape recorder spin.

Eighty-Three

CHICAGO PULLED THE hat down to keep the sun out of her eyes and shifted in her nest of sleeping bags. It was reasonably comfortable, although the old truck was jolting terribly on the rough track.

Angelica was riding in the cab. In another couple of miles they would be on the highway, then an hour or so to Mérida. The farmer was singing along with the radio. He had a lot to be happy about. He had a beautiful, if grimy, blonde bouncing in his truck and one hundred U.S. dollars in his pocket. He was ready to drive them all the way to Washington for that amount.

Chicago tried to work out their next move. Once they got to Mérida, there would be a hospital, a telephone, maybe a U.S. consulate. She closed her eyes and rested her hand on Alex's shoulder. They had inflated the plane's life raft and turned it upside down for a bed. His wounds had started bleeding again, and she wasn't sure he could take a lot of bumping around. She felt incredibly tired. Her legs ached, and she had blisters from her long trek to the road. She rested her cheek on the pontoon next to Alex's arm. It was warm from the sun, and the rubbery smell was familiar and comforting.

The water was so clear, so warm, so clean. Chicago spread her fingers and felt the luxurious sensation of water flowing through them. She was floating effortlessly in midwater, stretching her limbs in freedom, feeling the clean motion. Everything was quiet. The sunlight rippled on coral of the most intense colors, cobalt blue and scarlet and mossy green. Little jeweled fish darted in and out of the reef, young damselfish, with their iridescent blue spots browsed among the branches of orange staghorn coral. A pair of moorish idols swam along in regal disregard. A sparkling school of little fish engulfed her like a rainstorm. It was like being inside a diamond.

Then from out of the deep blue beyond, a manta ray appeared, ten feet across and black as the night, with a creamy white underbelly. It tipped its wings and sailed beneath her. She dove down to the creature, and it paused, letting her slide her own body on top of it. The manta's skin was soft and silky, and Chicago could feel the undulating muscles, feel the ripple of ocean power under her own earth limbs as it carried her along. On the back of the manta ray she flew past the bright reefs, through a forest of kelp where she looked up to see the sunlight through the waving emerald leaves. The manta took her past enormous underwater caves, white limestone caves with frosted pillars. They soared over deep crevices where she could see orange starfish on the bottom ten miles below. A school of dolphins appeared as escort, their sleek silver bodies weaving over and around, playing with her, sounding their chirps and squeals of friendship.

She felt so happy. She was alone in her ocean, in all the oceans at once, riding the giant manta ray. But suddenly there was a noise, a low growl, the distant whine of an engine. Chicago looked up and saw a boat on the surface. It was chasing her; bullets were flying through the water like a hailstorm. She clutched the manta, grabbing hold of his curved feelers. She pushed down, willing the creature to dive, dive to the bottom of the sea. It dove, but she couldn't stand the pressure. She pulled back, and it rose up again. Now she couldn't control it; they were soaring up toward the surface. Suddenly she felt a powerful contraction as the body arched beneath her, and with a tremendous surge, the manta leaped from the water into the sky, shaking her off like a parasite.

She cried out, a desperate protest, but the sound fell away into the thin air. The noise grew louder. She jerked awake in a panic, her face still warm from the rubber raft. She sat up against the cab and grabbed the gun. The engine noise filled the sky. She looked up and saw the plane. It circled lower. Her heart pounded. The plane banked and passed over them once again. She saw a face in the window: a large, heavy-boned face framed in a thick mat of yellow hair. As she watched, the plane turned abruptly and streaked off toward Mérida. Just before the wing tipped up, Chicago saw Sophie smile at her and wave.

Eighty-Four

THE FIRST SENSE to return was smell—a queer, antiseptic smell, a disconcerting mix of purity and disease. Next, the sense of touch crept back: soft sheets under his fingers, some kind of weight on one arm, something bulky and stiff around his chest. Sound was suddenly there: muffled bustling hallway sounds, creaky wheels, voices, distant phones ringing. And more immediately the small accidental sounds of another person in the room. Alex opened his eyes.

He saw a grayish ceiling in need of new paint. An IV pole, an enamel-topped wooden table against the wall with a small metal basin, a bottle of water, a cup. A picture of Jesus with a fiery heart in his hands. The fog in his head began to clear; he remembered swimming at night, then the cold sting of spray in a boat ride, then a long dreamlike stage. Throughout it all were shadows of Chicago.

A noise, a chair scraping; Alex lifted his head, ready to see her. Instead he saw a man sitting quietly on the chair, a thin film of perspiration on his forehead. It was a broad forehead with a receding hairline, jowly cheeks, and a wide rounded chin. Eyes, nose, and mouth seemed to have gravitated toward the center like pebbles in a slowly collapsing sinkhole. His thick glasses distorted his small eyes.

When he saw Alex was awake he stood.

"Ruthwilde."

"Ah, so you know me." The man's face made what was probably a smile.

"What's the matter?" Alex asked softly. "All your hit men busy today? You had to come down here yourself?" His free hand was sliding slowly beneath the sheet, feeling for the call button.

Ruthwilde sighed and looked genuinely sad.

"I have no desire to see you dead, Mr. Sandars. However, it doesn't matter much to me one way or the other." Ruthwilde stood and walked close to the bed. "I've been here twenty minutes. Killing you would have been simple if that was my goal. And the call button is on this side." Ruthwilde held it up. "Shall I push it for you? Are you in pain?" Alex felt dizzy, and realized he was holding his breath.

"I'm offering you a simple arrangement," Ruthwilde went on. "Give me Angelica, and I'll see to it that nobody kills you or your exotic little girlfriend." Ruthwilde paused. "You were a little surprised not to see her waiting here by your bedside, weren't you?"

Alex felt a stab of panic. Could Ruthwilde already have captured Chicago? Why wasn't she here? Not that he expected her to be chained to his side . . . but, well, a guy gets shot, he does sort of expect a little bedside vigil. What had happened? He forced his voice to stay steady.

"First of all, if you had tried to mess with Chicago you would have a few scars to show for it. Secondly, I told you, Angelica won't do you any good. The whole thing is over. You can't stop it now."

"I'm a realist, Mr. Sandars. And you are right; the thing is going to come out one way or another now. But I don't intend to wait around for the indictments."

"Don't let me keep you then." Alex waved his free hand toward the door.

Ruthwilde ignored his sarcasm. "I don't care what happens to Senator Wattles's political career; I need Angelica for myself. Although I am not an outwardly emotional man, Mr. Sandars, I do have certain hobbies which give me pleasure in life." It was the most passionate speech the man had made, and his fleshy face was still wobbling with fervor.

"You've obviously had a taste of what our German friends can do," he said bitterly, waving one small hand at Alex's bandages. "I enjoy no special favoritism. I have no loyalties. I am simply a middleman, an arranger. I am as expendable at this point as the rest of you. So here it is, all very simple. You give Angelica to me and I don't kill you. I give her to the Germans and they don't kill me. Wattles gives them their chemicals and they don't kill her."

"Damn." Alex sighed. "To look at the world today, you wouldn't know it was so easy for everybody not to get killed."

Ruthwilde picked his suit coat up off the chair. "Think about it. I had very little trouble tracking you here. I have no doubt the delicate Miss Sophie will find it even easier. I'll be back." With that Ruthwilde slipped out the door.

Alex fell back against the pillow in a wave of exhaustion. Not ten minutes later the door opened again and Chicago flew into the room.

"What are you doing?" "Where have you been!" They both spoke at once, exclamations that sliced across one another in midair like crossed swords and sent a shower of sparks.

"What the hell do you mean where have I been?"

"I didn't mean that—"

"I'll tell you where the hell I've been—"

"I'm sorry . . . I didn't mean—"

"I've been walking around the goddamn whole Yucatán—"

"Stop . . . calm down." Alex caught her arm and pulled her to him, and Chicago burst into tears as if a dam had broken. She pressed her face into his neck. He fell back on the bed, pulling her with him, overwhelmed by the fact of their bodies still alive. Her hair was wet; she smelled of cheap yellow soap. Her hands clutched hard at his pillow, her shoulders heaving.

"Illy . . . Illy, it's all right." He patted her hair. Gradually her sobs quieted and she sat up. Her face looked pale and sunken. "You did good," he whispered.

"Shut up," she snuffled into his chest. "You shit—I've cried more since I met you than in my whole life put together."

"It's good for you." Alex smiled.

Chicago shook her head and wiped her nose on the corner of his sheet. "I just don't know how to do this stuff." She touched him as she talked, stiff fingers stroking him urgently as if only enough touch would make him really there. "I don't know what to do. Sophie knows we're in the city. She saw us in the truck."

"I know." Alex pushed himself up again and caught her hand. "We need to get out of here now. Sophie's not the only one. Where's Angelica?"

"You can't go anywhere! You just had surgery!"

"So I'm all fixed up, right?" He swung his legs out of the bed and tested their stability. "Do I have any clothes here?"

"No. Alex, don't be stupid. You almost died."

"Naw." He gave her that dangerous grin. "Not even close. Not even a minor out-of-body experience. No long hallways and angels beckoning. Now go. We have to move fast. What time is it?"

"Around noon."

"When did we get here?"

"Yesterday afternoon."

"Shit."

"No one knows you're here. I mean, they don't know you're you, that you're an American even. I told them you were my husband; you got shot in a fight. Just don't speak any English and we'll be safe."

"That's good, but Ruthwilde found us. Sophie can't be far behind. Now please, Illy—go find me some clothes. Try another room, steal some. Where's Angelica?"

"I got us a room in a sleazy hotel, down by the bus station. I just went back to check on her. I took a shower," she added almost apologetically. "She doesn't speak Spanish and she's scared to go outside. I took all her clothes and everything and locked her in and paid a kid to watch the room. But I don't want to leave her too long. She wants to call Daddy."

"Did you call anyone? Finneaus, Shana?"

Chicago shook her head. "I didn't know if I should. I almost did, then I thought—what if someone's listening? I didn't know what to do. I'm sorry—"

"Don't," Alex broke in. "You did great. We'll go get Angelica, then call the States. Have you told her the real story?"

Chicago shook her head. "Not all of it. I didn't know how she would take it. She hates me enough already, Alex." Chicago stared as Alex began to peel the tape off the IV board.

"Alex, don't—just wait another day."

He shook his head. "We can't. Ethan Ruthwilde is here. He's coming back."

"What . . . how?"

"I'll tell you later. Go now. Find a wheelchair and some clothes." He gently pulled the needle out of his arm. Chicago stared. She had already seen, in horrible detail, the extent of his wounds. She had been up to her elbows in his blood, but this small act—the slow emergence of the fat needle from the swollen vein, the tiny drop of blood that beaded on the skin—made her faint.

Eighty-Five

SENATOR WATTLES WAS slouched in his chair staring at a soap opera. Over the past couple of days he had come to depend on the TV images. They were a constant presence, a silent but vital constituency. Their little programmed dramas were small and constant and absurd. He did not know any of the stories, but had developed a need to see the same faces recur day after day. Since Tobo had called from Belize, Wattles had not been able to go into the office. He would not leave his house. He had to be ready, here by the phone, whenever word came in. What was going on? Where was Angelica now? The worst part was not knowing. They got her off the island. There was gunfire at the airport. Sophie had disappeared. Then nothing.

He desperately wanted a drink, but was trying to stay as sober as possible. He had taken to sipping dry vermouth in soda water. It kept the edge off but left him alert. When the phone rang he looked at it for several rings. He slowly lifted the receiver.

"AT and T international operator." The voice was crackly and faint. His heart lurched. "I have a collect call from Angelica Wattles in Mérida—"

"Daddy? Daddy!" He could hear Angelica's voice beyond the operator's nasal tone.

"—in Mérida, Mexico. Will you accept the charges?"

"Angelica? Angel baby!"

"Will you accept the charges?"

"Yes!" he shouted. "Yes, of course."

"One moment please." Clicks and a buzz—a terrible pause, a lump of silence in which he feared they had been disconnected—then his daughter's voice.

"Daddy! Daddy, I got away. Daddy, this is all so horrible, you've got to get me out of here!"

Wattles felt his heart racing.

"Angel, oh, God, Angel. Where are you?"

"She's not here." Chicago flung open the little closet, checked the tiny bathroom, and looked under the bed. "I can't believe it. The door was padlocked. How could she get out?" She slammed the door so hard the room shook. She felt angry and stupid. Alex limped to the window. There was a fairly wide ledge, and the room next door had an iron balcony only a few feet away. It would not have been difficult to climb across.

"But she didn't have any clothes!"

Alex caught her arm. "It's not your fault."

"She was in her underwear!" Chicago brushed past him and leaned out the window. There was Juan, the boy she had paid to watch Angelica hanging out across the street, watching them.

"Hey," she shouted in Spanish, "what the hell is going on? Where is my cousin?"

The boy smiled and shrugged. "You little shit," Chicago yelled. "I'm going to chop your head off like a chicken and hold your feet while your body flops around in the dirt. Tell me what happened!" The boy just shoved his hands in his pockets.

"Maybe an angel took her," he replied insolently.

"Hey, amigo." Alex leaned out the window and a torn half of a five-dollar bill fluttered down to the street. "Come talk to me." Juan snatched up the money, thought about it for only a second, then they heard his light footsteps sprinting up the stairs. He appeared at the door of the room, a skinny boy of twelve, hanging back warily.

"Keep that chicken chopper lady away from me," he warned Alex.

"What happened to the girl?" Alex asked.

"She climbed out the window and ran away."

"What was she wearing?" Alex pressed.

"Clothes."

"What kind of clothes?"

"A dress."

"And where would she have found this dress?" Alex went on.

"On a clothesline."

Alex almost smiled, despite the frustration. He could appreciate the urchin's streetwise manner. He held out the other half of the bill. "She got this all by herself?"

The boy laughed. "Oh, I think someone felt sorry for her and brought it to her."

"Uh-huh. OK. Here you go." Alex held out the money. The boy was quick, but Alex was quicker. As the skinny fingers snatched the bill, Alex snatched him by the wrist. He twisted the arm just enough, then stuck his hand into the boy's pocket. He felt around and drew out a thin gold chain.

"Wheew," Alex whistled. "I hope you threw in a matching bag for this."

"Goddamnit!" Chicago muttered.

"Hey, she didn't look like no cousin to her!" Juan pointed at Chicago. "She had hands like a rich lady. I think she's been kidnapped and I have to help a kidnapped lady." His face was a brew of innocence and guile.

"You're a real gentleman, kid." Alex sighed. He handed the necklace back to the boy, and tucked the rest of the five-dollar bill into his surprised hand.

"The girl is in danger. I need to find her."

Juan hesitated for a second, glanced at Chicago, then back to Alex. "She didn't talk Spanish. But she did like she wanted a telephone." He mimed the action. "I got her a taxi and told the driver to go to Holiday Inn. I paid the taxi myself, mister. See, I'm not a thief. I know the necklace was worth more than just my sister's dress!"

"How long ago was this?"

"About one, two hours."

"Go on—get lost." Alex let go and the boy took off down the dim hallway like a flash.

"Goddamnit, Alex, I never thought about jewelry." Chicago's tone was crushed and heavy with self-chastisement. "I just—I didn't even notice it."

"Come on, you can beat yourself up later. We've got to find Angelica."

Eighty-Six

SENATOR WATTLES'S HANDS were shaking so badly he could hardly punch in his own office number. It rang once, twice.

"Senator Wattles's office."

"Give me Darcy right away."

"Yes, sir."

On the TV two soap opera people were floundering around on a desert island after a plane crash. Wattles felt tears of relief welling up.

"Darcy, it's me. Angelica's in Mexico. You got to help me. I—I can't even think straight. Please, you have to help me. She got away. She's all alone."

Darcy sat up and grabbed a pen. "Calm down, Senator. Tell me everything she said."

"She's in Mérida, at the Holiday Inn. I told her to stay there. I talked to the desk manager. I gave him my credit card number and tried to explain, but I don't know how much he understood. Who do we call? I need to get someone there right away! What about the CIA? We must have some people down there. Anybody! I need some Americans! I've got to get her out of there!"

"Hold it, hold it; just calm down."

"The embassy! Where the hell is our embassy down there?"

"Good, that's right. You call the embassy. I'll talk to Johnson over at State, then I'll find out about flights out of there." As he talked Sullevin was already making plans. "Keep this line open,

Senator, and I'll call you back in fifteen minutes. We'll get her out tonight, sir—I promise."

Sullevin hung up and pulled out his Filofax, flipped to yesterday's page. The message had been on his machine when he'd gotten home after work. Ethan Ruthwilde—Holiday Inn, Mérida, Mexico . . . phone number—Sullevin couldn't believe his luck. But wait. He stopped. He had to really think this through. Was it really to his advantage to have Angelica brought home now? Was there a chance Sophie could still get her? That might be the best option; but no, Wattles was ready to talk anyway. Having Angelica around would be a good sympathy move.

Sullevin nervously sketched lines and boxes on his notepad. Worst-case scenario was that Alex would bring her home. How could they avoid that? After a few minutes, Sullevin was ready to make his phone calls. It was 1:30 in Washington; Mexico was an hour or two behind, Ruthwilde should just be checking back at the hotel. Boy, did he have a surprise waiting for him there.

Eighty-Seven

CLEAN. EVERYTHING WAS finally clean. The floor was clean, the shower was clean, the shiny white tile, the fluffy towels, her fingernails, her hair, everything was clean and wonderful. Angelica sang to herself as she flung open the bathroom door and stepped out in a cloud of steam, still vigorously toweling her hair. She tossed the towel on the bed and flipped her hair back.

There was a knock on the door. Great, she thought, room service—a hamburger, Diet Pepsi, and ice cream. She was reveling in newfound civilization. She wrapped the towel around her body and flung open the door. Then she screamed. She tried to slam it shut, but the man was halfway in.

"Miss Wattles, I'm sorry—please don't be alarmed." Angelica ran back in the bathroom and slammed the door shut. Her heart was racing, her bare feet slid slowly on the damp floor, and her knees felt like Jell-O. Would this nightmare ever end?

"Angelica, I'm terribly sorry to frighten you." Ethan Ruthwilde's voice came from close beyond the door. "Please don't be afraid. I work for your father."

"Go away! Get out of here! Help! Somebody help!" she screamed.

"Please, dear. Your father just called me."

"Oh, stop it!" Angelica shouted angrily. "I'm not stupid, you know. I just talked to him an hour ago. You couldn't get here so fast."

"I was already down here, honey. I came to get you on Turtle Island, but I'm afraid I was too late. I had tracked you to Mérida when your father contacted me. I was already staying here at the hotel. I'm so sorry, dear, but please come out and let me help you now." He could almost hear her heart beating through the door.

"How do I know you work for my father?" Her voice was small.

"Well, if you open the door you might recognize me. I'm Ethan Ruthwilde. I'm a lobbyist. We've met twice at least. At a fund-raiser, I believe—Mrs. Dellacorte's affair in Baton Rouge last April."

Angelica hesitated. She had met hundreds of her father's political cronies. She vaguely remembered Mrs. Dellacorte's garden party, however. Well, she remembered the woman's grandson anyway, and his personal tour of the greenhouse.

"What was I wearing?" she asked. It seemed to Angelica a good proof. Ethan rolled his eyes and tried to check his exasperation. What the hell were Southern girls wearing to garden parties in the spring of 1990?

"It was a pretty little dress as I recall," he groped. "Colorful—a floral print wasn't it? With some sort of puffy sleeves." Ooh, watch out. Did ladies wear puffs that season? "Uh, full sleeves," he amended quickly. "It had a little ruffle." Ninety to one hundred on that one, he figured, although he didn't specify where this ruffle would have been. "And it fit you very well." *Bows,* he thought suddenly; there were a lot of bows around lately. "And I think I remember a—a sash, tied in the back in a bow."

Pretty close, Angelica thought with rising hope, although the bow tied in front. Well, come to think of it, after that little visit to the greenhouse with—what was his name?—the bow might have been anywhere.

"Tell me . . . tell me what's on my father's desk . . . in his office in Washington. What's unusual, I mean?" she pressed for further proof.

Ruthwilde spun his mind over the distant picture, reviewing each object: the photos, the marble ashtray, a carved decoy duck made into a planter. He smiled. "Do you mean the fish?" Angelica felt a sweet flush of relief. "The little mounted catfish about six inches long? The first fish you ever caught with your daddy?"

She flung open the door. Her joy at being rescued was muted by the appearance of her rescuer—this flabby, ugly little man. Heroes never looked like this on TV.

"Oh—oh, I do remember you. I think!" Good manners carry one through, she reminded herself and forced a smile. "I do thank you for coming to my rescue, Mr. Ruthwilde. Now will you please tell me what is going on!"

The fresh burst of steam fogged his glasses, and he plucked them off. "I'll tell you all about it on the way to the airport. We need to hurry. There's a flight to Dallas at three." He glanced at his watch. "If we miss that one, there's a five o'clock to Miami. Wherever—we'll get a private jet then to take us on to Washington."

"But I need some clothes," Angelica protested. "All I have is that ragged little dress. And I don't have my passport. How am I going to get out of this country?"

"We'll take care of all that. Your father's making some arrangements."

"But I can't go like this!"

Ruthwilde sighed and kept calm. "There's a shop in the hotel. I'll run down and get you some things."

"I need a brush . . . oh and some lotion . . . and . . . can you get me some mascara? Not the cheap kind though. . . . Here, let me just go—"

"No. Stay here. It's not safe, Angelica. I'll be back in ten minutes."

Eighty-Eight

"THEY JUST LEFT, sir. Just about ten minutes ago." The desk clerk spoke in a florid hotel English.

Alex leaned heavily on the counter and watched the clock on the wall behind the clerk fade in and out of focus.

"They? Who is they? Someone was with the woman?"

"Of course. The man her father sent."

"What did he look like?" Chicago pressed. "Did he tell you his name? Where did they go?"

"To the airport . . . he . . ." The man's eyes narrowed suspiciously.

Alex pushed away from the desk and squeezed Chicago's arm. "Thanks. Come on. Let's go." What little color he had drained from his face. She steered him to a couch.

"What the hell do you plan to do, Alex? One taxi ride and a couple of phone calls and you're already about to drop."

"That's what I like about you, baby," he whispered as he tried to push back the waves of pain. "You really know how to bolster a guy's confidence."

"It's not your confidence I'm worried about!" she whispered fiercely. "What's your big plan now? You going to chase them through the airport?" She patted his wounded leg. "Good idea. Or maybe we could have another shootout! Damn—they don't even have to shoot you. You can shoot at *them* and the kick will be enough to kill you. Alex, look at you—a Chihuahua could knock you down!"

He smiled and took her hand. "So you take the big gun this time."

"Shit."

"Come here." She tried to get up, but he held her there. "We've come too far. Besides, what about Sophie? You think Ruthwilde is going to be much of a match for her if she decides she wants to snatch Angelica herself?"

Chicago frowned. "So what now?"

"We go to the airport, and we save her one more time."

Eighty-Nine

"THAT'S ALL I know, Shana. Honestly, that's all he told me," Philip Greenway explained. There were two FBI agents in the office, and his lawyers had just arrived to prepare an exhumation order.

"They're on their way to the airport in Mérida. We're trying to get them some help."

"Who—what kind of help?" Shana pressed.

"I don't know yet. We've got the FBI here. It's going to take a while to sort this out. I'll call you again as soon as I know anything."

Shana hung up and jumped out of her chair. She sprinted to Harland's office and burst in without knocking.

"Alex and Chicago got Angelica out of Belize. They've got the feds in, Joe. We've got to break it now or it'll be all over the place."

"Slow down, Shana. What's going on?"

"I want to go live on the four o'clock newsbreak. Right now Ruthwilde has Angelica in Mexico. I don't know what's going on, but she's probably coming home tonight one way or another. Philip Greenway is getting an order to dig up the body. Who do we have in Louisiana? Can we get a crew there to film it?"

"Hold on."

"We *can't* hold on, Joe! Every station is going to pick this up now!" She felt an incredible energy, somewhere between delirium and panic. "Let's blurb it at four and break the story at six. So, OK, we lose the exclusive at the airport, but by then everyone will be watching us anyway. Maybe I can tape the senator this afternoon. Let me call him."

"Shana"—Harland grabbed the phone—"we have to be careful. Two days ago they tried to kill you."

"*Scare me,* Harland—"

"Whatever. We have to think about this."

"No, we don't." He saw her resolve. "This is it. No more overcrowded day-care centers and consumer rip-offs. This is the big one. Besides, the more exposure I have, the less likely anyone is to get away with murdering me."

Harland shook his head and glanced at the clock. It was quarter to four.

"I'll call the newsroom."

"Have you reached the ambassador yet?" Wattles's voice was growing hoarse from stress and overuse. He clutched the telephone like a drowning man on a lifeline.

"We're still trying, sir." Darcy's voice was steady, but it failed to reassure the senator this time. "He's away at some function, but they're sending word."

"Well, goddamn it, man, what about the rest of them?"

"I've talked to the police in Mérida. We'll have every available officer at the airport. Did the FBI show up yet?"

Wattles mopped his forehead and watched the November wind stir branches against his windows. "Yes." He turned back to the man in the room. "Yes, we're talking now. They may want to talk to you too, Darcy." The agent shook his head. "Well, call me as soon as you know anything," Wattles went on, "or hear anything. I've got to get back with this guy . . . Right . . . yes—as soon as you hear." Wattles hung up the phone.

"Now will you get this thing going!" he yelled at the agent. Half pleading, half commanding. "I know we have people down there; there must be somebody you can call!"

"Senator, we intend to take all possible action, but first of all, you have to understand there are limits to our jurisdiction in this case." Wattles was about to break in but the agent stopped him. "Secondly, I want you to understand, sir, that as it now stands, you don't have to tell me anything more without an attorney being present. You have, in fact, the right to remain silent."

Wattles felt a cold chill start at the base of his spine.

"You have already admitted to illegal trade and involvement in a conspiracy. Those are federal crimes. I must inform you that anything you say can and will be used against you in a court of law."

Wattles nodded. He stepped back and motioned toward the telephone. "Please." His voice was humble now. "I'm aware of . . . that. Please help me."

The agent picked up the phone and called the section chief. Briefly he explained the situation. "Call the consulate in Mérida about exit papers for Angelica, then get whoever you can at the airport. I want the airport sealed off. And I need an arrest warrant issued for Alex Sanders. S-a-n-d-e-r-s." He spelled it. "The charge is kidnapping."

Ninety

ALEX PAUSED JUST inside the airport entrance and drew Chicago up against a wall. Casually he scanned the area.

"Here"—he handed her some airline ticket folders that he had snatched out of the wastebasket at the hotel. "Try to look like a tourist. Come on." Alex led her across the wide corridor, weaving among baggage carts and little bundles of tourists, his walk steadier now. He waved away the shoeshine boys who flickered out of the crowd like sooty birds, and headed for the duty-free shop.

"What kind of perfume do you like?"

"What? You know I don't wear that shit. What are you talking about?"

"Here we go, honey." He took Chicago's elbow and steered her toward the perfume counter. She was too puzzled to protest.

"Let's see, Opium, Passion, Tabu. I guess virtue doesn't sell so well, huh? Try this one." Chicago recoiled instinctively as he sprayed a sample on her neck.

"Excuse me." A stranger approached. He was tall and tanned, dressed in casual slacks, a light blue sport coat, and deck shoes. He spoke with a Texas drawl.

"Hey, there. Y'all are Americans, right? Hey, I hope you don't mind, don't mean to interrupt you there, but I wonder if you might know about this duty-free stuff." He grinned and pointed to a shopping bag which contained two cardboard boxes of fancy liquor. "I forgot how much of this stuff I'm allowed to take home with me. I'm on my way back to Dallas this afternoon," he explained.

"I think it's four bottles," Alex replied casually as he opened another sample bottle and sniffed it.

"Shoot, I thought sure it was six."

"I'm quite certain it's four." He held the bottle to Chicago's nose.

"You like this one?"

"No."

"Hey, that's a good one. My girlfriend wears that kind. That's the one with the godawful name you can't pronounce, right?"

"Xias Xiana?" Alex suggested casually.

"Yeah, that's it. That's the one."

Alex looked at him, glanced back out at the airport bustle, and nodded. "Yes, it is. Come on, darling." He smiled at Chicago, took her by the elbow, and steered her out of the shop.

"Alex, what the hell—"

"Shhh. Let's sit down a minute." He nodded toward an empty waiting area.

"Alex, what the hell was that perfume crap all about? What's going on?"

"Shhhhh, sit. God, that stuff really stinks, doesn't it?" He waved his palm and wrinkled his nose at the smell of her. "I didn't want to get your hopes up in case nothing came through, but I called in a favor." His explanation was interrupted as the tourist from the duty-free shop suddenly joined them. He sat down next to Alex and placed his shopping bag on the ground between them.

"Well, glad to meet you, but damned if I know what's going on!" He looked different now that he had dropped the tourist pose. His clothes looked less stupid, his grin sharper.

"Name's Scotch," he said quietly as he kept watching the terminal, "like the tape. Whoever the hell you are, you've got some mean friends in high places."

"I'm Alex Sandars. This is Chicago."

Scotch leaned across and nodded. "Nice to meet you, ma'am." His eyes appraised her with a professional glance. "They described you perfectly." She was too surprised to ask exactly how that was, and then she didn't have time. Alex's tone was urgent and serious.

"Scotch is with the DEA," he explained to her. He turned back to Scotch. "I appreciate the help."

"They told me you earned it. Here's an ID and a badge. It's worthless but looks good."

"Do I have a plane?"

"Negative. DEA doesn't keep one here."

"Charter?"

"Come on, we need more than an hour . . ."

"OK—I'm not complaining. If we get rid of the bad guys, we can fly commercial. But I'll need some more finesse now. Can you do anything with customs? We pulled Angelica off an island; we don't have her passport."

"My boss is working hard for you, but don't expect miracles." Scotch looked Alex up and down.

"So call the shots, buddy. It's a kidnapping?"

"The girl is Angelica Wattles, daughter of Senator Wattles of Louisiana. She's with a stocky man in his fifties—Ethan Ruthwilde. He's noticeable—big round head, thick glasses. I don't know if he's armed. She probably thinks he's a good guy, probably trusts him. She also probably doesn't trust either one of us, and may be reluctant to accompany us anywhere."

"She probably will scream," Chicago added with a dry imitation of Alex's recitation, "and try to scratch my eyes out."

"There are two other people also after the girl, who may or may not be in collusion with Ruthwilde. A woman named Sophie—six one, about one-eighty, long blond hair. And maybe an American guy—shorter, built like a wrestler. Sophie is our main concern. Consider her well armed and extremely dangerous."

Scotch whistled in surprise. "Well, I can't imagine a six-foot-tall blond lady sneaking around Mexico."

"She's a pro," Alex warned.

"How about the girl—do they all want her alive?"

"I hope so." Alex shrugged. Chicago felt her palms sweating and her knees starting to shake as the reality of what could be about to happen began to dawn on her.

"I'd like you to approach Ruthwilde and Angelica. Flash your badge, take them aside. Then you can turn Angelica over to us. Hopefully quietly," he added. "I really would like to go home today without shooting up the airport." Scotch nodded. "Hell of a lot of paperwork that kind of thing."

"I'll give it a try," Alex said. "Can you hang on to Ruthwilde?"

"For a little while. You'll still need to get your butt out fast."

"There's a flight to Dallas in twenty minutes. I'm expecting Ruthwilde will try to board. If we get Angelica, we'll get out on the next plane anywhere."

"OK," Scotch said quietly. "There's a Taurus eighty-five in the Grand Marnier box."

Alex stood and picked up the duty-free bag. "Let's go." He pulled out a slip of paper and handed it to Scotch. "If we should get away without having a chance to make any phone calls, contact any one of these people and let them know what's going on."

"Sure." He looked over the numbers and tucked it into his shirt pocket.

"Especially Shana Phillips," Chicago added.

"You ready?" Alex turned to her and touched her lightly on the arm. Chicago nodded.

Ninety-One

ANGELICA AND RUTHWILDE sat on the hard wooden bench inside the customs office, nervously watching the clock. Only fifteen minutes until the flight. "Don't worry, dear." Ruthwilde tried to be comforting. "If we miss this, it's only another couple of hours."

"What if we're stuck here all night? I can't bear another night here, even at the Holiday Inn. I just can't bear it!" She wept.

The official just sat at his desk going through papers. In his many years of government service he had heard every story and twice as many excuses. When the proper documents arrived he would stamp the exit papers. There was a sharp knock on the door, then it swung open. A breathless young American man hurried in.

"Mr. Ruthwilde?"

Ruthwilde stood. Angelica wiped her eyes and jumped up happily.

"I'm from the U.S. consulate. This fax just arrived. I was told it was urgent."

Ruthwilde snatched the papers, glanced at them briefly, then handed them to the official. "Here they are. Now, please—we only have ten minutes."

Scotch stood near the boarding gate while Alex and Chicago waited silently on opposite sides of the throughway where they could watch everyone approaching. No sign yet of Sophie. Chicago felt relieved, but the back of her neck prickled. It was a feeling she had come to associate with Sophie. What would she do? Could it be that they really lost her? Doubtful. She would have checked the hospital. From there they had left no trail, but this was the most logical place to be.

Scotch saw them first. The petite blond almost skipping through the terminal and a much-beleaguered Ruthwilde looking around nervously. Alex and Chicago saw them, too. Alex ducked back into a doorway and winced as the pistol in his shoulder holster rubbed against his wound. The adrenaline was pumping, but he was still feeling shaky. Across the hall, Chicago pulled the hat down low over her brow and gazed casually around the seating area. It was crowded. She felt safe here, blending into the background, just waiting for Scotch to make his move.

There was a Mexican family with five children and huge vinyl suitcases. There was a flock of elderly tourists, some fanning themselves with magazines. A fat man in a loud Hawaiian-print shirt and polyester pants, was reading a copy of the *National Enquirer*, a gaudy souvenir sombrero pushed down on his head. There were three nuns, one playing peek-a-boo with a baby drooling on her father's shoulder.

Angelica and Ruthwilde were just about to present their tickets when Scotch stepped up behind them. "Excuse me, sir—DEA," he said in a quiet, authoritative voice while he displayed his badge. "I need to ask you a few questions. Will you step over here please?"

Ruthwilde turned crimson. "You have the wrong person. We're boarding this flight right now."

"I'm sorry, sir. It will just take a minute."

"Oh, my God, I cayn't believe this!" Angelica's shrill voice carried far. "We aren't *smugglehs!* Tell him, Ethan! Tell him who I am!" Angelica turned to Scotch and jabbed an indignant little finger at him. "My father is a United States senator." It was seeming to mean less and less. She moved toward the gate, but Scotch caught her arm.

"Please stop over here, miss. I'm sorry, but I'll need to see some identification."

"You don't understand." Angelica smiled sweetly at the man, flirting as natural a response for her as breathing. "I was kidnapped and suffered terrible things, and now this man is rescuing me!"

"Oh, blast it, man, this is outrageous. Look here . . ."

Chicago couldn't hear what they were saying, but she watched with delight as Ruthwilde's jowls trembled in indignation. He began to fumble in his jacket pocket to find the faxed papers. Then out of the corner of her eye, Chicago saw the fat man in the Hawaiian shirt leave his seat. With surprising agility he squeezed between the nun and the drooling baby and started toward the gate. His step was purposeful; he was quick for a man with that much gut; his step was familiar—his walk . . ."

"Sophie!" Chicago screamed. The man's shoulder dipped as he reached for a gun. "It's Sophie!" Chicago screamed.

Everything happened at once. People screamed as Alex burst around the corner with his own gun in the air. Scotch grabbed Angelica and shoved her down behind the counter. The ticket agent started screaming. Chaos erupted in the corridor, and people in the waiting area started ducking under the chairs.

The fat man's sombrero fell off and a blond ponytail dropped out as Sophie whirled and fired at Alex. Her bullet cracked the plaster wall, while Alex took more careful aim. Sophie clutched her leg and fell to the polished floor, spinning a half turn from the impact of his bullet. Her gunshot cracked the air, and all over the terminal people went diving for cover. Then Alex was on top of her, his feet spread, his arms steady, his gun pointed right at Sophie's formidable chest.

"Alto! Policia!" But it wasn't Alex shouting commands now. Chicago spun around and saw four Mexican cops running through the terminal with rifles and pistols drawn. Alex looked up in surprise.

"Policia!" A Mexican officer trained his gun on Alex, while another pointed a shotgun at Scotch who held up his badge and kept shouting at them not to shoot. There were already too many guns and too much confusion when a phalanx of airport security guards suddenly appeared on the mezzanine above, pointing a row of pistols over the balcony.

"I am a United States officer," Alex told the nearest Mexican in Spanish. He flashed the bogus badge. "This woman is my prisoner." The cop glanced toward Scotch who still held his badge in one hand and the gun in another. Suddenly a side door burst open and another small army burst in.

"Everybody freeze!" Six men spread out and trained a new set of weapons on the already frozen tableau.

"Boarder patrol?" Scotch muttered in astonishment. "What the hell . . . ?" Who's next he wondered, Fish and Game?

There was a long pause, oddly polite, as everyone glanced at everyone else. Sophie lay on the floor, with the alert coiled repose of a lion, no reflection of pain on her face despite the bleeding wound. Chicago was just outside the fringe of the drama, and slowly she eased back toward her seat. What do I do? she thought in a panic. Call the police?

"This is a DEA investigation." Scotch spoke first, holding up his badge. "I'm Officer Scotter." He smiled. "I appreciate all the help, fellows, but the situation is ah . . . under control." He could hear Angelica whimpering on the floor.

One of the U.S. border patrol agents spoke up. "Which one of you is Alex Sanders?" Alex kept his eye on Sophie and considered his options. There weren't many.

"I am," he said quietly, still holding his gun on the prostrate Sophie.

"Mr. Sanders, put down your weapon. I have a warrant for your arrest."

"He's with us," Scotch told the man.

"He is not!" Angelica peeked out from behind the ticket counter and screamed. "They tried to kidnap me! You arrest them all!" She sprinted from the desk. Scotch reached for her, but she pulled away and ran.

As all attention turned to Angelica, Sophie came alive. In a flash she gave a vicious kick and slammed Alex in the knee. He fired as his leg buckled, but she twisted away and followed through with a kick to his wounded side. An unimaginable pain shot through his body, and Alex crumpled like a sack of spaghetti. One of the Mexican cops kicked Alex's gun hand and the pistol went flying, but before anyone could control Sophie she pulled another pistol from the voluminous Hawaiian shirt just as the screeching Angelica was scampering toward the police. Sophie jumped to her feet and aimed the pistol at Angelica. She caught the girl around the neck and jabbed the gun into her ribs.

"OK. Now it's my turn," she said, grinning. "How does it go? Everybody freeze!" She was breathing hard and leaning on Angelica to stay off her wounded leg, but there was no doubt Sophie was back in business.

"Drop your gun and get back against that wall," she ordered Scotch. To Ruthwilde she just gave a cold smile. "Thanks for getting her this far, baby. I'll take over now."

Sophie was leaning on Angelica, her leg bleeding heavily. She glanced over her shoulder toward the distant exit where Grant was waiting with the car. It was a long way to walk, and she would be very exposed. If they had any sharpshooters she would be an easy target, even with her hostage. She saw the little baggage carts zipping around the waiting airplane, and decided that offered a better escape. There was an emergency exit close by with steps down to the tarmac.

"Come on now, little angel pie." She tightened her grip and poked her toward the door. "Let's take you home to Daddy."

Sophie dragged her hostage, sidestepping along the window until they were almost to the door. The various cops looked to one another for direction. Chicago crept back to her seat where the duty-free bag still sat with the second pistol. Her heart was racing.

Alex was still lying on the floor, a dark stain spreading through his shirt. From the waiting area came the hushed rustles of fear; in the background was the low rumble of baggage carousels. Sophie dragged Angelica up to the door and edged her hips up against the bar. "I will leave now. And you men may finish your game." Her face twisted into a contemptuous smile. She thrust her hip against the bar and the door latch unclicked. The emergency alarm sounded. Then Angelica fainted.

Dead weight, even a slight one hundred ten pounds of it, is still dead weight, and Sophie wasn't expecting it. Her wounded leg crumpled, her butt pushed the door open, and she tumbled backward just as the more alert officers opened fire. Scotch dove to the floor and pulled Angelica out of the way.

"Hold your fire!" he shouted. *"Alto! alto! basta!"* He jumped up and held his arms up, trying desperately to control the situation. Half the cops ran toward the open door where Sophie had fallen, half the rest were pointing guns at each other and looking for some kind of direction. Chicago snatched up the bag and with trembling fingers opened the Grand Marnier box.

"Oh, my God, is she dead?" Angelica cried.

"Stay right there, honey," Scotch whispered. "Don't move," he commanded. "Are you all right?"

Alex caught Chicago's eye and nodded his head a fraction toward the emergency exit. Then, summoning all his strength, he sprang up and kicked away the Mexican cop's gun. Chicago pulled the pistol out of the box, and trying to hold it as if she knew what she was doing, ran to his side.

"Freeze." It was a chorus of commands in English and Spanish, accompanied by the multiple clicking of guns.

"Oh, enough with the 'freeze' shit!" Chicago burst out angrily. She pulled Alex's arm across her shoulder.

"Take this thing." She thrust the pistol toward him. He smiled and leaned on her heavily, still keeping the weapon trained toward the assorted, confused cops.

"You are under arrest, Mr. Sandars," the border patrol officer repeated.

"Oh shut up!" Scotch demanded. "Anyway, we got him first. This is a DEA bust. Get over here." Alex and Chicago walked slowly toward Scotch.

"You better be saving the whole fucking world for all the trouble this is causing me!" he hissed. He saw the blood spreading on Alex's shirt. "Are you shot?"

"Not lately."

"Mr. Sandars, I advise you not to move." An officer tried to put force in his command.

"What's going on, Alex?" Scotch whispered suspiciously. "You didn't mention any of this. I need to know what the hell is going on."

"Same as before," he answered weakly. "We need to get the girl out of here."

"You are under arrest, Mr. Sandars," someone shouted threateningly. "You are charged with kidnapping." The tone was getting edgy.

"He kidnapped me!" Angelica cut in.

"Oh, stop it!" Chicago snapped. "Why did you have to wake up already?"

"I didn't even really faint! I just pretended. I thought about it long ago when there would always be these movies with hostages, and I thought, well what if they just pretended to faint—"

"Shut up." Scotch glared at her. "What's with the kidnapping?"

"The girl's father is being blackmailed," Alex explained as succinctly as he could. "I guess when Wattles found out she was safe he made up the kidnapping charges to try and shut me up."

"It's true," Chicago broke in. She couldn't tell if Scotch believed them or not. "Please, you've got to let us go."

They could hear sirens in the background.

"Shit." Alex turned suddenly. He winced with the pain. "Where's Ruthwilde?" They all looked toward the counter where he had been standing silently during all the mayhem. He was nowhere to be seen.

"You've got to get him."

Scotch glanced out to the tarmac, thinking. He had been dropped into something with nothing to go on now except directions to be loyal.

"What the hell did you ever do for us anyway?" Scotch asked suspiciously.

"Loggins and Dane," Alex replied simply. Scotch stared at him.

"That was you? You got them out?" Alex shrugged.

"OK." Scotch tried to figure out a plan. He saw a small plane out by the runway. A man was removing the blocks from the wheels. On the tail of the plane was the logo that so many people in rural areas had come to rejoice in; the Wings of Hope air ambulance. Scotch saw the pilot draw off his fuel sample, preparing for takeoff.

"Shit. Whatever I do now—I'm gonna get screwed," he growled.

Alex smiled and nodded. "But if you help us I can get you unscrewed."

The man sighed. "There's a plane over there. I know the pilot. We'll get him to fly you to Cancun; from there you can get a commercial flight out. I'll try to hold off your friends here."

Alex nodded. Scotch straightened up and addressed the collection of officers in Spanish. "I'm sorry, my friends. These people are my prisoners. I have to take them in myself. We can sort out the rest of the warrants later."

Gabriel Jimenez turned and saw the odd little group approaching—two women, an injured man, and lots of guns. What was going on? Then he recognized Scotch.

"Gabriel, amigo. I need your help, man." Scotch spoke with a drawl even in Spanish.

"Gabriel?" Chicago and Angelica looked at the plane, at the pilot, at each other in surprise. As soon as he spoke, they recognized his voice. Scotch and Alex watched astonished as the two women threw their arms around the surprised pilot.

"It's us!" Angelica screamed. "It was us you told how to fly the plane!"

Only the approaching sirens broke up the happy meeting.

"You better get out while you still can," Scotch warned them.

Ninety-Two

PHILIP GREENWAY SAT alone in his study, waiting for his wife. For five days now, he had been remarkably calm. At first he hadn't thought he would be able to keep the news about Clara to himself, but he had. There was an amazing strength in action. As long as the search for Angelica was going on, the photos of Clara seemed less real, and there had been a flicker of hope.

In his mind, his daughter was still alive. He often found himself forgetting it was not Clara that Alex had gone to rescue, but some other man's daughter. Now it was final. He heard his wife come in through the kitchen and got up. She had been out walking the dog and her face was rosy, her hair windblown.

"Phil, what are you doing home this early?" she asked in surprise, then stopped. Married twenty-five years, she knew when something was wrong. She held the dog leash limply and clutched her jacket instead of taking it off. Philip felt his eyes fill with tears. She walked slowly into the room like the floor was shaky.

"It's Clara, isn't it? You've heard something." Sadly, he nodded.

Shana nervously slid her bracelet on and off, on and off as Finneaus drove to Dulles Airport. Her mouth was dry and her heart was skipping; her confidence was crumbling despite Jacquie's ongoing pep talk. It was a little after seven. The plane would arrive at ten twenty-five. That gave Shana almost an hour to tape an interview with Wattles and send that back to the station, then wait to go live for the eleven o'clock news.

Since the four o'clock bulletin Washington had gone crazy. It was the best of all possible scandals—kidnapping, body switching, treason; and best of all, it seemed to be pretty clear-cut as far as the bad guys went. There were plenty of the snaking tendrils that made for a rich story, but none of the technical tangles that ruined the S and L scandals. The story was weak on the sex angle, but Shana was sure someone would work that in sooner or later.

Her station had run a special hour-long edition at six o'clock. They had bounced most of the national news and all of the local. A fluff piece on senior citizens knitting scarves for troops in the Gulf was jettisoned; the satellite photos were lopped off the weather; even the sports was compressed.

The broadcast was rough. Some of the file photos were mixed up, and they didn't have a lot of visuals. Shana hadn't had time to organize as she wanted to, but the urgency gave it all a vibrant raw edge. They had managed to get some talking heads for background, and ran some old file footage of Peter Valascheck's arrest at Alsak Chemicals two years ago. They were still searching for any information on Hans Goerbel.

When the story broke, there were a few minutes of jammed phone lines throughout the whole city as those who were watching channel seven started phoning those who might not be. Marcy DeLour of rival station five was taken ill and retired to her bedroom alone with a bottle of cheap merlot.

Shana felt worse and worse the closer they got to the airport. This would be the biggest story of her life. She was going to stand up there in the bright lights as Angelica Wattles came off the plane, and she was going to . . . go blank.

Finneaus pulled up in back of the channel seven remote van. The road was packed with news teams from every station. Technicians ran with cables; broadcasters discussed their scanty notes, still trying to figure out what was going on. Shana suddenly had a burst of confidence. Sam her cameraman came running up to the car.

"We're all set up in the VIP lounge. Wattles is there. He's ripe and he's all ours."

It was a subdued Angelica who walked out of the gate into the glaring television lights. On the flight from Cancun, Alex and Chicago had told her the whole story. Sam caught the angle just right, focusing not on the logical wide shot of father and daughter running into one another's arms, but on the girl's face at the first moment she saw him. This was not the same face that had beamed out at viewers from the videos and prom-queen photos. This was an older face. Shifting emotions glanced across her eyes like clouds in a windy sky as she met her father's gaze: relief, regret, accusation, sadness, and joy.

They embraced, then were whisked away by security as the TV cameras followed them out. Shana came over to Finneaus and Jacquie. "Alex and Chicago are still in the plane. Evidently there's still some problem."

"Problem? What kind of problem?"

The crowd had disappeared, and the equipment was being packed away. "Well, like Alex is hurt and under arrest."

Darcy Sullevin watched the drama on television with an edgy sort of glee. So far he had managed to escape the worst, although his name had been mentioned, as "unavailable for comment." Tomorrow would be tough, but he had the tapes ready, his journals adjusted. There was nothing on paper to tie him to the chemical end of it. The body switch business would be bad. There was no way to get around that, but he knew that alone would not kill him. In a short time, when things cooled off enough, he would be remembered in the right circles as someone who displayed extreme loyalty to his boss.

What else? What else could there be? He had spent three hours with his lawyer going over the possible charges. Obstruction of justice was a nasty one, but again, they probably stood a good chance with the defense that it was all to protect Angelica. He rested the clipboard on his lap and worked out the finishing touches on his press statement.

Ninety-Three

U.S. SENATOR SELLS NERVE GAS TO IRAQ, the *Washington Post* headlines screamed across page one the next morning. By noon, Senator Wattles had received so many death threats he and Angelica were taken away to a secret location.

"They got Ruthwilde right after you left," Shana explained to Alex when she came by to visit. "He couldn't slink very far with all those cops in the airport. And Sophie's going to be OK. She took six shots, all in the flesh."

Chicago shuddered at the mention of Sophie. Although Alex had suffered major physical injury, he seemed in better shape than Chicago right now. She had lost ten pounds, her eyes looked hollow, and she couldn't sleep. She jumped at every noise. Alex had been repaired and released, both from the hospital and from the kidnapping charges, and they were hiding out at Finneaus's and Jacquie's.

"What about Grant? Any news on him?"

"They picked him up this morning, still in Mérida. He says he abandoned Sophie at the airport, and was planning to lie low for a couple of days then make his own way home. He's claiming he was a pawn in the whole thing. That Ruthwilde and the senator set him up for the body switch, and then Sophie forced him to go along to Belize."

"Speaking of lying low," Alex said, "what are the chances of us skipping town with no publicity?"

Shana looked doubtful. "The press are ferocious, Alex, and you guys are the secret-agent glamor angle. We've had to hire a temp at the station just to fend off phone calls. They're offering me bribes just for your name—bidding started at five thousand."

Alex's eyes brightened. "Make it ten and we'll take it."

Shana laughed. "I think you're OK for a couple of days. I snuck through the alleys and Jacquie let me in the back, but I don't think

I'll try it again. We're covering you up as much as we can, but too many people know about you already."

"We really want to go home." Chicago's voice was almost pleading. Alex squeezed her hand, it felt cold and bony.

"What about the cops?" Shana asked.

"They want at least a couple of days until they get a handle on everything," Alex explained. "But Wattles is being cooperative. He even apologized for the kidnapping charge, although he claims that was Sullevin's idea."

"Big of him," Shana observed dryly. "Look, I have to run. I've got an interview with Philip Greenway. Clara was exhumed this morning. They're going to do an autopsy, but Willie Wallace has made a statement swearing it's her. I don't know when I'll get back to see you, but I'll give you a call."

Ninety-Four

THE STORY KEPT opening and fluttering around them like scarves from a magician's sleeve. For days the whole country buzzed with the drama. You could not turn on a talk show without running into it. The body switch, with its titillating mutilation aspect, played well on "Hard Copy," "Inside Edition," and "Crimewatch"; while "Meet the Press" pontificated about the role of the media in exposing criminal activity. "Rescue 911" did a reenactment of Angelica's night rescue through the reef, and all over the country, dive shops found their phones ringing off the hooks with people wanting to learn scuba. TV cameras exploited every detail of the exhumation and shipment of Clara Greenway's body.

Experts were dredged up to discuss international chemical trade regulations and chemical weapon production. Psychologists analyzed the main characters (much was made of Ruthwilde's hummingbird garden).

Oprah Winfrey interviewed Willie Wallace. "So there you were, cutting this dead girl's head off—and what was going through your mind?"

So far Willie had not been charged with anything, and Grant's fate was tangled in questions of complicity, foreknowledge, and jurisdiction. The new autopsy of Clara Greenway had found bruises and other signs of a struggle, but so far Grant was sticking to his story of her accidental fall down the stairs.

Alex and Chicago hid out for a couple of days with Finneaus and Jacquie until the last of their official statements had been given and the web of zealous reporters started tracking close to home. They decided it was time to head south. Chicago in particular was not eager to fly, and they decided to take an overnight train back to Miami.

"And then what?" Jacquie asked as they shared an early dinner before departure. Chicago and Alex looked at each other.

"We're . . . we . . . we're thinking about sailing," she explained tentatively.

"Somewhere," Alex added.

"For a little while, maybe," she qualified, "just to try it out."

"Yeah—I've always wanted to try it."

"And my boat's all ready. I need a crew . . ."

"And I found out about these great new seasick pills," Alex added hopefully.

Finneaus laughed. "You make it all sound so romantic."

The story dogged them on the slow passage south. There was a *Time* magazine left behind in their sleeper; overheard discussions in the dining car; a child, who upon seeing a picture of Ethan Ruthwilde in the newspaper, pointed him out as "the gas man."

When Umbi picked them up at the station, there was a copy of the *Miami Herald* in the truck, featuring a full-page story on the international chemical warfare business.

Sophie became the stuff of legend, although her story did not test the creative mettle of the tabloid reporters since so little exaggeration was needed. Three days after she was shot, she escaped from the hospital in Mérida and kidnapped one of her guards. She forced him to drive her to the port city of Progreso where she pirated a speed boat and was last seen heading out into open seas in the direction of Cuba.

Thanks to modern communications, the details reached across the globe, even to the Raj Suite in the Governor's Palace Hotel in Madras, India. Hans Goerbel was starting to realize that India did not have to be such a dreadful place. For half the price he usually paid in Vienna or Paris, he had rooms in a real palace, with gold brocade draperies and marble floors. Granted, it was unpleasant to have to go anywhere in the stinking hot city even in a limousine, but fortunately his business here did not require much travel.

People were happy to come to him. There was an excellent conference room complete with fax, telephones, and modem right in his suite. Goerbel rang the bell and immediately the steward entered. He was a handsome Indian boy in glittering turban.

"More ice, please," Goerbel ordered as he poured himself another drink. Much as he was enjoying the sumptuous surroundings and the respite from the tensions of the past week, he was eager to return to Western civilization. One could only take so much of this culture.

But he had to finish his business here first, and there was also the issue of his safety. He did not know yet if Abu Tahile had been fully appeased. While Goerbel had not been able to arrange the shipment of chemicals Tahile wanted, he had been able to come through with a respectable supply of surplus mustard gas shells. They were old, more dangerous to handle, and more likely to fail, but it was a start. If the man was satisfied and called off his threats, Goerbel would be free to leave this godforsaken country.

Hopefully, it would only take a month or so, then maybe St. Moritz for Christmas. He needed to drop by Switzerland to straighten out his banking anyway; the shutdown in Hamburg had happened so quickly, he was still not clear on some of the transfers.

There was a knock on the door, and the steward announced his visitor. Peter Valascheck came in, a broad smile of triumph on his face.

"A good meeting?" Goerbel greeted him.

"Very good." Valascheck dropped a folder on the table. "We've contracted with two plants, one in Nellore, just up the coast, and one in Thanjavur. Nellore has connections to Bhopal, and could start getting raw materials within two weeks. We have lunch tomorrow with a shipper in Thanjavur." The man raised his eyebrows and gave a little shrug that seemed to say, so why did you ever worry?

Ninety-Five

"DIS WHOLE STORY tax'n my brain." Umbi sighed as they sat on the deck of the *Tassia Far*, catching up. Chicago was thrilled to be home. Umbi had taken good care of the boat and of Lassie, who had shed while they were gone and now shimmered with iridescent purple and green highlights. Chicago sat with the snake curled on her lap, idly scratching its head. Once back in her own world, the raw scrape of the violence had begun to fade.

"So the senator kidnap his own daughter, to protect her from de real kidnappers, but dey get her anyway, so you kidnap her back from dem?"

"Something like that," Alex explained. "Only then she escapes from us, and we start the whole thing over again."

"And now they'll all get fancy rich lawyers," Chicago explained. "And make them richer trying to get their asses out of all this, and some other greedy bastard will step in and supply the chemicals and—"

"Hey," Alex interrupted, "can't we pretend, just for a couple of days anyway, that we made the world safe for democracy?" There was clear irony in his tone, but no bitterness. Alex's tolerance was much higher than Chicago's.

"No."

"Well how about we saved the girl?"

"Dat's always a good one," Umbi offered. "So when you leaving on dis big sailing voyage?"

"Couple of days," Chicago told him. "You know you're welcome to come along. We can always use another bilge rat," she invited.

Umbi laughed. "You think I'm crazy? You guys have no kinda normal life. You think I be stepping my big foot in there?" He shook his head grandly.

"Well, I'll talk to Albert," Chicago offered. "Maybe he'll give you my job. Hell, you know as much about running the marina by now as I do."

Umbi was smiling. "Actually, I got me a job offer." The smile slipped a little, as it was mixed with sadness. "Brian's place in Key Largo needing an instructor. They offered to pay my training and exam fees and then I work for them."

"Oh, Umbi, that's great!" Chicago didn't know what to feel. There was the thrill of starting a new adventure, mixed with the sadness of closing chapters with old friends. She looked around the marina. It had been a good couple of years here, all things considered. She shivered, and Alex put his arm around her shoulders.

Ninety-Six

CHICAGO WOKE SUDDENLY: the odd rare awakening when you are suddenly fully alert but strangely calm. She opened her eyes and saw the crescent moon shining through the hatch, bathing the bow cabin with a white glow. She turned her head and saw Alex, leaning up on one elbow, watching her. He smiled. The boat rocked gently at anchor. It was a feeling so delicious and so long forgotten. Two years in dock; it had seemed like forever, but now felt like no time at all.

They had set sail three days ago, the snap of the full sails like a thump to a dead heart. Now they were anchored near the reef off Islamorada in the Keys.

"How you doing?" she whispered, reaching to touch the side of his face. "You seasick?"

Alex smiled and shook his head. The moon was blocked as he bent to kiss her. A cool breeze slipped in the open hatch. Chicago could hear the familiar creaks and clanks of her boat, the distant muffled slap of water against the hull. How odd to have him in this place again, to have his body here beside her, his sounds, his smells, his motion.

"Hey." She looked at him suddenly, her eyes wide with excitement. "You want to do a dive?"

"Right now?" he laughed.

Chicago nodded. "It's the best. The sun rises in another hour. Come on."

Silently she slid out of the bunk and crept through the salon. Alex followed. They did not speak as they set up their tanks and pulled on the wet suits, still damp from an earlier dive. Such a forgotten sweet feeling, the delicious thrill of sneaking out at night. The worst part of being a grown-up is that the rules you have left aren't really much fun to break.

The water was almost flat. Chicago handed him one of the flashlights, and quietly they slipped into the water. The reef at night is a place of small accidental beauty. In the darkness the world is only what you see in a small beam of light: the delicate striped shrimp with its ballet poise, the brilliant red starfish, the big-eyed squirrel fish.

They swam slowly over the coral. The colors were sharp, lusty, not as riotous as in the day, but denser. Then slowly, barely perceptibly, the sea began to lighten. The outline of the reef was visible. Chicago switched off her light. They could see their own shapes now, swimming close, almost touching. Shades of blue grew paler, then suddenly the water was crowded. It was like a chorus of cherubim breaking in after a long prelude. Butterfly fish and chromis, triggers, durgons, snappers, a whole school of little grunts —beautiful fish all around them like a great colored snowfall. Alex watched as Chicago hovered in the middle of them, her eyes bright through her mask, her hands extended as if they would perch on her fingers like birds.

He saw a shimmer and a bright arching stripe in the sky through the water. Chicago turned and they watched a rim of gold appear on the distant horizon, curved by the water into a goblet of sun. Alex swam up beside her, and they just stayed that way, watching the sun rise through the water and the reef come alive, their arms just sometimes touching.